Cheerful
By Request

Edna Ferber

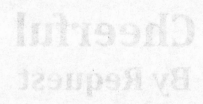

Cheerful—By Request

The present edition is a reproduction of previous publication of this classic work. Minor typographical errors may have been corrected without note; however, for an authentic reading experience the spelling, punctuation, and capitalization have been retained from the original text.

ISBN: 979-8-88830-076-3

CONTENTS

I	CHEERFUL—BY REQUEST	1
II	THE GAY OLD DOG	20
III	THE TOUGH GUY	39
IV	THE ELDEST	61
V	THAT'S MARRIAGE	77
VI	THE WOMAN WHO TRIED TO BE GOOD	98
VII	THE GIRL WHO WENT RIGHT	108
VIII	THE HOOKER-UP-THE-BACK	121
IX	THE GUIDING MISS GOWD	136
X	SOPHY-AS-SHE-MIGHT-HAVE-BEEN	152
XI	THE THREE OF THEM	167
XII	SHORE LEAVE	180

I

CHEERFUL—BY REQUEST

The editor paid for the lunch (as editors do). He lighted his seventh cigarette and leaned back. The conversation, which had zigzagged from the war to Zuloaga, and from Rasputin the Monk to the number of miles a Darrow would go on a gallon, narrowed down to the thin, straight line of business.

"Now don't misunderstand. Please! We're not presuming to dictate. Dear me, no! We have always felt that the writer should be free to express that which is in his—ah—heart. But in the last year we've been swamped with these drab, realistic stories. Strong, relentless things, you know, about dishwashers, with a lot of fine detail about the fuzz of grease on the rim of the pan. And then those drear and hopeless ones about fallen sisters who end it all in the East River. The East River must be choked up with 'em. Now, I know that life is real, life is earnest, and I'm not demanding a happy ending, exactly. But if you could—that is—would you—do you see your way at all clear to giving us a fairly cheerful story? Not necessarily Glad, but not so darned Russian, if you get me. Not pink, but not all grey either. Say—mauve."...

That was Josie Fifer's existence. Mostly grey, with a dash of pink. Which makes mauve.

Unless you are connected (which you probably are not) with the great firm of Hahn & Lohman, theatrical producers, you never will have heard of Josie Fifer.

There are things about the theatre that the public does not know. A statement, at first blush, to be disputed. The press agent, the special writer, the critic, the magazines, the Sunday supplement, the divorce courts—what have they left untold? We know the make of car Miss Billboard drives; who her husbands are and were; how much the movies have offered her; what she wears, reads, says, thinks, and eats for breakfast. Snapshots of author writing play at place on Hudson; pictures of the play in rehearsal; of the director directing it; of the stage hands rewriting it—long before the opening night we know more about the piece than does the playwright himself, and are ten times less eager to see it.

Josie Fifer's knowledge surpassed even this. For she was keeper of the ghosts of the firm of Hahn & Lohman. Not only was she present at the birth of a play; she officiated at its funeral. She carried the keys to the closets that housed the skeletons of the firm.

When a play died of inanition, old age, or—as was sometimes the case—before it was born, it was Josie Fifer who laid out its remains and followed it to the grave.

Her notification of its demise would come thus:

"Hello, Fifer! This is McCabe" (the property man of H. & L. at the phone).

"Well?"

"A little waspish this morning, aren't you, Josephine?"

"I've got twenty-five bathing suits for the No. 2 'Ataboy' company to mend and clean and press before five this afternoon. If you think I'm going to stand here wasting my—"

"All right, all right! I just wanted to tell you that 'My Mistake' closes Saturday. The stuff'll be up Monday morning early."

A sardonic laugh from Josie. "And yet they say 'What's in a name!'"

The unfortunate play had been all that its title implies. Its purpose was to star an actress who hadn't a glint. Her second-act costume alone had cost $700, but even Russian sable bands can't carry a bad play. The critics had pounced on it with the savagery of their kind and hacked it, limb from limb, leaving its carcass to rot under the pitiless white glare of Broadway. The dress with the Russian sable bands went the way of all Hahn & Lohman tragedies. Josie Fifer received it, if not reverently, still appreciatively.

"I should think Sid Hahn would know by this time," she observed sniffily, as her expert fingers shook out the silken folds and smoothed the fabulous fur, "that auburn hair and a gurgle and a Lucille dress don't make a play. Besides, Fritzi Kirke wears the biggest shoe of any actress I ever saw. A woman with feet like that"—she picked up a satin slipper, size 7½ C—"hasn't any business on the stage. She ought to travel with a circus. Here, Etta. Hang this away in D, next to the amethyst blue velvet, and be sure and lock the door."

McCabe had been right. A waspish wit was Josie's.

The question is whether to reveal to you now where it was that Josie Fifer reigned thus, queen of the cast-offs; or to take you back to the days that led up to her being there—the days when she was José Fyfer on the programme.

Her domain was the storage warehouse of Hahn & Lohman, as you may have guessed. If your business lay Forty-third Street way, you might have passed the building a hundred times without once giving it a seeing glance. It was not Forty-third Street of the small shops, the smart crowds, and the glittering motors. It was the Forty-third lying east of the Grand Central sluice gates; east of fashion; east, in a word, of Fifth Avenue—a great square brick building

2

smoke-grimed, cobwebbed, and having the look of a cold-storage plant or a car barn fallen into disuse; dusty, neglected, almost eerie. Yet within it lurks Romance, and her sombre sister Tragedy, and their antic brother Comedy, the cut-up.

A worn flight of wooden steps leads up from the sidewalk to the dim hallway; a musty-smelling passage wherein you are met by a genial sign which reads:

"No admittance. Keep out. This means you."

To confirm this, the eye, penetrating the gloom, is confronted by a great blank metal door that sheathes the elevator. To ride in that elevator is to know adventure, so painfully, so protestingly, with such creaks and jerks and lurchings does it pull itself from floor to floor, like an octogenarian who, grunting and groaning, hoists himself from his easy-chair by slow stages that wring a protest from ankle, knee, hip, back and shoulder. The corkscrew stairway, broken and footworn though it is, seems infinitely less perilous.

First floor—second—third—fourth. Whew! And there you are in Josie Fifer's kingdom—a great front room, unexpectedly bright and even cosy with its whir of sewing machines: tables, and tables, and tables, piled with orderly stacks of every sort of clothing, from shoes to hats, from gloves to parasols; and in the room beyond this, and beyond that, and again beyond that, row after row of high wooden cabinets stretching the width of the room, and forming innumerable aisles. All of Bluebeard's wives could have been tucked away in one corner of the remotest and least of these, and no one the wiser. All grimly shut and locked, they are, with the key in Josie's pocket. But when, at the behest of McCabe, or sometimes even Sid Hahn himself, she unlocked and opened one of these doors, what treasures hung revealed! What shimmer and sparkle and perfume— and moth balls! The long-tailed electric light bulb held high in one hand, Josie would stand at the door like a priestess before her altar.

There they swung, the ghosts and the skeletons, side by side. You remember that slinking black satin snakelike sheath that Gita Morini wore in "Little Eyolf"? There it dangles, limp, invertebrate, yet how eloquent! No other woman in the world could have worn that gown, with its unbroken line from throat to hem, its smooth, high, black satin collar, its writhing tail that went slip-slip-slipping after her. In it she had looked like a sleek and wicked python that had fasted for a long, long time.

Dresses there are that have made stage history. Surely you remember the beruffled, rose-strewn confection in which the beautiful Elsa Marriott swam into our ken in "Mississipp'"? She used to say, wistfully, that she always got a hand on her entrance in

3

that dress. It was due to the sheer shock of delight that thrilled audience after audience as it beheld her loveliness enhanced by this floating, diaphanous tulle cloud. There it hangs, time-yellowed, its pristine freshness vanished quite, yet as fragrant with romance as is the sere and withered blossom of a dead white rose pressed within the leaves of a book of love poems. Just next it, incongruously enough, flaunt the wicked froufrou skirts and the low-cut bodice and the wasp waist of the abbreviated costume in which Cora Kassell used so generously to display her charms. A rich and portly society matron of Pittsburgh now—she whose name had been a synonym for pulchritude these thirty years; she who had had more cold creams, hats, cigars, corsets, horses, and lotions named for her than any woman in history! Her ample girth would have wrought sad havoc with that eighteen-inch waist now. Gone are the chaste curves of the slim white silk legs that used to kick so lithely from the swirl of lace and chiffon. Yet there it hangs, pertly pathetic, mute evidence of her vanished youth, her delectable beauty, and her unblushing confidence in those same.

Up one aisle and down the next—velvet, satin, lace and broadcloth—here the costume the great Canfield had worn in Richard III; there the little cocked hat and the slashed jerkin in which Maude Hammond, as Peterkins, winged her way to fame up through the hearts of a million children whose ages ranged from seven to seventy. Brocades and ginghams; tailor suits and peignoirs; puffed sleeves and tight—dramatic history, all, they spelled failure, success, hope, despair, vanity, pride, triumph, decay. Tragic ghosts, over which Josie Fifer held grim sway!

Have I told you that Josie Fifer, moving nimbly about the great storehouse, limped as she went? The left leg swung as a normal leg should. The right followed haltingly, sagging at hip and knee. And that brings us back to the reason for her being where she was. And what.

The story of how Josie Fifer came to be mistress of the cast-off robes of the firm of Hahn & Lohman is one of those stage tragedies that never have a public performance. Josie had been one of those little girls who speak pieces at chicken-pie suppers held in the basement of the Presbyterian church. Her mother had been a silly, idle woman addicted to mother hubbards and paper-backed novels about the house. Her one passion was the theatre, a passion that had very scant opportunity for feeding in Wapello, Iowa. Josie's piece-speaking talent was evidently a direct inheritance. Some might call it a taint.

Two days before one of Josie's public appearances her mother would twist the child's hair into innumerable rag curlers that stood

4

out in grotesque, Topsy-like bumps all over her fair head. On the eventful evening each rag chrysalis would burst into a full-blown butterfly curl. In a pale-blue, lace-fretted dress over a pale-blue slip, made in what her mother called "Empire style," Josie would deliver herself of "Entertaining Big Sister's Beau" and other sophisticated classics with an incredible ease and absence of embarrassment. It wasn't a definite boldness in her. She merely liked standing there before all those people, in her blue dress and her toe slippers, speaking her pieces with enhancing gestures taught her by her mother in innumerable rehearsals.

Any one who has ever lived in Wapello, Iowa, or its equivalent, remembers the old opera house on the corner of Main and Elm, with Schroeder's drug store occupying the first floor. Opera never came within three hundred miles of Wapello, unless it was the so-called comic kind. It was before the day of the ubiquitous moving-picture theatre that has since been the undoing of the one-night stand and the ten-twenty-thirty stock company. The old red-brick opera house furnished unlimited thrills for Josie and her mother. From the time Josie was seven she was taken to see whatever Wapello was offered in the way of the drama. That consisted mostly of plays of the tell-me-more-about-me-mother type.

By the time she was ten she knew the whole repertoire of the Maude La Vergne Stock Company by heart. She was blasé with "East Lynne" and "The Two Orphans," and even "Camille" left her cold. She was as wise to the trade tricks as is a New York first nighter. She would sit there in the darkened auditorium of a Saturday afternoon, surveying the stage with a judicious and undeceived eye, as she sucked indefatigably at a lollipop extracted from the sticky bag clutched in one moist palm. (A bag of candy to each and every girl; a ball or a top to each and every boy!) Josie knew that the middle-aged soubrette who came out between the first and second acts to sing a gingham-and-sunbonnet song would whisk off to reappear immediately in knee-length pink satin and curls. When the heroine left home in a shawl and a sudden snowstorm that followed her upstage and stopped when she went off, Josie was interested, but undeceived. She knew that the surprised-looking white horse used in the Civil War comedy-drama entitled "His Southern Sweetheart" came from Joe Brink's livery stable in exchange for four passes, and that the faithful old negro servitor in the white cotton wig would save somebody from something before the afternoon was over.

In was inevitable that as Josie grew older she should take part in home-talent plays. It was one of these tinsel affairs that had made clear to her just where her future lay. The Wapello Daily Courier

5

helped her in her decision. She had taken the part of a gipsy queen, appropriately costumed in slightly soiled white satin slippers with four-inch heels, and a white satin dress enhanced by a red sash, a black velvet bolero, and large hoop earrings. She had danced and sung with a pert confidence, and the Courier had pronounced her talents not amateur, but professional, and had advised the managers (who, no doubt, read the Wapello Courier daily, along with their Morning Telegraph) to seek her out, and speedily.

Josie didn't wait for them to take the hint. She sought them out instead. There followed seven tawdry, hard-working, heartbreaking years. Supe, walk-on, stock, musical comedy—Josie went through them all. If any illusions about the stage had survived her Wapello days, they would have vanished in the first six months of her dramatic career. By the time she was twenty-four she had acquired the wisdom of fifty, a near-seal coat, a turquoise ring with a number of smoky-looking crushed diamonds surrounding it, and a reputation for wit and for decency. The last had cost the most.

During all these years of cheap theatrical boarding houses (the most soul-searing cheapness in the world), of one-night stands, of insult, disappointment, rebuff, and something that often came perilously near to want, Josie Fifer managed to retain a certain humorous outlook on life. There was something whimsical about it. She could even see a joke on herself. When she first signed her name José Fyfer, for example, she did it with, an appreciative giggle and a glint in her eye as she formed the accent mark over the e.

"They'll never stop me now," she said. "I'm made. But I wish I knew if that J was pronounced like H, in humbug. Are there any Spanish blondes?"

It used to be the habit of the other women in the company to say to her: "Jo, I'm blue as the devil to-day. Come on, give us a laugh."

She always obliged.

And then came a Sunday afternoon in late August when her laugh broke off short in the middle, and was forever after a stunted thing.

She was playing Atlantic City in a second-rate musical show. She had never seen the ocean before, and she viewed it now with an appreciation that still had in it something of a Wapello freshness.

They all planned to go in bathing that hot August afternoon after rehearsal. Josie had seen pictures of the beauteous bathing girl dashing into the foaming breakers. She ran across the stretch of glistening beach, paused and struck a pose, one toe pointed waterward, her arms extended affectedly.

"So!" she said mincingly. "So this is Paris!"

6

It was a new line in those days, and they all laughed, as she had meant they should. So she leaped into the water with bounds and shouts and much waving of white arms. A great floating derelict of a log struck her leg with its full weight, and with all the tremendous force of the breaker behind it. She doubled up ridiculously, and went down like a shot. Those on the beach laughed again. When she came up, and they saw her distorted face they stopped laughing, and fished her out. Her leg was broken in two places, and mashed in a dozen.

José Fyfer's dramatic career was over. (This is not the cheery portion of the story.)

When she came out of the hospital, three months later, she did very well indeed with her crutches. But the merry-eyed woman had vanished—she of the Wapello colouring that had persisted during all these years. In her place limped a wan, shrunken, tragic little figure whose humour had soured to a caustic wit. The near-seal coat and the turquoise-and-crushed-diamond ring had vanished too.

During those agonized months she had received from the others in the company such kindness and generosity as only stage folk can show—flowers, candy, dainties, magazines, sent by every one from the prima donna to the call boy. Then the show left town. There came a few letters of kind inquiry, then an occasional post card, signed by half a dozen members of the company. Then these ceased. Josie Fifer, in her cast and splints and bandages and pain, dragged out long hospital days and interminable hospital nights. She took a dreary pleasure in following the tour of her erstwhile company via the pages of the theatrical magazines.

"They're playing Detroit this week," she would announce to the aloof and spectacled nurse. Or: "One-night stands, and they're due in Muncie, Ind., to-night. I don't know which is worse—playing Muncie for one night or this moan factory for a three month's run."

When she was able to crawl out as far as the long corridor she spoke to every one she met. As she grew stronger she visited here and there, and on the slightest provocation she would give a scene ranging all the way from "Romeo and Juliet" to "The Black Crook." It was thus she first met Sid Hahn, and felt the warming, healing glow of his friendship.

Some said that Sid Hahn's brilliant success as a manager at thirty-five was due to his ability to pick winners. Others thought it was his refusal to be discouraged when he found he had picked a failure. Still others, who knew him better, were likely to say: "Why, I don't know. It's a sort of—well, you might call it charm—and yet—. Did you ever see him smile? He's got a million-dollar grin. You can't resist it."

None of them was right. Or all of them. Sid Hahn, erstwhile usher, call boy, press agent, advance man, had a genius for things theatrical. It was inborn. Dramatic, sensitive, artistic, intuitive, he was often rendered inarticulate by the very force and variety of his feelings. A little, rotund, ugly man, Sid Hahn, with the eyes of a dreamer, the wide, mobile mouth of a humourist, the ears of a comic ol'-clo'es man. His generosity was proverbial, and it amounted to a vice.

In September he had come to Atlantic City to try out "Splendour." It was a doubtful play, by a new author, starring Sarah Haddon for the first time. No one dreamed the play would run for years, make a fortune for Hahn, lift Haddon from obscurity to the dizziest heights of stardom, and become a classic of the stage.

Ten minutes before the curtain went up on the opening performance Hahn was stricken with appendicitis. There was not even time to rush him to New York. He was on the operating table before the second act was begun. When he came out of the ether he said: "How did it go?"

"Fine!" beamed the nurse. "You'll be out in two weeks."

"Oh, hell! I don't mean the operation. I mean the play."

He learned soon enough from the glowing, starry-eyed Sarah Haddon and from every one connected with the play. He insisted on seeing them all daily, against his doctor's orders, and succeeded in working up a temperature that made his hospital stay a four weeks' affair. He refused to take the tryout results as final.

"Don't be too bubbly about this thing," he cautioned Sarah Haddon. "I've seen too many plays that were skyrockets on the road come down like sticks when they struck New York."

The company stayed over in Atlantic City for a week, and Hahn held scraps of rehearsals in his room when he had a temperature of 102. Sarah Haddon worked like a slave. She seemed to realise that her great opportunity had come—the opportunity for which hundreds of gifted actresses wait a lifetime. Haddon was just twenty-eight then—a year younger than Josie Fifer. She had not yet blossomed into the full radiance of her beauty. She was too slender, and inclined to stoop a bit, but her eyes were glorious, her skin petal-smooth, her whole face reminding one, somehow, of an intelligent flower. Her voice was a golden, liquid delight.

Josie Fifer, dragging herself from bed to chair, and from chair to bed, used to watch for her. Hahn's room was on her floor. Sarah Haddon, in her youth and beauty and triumph, represented to Josie all that she had dreamed of and never realised; all that she had hoped for and never could know. She used to insist on having her door open, and she would lie there for hours, her eyes fixed on that

8

spot in the hall across which Haddon would flash for one brief instant on her way to the room down the corridor. There is about a successful actress a certain radiant something—a glamour, a luxuriousness, an atmosphere that suggest a mysterious mixture of silken things, of perfume, of adulation, of all that is rare and costly and perishable and desirable.

Josie Fifer's stage experience had included none of this. But she knew they were there. She sensed that to this glorious artist would come all those fairy gifts that Josie Fifer would never possess. All things about her—her furs, her gloves, her walk, her hats, her voice, her very shoe ties—were just what Josie would have wished for. As she lay there she developed a certain grim philosophy.

"She's got everything a woman could wish for. Me, I haven't got a thing. Not a blamed thing! And yet they say everything works out in the end according to some scheme or other. Well, what's the answer to this, I wonder? I can't make it come out right. I guess one of the figures must have got away from me."

In the second week of Sid Hahn's convalescence he heard, somehow, of Josie Fifer. It was characteristic of him that he sent for her. She put a chiffon scarf about the neck of her skimpy little kimono, spent an hour and ten minutes on her hair, made up outrageously with that sublime unconsciousness that comes from too close familiarity with rouge pad and grease jar, and went. She was trembling as though facing a first-night audience in a part she wasn't up on. Between the crutches, the lameness, and the trembling she presented to Sid Hahn, as she stood in the doorway, a picture that stabbed his kindly, sensitive heart with a quick pang of sympathy.

He held out his hand. Josie's crept into it. At the feel of that generous friendly clasp she stopped trembling. Said Hahn:

"My nurse tells me that you can do a bedside burlesque of 'East Lynne' that made even that Boston-looking interne with the thick glasses laugh. Go on and do it for me, there's a good girl. I could use a laugh myself just now."

And Josie Fifer caught up a couch cover for a cloak, with the scarf that was about her neck for a veil, and, using Hahn himself as the ailing chee-ild, gave a biting burlesque of the famous bedside visit that brought the tears of laughter to his eyes, and the nurse flying from down the hall. "This won't do," said that austere person.

"Won't, eh? Go on and stick your old thermometer in my mouth. What do I care! A laugh like that is worth five degrees of temperature."

When Josie rose to leave he eyed her keenly, and pointed to the dragging leg.

9

"How about that? Temporary or permanent?"

"Permanent."

"Oh, fudge! Who's telling you that? These days they can do—"

"Not with this, though. That one bone was mashed into about twenty-nine splinters, and when it came to putting 'em together again a couple of pieces were missing. I must've mislaid 'em somewhere. Anyway, I make a limping exit—for life."

"Then no more stage for you—eh, my girl?"

"No more stage."

Hahn reached for a pad of paper on the table at his bedside, scrawled a few words on it, signed it "S.H." in the fashion which became famous, and held the paper out to her.

"When you get out of here," he said, "you come to New York, and up to my office; see? Give 'em this at the door. I've got a job for you—if you want it."

And that was how Josie Fifer came to take charge of the great Hahn & Lohman storehouse. It was more than a storehouse. It was a museum. It housed the archives of the American stage. If Hahn & Lohman prided themselves on one thing more than on another, it was the lavish generosity with which they invested a play, from costumes to carpets. A period play was a period play when they presented it. You never saw a French clock on a Dutch mantel in a Hahn & Lohman production. No hybrid hangings marred their back drop. No matter what the play, the firm provided its furnishings from the star's slippers to the chandeliers. Did a play last a year or a week, at the end of its run furniture, hangings, scenery, rugs, gowns, everything, went off in wagonloads to the already crowded storehouse on East Forty-third Street.

Sometimes a play proved so popular that its original costumes, outworn, had to be renewed. Sometimes the public cried "Thumbs down!" at the opening performance, and would have none of it thereafter. That meant that costumes sometimes reached Josie Fifer while the wounds of the dressmaker's needle still bled in them. And whether for a week or a year fur on a Hahn & Lohman costume was real fur; its satin was silk-backed, its lace real lace. No paste, or tinsel, or cardboard about H. & L.! Josie Fifer could recall the scenes in a play, step by step from noting with her keen eye the marks left on costume after costume by the ravages of emotion. At the end of a play's run she would hold up a dress for critical inspection, turning it this way and that.

"This is the dress she wore in her big scene at the end of the second act where she crawls on her knees to her wronged husband and pounds on the door and weeps. She certainly did give it some hard wear. When Marriott crawls she crawls, and when she bawls she bawls. I'll say that for her. From the looks of this front breadth she must have worn a groove in the stage at the York."

No gently sentimental reason caused Hahn & Lohman to house these hundreds of costumes, these tons of scenery, these forests of furniture. Neither had Josie Fifer been hired to walk wistfully among them like a spinster wandering in a dead rose garden. No, they were stored for a much thriftier reason. They were stored, if you must know, for possible future use. H. & L. were too clever not to use a last year's costume for a this year's road show. They knew what a coat of enamel would do for a bedroom set. It was Josie Fifer's duty not only to tabulate and care for these relics, but to refurbish them when necessary. The sewing was done by a little corps of assistants under Josie's direction.

But all this came with the years. When Josie Fifer, white and weak, first took charge of the H. & L. lares et penates, she told herself it was only for a few months—a year or two at most. The end of sixteen years found her still there.

When she came to New York, "Splendour" was just beginning its phenomenal three years' run. The city was mad about the play. People came to see it again and again—a sure sign of a long run. The Sarah Haddon second-act costume was photographed, copied (unsuccessfully), talked about, until it became as familiar as a uniform. That costume had much to do with the play's success, though Sarah Haddon would never admit it. "Splendour" was what is known as a period play. The famous dress was of black velvet, made with a quaint, full-gathered skirt that made Haddon's slim waist seem fairylike and exquisitely supple. The black velvet bodice outlined the delicate swell of the bust. A rope of pearls enhanced the whiteness of her throat. Her hair, done in old-time scallops about her forehead, was a gleaming marvel of simplicity, and the despair of every woman who tried to copy it. The part was that of an Italian opera singer. The play pulsated with romance and love, glamour and tragedy. Sarah Haddon, in her flowing black velvet robe and her pearls and her pallor, was an exotic, throbbing, exquisite realisation of what every woman in the audience dreamed of being and every man dreamed of loving.

Josie Fifer saw the play for the first time from a balcony seat given her by Sid Hahn. It left her trembling, red-eyed, shaken. After that she used to see it, by hook or crook whenever possible. She used to come in at the stage door and lurk back of the scenes and in the wings when she had no business there. She invented absurd errands to take her to the theatre where "Splendour" was playing. Sid Hahn always said that after the big third-act scene he liked to watch the audience swim up the aisle. Josie, hidden in the backstage shadows, used to watch, fascinated, breathless. Then, one night, she indiscreetly was led, by her, absorbed interest, to venture too far into the wings. It was during the scene where Haddon, hearing a broken-down street singer cracking the golden notes of "Aïda" into a thousand mutilated fragments, throws open her window and, leaning far out, pours a shower of Italian and broken English and laughter and silver coin upon her amazed compatriot below.

When the curtain went down she came off raging.

"What was that? Who was that standing in the wings? How dare any one stand there! Everybody knows I can't have any one in the wings. Staring! It ruined my scene to-night. Where's McCabe? Tell Mr. Hahn I want to see him. Who was it? Staring at me like a ghost!"

Josie had crept away, terrified, contrite, and yet resentful. But the next week saw her back at the theatre, though she took care to stay in the shadows.

She was waiting for the black velvet dress. It was more than a dress to her. It was infinitely more than a stage costume. It was the habit of glory. It epitomised all that Josie Fifer had missed of beauty and homage and success.

The play ran on, and on, and on. Sarah Haddon was superstitious about the black gown. She refused to give it up for a new one. She insisted that if ever she discarded the old black velvet for a new the run of the play would stop. She assured Hahn that its shabbiness did not show from the front. She clung to it with that childish unreasonableness that is so often found in people of the stage.

But Josie waited patiently. Dozens of costumes passed through her hands. She saw plays come and go. Dresses came to her whose lining bore the mark of world-famous modistes. She hung them away, or refurbished them if necessary with disinterested conscientiousness. Sometimes her caustic comment, as she did so, would have startled the complacency of the erstwhile wearers of the garments. Her knowledge of the stage, its artifices, its pretence, its narrowness, its shams, was widening and deepening. No critic in bone-rimmed glasses and evening clothes was more scathingly severe than she. She sewed on satin. She mended fine lace. She polished stage jewels. And waited. She knew that one day her patience would be rewarded. And then, at last came the familiar voice over the phone: "Hello, Fifer! McCabe talking."

"Well?"

"'Splendour' closes Saturday. Haddon says she won't play in

12

this heat. They're taking it to London in the autumn. The stuff'll be up Monday, early."

Josie Fifer turned away from the telephone with a face so radiant that one of her sewing women, looking up, was moved to comment.

"Got some good news, Miss Fifer?"

"'Splendour' closes this week."

"Well, my land! To look at you a person would think you'd been losing money at the box office every night it ran."

The look was still on her face when Monday morning came. She was sewing on a dress just discarded by Adelaide French, the tragédienne. Adelaide's maid was said to be the hardest-worked woman in the profession. When French finished with a costume it was useless as a dress; but it was something historic, like a torn and tattered battle flag—an emblem.

McCabe, box under his arm, stood in the doorway. Josie Fifer stood up so suddenly that the dress on her lap fell to the floor. She stepped over it heedlessly, and went toward McCabe, her eyes on the pasteboard box. Behind McCabe stood two more men, likewise box-laden.

"Put them down here," said Josie. The men thumped the boxes down on the long table. Josie's fingers were already at the strings. She opened the first box, emptied its contents, tossed them aside, passed on to the second. Her hands busied themselves among the silks and broadcloth of this; then on to the third and last box. McCabe and his men, with scenery and furniture still to unload and store, turned to go. Their footsteps echoed hollowly as they clattered down the worn old stairway. Josie snapped the cord that bound the third box. Her cheeks were flushed, her eyes bright. She turned it upside down. Then she pawed it over. Then she went back to the contents of the first two boxes, clawing about among the limp garments with which the table was strewn. She was breathing quickly. Suddenly: "It isn't here!" she cried. "It isn't here!" She turned and flew to the stairway. The voices of the men came up to her. She leaned far over the railing. "McCabe! McCabe!"

"Yeh? What do you want?"

"The black velvet dress! The black velvet dress! It isn't there."

"Oh, yeh. That's all right. Haddon, she's got a bug about that dress, and she says she wants to take it to London with her, to use on the opening night. She says if she wears a new one that first night, the play'll be a failure. Some temperament, that girl, since she's got to be a star!"

Josie stood clutching the railing of the stairway. Her disappointment was so bitter that she could not weep. She felt

13

cheated, outraged. She was frightened at the intensity of her own sensations. "She might have let me have it," she said aloud in the dim half light of the hallway. "She's got everything else in the world. She might have let me have that."

Then she went back into the big, bright sewing room. "Splendour" ran three years in London.

During those three years she saw Sid Hahn only three or four times. He spent much of his time abroad. Whenever opportunity presented itself she would say: "Is 'Splendour' still playing in London?"

"Still playing."

The last time Hahn, intuitive as always, had eyed her curiously. "You seem to be interested in that play."

"Oh, well," Josie had replied with assumed carelessness, "it being in Atlantic City just when I had my accident, and then meeting you through that, and all, why, I always kind of felt a personal interest in it." ...

At the end of three years Sarah Haddon returned to New York with an English accent, a slight embonpoint, and a little foreign habit of rushing up to her men friends with a delighted exclamation (preferably French) and kissing them on both cheeks. When Josie Fifer, happening back stage at a rehearsal of the star's new play, first saw her do this a grim gleam came into her eyes.

"Bernhardt's the only woman who can spring that and get away with it," she said to her assistant. "Haddon's got herself sized up wrong. I'll gamble her next play will be a failure."

And it was.

The scenery, props, and costumes of the London production of "Splendour" were slow in coming back. But finally they did come. Josie received them with the calmness that comes of hope deferred. It had been three years since she last saw the play. She told herself, chidingly, that she had been sort of foolish over that play and this costume. Her recent glimpse of Haddon had been somewhat disillusioning. But now, when she finally held the gown itself in her hand—the original "Splendour" second-act gown, a limp, soft black mass: just a few yards of worn and shabby velvet—she found her hands shaking. Here was where she had hugged the toy dog to her breast. Here where she had fallen on her knees to pray before the little shrine in her hotel room. Every worn spot had a meaning for her. Every mark told a story. Her fingers smoothed it tenderly.

"Not much left of that," said one of the sewing girls, glancing up. "I guess Sarah would have a hard time making the hooks and eyes meet now. They say she's come home from London looking a little too prosperous."

14

Josie did not answer. She folded the dress over her arm and carried it to the wardrobe room. There she hung it away in an empty closet, quite apart from the other historic treasures. And there it hung, untouched, until the following Sunday.

On Sunday morning East Forty-third Street bears no more resemblance to the week-day Forty-third than does a stiffly starched and subdued Sabbath-school scholar to his Monday morning self. Strangely quiet it is, and unfrequented. Josie Fifer, scurrying along in the unwonted stillness, was prompted to throw a furtive glance over her shoulder now and then, as though afraid of being caught at some criminal act. She ran up the little flight of steps with a rush, unlocked the door with trembling fingers, and let herself into the cool, dank gloom of the storehouse hall. The metal door of the elevator stared inquiringly after her. She fled past it to the stairway. Every step of that ancient structure squeaked and groaned. First floor, second, third, fourth. The everyday hum of the sewing machines was absent. The room seemed to be holding its breath. Josie fancied that the very garments on the worktables lifted themselves inquiringly from their supine position to see what it was that disturbed their Sabbath rest. Josie, a tense, wide-eyed, frightened little figure, stood in the centre of the vast room, listening to she knew not what. Then, relaxing, she gave a nervous little laugh and, reaching up, unpinned her hat. She threw it on a near-by table and disappeared into the wardrobe room beyond.

Minutes passed—an hour. She did not come back. From the room beyond came strange sounds—a woman's voice; the thrill of a song; cries; the anguish of tears; laughter, harsh and high, as a desperate and deceived woman laughs—all this following in such rapid succession that Sid Hahn, puffing laboriously up the four flights of stairs leading to the wardrobe floor, entered the main room unheard. Unknown to any one, he was indulging in one of his unsuspected visits to the old wareroom that housed the evidence of past and gone successes—successes that had brought him fortune and fame, but little real happiness, perhaps. No one knew that he loved to browse among these pathetic rags of a forgotten triumph. No one would have dreamed that this chubby little man could glow and weep over the cast-off garment of a famous Cyrano, or the faded finery of a Zaza.

At the doorway he paused now, startled. He was listening with every nerve of his taut body. What? Who? He tiptoed across the room with a step incredibly light for one so stout, peered cautiously around the side of the doorway, and leaned up against it weakly. Josie Fifer, in the black velvet and mock pearls of "Splendour," with her grey-streaked blonde hair hidden under the romantic scallops of

15

a black wig, was giving the big scene from the third act. And though it sounded like a burlesque of that famous passage, and though she limped more than ever as she reeled to an imaginary shrine in the corner, and though the black wig was slightly askew by now, and the black velvet hung with bunchy awkwardness about her skinny little body, there was nothing of mirth in Sid Hahn's face as he gazed. He shrank back now.

She was coming to the big speech at the close of the act—the big renunciation speech that was the curtain. Sid Hahn turned and tiptoed painfully, breathlessly, magnificently, out of the big front room, into the hallway, down the creaking stairs, and so to the sunshine of Forty-third Street, with its unaccustomed Sunday-morning quiet. And he was smiling that rare and melting smile of his—the smile that was said to make him look something like a kewpie, and something like a cupid, and a bit like an imp, and very much like an angel. There was little of the first three in it now, and very much of the last. And so he got heavily into his very grand motor car and drove off.

"Why, the poor little kid," said he—"the poor, lonely, stifled little crippled-up kid."

"I beg your pardon, sir?" inquired his chauffeur.

"Speak when you're spoken to," snapped Sid Hahn.

And here it must be revealed to you that Sid Hahn did not marry the Cinderella of the storage warehouse. He did not marry anybody, and neither did Josie. And yet there is a bit more to this story—ten years more, if you must know—ten years, the end of which found Josie a sparse, spectacled, and agile little cripple, as alert and caustic as ever. It found Sid Hahn the most famous theatrical man of his day. It found Sarah Haddon at the fag-end of a career that had blazed with triumph and adulation. She had never had a success like "Splendour." Indeed, there were those who said that all the plays that followed had been failures, carried to semi-success on the strength of that play's glorious past. She eschewed low-cut gowns now. She knew that it is the telltale throat which first shows the marks of age. She knew, too, why Bernhardt, in "Camille," always died in a high-necked nightgown. She took to wearing high, ruffled things about her throat, and softening, kindly chiffons.

And then, in a mistaken moment, they planned a revival of "Splendour." Sarah Haddon would again play the part that had become a classic. Fathers had told their children of it—of her beauty, her golden voice, the exquisite grace of her, the charm, the tenderness, the pathos. And they told them of the famous black velvet dress, and how in it she had moved like a splendid, buoyant bird.

16

So they revived "Splendour." And men and women brought their sons and daughters to see. And what they saw was a stout, middle-aged woman in a too-tight black velvet dress that made her look like a dowager. And when this woman flopped down on her knees in the big scene at the close of the last act she had a rather dreadful time of it getting up again. And the audience, resentful, bewildered, cheated of a precious memory, laughed. That laugh sealed the career of Sarah Haddon. It is a fickle thing, this public that wants to be amused; fickle and cruel and—paradoxically enough—true to its superstitions. The Sarah Haddon of eighteen years ago was one of these. They would have none of this fat, puffy, ample-bosomed woman who was trying to blot her picture from their memory. "Away with her!" cried the critics through the columns of next morning's paper. And Sarah Haddon's day was done.

"It's because I didn't wear the original black velvet dress!" cried she, with the unreasoning rage for which she had always been famous. "If I had worn it, everything would have been different. That dress had a good-luck charm. Where is it? I want it. I don't care if they do take off the play. I want it. I want it."

"Why, child," Sid Hahn said soothingly, "that dress has probably fallen into dust by this time."

"Dust! What do you mean? How old do you think I am? That you should say that to me! I've made millions for you, and now—"

"Now, now, Sally, be a good girl. That's all rot about that dress being lucky. You've grown out of this part; that's all. We'll find another play—"

"I want that dress."

Sid Hahn flushed uncomfortably. "Well, if you must know, I gave it away."

"To whom?"

"To—to Josie Fifer. She took a notion to it, and so I told her she could have it." Then, as Sarah Haddon rose, dried her eyes, and began to straighten her hat: "Where are you going?" He trailed her to the door worriedly. "Now, Sally, don't do anything foolish. You're just tired and overstrung. Where are you—"

"I am going to see Josie Fifer."

"Now, look here, Sarah!"

But she was off, and Sid Hahn could only follow after, the showman in him anticipating the scene that was to follow. When he reached the fourth floor of the storehouse Sarah Haddon was there ahead of him. The two women—one tall, imperious, magnificent in furs; the other shrunken, deformed, shabby—stood staring at each

17

other from opposites sides of the worktable. And between them, in a crumpled, grey-black heap, lay the velvet gown.

"I don't care who says you can have it," Josie Fifer's shrill voice was saying. "It's mine, and I'm going to keep it. Mr. Hahn himself gave it to me. He said I could cut it up for a dress or something if I wanted to. Long ago." Then, as Sid Hahn himself appeared, she appealed to him. "There he is now. Didn't you, Mr. Hahn? Didn't you say I could have it? Years ago?"

"Yes, Jo," said Sid Hahn. "It's yours, to do with as you wish."

Sarah Haddon, who never had been denied anything in all her pampered life, turned to him now. Her bosom rose and fell. She was breathing sharply. "But S.H.!" she cried, "S.H., I've got to have it. Don't you see, I want it! It's all I've got left in the world of what I used to be. I want it!" She began to cry, and it was not acting.

Josie Fifer stood staring at her, her eyes wide with horror and unbelief.

"Why, say, listen! Listen! You can have it. I didn't know you wanted it as bad as that. Why, you can have it. I want you to take it. Here."

She shoved it across the table. Sarah reached out for it quickly. She rolled it up in a tight bundle and whisked off with it without a backward glance at Josie or at Hahn. She was still sobbing as she went down the stairs.

The two stood staring at each other ludicrously. Hahn spoke first.

"I'm sorry, Josie. That was nice of you, giving it to her like that."

But Josie did not seem to hear. At least she paid no attention to his remark. She was staring at him with that dazed and wide-eyed look of one upon whom a great truth has just dawned. Then, suddenly, she began to laugh. She laughed a high, shrill laugh that was not so much an expression of mirth as of relief.

Sid Hahn put up a pudgy hand in protest. "Josie! Please! For the love of Heaven don't you go and get it. I've had to do with one hysterical woman to-day. Stop that laughing! Stop it!"

Josie stopped, not abruptly, but in a little series of recurring giggles. Then these subsided and she was smiling. It wasn't at all her usual smile. The bitterness was quite gone from it. She faced Sid Hahn across the table. Her palms were outspread, as one who would make things plain. "I wasn't hysterical. I was just laughing. I've been about seventeen years earning that laugh. Don't grudge it to me."

"Let's have the plot," said Hahn.

"There isn't any. You see, it's just—well, I've just discovered how it works out. After all these years! She's had everything she

18

wanted all her life. And me, I've never had anything. Not a thing. She's travelled one way, and I've travelled in the opposite direction, and where has it brought us? Here we are, both fighting over an old black velvet rag. Don't you see? Both wanting the same—" She broke off, with the little twisted smile on her lips again. "Life's a strange thing, Mr. Hahn."

"I hope, Josie, you don't claim any originality for that remark," replied Sid Hahn dryly.

"But," argued the editor, "you don't call this a cheerful story, I hope."

"Well, perhaps not exactly boisterous. But it teaches a lesson, and all that. And it's sort of philosophical and everything, don't you think?"

The editor shuffled the sheets together decisively, so that they formed a neat sheaf. "I'm afraid I didn't make myself quite clear. It's entertaining, and all that, but—ah—in view of our present needs, I'm sorry to say we—"

II

THE GAY OLD DOG

Those of you who have dwelt—or even lingered—in Chicago, Illinois (this is not a humorous story), are familiar with the region known as the Loop. For those others of you to whom Chicago is a transfer point between New York and San Francisco there is presented this brief explanation:

The Loop is a clamorous, smoke-infested district embraced by the iron arms of the elevated tracks. In a city boasting fewer millions, it would be known familiarly as downtown. From Congress to Lake Street, from Wabash almost to the river, those thunderous tracks make a complete circle, or loop. Within it lie the retail shops, the commercial hotels, the theatres, the restaurants. It is the Fifth Avenue (diluted) and the Broadway (deleted) of Chicago. And he who frequents it by night in search of amusement and cheer is known, vulgarly, as a Loop-hound.

Jo Hertz was a Loop-hound. On the occasion of those sparse first nights granted the metropolis of the Middle West he was always present, third row, aisle, left. When a new loop café was opened Jo's table always commanded an unobstructed view of anything worth viewing. On entering he was wont to say, "Hello, Gus," with careless cordiality to the head waiter, the while his eye roved expertly from table to table as he removed his gloves. He ordered things under glass, so that his table, at midnight or thereabouts, resembled a hot-bed that favours the bell system. The waiters fought for him. He was the kind of man who mixes his own salad dressing. He liked to call for a bowl, some cracked ice, lemon, garlic, paprika, salt, pepper, vinegar, and oil and make a rite of it. People at near-by tables would lay down their knives and forks to watch, fascinated. The secret of it seemed to lie in using all the oil in sight and calling for more.

That was Jo—a plump and lonely bachelor of fifty. A plethoric, roving-eyed and kindly man, clutching vainly at the garments of a youth that had long slipped past him. Jo Hertz, in one of those pinch-waist belted suits and a trench coat and a little green hat, walking up Michigan Avenue of a bright winter's afternoon, trying to take the curb with a jaunty youthfulness against which every one of his fat-encased muscles rebelled, was a sight for mirth or pity, depending on one's vision.

The gay-dog business was a late phase in the life of Jo Hertz.

He had been a quite different sort of canine. The staid and harassed brother of three unwed and selfish sisters is an under dog. The tale of how Jo Hertz came to be a Loop-hound should not be compressed within the limits of a short story. It should be told as are the photo plays, with frequent throwbacks and many cut-ins. To condense twenty-three years of a man's life into some five or six thousand words requires a verbal economy amounting to parsimony.

At twenty-seven Jo had been the dutiful, hard-working son (in the wholesale harness business) of a widowed and gummidging mother, who called him Joey. If you had looked close you would have seen that now and then a double wrinkle would appear between Jo's eyes—a wrinkle that had no business there at twenty-seven. Then Jo's mother died, leaving him handicapped by a death-bed promise, the three sisters and a three-story-and-basement house on Calumet Avenue. Jo's wrinkle became a fixture.

Death-bed promises should be broken as lightly as they are seriously made. The dead have no right to lay their clammy fingers upon the living.

"Joey," she had said, in her high, thin voice, "take care of the girls."

"I will, Ma," Jo had choked.

"Joey," and the voice was weaker, "promise me you won't marry till the girls are all provided for." Then as Joe had hesitated, appalled: "Joey, it's my dying wish. Promise!"

"I promise, Ma," he had said.

Whereupon his mother had died, comfortably, leaving him with a completely ruined life.

They were not bad-looking girls, and they had a certain style, too. That is, Stell and Eva had. Carrie, the middle one, taught school over on the West Side. In those days it took her almost two hours each way. She said the kind of costume she required should have been corrugated steel. But all three knew what was being worn, and they wore it—or fairly faithful copies of it. Eva, the housekeeping sister, had a needle knack. She could skim the State Street windows and come away with a mental photograph of every separate tuck, hem, yoke, and ribbon. Heads of departments showed her the things they kept in drawers, and she went home and reproduced them with the aid of a two-dollar-a-day seamstress. Stell, the youngest, was the beauty. They called her Babe. She wasn't really a beauty, but some one had once told her that she looked like Janice Meredith (it was when that work of fiction was at the height of its popularity). For years afterward, whenever she went to parties, she

21

affected a single, fat curl over her right shoulder, with a rose stuck through it.

Twenty-three years ago one's sisters did not strain at the household leash, nor crave a career. Carrie taught school, and hated it. Eva kept house expertly and complainingly. Babe's profession was being the family beauty, and it took all her spare time. Eva always let her sleep until ten.

This was Jo's household, and he was the nominal head of it. But it was an empty title. The three women dominated his life. They weren't consciously selfish. If you had called them cruel they would have put you down as mad. When you are the lone brother of three sisters, it means that you must constantly be calling for, escorting, or dropping one of them somewhere. Most men of Jo's age were standing before their mirror of a Saturday night, whistling blithely and abstractedly while they discarded a blue polka-dot for a maroon tie, whipped off the maroon for a shot-silk, and at the last moment decided against the shot-silk in favor of a plain black-and-white, because she had once said she preferred quiet ties. Jo, when he should have been preening his feathers for conquest, was saying:

"Well, my God, I am hurrying! Give a man time, can't you? I just got home. You girls have been laying around the house all day. No wonder you're ready."

He took a certain pride in seeing his sisters well dressed, at a time when he should have been reveling in fancy waistcoats and brilliant-hued socks, according to the style of that day, and the inalienable right of any unwed male under thirty, in any day. On those rare occasions when his business necessitated an out-of-town trip, he would spend half a day floundering about the shops, selecting handkerchiefs, or stockings, or feathers, or fans, or gloves for the girls. They always turned out to be the wrong kind, judging by their reception.

From Carrie, "What in the world do I want of a fan!"

"I thought you didn't have one," Jo would say.

"I haven't. I never go to dances."

Jo would pass a futile hand over the top of his head, as was his way when disturbed. "I just thought you'd like one. I thought every girl liked a fan. Just," feebly, "just to—to have."

"Oh, for pity's sake!"

And from Eva or Babe, "I've got silk stockings, Jo." Or, "You brought me handkerchiefs the last time."

There was something selfish in his giving, as there always is in any gift freely and joyfully made. They never suspected the exquisite pleasure it gave him to select these things; these fine, soft, silken things. There were many things about this slow-going, amiable

22

brother of theirs that they never suspected. If you had told them he was a dreamer of dreams, for example, they would have been amused. Sometimes, dead-tired by nine o'clock, after a hard day down town, he would doze over the evening paper. At intervals he would wake, red-eyed, to a snatch of conversation such as, "Yes, but if you get a blue you can wear it anywhere. It's dressy, and at the same time it's quiet, too." Eva, the expert, wrestling with Carrie over the problem of the new spring dress. They never guessed that the commonplace man in the frayed old smoking-jacket had banished them all from the room long ago; had banished himself, for that matter. In his place was a tall, debonair, and rather dangerously handsome man to whom six o'clock spelled evening clothes. The kind of man who can lean up against a mantel, or propose a toast, or give an order to a man-servant, or whisper a gallant speech in a lady's ear with equal ease. The shabby old house on Calumet Avenue was transformed into a brocaded and chandeliered rendezvous for the brilliance of the city. Beauty was here, and wit. But none so beautiful and witty as She. Mrs.—er—Jo Hertz. There was wine, of course; but no vulgar display. There was music; the soft sheen of satin; laughter. And he the gracious, tactful host, king of his own domain—

"Jo, for heaven's sake, if you're going to snore go to bed!"

"Why—did I fall asleep?"

"You haven't been doing anything else all evening. A person would think you were fifty instead of thirty."

And Jo Hertz was again just the dull, grey, commonplace brother of three well-meaning sisters.

Babe used to say petulantly, "Jo, why don't you ever bring home any of your men friends? A girl might as well not have any brother, all the good you do."

Jo, conscience-stricken, did his best to make amends. But a man who has been petticoat-ridden for years loses the knack, somehow, of comradeship with men. He acquires, too, a knowledge of women, and a distaste for them, equalled only, perhaps, by that of an elevator-starter in a department store.

Which brings us to one Sunday in May. Jo came home from a late Sunday afternoon walk to find company for supper. Carrie often had in one of her school-teacher friends, or Babe one of her frivolous intimates, or even Eva a staid guest of the old-girl type. There was always a Sunday night supper of potato salad, and cold meat, and coffee, and perhaps a fresh cake. Jo rather enjoyed it, being a hospitable soul. But he regarded the guests with the undazzled eyes of a man to whom they were just so many petticoats, timid of the night streets and requiring escort home. If you had

23

suggested to him that some of his sisters' popularity was due to his own presence, or if you had hinted that the more kittenish of these visitors were probably making eyes at him, he would have stared in amazement and unbelief.

This Sunday night it turned out to be one of Carrie's friends.

"Emily," said Carrie, "this is my brother, Jo."

Jo had learned what to expect in Carrie's friends. Drab-looking women in the late thirties, whose facial lines all slanted downward.

"Happy to meet you," said Jo, and looked down at a different sort altogether. A most surprisingly different sort, for one of Carrie's friends. This Emily person was very small, and fluffy, and blue-eyed, and sort of—well, crinkly looking. You know. The corners of her mouth when she smiled, and her eyes when she looked up at you, and her hair, which was brown, but had the miraculous effect, somehow, of being golden.

Jo shook hands with her. Her hand was incredibly small, and soft, so that you were afraid of crushing it, until you discovered she had a firm little grip all her own. It surprised and amused you, that grip, as does a baby's unexpected clutch on your patronising forefinger. As Jo felt it in his own big clasp, the strangest thing happened to him. Something inside Jo Hertz stopped working for a moment, then lurched sickeningly, then thumped like mad. It was his heart. He stood staring down at her, and she up at him, until the others laughed. Then their hands fell apart, lingeringly.

"Are you a school-teacher, Emily?" he said.

"Kindergarten. It's my first year. And don't call me Emily, please."

"Why not? It's your name. I think it's the prettiest name in the world." Which he hadn't meant to say at all. In fact, he was perfectly aghast to find himself saying it. But he meant it.

At supper he passed her things, and stared, until everybody laughed again, and Eva said acidly, "Why don't you feed her?"

It wasn't that Emily had an air of helplessness. She just made you feel you wanted her to be helpless, so that you could help her.

Jo took her home, and from that Sunday night he began to strain at the leash. He took his sisters out, dutifully, but he would suggest, with a carelessness that deceived no one, "Don't you want one of your girl friends to come along? That little What's-her-name—Emily, or something. So long's I've got three of you, I might as well have a full squad."

For a long time he didn't know what was the matter with him. He only knew he was miserable, and yet happy. Sometimes his heart seemed to ache with an actual physical ache. He realised that he wanted to do things for Emily. He wanted to buy things for Emily—

24

useless, pretty, expensive things that he couldn't afford. He wanted to buy everything that Emily needed, and everything that Emily desired. He wanted to marry Emily. That was it. He discovered that one day, with a shock, in the midst of a transaction in the harness business. He stared at the man with whom he was dealing until that startled person grew uncomfortable.

"What's the matter, Hertz?"

"Matter?"

"You look as if you'd seen a ghost or found a gold mine. I don't know which."

"Gold mine," said Jo. And then, "No. Ghost."

For he remembered that high, thin voice, and his promise. And the harness business was slithering downhill with dreadful rapidity, as the automobile business began its amazing climb. Jo tried to stop it. But he was not that kind of business man. It never occurred to him to jump out of the down-going vehicle and catch the up-going one. He stayed on, vainly applying brakes that refused to work.

"You know, Emily, I couldn't support two households now. Not the way things are. But if you'll wait. If you'll only wait. The girls might—that is, Babe and Carrie—"

She was a sensible little thing, Emily. "Of course I'll wait. But we mustn't just sit back and let the years go by. We've got to help."

She went about it as if she were already a little match-making matron. She corralled all the men she had ever known and introduced them to Babe, Carrie, and Eva separately, in pairs, and en masse. She arranged parties at which Babe could display the curl. She got up picnics. She stayed home while Jo took the three about. When she was present she tried to look as plain and obscure as possible, so that the sisters should show up to advantage. She schemed, and planned, and contrived, and hoped; and smiled into Jo's despairing eyes.

And three years went by. Three precious years. Carrie still taught school, and hated it. Eva kept house, more and more complainingly as prices advanced and allowance retreated. Stell was still Babe, the family beauty; but even she knew that the time was past for curls. Emily's hair, somehow, lost its glint and began to look just plain brown. Her crinkliness began to iron out.

"Now, look here!" Jo argued, desperately, one night. "We could be happy, anyway. There's plenty of room at the house. Lots of people begin that way. Of course, I couldn't give you all I'd like to, at first. But maybe, after a while—"

No dreams of salons, and brocade, and velvet-footed servitors, and satin damask now. Just two rooms, all their own, all alone, and

25

Emily to work for. That was his dream. But it seemed less possible than that other absurd one had been.

You know that Emily was as practical a little thing as she looked fluffy. She knew women. Especially did she know Eva, and Carrie, and Babe. She tried to imagine herself taking the household affairs and the housekeeping pocketbook out of Eva's expert hands. Eva had once displayed to her a sheaf of aigrettes she had bought with what she saved out of the housekeeping money. So then she tried to picture herself allowing the reins of Jo's house to remain in Eva's hands. And everything feminine and normal in her rebelled. Emily knew she'd want to put away her own freshly laundered linen, and smooth it, and pat it. She was that kind of woman. She knew she'd want to do her own delightful haggling with butcher and vegetable pedlar. She knew she'd want to muss Jo's hair, and sit on his knee, and even quarrel with him, if necessary, without the awareness of three ever-present pairs of maiden eyes and ears.

"No! No! We'd only be miserable. I know. Even if they didn't object. And they would, Jo. Wouldn't they?"

His silence was miserable assent. Then, "But you do love me, don't you, Emily?"

"I do, Jo. I love you—and love you—and love you. But, Jo, I—can't."

"I know it, dear. I knew it all the time, really. I just thought, maybe, somehow—"

The two sat staring for a moment into space, their hands clasped. Then they both shut their eyes, with a little shudder, as though what they saw was terrible to look upon. Emily's hand, the tiny hand that was so unexpectedly firm, tightened its hold on his, and his crushed the absurd fingers until she winced with pain.

That was the beginning of the end, and they knew it.

Emily wasn't the kind of girl who would be left to pine. There are too many Jo's in the world whose hearts are prone to lurch and then thump at the feel of a soft, fluttering, incredibly small hand in their grip. One year later Emily was married to a young man whose father owned a large, pie-shaped slice of the prosperous state of Michigan.

That being safely accomplished, there was something grimly humorous in the trend taken by affairs in the old house on Calumet. For Eva married. Of all people, Eva! Married well, too, though he was a great deal older than she. She went off in a hat she had copied from a French model at Field's, and a suit she had contrived with a home dressmaker, aided by pressing on the part of the little tailor in the basement over on Thirty-first Street. It was the last of that, though. The next time they saw her, she had on a hat that even she would have despaired of copying, and a suit that sort of melted into your gaze. She moved to the North Side (trust Eva for that), and Babe assumed the management of the household on Calumet Avenue. It was rather a pinched little household now, for the harness business shrank and shrank.

"I don't see how you can expect me to keep house decently on this!" Babe would say contemptuously. Babe's nose, always a little inclined to sharpness, had whittled down to a point of late. "If you knew what Ben gives Eva."

"It's the best I can do, Sis. Business is something rotten."

"Ben says if you had the least bit of—" Ben was Eva's husband, and quotable, as are all successful men.

"I don't care what Ben says," shouted Jo, goaded into rage. "I'm sick of your everlasting Ben. Go and get a Ben of your own, why don't you, if you're so stuck on the way he does things."

And Babe did. She made a last desperate drive, aided by Eva, and she captured a rather surprised young man in the brokerage way, who had made up his mind not to marry for years and years. Eva wanted to give her her wedding things, but at that Jo broke into sudden rebellion.

"No sir! No Ben is going to buy my sister's wedding clothes, understand? I guess I'm not broke—yet. I'll furnish the money for her things, and there'll be enough of them, too."

Babe had as useless a trousseau, and as filled with extravagant pink-and-blue and lacy and frilly things as any daughter of doting parents. Jo seemed to find a grim pleasure in providing them. But it left him pretty well pinched. After Babe's marriage (she insisted that they call her Estelle now) Jo sold the house on Calumet. He and Carrie took one of those little flats that were springing up, seemingly over night, all through Chicago's South Side.

There was nothing domestic about Carrie. She had given up teaching two years before, and had gone into Social Service work on the West Side. She had what is known as a legal mind—hard, clear, orderly—and she made a great success of it. Her dream was to live at the Settlement House and give all her time to the work. Upon the little household she bestowed a certain amount of grim, capable attention. It was the same kind of attention she would have given a piece of machinery whose oiling and running had been entrusted to her care. She hated it, and didn't hesitate to say so.

Jo took to prowling about department store basements, and household goods sections. He was always sending home a bargain in a ham, or a sack of potatoes, or fifty pounds of sugar, or a window clamp, or a new kind of paring knife. He was forever doing odd little jobs that the janitor should have done. It was the domestic in him claiming its own.

Then, one night, Carrie came home with a dull glow in her leathery cheeks, and her eyes alight with resolve. They had what she called a plain talk.

"Listen, Jo. They've offered me the job of first assistant resident worker. And I'm going to take it. Take it! I know fifty other girls who'd give their ears for it. I go in next month."

They were at dinner. Jo looked up from his plate, dully. Then he glanced around the little dining room, with its ugly tan walls and its heavy, dark furniture (the Calumet Avenue pieces fitted cumbersomely into the five-room flat).

"Away? Away from here, you mean—to live?" Carrie laid down her fork. "Well, really, Jo! After all that explanation."

"But to go over there to live! Why, that neighbourhood's full of dirt, and disease, and crime, and the Lord knows what all. I can't let you do that, Carrie."

Carrie's chin came up. She laughed a short little laugh. "Let me! That's eighteenth-century talk, Jo. My life's my own to live. I'm going."

And she went.

Jo stayed on in the apartment until the lease was up. Then he sold what furniture he could, stored or gave away the rest, and took a room on Michigan Avenue in one of the old stone mansions whose decayed splendour was being put to such purpose.

Jo Hertz was his own master. Free to marry. Free to come and go. And he found he didn't even think of marrying. He didn't even want to come or go, particularly. A rather frumpy old bachelor, with thinning hair and a thickening neck. Much has been written about the unwed, middle-aged woman; her fussiness, her primness, her angularity of mind and body. In the male that same fussiness develops, and a certain primness, too. But he grows flabby where she grows lean.

Every Thursday evening he took dinner at Eva's, and on Sunday noon at Stell's. He tucked his napkin under his chin and openly enjoyed the home-made soup and the well-cooked meats. After dinner he tried to talk business with Eva's husband, or Stell's. His business talks were the old-fashioned kind, beginning:

"Well, now, looka here. Take, f'rinstance your raw hides and leathers."

But Ben and George didn't want to "take, f'rinstance, your raw hides and leathers." They wanted, when they took anything at all, to take golf, or politics or stocks. They were the modern type of business man who prefers to leave his work out of his play.

28

Business, with them, was a profession—a finely graded and balanced thing, differing from Jo's clumsy, downhill style as completely as does the method of a great criminal detective differ from that of a village constable. They would listen, restively, and say, "Uh-uh," at intervals, and at the first chance they would sort of fade out of the room, with a meaning glance at their wives. Eva had two children now. Girls. They treated Uncle Jo with good-natured tolerance. Stell had no children. Uncle Jo degenerated, by almost imperceptible degrees, from the position of honoured guest, who is served with white meat, to that of one who is content with a leg and one of those obscure and bony sections which, after much turning with a bewildered and investigating knife and fork, leave one baffled and unsatisfied.

Eva and Stell got together and decided that Jo ought to marry.

"It isn't natural," Eva told him. "I never saw a man who took so little interest in women."

"Me!" protested Jo, almost shyly. "Women!"

"Yes. Of course. You act like a frightened schoolboy."

So they had in for dinner certain friends and acquaintances of fitting age. They spoke of them as "splendid girls." Between thirty-six and forty. They talked awfully well, in a firm, clear way, about civics, and classes, and politics, and economics, and boards. They rather terrified Jo. He didn't understand much that they talked about, and he felt humbly inferior, and yet a little resentful, as if something had passed him by. He escorted them home, dutifully, though they told him not to bother, and they evidently meant it. They seemed capable, not only of going home quite unattended, but of delivering a pointed lecture to any highwayman or brawler who might molest them.

The following Thursday Eva would say, "How did you like her, Jo?"

"Like who?" Jo would spar feebly.

"Miss Matthews."

"Who's she?"

"Now, don't be funny, Jo. You know very well I mean the girl who was here for dinner. The one who talked so well on the emigration question."

"Oh, her! Why, I liked her all right. Seems to be a smart woman."

"Smart! She's a perfectly splendid girl."

"Sure," Jo would agree cheerfully.

"But didn't you like her?"

"I can't say I did, Eve. And I can't say I didn't. She made me think a lot of a teacher I had in the fifth reader. Name of Himes. As I

29

recall her, she must have been a fine woman. But I never thought of her as a woman at all. She was just Teacher."

"You make me tired," snapped Eva impatiently. "A man of your age. You don't expect to marry a girl, do you? A child!"

"I don't expect to marry anybody," Jo had answered.

And that was the truth, lonely though he often was.

The following spring Eva moved to Winnetka. Any one who got the meaning of the Loop knows the significance of a move to a north-shore suburb, and a house. Eva's daughter, Ethel, was growing up, and her mother had an eye on society.

That did away with Jo's Thursday dinner. Then Stell's husband bought a car. They went out into the country every Sunday. Stell said it was getting so that maids objected to Sunday dinners, anyway. Besides, they were unhealthy, old-fashioned things. They always meant to ask Jo to come along, but by the time their friends were placed, and the lunch, and the boxes, and sweaters, and George's camera, and everything, there seemed to be no room for a man of Jo's bulk. So that eliminated the Sunday dinners.

"Just drop in any time during the week," Stell said, "for dinner. Except Wednesday—that's our bridge night—and Saturday. And, of course, Thursday. Cook is out that night. Don't wait for me to phone."

And so Jo drifted into that sad-eyed, dyspeptic family made up of those you see dining in second-rate restaurants, their paper propped up against the bowl of oyster crackers, munching solemnly and with indifference to the stare of the passer-by surveying them through the brazen plate-glass window.

And then came the War. The war that spelled death and destruction to millions. The war that brought a fortune to Jo Hertz, and transformed him, over night, from a baggy-kneed old bachelor, whose business was a failure, to a prosperous manufacturer whose only trouble was the shortage in hides for the making of his product—leather! The armies of Europe called for it. Harnesses! More harnesses! Straps! Millions of straps. More! More!

The musty old harness business over on Lake Street was magically changed from a dust-covered, dead-alive concern to an orderly hive that hummed and glittered with success. Orders poured in. Jo Hertz had inside information on the War. He knew about troops and horses. He talked with French and English and Italian buyers—noblemen, many of them—commissioned by their countries to get American-made supplies. And now, when he said to Ben or George, "Take f'rinstance your raw hides and leathers," they listened with respectful attention.

And then began the gay-dog business in the life of Jo Hertz. He developed into a Loop-hound, ever keen on the scent of fresh pleasure. That side of Jo Hertz which had been repressed and crushed and ignored began to bloom, unhealthily. At first he spent money on his rather contemptuous nieces. He sent them gorgeous fans, and watch bracelets, and velvet bags. He took two expensive rooms at a downtown hotel, and there was something more tear-compelling than grotesque about the way he gloated over the luxury of a separate ice-water tap in the bathroom. He explained it.

"Just turn it on. Ice-water! Any hour of the day or night."

He bought a car. Naturally. A glittering affair; in colour a bright blue, with pale blue leather straps and a great deal of gold fittings, and wire wheels. Eva said it was the kind of thing a soubrette would use, rather than an elderly business man. You saw him driving about in it, red-faced and rather awkward at the wheel. You saw him, too, in the Pompeian room at the Congress Hotel of a Saturday afternoon when doubtful and roving-eyed matrons in kolinsky capes are wont to congregate to sip pale amber drinks. Actors grew to recognise the semi-bald head and the shining, round, good-natured face looming out at them from the dim well of the parquet, and sometimes, in a musical show, they directed a quip at him, and he liked it. He could pick out the critics as they came down the aisle, and even had a nodding acquaintance with two of them.

"Kelly, of the Herald," he would say carelessly. "Bean, of the Trib. They're all afraid of him."

So he frolicked, ponderously. In New York he might have been called a Man About Town.

And he was lonesome. He was very lonesome. So he searched about in his mind and brought from the dim past the memory of the luxuriously furnished establishment of which he used to dream in the evenings when he dozed over his paper in the old house on Calumet. So he rented an apartment, many-roomed and expensive, with a man-servant in charge, and furnished it in styles and periods ranging through all the Louises. The living room was mostly rose colour. It was like an unhealthy and bloated boudoir. And yet there was nothing sybaritic or uncleanly in the sight of this paunchy, middle-aged man sinking into the rosy-cushioned luxury of his ridiculous home. It was a frank and naïve indulgence of long-starved senses, and there was in it a great resemblance to the rolling eyed ecstasy of a schoolboy smacking his lips over an all-day sucker.

The War went on, and on, and on. And the money continued to roll in—a flood of it. Then, one afternoon, Eva, in town on shopping bent, entered a small, exclusive, and expensive shop on Michigan Avenue. Exclusive, that is, in price. Eva's weakness, you may remember, was hats. She was seeking a hat now. She described what she sought with a languid conciseness, and stood looking about her after the saleswoman had vanished in quest of it. The room was becomingly rose-illumined and somewhat dim, so that some minutes had passed before she realised that a man seated on a raspberry brocade settee not five feet away—a man with a walking stick, and yellow gloves, and tan spats, and a check suit—was her brother Jo. From him Eva's wild-eyed glance leaped to the woman who was trying on hats before one of the many long mirrors. She was seated, and a saleswoman was exclaiming discreetly at her elbow.

Eva turned sharply and encountered her own saleswoman returning, hat-laden. "Not to-day," she gasped. "I'm feeling ill. Suddenly." And almost ran from the room.

That evening she told Stell, relating her news in that telephone pidgin-English devised by every family of married sisters as protection against the neighbours and Central. Translated, it ran thus:

"He looked straight at me. My dear, I thought I'd die! But at least he had sense enough not to speak. She was one of those limp, willowy creatures with the greediest eyes that she tried to keep softened to a baby stare, and couldn't, she was so crazy to get her hands on those hats. I saw it all in one awful minute. You know the way I do. I suppose some people would call her pretty. I don't. And her colour! Well! And the most expensive-looking hats. Aigrettes, and paradise, and feathers. Not one of them under seventy-five. Isn't it disgusting! At his age! Suppose Ethel had been with me!"

The next time it was Stell who saw them. In a restaurant. She said it spoiled her evening. And the third time it was Ethel. She was one of the guests at a theatre party given by Nicky Overton II. You know. The North Shore Overtons. Lake Forest. They came in late, and occupied the entire third row at the opening performance of "Believe Me!" And Ethel was Nicky's partner. She was glowing like a rose. When the lights went up after the first act Ethel saw that her uncle Jo was seated just ahead of her with what she afterward described as a blonde. Then her uncle had turned around, and seeing her, had been surprised into a smile that spread genially all over his plump and rubicund face. Then he had turned to face forward again, quickly.

"Who's the old bird?" Nicky had asked. Ethel had pretended not to hear, so he had asked again.

"My Uncle," Ethel answered, and flushed all over her delicate face, and down to her throat. Nicky had looked at the blonde, and his eyebrows had gone up ever so slightly.

It spoiled Ethel's evening. More than that, as she told her mother of it later, weeping, she declared it had spoiled her life.

Eva talked it over with her husband in that intimate, kimonoed hour that precedes bedtime. She gesticulated heatedly with her hair brush.

"It's disgusting, that's what it is. Perfectly disgusting. There's no fool like an old fool. Imagine! A creature like that. At his time of life."

There exists a strange and loyal kinship among men. "Well, I don't know," Ben said now, and even grinned a little. "I suppose a boy's got to sow his wild oats some time."

"Don't be any more vulgar than you can help," Eva retorted. "And I think you know, as well as I, what it means to have that Overton boy interested in Ethel."

"If he's interested in her," Ben blundered, "I guess the fact that Ethel's uncle went to the theatre with some one who wasn't Ethel's aunt won't cause a shudder to run up and down his frail young frame, will it?"

"All right," Eva had retorted. "If you're not man enough to stop it, I'll have to, that's all. I'm going up there with Stell this week."

They did not notify Jo of their coming. Eva telephoned his apartment when she knew he would be out, and asked his man if he expected his master home to dinner that evening. The man had said yes. Eva arranged to meet Stell in town. They would drive to Jo's apartment together, and wait for him there.

When she reached the city Eva found turmoil there. The first of the American troops to be sent to France were leaving. Michigan Boulevard was a billowing, surging mass: Flags, pennants, banners crowds. All the elements that make for demonstration. And over the whole—quiet. No holiday crowd, this. A solid, determined mass of people waiting patient hours to see the khaki-clads go by. Three years of indefatigable reading had brought them to a clear knowledge of what these boys were going to.

"Isn't it dreadful!" Stell gasped.

"Nicky Overton's only nineteen, thank goodness."

Their car was caught in the jam. When they moved at all it was by inches. When at last they reached Jo's apartment they were flushed, nervous, apprehensive. But he had not yet come in. So they waited.

No, they were not staying to dinner with their brother, they told the relieved houseman.

Jo's home has already been described to you. Stell and Eva, sunk in rose-coloured cushions, viewed it with disgust, and some mirth. They rather avoided each other's eyes.

33

"Carrie ought to be here," Eva said. They both smiled at the thought of the austere Carrie in the midst of those rosy cushions, and hangings, and lamps. Stell rose and began to walk about, restlessly. She picked up a vase and laid it down; straightened a picture. Eva got up, too, and wandered into the hall. She stood there a moment, listening. Then she turned and passed into Jo's bedroom. And there you knew Jo for what he was.

This room was as bare as the other had been ornate. It was Jo, the clean-minded and simple-hearted, in revolt against the cloying luxury with which he had surrounded himself. The bedroom, of all rooms in any house, reflects the personality of its occupant. True, the actual furniture was panelled, cupid-surmounted, and ridiculous. It had been the fruit of Jo's first orgy of the senses. But now it stood out in that stark little room with an air as incongruous and ashamed as that of a pink tarleton danseuse who finds herself in a monk's cell. None of those wall-pictures with which bachelor bedrooms are reputed to be hung. No satin slippers. No scented notes. Two plain-backed military brushes on the chiffonier (and he so nearly hairless!). A little orderly stack of books on the table near the bed. Eva fingered their titles and gave a little gasp. One of them was on gardening.

"Well, of all things!" exclaimed Stell. A book on the War, by an Englishman. A detective story of the lurid type that lulls us to sleep. His shoes ranged in a careful row in the closet, with a shoe-tree in every one of them. There was something speaking about them. They looked so human. Eva shut the door on them, quickly. Some bottles on the dresser. A jar of pomade. An ointment such as a man uses who is growing bald and is panic-stricken too late. An insurance calendar on the wall. Some rhubarb-and-soda mixture on the shelf in the bathroom, and a little box of pepsin tablets.

"Eats all kinds of things at all hours of the night," Eva said, and wandered out into the rose-coloured front room again with the air of one who is chagrined at her failure to find what she has sought. Stell followed her furtively.

"Where do you suppose he can be?" she demanded. "It's"—she glanced at her wrist—"why, it's after six!"

And then there was a little click. The two women sat up, tense. The door opened. Jo came in. He blinked a little. The two women in the rosy room stood up.

"Why—Eve! Why, Babe! Well! Why didn't you let me know?"

"We were just about to leave. We thought you weren't coming home."

Joe came in, slowly.

"I was in the jam on Michigan, watching the boys go by." He sat

34

down, heavily. The light from the window fell on him. And you saw that his eyes were red.

And you'll have to learn why. He had found himself one of the thousands in the jam on Michigan Avenue, as he said. He had a place near the curb, where his big frame shut off the view of the unfortunates behind him. He waited with the placid interest of one who has subscribed to all the funds and societies to which a prosperous, middle-aged business man is called upon to subscribe in war time. Then, just as he was about to leave, impatient at the delay, the crowd had cried, with a queer dramatic, exultant note in its voice, "Here they come! Here come the boys!"

Just at that moment two little, futile, frenzied fists began to beat a mad tattoo on Jo Hertz's broad back. Jo tried to turn in the crowd, all indignant resentment. "Say, looka here!"

The little fists kept up their frantic beating and pushing. And a voice—a choked, high little voice—cried, "Let me by! I can't see! You man, you! You big fat man! My boy's going by—to war—and I can't see! Let me by!"

Jo scrooged around, still keeping his place. He looked down. And upturned to him in agonised appeal was the face of little Emily. They stared at each other for what seemed a long, long time. It was really only the fraction of a second. Then Jo put one great arm firmly around Emily's waist and swung her around in front of him. His great bulk protected her. Emily was clinging to his hand. She was breathing rapidly, as if she had been running. Her eyes were straining up the street.

"Why, Emily, how in the world!—"

"I ran away. Fred didn't want me to come. He said it would excite me too much."

"Fred?"

"My husband. He made me promise to say good-bye to Jo at home."

"Jo?"

"Jo's my boy. And he's going to war. So I ran away. I had to see him. I had to see him go."

She was dry-eyed. Her gaze was straining up the street.

"Why, sure," said Jo. "Of course you want to see him." And then the crowd gave a great roar. There came over Jo a feeling of weakness. He was trembling. The boys went marching by.

"There he is," Emily shrilled, above the din. "There be is! There he is! There he—" And waved a futile little hand. It wasn't so much a wave as a clutching. A clutching after something beyond her reach.

"Which one? Which one, Emily?"

35

"The handsome one. The handsome one. There!" Her voice quavered and died.

Jo put a steady hand on her shoulder. "Point him out," he commanded. "Show me." And the next instant. "Never mind. I see him."

Somehow, miraculously, he had picked him from among the hundreds. Had picked him as surely as his own father might have. It was Emily's boy. He was marching by, rather stiffly. He was nineteen, and fun-loving, and he had a girl, and he didn't particularly want to go to France and—to go to France. But more than he had hated going, he had hated not to go. So he marched by, looking straight ahead, his jaw set so that his chin stuck out just a little. Emily's boy.

Jo looked at him, and his face flushed purple. His eyes, the hard-boiled eyes of a Loop-hound, took on the look of a sad old man. And suddenly he was no longer Jo, the sport; old J. Hertz, the gay dog. He was Jo Hertz, thirty, in love with life, in love with Emily, and with the stinging blood of young manhood coursing through his veins.

Another minute and the boy had passed on up the broad street—the fine, flag-bedecked street—just one of a hundred service-hats bobbing in rhythmic motion like sandy waves lapping a shore and flowing on.

Then he disappeared altogether.

Emily was clinging to Jo. She was mumbling something, over and over. "I can't. I can't. Don't ask me to. I can't let him go. Like that. I can't."

Jo said a queer thing.

"Why, Emily! We wouldn't have him stay home, would we? We wouldn't want him to do anything different, would we? Not our boy. I'm glad he enlisted. I'm proud of him. So are you glad."

Little by little he quieted her. He took her to the car that was waiting, a worried chauffeur in charge. They said good-bye, awkwardly. Emily's face was a red, swollen mass.

So it was that when Jo entered his own hallway half an hour later he blinked, dazedly, and when the light from the window fell on him you saw that his eyes were red.

Eva was not one to beat about the bush. She sat forward in her chair, clutching her bag rather nervously.

"Now, look here, Jo. Stell and I are here for a reason. We're here to tell you that this thing's got to stop."

"Thing? Stop?"

"You know very well what I mean. You saw me at the milliner's that day. And night before last, Ethel. We're all disgusted. If you

36

must go about with people like that, please have some sense of decency."

Something gathering in Jo's face should have warned her. But he was slumped down in his chair in such a huddle, and he looked so old and fat that she did not heed it. She went on. "You've got us to consider. Your sisters. And your nieces. Not to speak of your own—"

But he got to his feet then, shaking, and at what she saw in his face even Eva faltered and stopped. It wasn't at all the face of a fat, middle-aged sport. It was a face Jovian, terrible.

"You!" he began, low-voiced, ominous. "You!" He raised a great fist high. "You two murderers! You didn't consider me, twenty years ago. You come to me with talk like that. Where's my boy! You killed him, you two, twenty years ago. And now he belongs to somebody else. Where's my son that should have gone marching by to-day?" He flung his arms out in a great gesture of longing. The red veins stood out on his forehead. "Where's my son! Answer me that, you two selfish, miserable women. Where's my son!" Then, as they huddled together, frightened, wild-eyed. "Out of my house! Out of my house! Before I hurt you!"

They fled, terrified. The door banged behind them.

Jo stood, shaking, in the centre of the room. Then he reached for a chair, gropingly, and sat down. He passed one moist, flabby hand over his forehead and it came away wet. The telephone rang. He sat still. It sounded far away and unimportant, like something forgotten. I think he did not even hear it with his conscious ear. But it rang and rang insistently. Jo liked to answer his telephone, when at home.

"Hello!" He knew instantly the voice at the other end.

"That you, Jo?" it said.

"Yes."

"How's my boy?"

"I'm—all right."

"Listen, Jo. The crowd's coming over to-night. I've fixed up a little poker game for you. Just eight of us."

"I can't come to-night, Gert."

"Can't! Why not?"

"I'm not feeling so good."

"You just said you were all right."

"I am all right. Just kind of tired."

The voice took on a cooing note. "Is my Joey tired? Then he shall be all comfy on the sofa, and he doesn't need to play if he don't want to. No, sir."

Jo stood staring at the black mouth-piece of the telephone. He

37

was seeing a procession go marching by. Boys, hundreds of boys, in khaki.

"Hello! Hello!" the voice took on an anxious note. "Are you there?"

"Yes," wearily.

"Jo, there's something the matter. You're sick. I'm coming right over."

"No!"

"Why not? You sound as if you'd been sleeping. Look here—"

"Leave me alone!" cried Jo, suddenly, and the receiver clacked onto the hook. "Leave me alone. Leave me alone." Long after the connection had been broken.

He stood staring at the instrument with unseeing eyes. Then he turned and walked into the front room. All the light had gone out of it. Dusk had come on. All the light had gone out of everything. The zest had gone out of life. The game was over—the game he had been playing against loneliness and disappointment. And he was just a tired old man. A lonely, tired old man in a ridiculous, rose-coloured room that had grown, all of a sudden, drab.

III

THE TOUGH GUY

You could not be so very tough in Chippewa, Wisconsin. But Buzz Werner managed magnificently with the limited means at hand. Before he was nineteen mothers were warning their sons against him, and brothers their sisters. Buzz Werner not only was tough—he looked tough. When he spoke—which was often—his speech slid sinisterly out of the extreme left corner of his mouth. He had a trick of hitching himself up from the belt—one palm on the stomach and a sort of heaving jerk from the waist, as a prize fighter does it—that would have made a Van Bibber look rough.

His name was not really Buzz, but quotes are dispensed with because no one but his mother remembered what it originally had been. His mother called him Ernie and she alone, in all Chippewa, Wisconsin, was unaware that her son was the town tough guy. But even she sometimes mildly remonstrated with him for being what she called kind of wild. Buzz had yellow hair with a glint in it, and it curled up into a bang at the front. No amount of wetting or greasing could subdue that irrepressible forelock. A boy with hair like that never grows up in his mother's eyes.

If Buzz's real name was lost in the dim mists of boyhood, the origin and fitness of his nickname were apparent after two minutes' conversation with him. Buzz Werner was called Buzz not only because he talked too much, but because he was a braggart. His conversation bristled with the perpendicular pronoun, and his pet phrase was, "I says to him—"

He buzzed.

By the time Buzz was fourteen he was stealing brass from the yards of the big paper mills down in the Flats and selling it to the junk man. How he escaped the reform school is a mystery. Perhaps it was the blond forelock. At nineteen he was running with the Kearney girl.

Twenty-five years hence Chippewa will have learned to treat the Kearney-girl type as a disease, and a public menace. Which she was. The Kearney girl ran wild in Chippewa, and Chippewa will be paying taxes on the fruit of her liberty for a hundred years to come. The Kearney girl was a beautiful idiot, with a lovely oval face, and limpid, rather wistful blue eyes, and fair, fine hair, and a long slim neck. She looked very much like those famous wantons of history, from Lucrezia Borgia to Nell Gwyn, that you see pictured in the

39

galleries of Europe—all very mild and girlish, with moist red mouths, like a puppy's, so that you wonder if they have not been basely defamed through all the centuries.

The Kearney girl's father ran a saloon out on Second Avenue, and every few days the Chippewa paper would come out with a story of a brawl, a knifing, or a free-for-all fight following a Saturday night in Kearney's. The Kearney girl herself was forever running up and down Grand Avenue, which was the main business street. She would trail up and down from the old Armory to the post-office and back again. When she turned off into the homeward stretch on Outagamie Street there always slunk after her some stoop-shouldered, furtive, loping youth. But he never was seen with her on Grand Avenue. She had often been up before old Judge Colt for some nasty business or other. At such times the shabby office of the Justice of the Peace would be full of shawled mothers and heavy-booted, work-worn fathers, and an aunt or two, and some cousins, and always a slinking youth fumbling with the hat in his hands, his glance darting hither and thither, from group to group, but never resting for a moment within any one else's gaze. Of all these present, the Kearney girl herself was always the calmest. Old Judge Colt meted out justice according to his lights. Unfortunately, the wearing of a yellow badge on the breast was a custom that had gone out some years before.

This nymph it was who had taken a fancy to Buzz Werner. It looked very black for his future.

The strange part of it was that the girl possessed little attraction for Buzz. It was she who made all the advances. Buzz had sprung from very decent stock, as you shall see. And something about the sultry unwholesomeness of this girl repelled him, though he was hardly aware that this was so. Buzz and his gang would meet down town of a Saturday night, very moist as to hair and clean as to soft shirt. They would lounge on the corner of Grand and Outagamie, in front of Schroeder's brightly lighted drug store, watching the girls go by. They were, for the most part, a pimply-faced lot. They would shuffle their feet in a slow jig, hands in pockets. When a late comer joined them it was considered au fait to welcome him by assuming a fistic attitude, after the style of the pugilists pictured in the barber-shop magazines, and spar a good-natured and make-believe round with him, with much agile dancing about in a circle, head held stiffly, body crouching, while working a rapid and facetious right.

This corner, or Donovan's pool-shack, was their club, their forum. Here they recounted their exploits, bragged of their triumphs, boasted of their girls, flexed their muscles to show their strength. And all through their talk there occurred again and again a certain term whose use is common to their kind. Their remarks were prefaced and interlarded and concluded with it, so that it was no longer an oath or a blasphemy.

"Je's, I was sore at 'm. I told him where to get off at. Nobody can talk to me like that. Je's, I should say not."

So accustomed had it grown that it was not even thought of as profanity.

If Buzz's family could have heard him in his talk with his street-corner companions they would not have credited their ears. A mouthy braggart in company is often silent in his own home, and Buzz was no exception to this rule. Fortunately, Buzz's braggadocio carried with it a certain conviction. He never kept a job more than a month, and his own account of his leave-taking was always as vainglorious as it was dramatic.

"'G'wan!' I says to him, 'Who you talkin' to? I don't have to take nothin' from you nor nobody like you,' I says. 'I'm as good as you are any day, and better. You can have your dirty job,' I says. And with that I give him my time and walked out on 'm. Je's, he was sore!"

They would listen to him, appreciatively, but with certain mental reservations; reservations inevitable when a speaker's name is Buzz. One by one they would melt away as their particular girl, after flaunting by with a giggle and a sidelong glance for the dozenth time, would switch her skirts around the corner of Outagamie Street past the Brill House, homeward bound.

"Well, s'long," they would say. And lounging after her, would overtake her in the shadow of the row of trees in front of the Agassiz School.

If the Werner family had been city folk they would, perforce, have burrowed in one of those rabbit-warren tenements that line block after block of city streets. But your small-town labouring man is likely to own his two-story frame house with a garden patch in the back and a cement walk leading up to the front porch, and pork roast on Sundays. The Werners had all this, no thanks to Pa Werner; no thanks to Buzz, surely; and little to Minnie Werner who clerked in the Sugar Bowl Candy Store and tried to dress like Angie Hatton whose father owned the biggest Pulp and Paper mill in the Fox River Valley. No, the house and the garden, the porch and the cement sidewalk, and the pork roast all had their origin in Ma Werner's tireless energy, in Ma Werner's thrift; in her patience and unremitting toil, her nimble fingers and bent back, her shapeless figure and unbounded and unexpressed (verbally, that is) love for her children. Pa Werner—sullen, lazy, brooding, tyrannical—she soothed and mollified for the children's sake, or shouted down with a shrewish outburst, as the occasion required. An expert stone-

41

mason by trade, Pa Werner could be depended on only when he was not drinking, or when he was not on strike, or when he had not quarrelled with the foreman. An anarchist, Pa—dissatisfied with things as they were, but with no plan for improving them. His evil-smelling pipe between his lips, he would sit, stocking-footed, in silence, smoking and thinking vague, formless, surly thoughts. This sullen unrest and rebellion it was that, transmitted to his son, had made Buzz the unruly braggart that he was, and which, twenty or thirty years hence, would find him just such a one as his father—useless, evil-tempered, half brutal, defiant of order.

It was in May, a fine warm sunny day, that Ma Werner, looking up from the garden patch where she was spading, a man's old battered felt hat perched grotesquely atop her white head, saw Buzz lounging homeward, cutting across lots from Bates Street, his dinner pail glinting in the sun. It was four o'clock in the afternoon. Ma Werner straightened painfully and her over-flushed face took on a purplish tinge. She wiped her moist chin with an apron-corner.

As Buzz espied her his gait became a swagger. At sight of that swagger Ma knew. She dropped her spade and plodded heavily through the freshly turned earth to the back porch as Buzz turned in at the walk. She shifted her weight ponderously as she wiped first one earth-crusted shoe and then the other.

"What's the matter, Ernie? You ain't sick, are you?"

"Naw."

"What you home so early for?"

"Because I feel like it, that's why."

He took the back steps at a bound and slammed the kitchen door behind him. Ma Werner followed heavily after. Buzz was hanging his hat up behind the kitchen door. He turned with a scowl as his mother entered. She looked even more ludicrous in the house than she had outside, with her skirts tucked up to make spading the easier, so that there was displayed an unseemly length of thick ankle rising solidly above the old pair of men's side-boots that encased her feet. The battered hat perched rakishly atop her knob of gray-white hair gave her a jaunty, sporting look, as of a ponderous, burlesque Watteau.

She abandoned pretense. "Ernie, your pa'll be awful mad. You know the way he carried on the last time."

"Let him. He aint worked five days himself this month." Then, at a sudden sound from the front of the house, "He ain't home, is he?"

"That's the shade flapping."

Buzz turned toward the inside wooden stairway that led to the half-story above. But his mother followed, with surprising agility for

42

so heavy a woman. She put a hand on his arm. "Such a good-payin' job, Ernie. An' you said only yesterday you liked it. Somethin' must've happened."

There broke a grim little laugh from Buzz. "Believe me something happened good an' plenty." A little frightened look came into his eyes, "I just had a run-in with young Hatton."

The red faded from her face and a grey-white mask seemed to slip down over it. "You don't mean Hatton! Not Hatton's son. Ernie, you ain't done—"

A dash of his street-corner bravado came back to him. "Aw, keep your hair on, Ma. I didn't know it was young Hatton when I hit'm. An' anyway nobody his age is gonna tell me where to get off at. Say, w'en a guy who ain't twenty-three, hardly, and that never done a lick in his life except go to college, the sissy, tries t'—"

But the first sentence only had penetrated her brain. She grappled with it, dizzily. "Hit him! Ernie, you don't mean you hit him! Not Hatton's son! Ernie!"

"Sure I did. You oughta seen his face." But there was very little triumph or satisfaction in Buzz Werner's face or voice as he said it. "Course, I didn't know it was him when I done it. I dunno would it have made any difference if I had."

She seemed so old and so shrunken, in spite of her bulk, as she looked up at him. The look in her eyes was so strained. The way her hand brought her apron-corner up to her mouth, as though to stifle the fear that shook her, was so groping, somehow, so uncertain, that, paradoxically, the pitifulness of it reacted to make him savage.

When she quavered her next question, "What was he doin' in the mill?" he turned toward the stairway again, flinging his answer over his shoulder.

"Learnin' the business, that's what. From the ground up, see?" He turned at the first stair and leaned forward and down, one hand on the door-jamb. "Well, believe me he don't use me as no ground-dirt. An' when I'm takin' the screen off the big roll—see?—he comes up to me an' says I'm handlin' it rough an' it's a delicate piece of mechanism. 'Who're you?' I says. 'Never mind who I am' he says, 'I'm working' on this job,' he says, 'an' this is a paper mill you're workin' in,' he says, 'not a boiler factory. Treat the machinery accordin', like a real workman,' he says. The simp! I just stepped down off the platform of the big press, and I says, 'Well, you look like a kinda delicate piece of mechanism yourself,' I says, 'an' need careful handlin', so take that for a starter,' I says. An' with that I handed him one in the nose." Buzz laughed, but there was little mirth in it. "I bet he seen enough wheels an' delicate machinery that minute to set up a whole new plant."

43

There was nothing of mirth in the woman's drawn face. "Oh, Ernie, f'r God's sake! What they goin' to do to you!"

He was half way up the narrow stairway, she at the foot of it, peering up at him. "They won't do anything. I guess old Hatton ain't so stuck on havin' his swell golf club crowd know his little boy was beat up by one of the workmen."

He was clumping about upstairs now. So she turned toward the kitchen, dazedly. She glanced at the clock. Going on toward five. Still in the absurd hat she got out a panful of potatoes and began to peel them skilfuly, automatically. The seamed and hardened fingers had come honestly by their deftness. They had twirled and peeled pecks—bushels—tons of these brown balls in their time.

At five-thirty Pa came in. At six, Minnie. She had to go back to the Sugar Bowl until nine. Five minutes later the supper was steaming on the table.

"Ernie," called Ma, toward the ceiling. "Er-nie! Supper's on." The three sat down at the table without waiting. Pa had slipped off his shoes, and was in his stockinged feet. They ate in silence. It was a good meal. A European family of the same class would have considered it a banquet. There were meat and vegetables, butter and home-made bread, preserve and cake, true to the standards of the extravagant American labouring-class household. In the summer the garden supplied them with lettuce, beans, peas, onions, radishes, beets, potatoes, corn, thanks to Ma's aching back and blistered hands. They stored enough vegetables in the cellar to last through the winter.

Buzz usually cleaned up after supper. But to-night, when he came down, he was already clean-shaven, clean-shirted, and his hair was wet from the comb. He took his place in silence. His acid-stained work shoes had been replaced by his good tan ones. Evidently he was going down town after supper. Buzz never took any exercise for the sake of his body's good. Sometimes he and the Lembke boys across the way played a game of ball in the middle of the road, or in the vacant lot, but they did it out of the game instinct, and with no thought of their muscles' gain.

But to-night, evidently, there was to be no ball. Buzz ate little. His mother, forever between the stove and the table, ate less. But that was nothing unusual in her. She waited on the others, but mostly she hovered about the boy.

"Ernie, you ain't eaten your potatoes. Look how nice an' mealy they are."

"Don't want none."

"Ernie, would you rather have a baked apple than the raspberry preserve? I fixed a pan this morning."

"Naw. Lemme alone. I ain't hungry."

He slouched from the table. Minnie, teacup in hand, regarded him over its rim with wide, malicious eyes. "I saw that Kearney girl go by here before supper, and she rubbered in like everything."

"You're a liar," said Buzz, unemotionally.

"I did so! She went by and then she came back again. I saw her both times. Say, I guess I ought to know her. Anybody in town'd know Kearney."

Buzz had been headed toward the front porch. He hesitated and turned, now, and picked up the newspaper from the sitting-room sofa. Pa Werner, in trousers, shirt and suspenders, was padding about the kitchen with his pipe and tobacco. He came into the sitting room now and stood a moment, his lips twisted about the pipe-stem. The pipe's putt-putting gave warning that he was about to break into unaccustomed speech. He regarded Buzz with beady, narrowed eyes.

"You let me see you around with that Kearney girl and I'll break every bone in your body, and hers too. The hussy!"

"Oh, you will, will you?"

Ma, who had been making countless trips from the kitchen to the back garden with water pail and sprinkling can sagging from either arm, put in a word to stay the threatening storm. "Now, Pa! Now, Ernie!" The two men subsided into bristling silence.

Suddenly, "There she is again!" shrilled Minnie, from her bedroom. Buzz shrank back in his chair. Old man Werner, with a muttered oath, went to the open doorway and stood there, puffing savage little spurts of smoke streetward. The Kearney girl stared brazenly at him as she strolled slowly by, a slim and sinister figure. Old man Werner watched her until she passed out of sight.

"You go gettin' mixed up with dirt like that," threatened he, "and I'll learn you. She'll be hangin' around the mill yet, the brass-faced thing. If I hear of it I'll get the foreman to put her off the place. You'll stay home to-night. Carry a pail of water for your ma once."

"Carry it yourself."

Buzz, with a wary eye up the street, slouched out to the front porch, into the twilight of the warm May evening. Charley Lembke, from his porch across the street, called to him: "Goin' down town?"

"Yeh, I guess so."

"Ain't you afraid of bein' pinched?" Buzz turned his head quickly toward the room just behind him. He turned to go in. Charley's voice came again, clear and far-reaching. "I hear you had a run-in with Hatton's son, and knocked him down. Some class t' you, Buzz, even if it does cost you your job."

45

From within the sound of a newspaper hurled to the floor. Pa Werner was at the door. "What's that! What's that he's sayin'?"

Buzz, cornered, jutted a threatening jaw at his father and brazened it out. "Can't you hear good?"

"Come on in here."

Buzz hesitated a moment. Then he turned, slowly, and walked into the little sitting room with an attempt at a swagger that failed to convince even himself. He leaned against the side of the door, hands in pockets. Pa Werner faced him, black-browed. "Is that right, what he said? Lembke? Huh?"

"Sure it's right. I had a run-in with Hatton, an' licked him, and give'm my time. What you goin' to do about it?"

Ma Werner was in the room, now. Minnie, passing through on her way to work again, caught the electric current of the storm about to break and escaped it with a parting:

"Oh, for the land's sakes! You two. Always a-fighting."

The two men faced each other. The one a sturdy man-boy nearing twenty, with a great pair of shoulders and a clear eye, a long, quick arm and a deft hand—these last his assets as a workman. The other, gnarled, prematurely wrinkled, almost gnome-like. This one took his pipe from between his lips and began to speak. The drink he had had at Wenzel's on the way home sparked his speech.

He began with a string of epithets. They flowed from his lips, an acid stream. Pick and choose as I will, there is none that can be repeated here. Old Man Werner had, perhaps, been something of a tough guy himself, in his youth. As he reviled his son now you saw that son, at fifty, just such another stocking-footed, bitter old man, smoking a glum pipe on the back porch, summer evenings, and spitting into the fresh young grass.

I don't say that this thought came to Buzz as his father flayed him with his abuse. But there was something unusual, surely, in the non-resistance with which he allowed the storm to beat about his head. Something in his steady, unruffled gaze caused the other man to falter a little in his tirade, and finally to stop, almost apprehensively. He had paid no heed to Ma Werner's attempts at pacification. "Now, Pa!" she had said, over and over, her hand on his arm, though he shook it off again and again. "Now, Pa!—" But he stopped now, fist raised in a last profane period. Buzz stood regarding him with his unblinking stare.

Finally: "You through?" said Buzz.

"Ya-as," snarled Pa, "I'm through. Get to hell out of here. You'll be hung yet, you loafer. A good-for-nothing bum, that's what. Get out o' here!"

"I'm gettin'," said Buzz. He took his hat off the hook and wiped

46

it carefully with the lower side of his sleeve, round and round. He placed it on his head, jauntily. He stepped to the kitchen, took a tooth-pick from the little red-and-white glass holder on the table, and—with this emblem of insouciance, at an angle of ninety, between his teeth—strolled indolently, nonchalantly down the front steps, along the cement walk to the street and so toward town. The two old people, left alone in the sudden silence of the house, stared after the swaggering figure until the dim twilight blotted it out. And a sinister something seemed to close its icy grip about the heart of one of them. A vague premonition that she could only feel, not express, made her next words seem futile.

"Pa, you oughtn't to talked to him like that. He's just a little wild. He looked so kind of funny when he went out. I don'no, he looked so kind of—"

"He looked like the bum he is, that's what. No respect for nothing. For his pa, or ma, or nothing. Down on the corner with the rest of 'em, that's where he's goin'. Hatton ain't goin' to let this go by. You see."

But she, on her way to the kitchen, repeated, "I don'no, he looked so kind of funny. He looked so kind of—"

Considering all things—the happenings of the past few hours, at least—Buzz, as he strolled on down toward Grand Avenue with his sauntering, care-free gait, did undoubtedly look kind of funny. The red-hot rage of the afternoon and the white-hot rage of the evening had choked the furnace of brain and soul with clinkers so that he was thinking unevenly and disconnectedly. On the surface he was cool and unruffled. He stopped for a moment at the railroad tracks to talk with Stumpy Gans, the one-legged gateman. The little bell above Stumpy's shanty was ringing its warning, so he strolled leisurely over to the depot platform to see the 7:15 come in from Chicago. When the train pulled out Buzz went on down the street. His mind was darting here and there, planning this revenge, discarding it; seizing on another, abandoning that. He'd show'm. He'd show'm. Sick of the whole damn bunch, anyway.... Wonder was Hatton going to raise a shindy.... Let'm. Who cares?... The old man was a drunk, that's what.... Ma had looked kinda sick....

He put that uncomfortable thought out of his mind and slammed the door on it. Anyway, he'd show'm.

Out of the shadows of the great trees in front of the Agassiz School stepped the Kearney girl, like a lean and hungry cat. One hand clutched his arm.

Buzz jumped and said something under his breath. Then he laughed, shortly. "Might as well kill a guy as scare him to death!"

47

She thrust one hand through his arm and linked it with the other. "I've been waiting for you, Buzz."

"Yeh. Well, let me tell you something. You quit traipsing up and down in front of my house, see?"

"I wanted to see you. An' I didn't know whether you was coming down town to-night or not."

"Well, I am. So now you know." He pulled away from her, but she twined her arm the tighter about his.

"Ain't sore at me, are yuh, Buzz?"

"No. Leggo my arm."

"If you're sore because I been foolin' round with that little wart of a Donahue—" She turned wise eyes up to him, trying to make them limpid in the darkness.

"What do I care who you run with?"

"Don't you care, Buzz?" The words were soft but there was a steel edge to her utterance.

"No."

"Oh, Buzz, I'm batty about you. I can't help it, can I? H'm? Look here, you go on to Grand, and hang around for an hour, maybe, and I'll meet you here an' we'll walk a ways. Will you? I got something to tell you."

"Naw, I can't to-night. I'm busy."

And then the steel edge cut. "Buzz, if you turn me down I'll have you up."

"Up?"

"Before old Colt. I can fix up charges. He'll believe it. Say, he knows me, Judge Colt does. I can name you an'—"

"Me!" Sheer amazement rang in his voice. "Me? You must be crazy. I ain't had anything to do with you. You make me sick."

"That don't make any difference. You can't prove it. I told you I was crazy about you. I told you—"

He jerked loose from her then and was off. He ran one block. Then, after a backward glance, fell into a quick walk that brought him past the Brill House and to Schroeder's drug store corner. There was his crowd—Spider, and Red, and Bing, and Casey. They took him literally unto their breasts. They thumped him on the back. They bestowed on him the low epithets with which they expressed admiration. Red worked at one of the bleaching vats in the Hatton paper mill. The story of Buzz's fistic triumph had spread through the big plant like a flame.

"Go on, Buzz, tell 'em about it," Red urged, now. "Je's, I like to died laughing when I heard it. He must of looked a sight, the poor boob. Go on, Buzz, tell 'em how you says to him he must be a kind of delicate piece of—you know; go on, tell 'em."

48

Buzz hitched himself up with a characteristic gesture, and plunged into his story. His audience listened entranced, interrupting him with an occasional "Je's!" of awed admiration. But the thing seemed to lack a certain something. Perhaps Casey put his finger on that something when, at the recital's finish he asked:

"Didn't he see you was goin' to hit him?"

"No. He never see a thing."

Casey ruminated a moment. "You could of give him a chanst to put up his dukes," he said at last. A little silence fell upon the group. Honour among thieves.

Buzz shifted uncomfortably. "He's a bigger guy than I am. I bet he's over six foot. The papers was always telling how he played football at that college he went to."

Casey spoke up again. "They say he didn't wait for this here draft. He's goin' to Fort Sheridan, around Chicago somewhere, to be made a officer."

"Yeh, them rich guys, they got it all their own way," Spider spoke up, gloomily. "They—"

From down the street came a dull, muffled thud-thud-thud-thud. Already Chippewa, Wisconsin, had learned to recognise it. Grand Avenue, none too crowded on this mid-week night, pressed to the curb to see. Down the street they stared toward the moving mass that came steadily nearer. The listless group on the corner stiffened into something like interest.

"Company G," said Red. "I hear they're leavin' in a couple of days."

And down the street they came, thud-thud-thud, Company G, headed for the new red-brick Armory for the building of which they had engineered everything from subscription dances and exhibition drills to turkey raffles. Chippewa had never taken Company G very seriously until now. How could it, when Company G was made up of Willie Kemp, who clerked in Hassell's shoe store; Fred Garvey, the reporter on the Chippewa Eagle; Hermie Knapp, the real-estate man, and Earl Hanson who came around in the morning for your grocery order.

Thud-thud-thud-thud. And to Chippewa, standing at the curb, quite suddenly these every-day men and boys were transformed into something remote and almost terrible. Something grim. Something sacrificial. Something sacred.

Thud-thud-thud-thud. Looking straight ahead.

"The poor boobs," said Spider, and spat, and laughed.

The company passed on down the street—vanished. Grand Avenue went its way.

49

A little silence fell upon the street-corner group. Bing was the first to speak.

"They won't git me in this draft. I got a mother an' two kid sisters to support."

"Yeh, a swell lot of supportin' you do!"

"Who says I don't! I can prove it."

"They'll get me all right," said Casey. "I ain't kickin'."

"I'm under age," from Red.

Spider said nothing. His furtive eyes darted here and there. Spider was of age. And Spider had no family to support. But Spider had reason to know that no examining board would pass him into the army of his country. And it was a reason of which one did not speak. "You're only twenty, ain't you, Buzz?" he asked, to cover the gap in the conversation.

"Yeh." Silence fell again. Then, "But I wouldn't mind goin'. Anything for a change. This place makes me sick."

Spider laughed. "You better be a hero and go and enlist."

Buzz's head came up with a jerk. "Je's, I never thought of that!"

Red struck an attitude, one hand on his breast. "Now's your chanct, Buzz, to save your country an' your flag. Enlistment office's right over the Golden Eagle clothing store. Step up. Don't crowd gents! This way!"

Buzz was staring at him, open-mouthed. His gaze was fixed, tense. Suddenly he seemed to gather all his muscles together as for a spring. But he only threw his cigarette into the gutter, yawned elaborately, and moved away. "S'long," he said; and lounged off. The others looked after him a moment, puzzled, speculative. Buzz was not usually so laconic. But evidently he was leaving with no further speech.

"I guess maybe he ain't so dead sure that Hatton bunch won't git him for this, anyway," Casey said. Then, raising his voice: "Goin' home, Buzz?"

"Yeh."

But he did not. If they had watched him they would have seen him change his lounging gait when he reached the corner. They would have seen him stand a moment, sending a quick glance this way and that, then turn, retrace his steps almost at a run, and dart into the doorway that led to the flight of wooden stairs at the side of the Golden Eagle clothing store.

A dingy room. A man at a bare table. Another seated at the window, his chair tipped back, his feet on the sill, a pipe between his teeth. Buzz, shambling, suddenly awkward, stood in the door.

"This the place where you enlist?"

50

The man at the table stood up. The chair in front of the open window came down on all-fours.

"Sure," said the first man. "What's your name?"

Buzz told him.

"Meet Sergeant Keith. He's a Canadian. Been through the whole game."

Five minutes later Buzz's fine white torso rose above his trousers like a great pillar. Unconsciously his sagging shoulders had straightened. His stomach was held in. His chest jutted, shelf-like. His ribs showed through the pink-white flesh.

"Get some of that pork off of him," observed Sergeant Keith, "and he'll do in a couple of Fritzes before he's through."

"Me!" blurted Buzz, struggling now with his shirt. "A couple! Say, you don't know me. Whaddyou mean, a couple? I can lick a whole regiment of them beerheads with one hand tied behind me an' my feet in a sack." He emerged from the struggle with his shirt, his face very red, his hair rumpled.

Sergeant Keith smiled a grim little smile. "Keep your shirt on, kid," he said, "and remember, this isn't a fist fight you're going into. It's war."

Buzz, fumbling with his hat, put his question. "When—when do I go?" For he had signed his name in his round, boyish, sixth-grade scrawl.

"To-morrow. Now listen to these instructions."

"T-to-morrow?" gasped Buzz.

He was still gasping as he reached the street and struck out toward home. To-morrow! When the Kearney girl again stepped out of the tree-shadows he stared at her as at something remote and trivial.

"I thought you tried to give me the slip, Buzz. Where you been?"

"Never mind where I've been."

She fell into step beside him, but had difficulty in matching his great strides. She caught at his arm. At that Buzz turned and stopped. It was too dark to see his face, but something in his voice— something new, and hard, and resolute—reached even the choked and slimy cells of this creature's consciousness.

"Now looka here. You beat it. I got somethin' on my mind to-night and I can't be bothered with no fool girl, see? Don't get me sore. I mean it."

Her hand dropped away from his arm. "I didn't mean what I said about havin' you up, Buzz; honest t' Gawd I didn't."

"I don't care what you meant."

'Will you meet me to-morrow night? Will you, Buzz?"

51

"If I'm in this town to-morrow night I'll meet you. Is that good enough?"

He turned and strode away. But she was after him. "Where you goin' to-morrow?"

"I'm goin' to war, that's where."

"Yes you are!" scoffed Miss Kearney. Then, at his silence: "You didn't go and do a fool thing like that?"

"I sure did."

"When you goin'?"

"To-morrow."

"Well, of all the big boobs," sneered Miss Kearney; "what did you go and do that for?"

"Search me," said Buzz, dully. "Search me."

Then he turned and went on toward home, alone. The Kearney girl's silly, empty laugh came back to him through the darkness. It might have been called a scornful laugh if the Kearney girl had been capable of any emotion so dignified as scorn.

The family was still up. The door was open to the warm May night. The Werners, in their moments of relaxation, were as unbuttoned and highly negligée as one of those group pictures you see of the Robert Louis Stevenson family. Pa, shirt-sleeved, stocking-footed, asleep in his chair. Ma's dress open at the front. Minnie, in an untidy kimono, sewing.

On this flaccid group Buzz burst, bomb-like. He hung his hat on the hook, wordlessly. The noise he made woke his father, as he had meant that it should. There came a muttered growl from the old man. Buzz leaned against the stairway door, negligently. The eyes of the three were on him.

"Well," he said, "I guess you won't be bothered with me much longer." Ma Werner's head came up sharply at that.

"What you done, Ernie?"

"Enlisted."

"Enlisted—for what?"

"For the war; what do you suppose?"

Ma Werner rose at that, heavily. "Ernie! You never!"

Pa Werner was wide awake now. Out of his memory of the old country, and soldier service there, he put his next question. "Did you sign to it?"

"Yeh."

"When you goin'?"

"To-morrow."

Even Pa Werner gasped at that.

In families like the Werners emotion is rarely expressed. But now, because of something in the stricken face and starting eyes of

52

the woman, and the open-mouthed dumbfoundedness of the old man, and the sudden tender fearfulness in the face of the girl; and because, in that moment, all these seemed very safe, and accustomed, and, somehow, dear, Buzz curled his mouth into the sneer of the tough guy and spoke out of the corner of that contorted feature.

"What did you think I was goin' to do? Huh? Stick around here and take dirt from the bunch of you! Nix! I'm through!"

There was nothing dramatic about Buzz's going. He seemed to be whisked away. One moment he was eating his breakfast at an unaccustomed hour, in his best shirt and trousers, his mother, only half understanding even now, standing over him with the coffee pot; the next he was standing with his cheap shiny suitcase in his hand. Then he was waiting on the depot platform, and Hefty Burke, the baggage man, was saying, "Where you goin', Buzz?"

"Goin' to fight the Germans."

Hefty had hooted hoarsely: "Ya-a-as you are, you big bluff!"

"Who you callin' a bluff, you baggage-smasher, you! I'm goin' to war, I'm tellin' you."

Hefty, still scoffing, turned away to his work. "Well, then, I guess it's as good as over. Give old Willie a swipe for me, will you?"

"You bet I will. Watch me!"

I think he more than half meant it.

And thus Buzz Werner went to war. He was vague about its locality. Somewhere in Europe. He was pretty sure it was France. A line from his Fourth Grade geography came back to him. "The French," it had said, "are a gay people, fond of dancing and light wines."

Well, that sounded all right.

The things that happened to Buzz Werner in the next twelve months cannot be detailed here. They would require the space of what the publishers call a 12-mo volume. Buzz himself could never have told you. Things happened too swiftly, too concentratedly.

Chicago first. Buzz had never seen Chicago. Now that he saw it, he hardly believed it. His first glimpse of it left him cowering, terrified. The noise, the rush, the glitter, the grimness, the vastness, were like blows upon his defenceless head. They beat the braggadocio and the self-confidence temporarily out of him. But only temporarily.

Then came a camp. A rough, temporary camp compared to which the present cantonments are luxurious. The United States Government took Buzz Werner by the slack of the trousers and the slack of the mind, and, holding him thus, shook him into shape— and into submission. And eventually—though it required months—

into an understanding of why that submission was manly, courageous, and fine. But before he learned that he learned many other things. He learned there was little good in saying, "Aw, g'wan!" to a dapper young lieutenant if they clapped you into the guard-house for saying it. There was little point to throwing down your shovel and refusing to shovel coal if they clapped you into the guard house for doing it; and made you shovel harder than ever when you came out. He learned what it was to rise at dawn and go thud-thud-thudding down a dirt road for endless weary miles. He became an olive-drab unit in an olive-drab village. He learned what it was to wake up in the morning so sore and lame that he felt as if he had been pulled apart, limb from limb, during the night, and never put together again. He stood out with a raw squad in the dirt of No Man's Land between barracks and went through exercises that took hold of his great slack muscles and welded them into whip-cords. And in front of him, facing him, stood a slim, six-foot whipper-snapper of a lieutenant, hatless, coatless, tireless, merciless—a creature whom Buzz at first thought he could snap between thumb and finger—like that!—who made life a hell for Buzz Werner. Until his muscles became used to it.

"One—two!—three! One—two—three! One—two—three!" yelled this person. And, "Inhale! Exhale! Inhale! Exhale!" till Buzz's lungs were bursting, his eyes were starting from his head, his chest carried a sledge hammer inside it, his thigh-muscles screamed, and his legs, arms, neck, were no longer parts of him, but horrid useless burdens, detached, yet clinging. He learned what this person meant when he shouted (always with the rising inflection), "Comp'ny! Right! Whup!" Buzz whupped with the best of 'em. The whipper-snapper seemed tireless. Long after Buzz felt that another moment of it would kill him the lithe young lieutenant would be leaping about like a faun, and pride kept Buzz going though he wanted to drop with fatigue, and his shirt and hair and face were wet with sweat.

So much for his body. It soon became accustomed to the routine, then hardened. His mind was less pliable. But that, too, was undergoing a change. He found that the topics of conversation that used to interest his little crowd on the street corner in Chippewa were not of much interest, here. There were boys from every part of the great country. And they talked of the places whence they had come and speculated about the places to which they were going. And Buzz listened and learned. There was strangely little talk about girls. There usually is when muscles and mind are being driven to the utmost. But he heard men—men as big as he—speak openly of things that he had always sneered at as soft. After one of these

54

conversations he wrote an awkward, but significant scrawl home to his mother.

"Well Ma," he wrote, "I guess maybe you would like to hear a few words from me. Well I like it in the army it is the life for me you bet. I am feeling great how are you all—"

Ma Werner wasted an entire morning showing it around the neighbourhood, and she read and reread it until it was almost pulp.

Six months of this. Buzz Werner was an intelligent machine composed of steel, cord, and iron. I think he had forgotten that the Kearney girl had ever existed. One day, after three months of camp life, the man in the next cot had thrown him a volume of Kipling. Buzz fingered it, disinterestedly. Until that moment Kipling had not existed for Buzz Werner. After that moment he dominated his leisure hours. The Y.M.C.A. hut had many battered volumes of this writer. Buzz read them all.

The week before Thanksgiving Buzz found himself on his way to New York. For some reason unexplained to him he was separated from his company in one of the great shake-ups performed for the good of the army. He never saw them again. He was sent straight to a New York camp. When he beheld his new lieutenant his limbs became fluid, and his heart leaped into his throat, and his mouth stood open, and his eyes bulged. It was young Hatton—Harry Hatton—whose aristocratic nose he had punched six months before, in the Hatton Pulp and Paper Mill.

And even as he stared young Hatton fixed him with his eye, and then came over to him and said, "It's all right, Werner."

Buzz Werner could only salute with awkward respect, while with one great gulp his heart slid back into normal place. He had not thought that Hatton was so tall, or so broad-shouldered, or so—

He no more thought of telling the other men that he had once knocked this man down than he thought of knocking him down again. He would almost as soon have thought of taking a punch at the President.

The day before Thanksgiving Buzz was told he might have a holiday. Also he was given an address and a telephone number in New York City and told that if he so desired he might call at that address and receive a bountiful Thanksgiving dinner. They were expecting him there. That the telephone exchange was Murray Hill, and the street Madison Avenue meant nothing to Buzz. He made the short trip to New York, floundered about the city, found every one willing and eager to help him find the address on the slip, and brought up, finally, in front of the house on Madison Avenue. It was a large, five-story stone place, and Buzz supposed it was a flat, of course. He stood off and surveyed it. Then he ascended the steps and rang the bell. They must have been waiting for him. The door was opened by a large amiable-looking, middle-aged man who said, "Well, well! Come in, come in, my boy!" a great deal as the folks in Chippewa, Wisconsin, might have said it. The stout old party also said he was glad to see him and Buzz believed it. They went upstairs, much to Buzz's surprise. In Buzz's experience upstairs always meant bedrooms. But in this case it meant a great bright sitting room, with books in it, and a fireplace, very cheerful. There were not a lot of people in the room. Just a middle-aged woman in a soft kind of dress, who came to him without any fuss and the first thing he knew he felt acquainted. Within the next fifteen minutes or so some other members of the family seemed to ooze in, unnoticeably. First thing you knew, there they were. They didn't pay such an awful lot of attention to you. Just took you for granted. A couple of young kids, a girl of fourteen, and a boy of sixteen who asked you easy questions about the army till you found yourself patronising him. And a tall black-haired girl who made you think of the vamps in the movies, only her eyes were different. And then, with a little rush, a girl about his own age, or maybe younger—he couldn't tell—who came right up to him, and put out her hand, and gave him a grip with her hard little fist, just like a boy, and said, "I'm Joyce Ladd."

"Pleased to meetcha," mumbled Buzz. And then he found himself talking to her quite easily. She knew a surprising lot about the army.

"I've two brothers over there," she said. "And all my friends, of course." He found out later, quite by accident, that this boyish, but strangely appealing person belonged to some sort of Motor Service League, and drove an automobile, every day, from eight to six, up and down and round and about New York, working like a man in the service of the country. He never would have believed that the world held that kind of girl.

Then four other men in uniform came in, and it turned out that three of them were privates like himself, and the other a sergeant. Their awkward entrance made him feel more than ever at ease, and ten minutes later they were all talking like mad, and laughing and joking as if they had known these people for years. They all went in to dinner. Buzz got panicky when he thought of the knives and forks, but that turned out all right, too, because they brought these as you needed them. And besides, the things they gave you to eat weren't much different from the things you had for Sunday or Thanksgiving dinner at home, and it was cooked the way his mother would have cooked it—even better, perhaps. And lots of it. And paper snappers and caps and things, and much laughter and talk. And Buzz Werner, who had never been shown any respect or deference in his life, was asked, politely, his opinion of the war, and the army, and when he thought it all would end; and he told them, politely, too.

After dinner Mrs. Ladd said, "What would you boys like to do? Would you like to drive around the city and see New York? Or would you like to go to a matinée, or a picture show? Or do you want to stay here? Some of Joyce's girl friends are coming in a little later."

And Buzz found himself saying, stumblingly, "I—I'd kind of rather stay and talk with the girls." Buzz, the tough guy, blushing like a shy schoolboy.

They did not even laugh at that. They just looked as if they understood that you missed girls at camp. Mrs. Ladd came over to him and put her hand on his arm and said, "That's splendid. We'll all go up to the ballroom and dance." And they did. And Buzz, who had learned to dance at places like Kearney's saloon, and at the mill shindigs, glided expertly about with Joyce Ladd of Madison Avenue, and found himself seated in a great cushioned window-seat, talking with her about Kipling. It was like talking to another fellow, almost, only it had a thrill in it. She said such comic things. And when she laughed she threw back her head and your eyes were dazzled by her slender white throat. They all stayed for supper. And when they left Mrs. Ladd and Joyce handed them packages that, later, turned out to be cigarettes, and chocolate, and books, and soap, and knitted things and a wallet. And when Buzz opened the wallet and found, with relief, that there was no money in it he knew that he had met and mingled with American royalty as its equal.

Three days later he sailed for France.

Buzz Werner, the Chippewa tough guy, in Paris! Buzz Werner at Napoleon's tomb, that glorious white marble poem. Buzz Werner in the Place de la Concorde. Eating at funny little Paris restaurants.

Then a new life. Life in a drab, rain-soaked, mud-choked little French village, sleeping in barns, or stables, or hen coops. If the French were "a gay people, fond of dancing and light wines," he'd like to know where it came in! Nothing but drill and mud, mud and drill, and rain, rain, rain! And old women with tragic faces, and young women with old eyes. And unbelievable stories of courage and sacrifice. And more rain, and more mud, and more drill. And then—into it!

Into it with both feet. Living in the trenches. Back home, in camp, they had refused to take the trenches seriously. They had played in them as children play bear under the piano or table, and had refused to keep their heads down. But Buzz learned to keep his down now, quickly enough. A first terrifying stretch of this, then back to the rear again. More mud and drill. Marches so long and arduous that walking was no longer walking but a dreadful mechanical motion. He learned what thirst was, did Buzz. He learned what it was to be obliged to keep your mind off the thought of pails of water—pails that slopped and brimmed over, so that you could put your head into them and lip around like a horse.

Then back into the trenches. And finally, over the top! Very little memory of what happened after that. A rush. Trampling over soft heaps that writhed. Some one yelling like an Indian with a voice somehow like his own. The German trench reached. At them with his bayonet! He remembered, automatically, how his manual had taught him to jerk out the steel, after you had driven it home. He did it. Into the very trench itself. A great six-foot German struggling with a slim figure that Buzz somehow recognised as his lieutenant, Hatton. A leap at him, like an enraged dog:

"G'wan! who you shovin', you big slob you" yelled Buzz (I regret to say). And he thrust at him, and through him. The man released his grappling hold of Hatton's throat, and grunted, and sat down. And Buzz laughed. And the two went on, Buzz behind his lieutenant, and then something smote his thigh, and he too sat down. The dying German had thrown his last bomb, and it had struck home.

Buzz Werner would never again do a double shuffle on Schroeder's drug-store corner.

Hospital days. Hospital nights. A wheel chair. Crutches. Home.

It was May once more when Buzz Werner's train came into the little red-brick depot at Chippewa, Wisconsin. Buzz, spick and span in his uniform, looked down rather nervously, and yet with a certain pride at his left leg. When he sat down you couldn't tell which was the real one. As the train pulled in at the Chippewa Junction, just before reaching the town proper, there was old Bart Ochsner ringing the bell for dinner at the Junction eating house. Well, for the love of Mike! Wouldn't that make you laugh. Ringing that bell, just like always, as if nothing had happened in the last year! Buzz leaned against the window, to see. There was some commotion in the train and some one spoke his name. Buzz turned, and there stood Old Man Hatton, and a lot of others, and he seemed to be making a speech, and kind of crying, though that couldn't be possible. And his father was there, very clean and shaved and queer. Buzz caught words about bravery, and Chippewa's pride, and he was fussed to death, and glad when the train pulled in at the Chippewa station. But there the commotion was worse than ever. There was a band, playing away like mad. Buzz's great hands grown very white, were fidgeting at his uniform buttons, and at the stripe on his sleeve, and the medal on his breast. They wouldn't let him carry a thing, and when he came out on the car platform to descend there went up a great sound that was half roar and half scream. Buzz Werner was the first of Chippewa's men to come back.

After that it was rather hazy. There was his mother. His sister Minnie, too. He even saw the Kearney girl, with her loose red mouth, and her silly eyes, and she was as a strange woman to him. He was in Hatton's glittering automobile, being driven down Grand Avenue. There were speeches, and a dinner, and, later, when he was allowed to go home, rather white, a steady stream of people pouring in and out of the house all day. That night, when he limped up the stairs to his hot little room under the roof he was dazed, spent, and not so very happy.

Next morning, though, he felt more himself, and inclined to joke. And then there was a talk with old Man Hatton; a talk that left Buzz somewhat numb, and the family breathless.

Visitors again, all that afternoon.

After supper he carried water for the garden, against his mother's outraged protests.

"What'll folks think!" she said, "you carryin' water for me?"

Afterward he took his smart visored cap off the hook and limped down town, his boots and leggings and uniform very spick and span from Ma Werner's expert brushing and rubbing. She refused to let Buzz touch them, although he tried to tell her that he had done that job for a year.

At the corner of Grand and Outagamie, in front of Schroeder's drug store, stood what was left of the gang, and some new members who had come during the year that had passed. Buzz knew them all.

They greeted him at first with a mixture of shyness and resentment. They eyed his leg, and his uniform, and the metal and ribbon thing that hung at his breast. Bing and Red and Spider were there. Casey was gone.

Finally Spider spat and said, "G'wan, Buzz, give us your spiel about how you saved young Hatton—the simp!"

"Who says he's a simp?" inquired Buzz, very quietly. But there was a look about his jaw.

"Well—anyway—the papers was full of how you was a hero. Say, is that right that old Hatton's goin' to send you to college? Huh? Je's!"

"Yeh," chorused the others, "go on, Buzz. Tell us."

Red put his question. "Tell us about the fightin', Buzz. Is it like they say?"

It was Buzz Werner's great moment. He had pictured it a thousand times in his mind as he lay in the wet trenches, as he plodded the muddy French roads, as he reclined in his wheel chair in the hospital garden. He had them in the hollow of his hand. His eyes brightened. He looked at the faces so eagerly fixed on his utterance.

"G'wan, Buzz," they urged.

Buzz opened his lips and the words he used were the words he might have used a year before, as to choice. "There's nothin' to tell. A guy didn't have no time to be scairt. Everything kind of come at once, and you got yours, or either you didn't. That's all there was to it. Je's, it was fierce!"

They waited. Nothing more. "Yeh, but tell us—"

And suddenly Buzz turned away. The little group about him fell back, respectfully. Something in his face, perhaps. A quietness, a new dignity.

"S'long, boys," he said. And limped off, toward home.

And in that moment Buzz, the bully and braggart, vanished forever. And in his place—head high, chest up, eyes clear—limped Ernest Werner, the man.

IV

THE ELDEST

The Self-Complacent Young Cub leaned an elbow against the mantel as you've seen it done in English plays, and blew a practically perfect smoke-ring. It hurtled toward me like a discus.

"Trouble with your stuff," he began at once (we had just been introduced), "is that it lacks plot. Been meaning to meet and tell you that for a long time. Your characterization's all right, and your dialogue. In fact, I think they're good. But your stuff lacks raison d'être—if you know what I mean.

"But"—in feeble self-defence—"people's insides are often so much more interesting than their outsides; that which they think or feel so much more thrilling than anything they actually do. Bennett—Wells—"

"Rot!" remarked the young cub, briskly. "Plot's the thing."

There is no plot to this because there is no plot to Rose. There never was. There never will be. Compared to the drab monotony of Rose's existence a desert waste is as thrilling as a five-reel film.

They had called her Rose, fatuously, as parents do their first-born girl. No doubt she had been normally pink and white and velvety. It is a risky thing to do, however. Think back hastily on the Roses you know. Don't you find a startling majority still clinging, sere and withered, to the family bush?

In Chicago, Illinois, a city of two millions (or is it three?), there are women whose lives are as remote, as grey, as unrelated to the world about them as is the life of a Georgia cracker's woman-drudge. Rose was one of these. An unwed woman, grown heavy about the hips and arms, as houseworking women do, though they eat but little, moving dully about the six-room flat on Sangamon Street, Rose was as much a slave as any black wench of plantation days.

There was the treadmill of endless dishes, dirtied as fast as cleansed; there were beds, and beds, and beds; gravies and soups and stews. And always the querulous voice of the sick woman in the front bedroom demanding another hot water bag. Rose's day was punctuated by hot water bags. They dotted her waking hours. She filled hot water bags automatically, like a machine—water half-way to the top, then one hand clutching the bag's slippery middle while the other, with a deft twist, ejected the air within; a quick twirl of the metal stopper, the bag released, squirming, and, finally, its plump and rufous cheeks wiped dry.

"Is that too hot for you, Ma? Where'd you want it—your head or your feet?"

A spinster nearing forty, living thus, must have her memories— one precious memory, at least—or she dies. Rose had hers. She hugged it, close. The L trains roared by, not thirty feet from her kitchen door. Alley and yard and street sent up their noises to her. The life of Chicago's millions yelped at her heels. On Rose's face was the vague, mute look of the woman whose days are spent indoors, at sordid tasks.

At six-thirty every night that look lifted, for an hour. At six-thirty they came home—Floss, and Al, and Pa—their faces stamped with the marks that come from a day spent in shop and factory. They brought with them the crumbs and husks of the day's happenings, and these they flung carelessly before the life-starved Rose and she ate them, gratefully.

They came in with a rush, hungry, fagged, grimed, imperious, smelling of the city. There was a slamming of doors, a banging of drawers, a clatter of tongues, quarrelling, laughter. A brief visit to the sick woman's room. The thin, complaining voice reciting its tale of the day's discomfort and pain. Then supper.

"Guess who I waited on to-day!" Floss might demand.

Rose, dishing up, would pause, interested. "Who?"

"Gladys Moraine! I knew her the minute she came down the aisle. I saw her last year when she was playing in 'His Wives.' She's prettier off than on, I think. I waited on her, and the other girls were wild. She bought a dozen pairs of white kids, and made me give 'em to her huge, so she could shove her hand right into 'em, like a man does. Two sizes too big. All the swells wear 'em that way. And only one ring—an emerald the size of a dime."

"What'd she wear?" Rose's dull face was almost animated.

"Ah yes!" in a dreamy falsetto from Al, "what did she wear?"

"Oh, shut up, Al! Just a suit, kind of plain, and yet you'd notice it. And sables! And a Gladys Moraine hat. Everything quiet, and plain, and dark; and yet she looked like a million dollars. I felt like a roach while I was waiting on her, though she was awfully sweet to me."

Or perhaps Al, the eel-like, would descend from his heights to mingle a brief moment in the family talk. Al clerked in the National Cigar Company's store at Clark and Madison. His was the wisdom of the snake, the weasel, and the sphinx. A strangely silent young man, this Al, thin-lipped, smooth-cheeked, perfumed. Slim of waist, flat of hip, narrow of shoulder, his was the figure of the born fox-trotter.

He walked lightly, on the balls of his feet, like an Indian, but without the Indian's dignity.

"Some excitement ourselves, to-day, down at the store, believe me. The Old Man's son started in to learn the retail selling end of the business. Back of the showcase with the rest of us, waiting on trade, and looking like a Yale yell."

Pa would put down his paper to stare over his reading specs at Al.

"Mannheim's son! The president!"

"Yep! And I guess he loves it, huh? The Old Man wants him to learn the business from the ground up. I'll bet he'll never get higher than the first floor. To-day he went out to lunch at one and never shows up again till four. Wears English collars, and smokes a brand of cigarettes we don't carry."

Thus was the world brought to Rose. Her sallow cheek would show a faint hint of colour as she sipped her tea.

At six-thirty on a Monday morning in late April (remember, nothing's going to happen) Rose smothered her alarm clock at the first warning snarl. She was wide-awake at once, as are those whose yesterdays, to-days and to-morrows are all alike. Rose never opened her eyes to the dim, tantalising half-consciousness of a something delightful or a something harrowing in store for her that day. For one to whom the wash-woman's Tuesday visitation is the event of the week, and in whose bosom the delivery boy's hoarse "Groc-rees!" as he hurls soap and cabbage on the kitchen table, arouses a wild flurry, there can be very little thrill on awakening.

Rose slept on the davenport-couch in the sitting-room. That fact in itself rises her status in the family. This Monday morning she opened her eyes with what might be called a start if Rose were any other sort of heroine. Something had happened, or was happening. It wasn't the six o'clock steam hissing in the radiator. She was accustomed to that. The rattle of the L trains, and the milkman's artillery disturbed her as little as does the chirping of the birds the farmer's daughter. A sensation new, yet familiar; delicious, yet painful, held her. She groped to define it, lying there. Her gaze, wandering over the expanse of the grey woollen blanket, fixed upon a small black object trembling there. The knowledge that came to her then had come, many weeks before, in a hundred subtle and exquisite ways, to those who dwell in the open places. Rose's eyes narrowed craftily. Craftily, stealthily, she sat up, one hand raised. Her eyes still fixed on the quivering spot, the hand descended, lightning-quick. But not quickly enough. The black spot vanished. It sped toward the open window. Through that window there came a balmy softness made up of Lake Michigan zephyr, and stockyards

63

smell, and distant budding things. Rose had failed to swat the first fly of the season. Spring had come.

As she got out of bed and thud-thudded across the room on her heels to shut the window she glanced out into the quiet street. Her city eyes, untrained to nature's hints, failed to notice that the scraggy, smoke-dwarfed oak that sprang, somehow, miraculously, from the mangey little dirt-plot in front of the building had developed surprising things all over its scrawny branches overnight. But she did see that the front windows of the flat building across the way were bare of the Chicago-grey lace curtains that had hung there the day before. House cleaning! Well, most decidedly spring had come.

Rose was the household's Aurora. Following the donning of her limp and obscure garments it was Rose's daily duty to tear the silent family from its slumbers. Ma was always awake, her sick eyes fixed hopefully on the door. For fourteen years it had been the same.

"Sleeping?"

"Sleeping! I haven't closed an eye all night."

Rose had learned not to dispute that statement.

"It's spring out! I'm going to clean the closets and the bureau drawers to-day. I'll have your coffee in a jiffy. Do you feel like getting up and sitting out on the back porch, toward noon, maybe?"

On her way kitchenward she stopped for a sharp tattoo at the door of the room in which Pa and Al slept. A sleepy grunt of remonstrance rewarded her. She came to Floss's door, turned the knob softly, peered in. Floss was sleeping as twenty sleeps, deeply, dreamlessly, one slim bare arm outflung, the lashes resting ever so lightly on the delicate curve of cheek. As she lay there asleep in her disordered bedroom, her clothes strewing chair, dresser, floor, Floss's tastes, mental equipment, spiritual make-up, innermost thoughts, were as plainly to be read by the observer as though she had been scientifically charted by a psycho-analyst, a metaphysician and her dearest girl friend.

"Floss! Floss, honey! Quarter to seven!" Floss stirred, moaned faintly, dropped into sleep again.

Fifteen minutes later, the table set, the coffee simmering, the morning paper brought from the back porch to Ma, Rose had heard none of the sounds that proclaimed the family astir—the banging of drawers, the rush of running water, the slap of slippered feet. A peep of enquiry into the depths of the coffee pot, the gas turned to a circle of blue beads, and she was down the hall to sound the second alarm.

"Floss, you know if Al once gets into the bathroom!" Floss sat up in bed, her eyes still closed. She made little clucking sounds with her tongue and lips, as a baby does when it wakes. Drugged with sleep, hair tousled, muscles sagging, at seven o'clock in the morning, the most trying hour in the day for a woman, Floss was still triumphantly pretty. She had on one of those absurd pink muslin nightgowns, artfully designed to look like crêpe de chine. You've seen them rosily displayed in the cheaper shop windows, marked ninety-eight cents, and you may have wondered who might buy them, forgetting that there is an imitation mind for every imitation article in the world.

Rose stooped, picked up a pair of silk stockings from the floor, and ran an investigating hand through to heel and toe. She plucked a soiled pink blouse off the back of a chair, eyed it critically, and tucked it under her arm with the stockings.

"Did you have a good time last night?"

Floss yawned elaborately, stretched her slim arms high above her head; then, with a desperate effort, flung back the bed-clothes, swung her legs over the side of the bed and slipped her toes into the shabby, pomponed slippers that lay on the floor.

"I say, did you have a g—"

"Oh Lord, I don't know! I guess so," snapped Floss. Temperamentally, Floss was not at her best at seven o'clock on Monday morning. Rose did not pursue the subject. She tried another tack.

"It's as mild as summer out. I see the Werners and the Burkes are housecleaning. I thought I'd start to-day with the closets, and the bureau drawers. You could wear your blue this morning, if it was pressed."

Floss yawned again, disinterestedly, and folded her kimono about her.

"Go as far as you like. Only don't put things back in my closet so's I can't ever find 'em again. I wish you'd press that blue skirt. And wash out the Georgette crêpe waist. I might need it."

The blouse, and skirt, and stockings under her arm, Rose went back to the kitchen to prepare her mother's breakfast tray. Wafted back to her came the acrid odour of Pa's matutinal pipe, and the accustomed bickering between Al and Floss over the possession of the bathroom.

"What do you think this is, anyway? A Turkish bath?"

"Shave in your own room!"

Between Floss and Al there existed a feud that lifted only when a third member of the family turned against either of them. Immediately they about-faced and stood united against the offender.

Pa was the first to demand breakfast, as always. Very neat, was

65

Pa, and fussy, and strangely young looking to be the husband of the grey-haired, parchment-skinned woman who lay in the front bedroom. Pa had two manias: the movies, and a passion for purchasing new and complicated household utensils—cream-whippers, egg-beaters, window-clamps, lemon-squeezers, silver-polishers. He haunted department store basements in search of them.

He opened his paper now and glanced at the head-lines and at the Monday morning ads. "I see the Fair's got a spring housecleaning sale. They advertise a new kind of extension curtain rod. And Scouro, three cakes for a dime."

"If you waste one cent more on truck like that," Rose protested, placing his breakfast before him, "when half the time I can't make the housekeeping money last through the week!"

"Your ma did it."

"Fourteen years ago liver wasn't thirty-two cents a pound," retorted Rose, "and besides—"

"Scramble 'em!" yelled Al, from the bedroom, by way of warning.

There was very little talk after that. The energies of three of them were directed toward reaching the waiting desk or counter on time. The energy of one toward making that accomplishment easy. The front door slammed once—that was Pa, on his way; slammed again—Al. Floss rushed into the dining-room fastening the waist-band of her skirt, her hat already on. Rose always had a rather special breakfast for Floss. Floss posed as being a rather special person. She always breakfasted last, and late. Floss's was a fastidiousness which shrinks at badly served food, a spotted table-cloth, or a last year's hat, while it overlooks a rent in an undergarment or the accumulated dust in a hairbrush. Her blouse was of the sheerest. Her hair shone in waves about her delicate checks. She ate her orange, and sipped her very special coffee, and made a little face over her egg that had been shirred in the oven or in some way highly specialised. Then the front door slammed again—a semi-slam, this time. Floss never did quite close a door. Rose followed her down the hall, shut and bolted it, Chicago fashion. The sick woman in the front bedroom had dropped into one of her fitful morning dozes. At eight o'clock the little flat was very still.

If you knew nothing about Rose; if you had not already been told that she slept on the sitting-room davenport; that she was taken for granted as the family drudge; that she was, in that household, merely an intelligent machine that made beds, fried eggs, filled hot water bags, you would get a characterization of her

66

from this: She was the sort of person who never has a closet or bureau drawer all her own. Her few and negligible garments hung apologetically in obscure corners of closets dedicated to her sister's wardrobe or her brother's, or her spruce and fussy old father's. Vague personal belongings, such as combings, handkerchiefs, a spectacle case, a hairbrush, were found tucked away in a desk pigeon-hole, a table drawer, or on the top shelf in the bathroom.

As she pulled the disfiguring blue gingham dust-cap over her hair now, and rolled her sleeves to her elbows, you would never have dreamed that Rose was embarking upon her great adventure. You would never have guessed that the semi-yearly closet cleaning was to give to Rose a thrill as delicious as it was exquisitely painful. But Rose knew. And so she teased herself, and tried not to think of the pasteboard box on the shelf in the hall closet, under the pile of reserve blankets, and told herself that she would leave that closet until the last, when she would have to hurry over it.

When you clean closets and bureau drawers thoroughly you have to carry things out to the back porch and flap them, Rose was that sort of housekeeper. She leaned over the porch railing and flapped things, so that the dust motes spun and swirled in the sunshine. Rose's arms worked up and down energetically, then less energetically, finally ceased their motion altogether. She leaned idle elbows on the porch railing and gazed down into the yard below with a look in her eyes such as no squalid Chicago back yard, with its dusty débris, could summon, even in spring-time.

The woman next door came out on her back porch that adjoined Rose's. The day seemed to have her in its spell, too, for in her hand was something woolly and wintry, and she began to flap it about as Rose had done. She had lived next door since October, had that woman, but the two had never exchanged a word, true to the traditions of their city training. Rose had her doubts of the woman next door. She kept a toy dog which she aired afternoons, and her kimonos were florid and numerous. Now, as the eyes of the two women met, Rose found herself saying, "Looks like summer."

The woman next door caught the scrap of conversation eagerly, hungrily. "It certainly does! Makes me feel like new clothes, and housecleaning."

"I started to-day!" said Rose, triumphantly.

"Not already!" gasped the woman next door, with the chagrin that only a woman knows who has let May steal upon her unawares.

From far down the alley sounded a chant, drawing nearer and nearer, until there shambled into view a decrepit horse drawing a dilapidated huckster's cart. Perched on the seat was a Greek who turned his dusky face up toward the two women leaning over the porch railings. "Rhubarb, leddy. Fresh rhubarb!"

"My folks don't care for rhubarb sauce," Rose told the woman next door.

"It makes the worst pie in the world," the woman confided to Rose.

Whereupon each bought a bunch of the succulent green and red stalks. It was their offering at the season's shrine.

Rose flung the rhubarb on the kitchen table, pulled her dust-cap more firmly about her ears, and hurried back to the disorder of Floss's dim little bedroom. After that it was dust-cloth, and soapsuds, and scrub-brush in a race against recurrent water bags, insistent doorbells, and the inevitable dinner hour. It was mid-afternoon when Rose, standing a-tiptoe on a chair, came at last to the little box on the top shelf under the bedding in the hall closet. Her hand touched the box, and closed about it. A little electric thrill vibrated through her body. She stepped down from the chair, heavily, listened until her acute ear caught the sound of the sick woman's slumbrous breathing; then, box in hand, walked down the dark hall to the kitchen. The rhubarb pie, still steaming in its pan, was cooling on the kitchen table. The dishes from the invalid's lunch-tray littered the sink. But Rose, seated on the kitchen chair, her rumpled dust-cap pushed back from her flushed, perspiring face, untied the rude bit of string that bound the old candy box, removed the lid, slowly, and by that act was wafted magically out of the world of rhubarb pies, and kitchen chairs, and dirty dishes, into that place whose air is the breath of incense and myrrh, whose paths are rose-strewn, whose dwellings are temples dedicated to but one small god. The land is known as Love, and Rose travelled back to it on the magic rug of memory.

A family of five in a six-room Chicago flat must sacrifice sentiment to necessity. There is precious little space for those pressed flowers, time-yellowed gowns, and ribbon-bound packets that figured so prominently in the days of attics. Into the garbage can with yesterday's roses! The janitor's burlap sack yawns for this morning's mail; last year's gown has long ago met its end at the hands of the ol'-clo'es man or the wash-woman's daughter. That they had survived these fourteen years, and the strictures of their owner's dwelling, tells more about this boxful of letters than could be conveyed by a battalion of adjectives.

Rose began at the top of the pile, in her orderly fashion, and read straight through to the last. It took one hour. Half of that time she was not reading. She was staring straight ahead with what is mistakenly called an unseeing look, but which actually pierces the

68

veil of years and beholds things far, far beyond the vision of the actual eye. They were the letters of a commonplace man to a commonplace woman, written when they loved each other, and so they were touched with something of the divine. They must have been, else how could they have sustained this woman through fifteen years of drudgery? They were the only tangible foundation left of the structure of dreams she had built about this man. All the rest of her house of love had tumbled about her ears fifteen years before, but with these few remaining bricks she had erected many times since castles and towers more exquisite and lofty and soaring than the original humble structure had ever been.

The story? Well, there really isn't any, as we've warned you. Rose had been pretty then in much the same delicate way that Floss was pretty now. They were to have been married. Rose's mother fell ill, Floss and Al were little more than babies. The marriage was put off. The illness lasted six months—a year—two years—became interminable. The breach into which Rose had stepped closed about her and became a prison. The man had waited, had grown impatient, finally rebelled. He had fled, probably, to marry a less encumbered lady. Rose had gone dully on, caring for the household, the children, the sick woman. In the years that had gone by since then Rose had forgiven him his faithlessness. She only remembered that he had been wont to call her his Röschen, his Rosebud, his pretty flower (being a German gentleman). She only recalled the wonder of having been first in some one's thoughts—she who now was so hopelessly, so irrevocably last.

As she sat there in her kitchen, wearing her soap-stained and faded blue gingham, and the dust-cap pushed back at a rakish angle, a simpering little smile about her lips, she was really very much like the disappointed old maids you used to see so cruelly pictured in the comic valentines. Had those letters obsessed her a little more strongly she might have become quite mad, the Freudians would tell you. Had they held less for her, or had she not been so completely the household's slave, she might have found a certain solace and satisfaction in viewing the Greek profile and marcel wave of the most-worshipped movie star. As it was, they were her ballast, her refuge, the leavening yeast in the soggy dough of her existence. This man had wanted her to be his wife. She had found favour in his eyes. She was certain that he still thought of her, sometimes, and tenderly, regretfully, as she thought of him. It helped her to live. Not only that, it made living possible.

A clock struck, a window slammed, or a street-noise smote her ear sharply. Some sound started her out of her reverie. Rose jumped, stared a moment at the letters in her lap, then hastily, almost shamefacedly, sorted them (she knew each envelope by heart) tied them, placed them in their box and bore them down the hall. There, mounting her chair, she scrubbed the top shelf with her soapy rag, placed the box in its corner, left the hall closet smelling of cleanliness, with never a hint of lavender to betray its secret treasure.

Were Rose to die and go to Heaven, there to spend her days thumbing a golden harp, her hands, by force of habit, would, drop harp-strings at quarter to six, to begin laying a celestial and unspotted table-cloth for supper. Habits as deeply rooted as that must hold, even in after-life.

To-night's six-thirty stampede was noticeably subdued on the part of Pa and Al. It had been a day of sudden and enervating heat, and the city had done its worst to them. Pa's pink gills showed a hint of purple. Al's flimsy silk shirt stuck to his back, and his glittering pompadour was many degrees less submissive than was its wont. But Floss came in late, breathless, and radiant, a large and significant paper bag in her hand. Rose, in the kitchen, was transferring the smoking supper from pot to platter. Pa, in the doorway of the sick woman's little room, had just put his fourteen-year-old question with his usual assumption of heartiness and cheer: "Well, well! And how's the old girl to-night? Feel like you could get up and punish a little supper, eh?" Al engaged at the telephone with some one whom he addressed proprietorially as Kid, was deep in his plans for the evening's diversion. Upon this accustomed scene Floss burst with havoc.

"Rose! Rose, did you iron my Georgette crêpe? Listen! Guess what!" All this as she was rushing down the hall, paper hat-bag still in hand. "Guess who was in the store to-day!"

Rose, at the oven, turned a flushed and interested face toward Floss.

"Who? What's that? A hat?"

"Yes. But listen—"

"Let's see it."

Floss whipped it out of its bag, defiantly. "There! But wait a minute! Let me tell you—"

"How much?"

Floss hesitated just a second. Her wage was nine dollars a week. Then, "Seven-fifty, trimmed." The hat was one of those tiny, head-hugging absurdities that only the Flosses can wear.

"Trimmed is right!" jeered Al, from the doorway.

Rose, thin-lipped with disapproval, turned to her stove again.

"Well, but I had to have it. I'm going to the theatre to-night. And guess who with! Henry Selz!"

70

Henry Selz was the unromantic name of the commonplace man over whose fifteen-year-old letters Rose had glowed and dreamed an hour before. It was a name that had become mythical in that household—to all but one. Rose heard it spoken now with a sense of unreality. She smiled a little uncertainly, and went on stirring the flour thickening for the gravy. But she was dimly aware that something inside her had suspended action for a moment, during which moment she felt strangely light and disembodied, and that directly afterward the thing began to work madly, so that there was a choked feeling in her chest and a hot pounding in her head.

"What's the joke?" she said, stirring the gravy in the pan.

"Joke nothing! Honest to God! I was standing back of the counter at about ten. The rush hadn't really begun yet. Glove trade usually starts late. I was standing there kidding Herb, the stock boy, when down the aisle comes a man in a big hat, like you see in the western pictures, hair a little grey at the temples, and everything, just like a movie actor. I said to Herb, 'Is it real?' I hadn't got the words out of my mouth when the fellow sees me, stands stock still in the middle of the aisle with his mouth open and his eyes sticking out. 'Register surprise,' I said to Herb, and looked around for the camera. And that minute he took two jumps over to where I was standing, grabbed my hands and says, 'Rose! Rose!' kind of choky. 'Not by about twenty years,' I said. 'I'm Floss, Rose's sister. Let go my hands!'"

Rose—a transfigured Rose, glowing, trembling, radiant—repeated, vibrantly, "You said, 'I'm Floss, Rose's sister. Let go my hands!' And—?"

"He looked kind of stunned, for just a minute. His face was a scream, honestly. Then he said, 'But of course. Fifteen years. But I had always thought of her as just the same.' And he kind of laughed, ashamed, like a kid. And the whitest teeth!"

"Yes, they were—white," said Rose. "Well?"

"Well, I said, 'Won't I do instead?' 'You bet you'll do!' he said. And then he told me his name, and how he was living out in Spokane, and his wife was dead, and he had made a lot of money—fruit, or real estate, or something. He talked a lot about it at lunch, but I didn't pay any attention, as long as he really has it a lot I care how—"

"At lunch?"

"Everything from grape-fruit to coffee. I didn't know it could be done in one hour. Believe me, he had those waiters jumping. It takes money. He asked all about you, and ma, and everything. And he kept looking at me and saying, 'It's wonderful!' I said, 'Isn't it!' but I meant the lunch. He wanted me to go driving this afternoon—auto and everything. Kept calling me Rose. It made me kind of mad, and I told him how you look. He said, 'I suppose so,' and asked me to go to a show to-night. Listen, did you press my Georgette? And the blue?"

"I'll iron the waist while you're eating. I'm not hungry. It only takes a minute. Did you say he was grey?"

"Grey? Oh, you mean—why, just here, and here. Interesting, but not a bit old. And he's got that money look that makes waiters and doormen and taxi drivers just hump. I don't want any supper. Just a cup of tea. I haven't got enough time to dress in, decently, as it is."

Al, draped in the doorway, removed his cigarette to give greater force to his speech. "Your story interests me strangely, little gell. But there's a couple of other people that would like to eat, even if you wouldn't. Come on with that supper, Ro. Nobody staked me to a lunch to-day."

Rose turned to her stove again. Two carmine spots had leaped suddenly to her cheeks. She served the meal in silence, and ate nothing, but that was not remarkable. For the cook there is little appeal in the meat that she has tended from its moist and bloody entrance in the butcher's paper, through the basting or broiling stage to its formal appearance on the platter. She saw that Al and her father were served. Then she went back to the kitchen, and the thud of her iron was heard as she deftly fluted the ruffles of the crêpe blouse. Floss appeared when the meal was half eaten, her hair shiningly coiffed, the pink ribbons of her corset cover showing under her thin kimono. She poured herself a cup of tea and drank it in little quick, nervous gulps. She looked deliriously young, and fragile and appealing, her delicate slenderness revealed by the flimsy garment she wore. Excitement and anticipation lent a glow to her eyes, colour to her cheeks. Al, glancing expertly at the ingenuousness of her artfully simple coiffure, the slim limpness of her body, her wide-eyed gaze, laughed a wise little laugh.

"Every move a Pickford. And so girlish withal."

Floss ignored him. "Hurry up with that waist, Rose!"

"I'm on the collar now. In a second." There was a little silence. Then: "Floss, is—is Henry going to call for you—here?"

"Well, sure! Did you think I was going to meet him on the corner? He said he wanted to see you, or something polite like that."

She finished her tea and vanished again. Al, too, had disappeared to begin that process from which he had always emerged incredibly sleek, and dapper and perfumed. His progress with shaving brush, shirt, collar and tie was marked by disjointed bars of the newest syncopation whistled with an uncanny precision and fidelity to detail. He caught the broken time, and tossed it lightly up again, and dropped it, and caught it deftly like a juggler playing with frail crystal globes that seem forever on the point of crashing to the ground.

Pa stood up, yawning. "Well," he said, his manner very casual, "guess I'll just drop around to the movie."

From the kitchen, "Don't you want to sit with ma a minute, first?"

"I will when I come back. They're showing the third installment of 'The Adventures of Aline,' and I don't want to come in in the middle of it."

He knew the selfishness of it, this furtive and sprightly old man. And because he knew it he attempted to hide his guilt under a burst of temper.

"I've been slaving all day. I guess I've got the right to a little amusement. A man works his fingers to the bone for his family, and then his own daughter nags him."

He stamped down the hall, righteously, and slammed the front door.

Rose came from the kitchen, the pink blouse, warm from the iron, in one hand. She prinked out its ruffles and pleatings as she went. Floss, burnishing her nails somewhat frantically with a dilapidated and greasy buffer, snatched the garment from her and slipped bare arms into it. The front door bell rang, three big, determined rings. Panic fell upon the household.

"It's him!" whispered Floss, as if she could be heard in the entrance three floors below. "You'll have to go."

"I can't!" Every inch of her seemed to shrink and cower away from the thought. "I can't!" Her eyes darted to and fro like a hunted thing seeking to escape. She ran to the hall. "Al! Al, go to the door, will you?"

"Can't," came back in a thick mumble. "Shaving."

The front door-bell rang again, three big, determined rings. "Rose!" hissed Floss, her tone venomous. "I can't go with my waist open. For heaven's sake! Go to the door!"

"I can't," repeated Rose, in a kind of wail. "I—can't." And went. As she went she passed one futile, work-worn hand over her hair, plucked off her apron and tossed it into; a corner, first wiping her flushed face with it.

Henry Selz came up the shabby stairs springily as a man of forty should. Rose stood at the door and waited for him. He stood in the doorway a moment, uncertainly.

"How-do, Henry."

His uncertainty became incredulity. Then, "Why, how-do, Rose!

73

Didn't know you—for a minute. Well, well! It's been a long time. Let's see—ten—fourteen—about fifteen years, isn't it?"

His tone was cheerfully conversational. He really was interested, mathematically. He was as sentimental in his reminiscence as if he had been calculating the lapse of time between the Chicago fire and the World's Fair.

"Fifteen," said Rose, "in May. Won't you come in? Floss'll be here in a minute."

Henry Selz came in and sat down on the davenport couch and dabbed at his forehead. The years had been very kind to him—those same years that had treated Rose so ruthlessly. He had the look of an outdoor man; a man who has met prosperity and walked with her, and followed her pleasant ways; a man who has learned late in life of golf and caviar and tailors, but who has adapted himself to these accessories of wealth with a minimum of friction.

"It certainly is warm, for this time of year." He leaned back and regarded Rose tolerantly. "Well, and how've you been? Did little sister tell you how flabbergasted I was when I saw her this morning? I'm darned if it didn't take fifteen years off my age, just like that! I got kind of balled up for one minute and thought it was you. She tell you?"

"Yes, she told me," said Rose.

"I hear your ma's still sick. That certainly is tough. And you've never married, eh?"

"Never married," echoed Rose.

And so they made conversation, a little uncomfortably, until there came quick, light young steps down the hallway, and Floss appeared in the door, a radiant, glowing, girlish vision. Youth was in her eyes, her cheeks, on her lips. She radiated it. She was miraculously well dressed, in her knowingly simple blue serge suit, and her tiny hat, and her neat shoes and gloves.

"Ah! And how's the little girl to-night?" said Henry Selz.

Floss dimpled, blushed, smiled, swayed. "Did I keep you waiting a terribly long time?"

"No, not a bit. Rose and I were chinning over old times, weren't we, Rose?" A kindly, clumsy thought struck him. "Say, look here, Rose. We're going to a show. Why don't you run and put on your hat and come along. H'm? Come on!"

Rose smiled as a mother smiles at a child that has unknowingly hurt her. "No, thanks, Henry. Not to-night. You and Floss run along. Yes, I'll remember you to Ma. I'm sorry you can't see her. But she don't see anybody, poor Ma."

Then they were off, in a little flurry of words and laughter. From force of habit Rose's near-sighted eyes peered critically at the hang of Floss's blue skirt and the angle of the pert new hat. She stood a moment, uncertainly, after they had left. On her face was the queerest look, as of one thinking, re-adjusting, struggling to arrive at a conclusion in the midst of sudden bewilderment. She turned mechanically and went into her mother's room. She picked up the tray on the table by the bed.

"Who was that?" asked the sick woman, in her ghostly, devitalised voice.

"That was Henry Selz," said Rose.

The sick woman grappled a moment with memory. "Henry Selz! Henry—oh, yes. Did he go out with Rose?"

"Yes," said Rose.

"It's cold in here," whined the sick woman.

"I'll get you a hot bag in a minute, Ma." Rose carried the tray down the hall to the kitchen. At that Al emerged from his bedroom, shrugging himself into his coat. He followed Rose down the hall and watched her as she filled the bag and screwed it and wiped it dry.

"I'll take that in to Ma," he volunteered. He was up the hall and back in a flash. Rose had slumped into a chair at the dining-room table, and was pouring herself a cup of cold and bitter tea. Al came over to her and laid one white hand on her shoulder.

"Ro, lend me a couple of dollars till Saturday, will you?"

"I should say not."

Al doused his cigarette in the dregs of a convenient teacup. He bent down and laid his powdered and pale cheek against Rose's sallow one. One arm was about her, and his hand patted her shoulder.

"Oh, come on, kid," he coaxed. "Don't I always pay you back? Come on! Be a sweet ol' sis. I wouldn't ask you only I've got a date to go to the White City to-night, and dance, and I couldn't get out of it. I tried." He kissed her, and his lips were moist, and he reeked of tobacco, and though Rose shrugged impatiently away from him he knew that he had won. Rose was not an eloquent woman; she was not even an articulate one, at times. If she had been, she would have lifted up her voice to say now:

"Oh, God! I am a woman! Why have you given me all the sorrows, and the drudgery, and the bitterness and the thanklessness of motherhood, with none of its joys! Give me back my youth! I'll drink the dregs at the bottom of the cup, but first let me taste the sweet!"

But Rose did not talk or think in such terms. She could not have put into words the thing she was feeling even if she had been able to diagnose it. So what she said was, "Don't you think I ever get sick and tired of slaving for a thankless bunch like you? Well, I do! Sick

75

and tired of it. That's what! You make me tired, coming around asking for money, as if I was a bank."

But Al waited. And presently she said, grudgingly, wearily, "There's a dollar bill and some small change in the can on the second shelf in the china closet."

Al was off like a terrier. From the pantry came the clink of metal against metal. He was up the hall in a flash, without a look at Rose. The front door slammed a third time.

Rose stirred her cold tea slowly, leaning on the table's edge and gazing down into the amber liquid that she did not mean to drink. For suddenly and comically her face puckered up like a child's. Her head came down among the supper things with a little crash that set the teacups, and the greasy plates to jingling, and she sobbed as she lay there, with great tearing, ugly sobs that would not be stilled, though she tried to stifle them as does one who lives in a paper-thin Chicago flat. She was not weeping for the Henry Selz whom she had just seen. She was not weeping for envy of her selfish little sister, or for loneliness, or weariness. She was weeping at the loss of a ghost who had become her familiar. She was weeping because a packet of soiled and yellow old letters on the top shelf in the hall closet was now only a packet of soiled and yellow old letters, food for the ash can. She was weeping because the urge of spring, that had expressed itself in her only this morning pitifully enough in terms of rhubarb, and housecleaning and a bundle of thumbed old love letters, had stirred in her for the last time.

But presently she did stop her sobbing and got up and cleared the table, and washed the dishes and even glanced at the crumpled sheets of the morning paper that she never found time to read until evening. By eight o'clock the little flat was very still.

V

THAT'S MARRIAGE

Theresa Platt (she that had been Terry Sheehan) watched her husband across the breakfast table with eyes that smouldered. When a woman's eyes smoulder at 7.30 a.m. the person seated opposite her had better look out. But Orville Platt was quite unaware of any smouldering in progress. He was occupied with his eggs. How could he know that these very eggs were feeding the dull red menace in Terry Platt's eyes?

When Orville Platt ate a soft-boiled egg he concentrated on it. He treated it as a great adventure. Which, after all, it is. Few adjuncts of our daily life contain the element of chance that is to be found in a three-minute breakfast egg.

This was Orville Platt's method of attack: First, he chipped off the top, neatly. Then he bent forward and subjected it to a passionate and relentless scrutiny. Straightening—preparatory to plunging his spoon therein—he flapped his right elbow. It wasn't exactly a flap; it was a pass between a hitch and a flap, and presented external evidence of a mental state. Orville Platt always gave that little preliminary jerk when he was contemplating a step, or when he was moved, or argumentative. It was a trick as innocent as it was maddening.

Terry Platt had learned to look for that flap—they had been married four years—to look for it, and to hate it with a morbid, unreasoning hate. That flap of the elbow was tearing Terry Platt's nerves into raw, bleeding fragments.

Her fingers were clenched tightly under the table, now. She was breathing unevenly. "If he does that again," she told herself, "if he flaps again when he opens the second egg, I'll scream. I'll scream. I'll scream! I'll sc—"

He had scooped the first egg into his cup. Now he picked up the second, chipped it, concentrated, straightened, then—up went the elbow, and down, with the accustomed little flap.

The tortured nerves snapped. Through the early morning quiet of Wetona, Wisconsin, hurtled the shrill, piercing shriek of Terry Platt's hysteria.

"Terry! For God's sake! What's the matter!"

Orville Platt dropped the second egg, and his spoon. The egg yolk trickled down his plate. The spoon made a clatter and flung a gay spot of yellow on the cloth. He started toward her.

Terry, wild-eyed, pointed a shaking finger at him. She was laughing, now, uncontrollably. "Your elbow! Your elbow!"

"Elbow?" He looked down at it, bewildered; then up, fright in his face. "What's the matter with it?"

She mopped her eyes. Sobs shook her. "You f-f-flapped it."

"F-f-f—" The bewilderment in Orville Platt's face gave way to anger. "Do you mean to tell me that you screeched like that because my—because I moved my elbow?"

"Yes."

His anger deepened and reddened to fury. He choked. He had started from his chair with his napkin in his hand. He still clutched it. Now he crumpled it into a wad and hurled it to the centre of the table, where it struck a sugar bowl, dropped back, and uncrumpled slowly, reprovingly. "You—you—" Then bewilderment closed down again like a fog over his countenance. "But why? I can't see—"

"Because it—because I can't stand it any longer. Flapping. This is what you do. Like this."

And she did it. Did it with insulting fidelity, being a clever mimic.

"Well, all I can say is you're crazy, yelling like that, for nothing."

"It isn't nothing."

"Isn't, huh? If that isn't nothing, what is?" They were growing incoherent. "What d'you mean, screeching like a maniac? Like a wild woman? The neighbours'll think I've killed you. What d'you mean, anyway!"

"I mean I'm tired of watching it, that's what. Sick and tired."

"Y'are, huh? Well, young lady, just let me tell you something—"

He told her. There followed one of those incredible quarrels, as sickening as they are human, which can take place only between two people who love each other; who love each other so well that each knows with cruel certainty the surest way to wound the other; and who stab, and tear, and claw at these vulnerable spots in exact proportion to their love.

Ugly words. Bitter words. Words that neither knew they knew flew between them like sparks between steel striking steel.

From him—"Trouble with you is you haven't got enough to do. That's the trouble with half you women. Just lay around the house, rotting. I'm a fool, slaving on the road to keep a good-for-nothing—"

"I suppose you call sitting around hotel lobbies slaving! I suppose the house runs itself! How about my evenings? Sitting here alone, night after night, when you're on the road."

Finally, "Well, if you don't like it," he snarled, and lifted his chair by the back and slammed it down, savagely, "if you don't like it, why don't you get out, h'm? Why don't you get out?"

78

And from her, her eyes narrowed to two slits, her cheeks scarlet:

"Why, thanks. I guess I will."

Ten minutes later he had flung out of the house to catch the 8.19 for Manitowoc. He marched down the street, his shoulders swinging rhythmically to the weight of the burden he carried—his black leather hand-bag and the shiny tan sample case, battle-scarred, both, from many encounters with ruthless porters and 'bus men and bell boys. For four years, as he left for his semi-monthly trip, he and Terry had observed a certain little ceremony (as had the neighbours). She would stand in the doorway watching him down the street, the heavier sample-case banging occasionally at his shin. The depot was only three blocks away. Terry watched him with fond, but unillusioned eyes, which proves that she really loved him. He was a dapper, well-dressed fat man, with a weakness for pronounced patterns in suitings, and addicted to brown derbies. One week on the road, one week at home. That was his routine. The wholesale grocery trade liked Platt, and he had for his customers the fondness that a travelling salesman has who is successful in his territory. Before his marriage to Terry Sheehan his little red address book had been overwhelming proof against the theory that nobody loves a fat man.

Terry, standing in the doorway, always knew that when he reached the corner, just where Schroeder's house threatened to hide him from view, he would stop, drop the sample case, wave his hand just once, pick up the sample case and go on, proceeding backward for a step or two, until Schroeder's house made good its threat. It was a comic scene in the eyes of the onlooker, perhaps because a chubby Romeo offends the sense of fitness. The neighbours, lurking behind their parlour curtains, had laughed at first. But after awhile they learned to look for that little scene, and to take it unto themselves, as if it were a personal thing. Fifteen-year wives whose husbands had long since abandoned flowery farewells used to get a vicarious thrill out of it, and to eye Terry with a sort of envy.

This morning Orville Platt did not even falter when he reached Schroeder's corner. He marched straight on, looking steadily ahead, the heavy bags swinging from either hand. Even if he had stopped—though she knew he wouldn't—Terry Platt would not have seen him. She remained seated at the disordered breakfast table, a dreadfully still figure, and sinister; a figure of stone and fire; of ice and flame. Over and over in her mind she was milling the things she might have said to him, and had not. She brewed a hundred vitriolic cruelties that she might have flung in his face. She would concoct one biting brutality, and dismiss it for a second, and abandon that

79

for a third. She was too angry to cry—a dangerous state in a woman. She was what is known as cold mad, so that her mind was working clearly and with amazing swiftness, and yet as though it were a thing detached; a thing that was no part of her.

She sat thus for the better part of an hour, motionless except for one forefinger that was, quite unconsciously, tapping out a popular and cheap little air that she had been strumming at the piano the evening before, having bought it down town that same afternoon. It had struck Orville's fancy, and she had played it over and over for him. Her right forefinger was playing the entire tune, and something in the back of her head was following it accurately, though the separate thinking process was going on just the same. Her eyes were bright, and wide, and hot. Suddenly she became conscious of the musical antics of her finger. She folded it in with its mates, so that her hand became a fist. She stood up and stared down at the clutter of the breakfast table. The egg—that fateful second egg—had congealed to a mottled mess of yellow and white. The spoon lay on the cloth. His coffee, only half consumed, showed tan with a cold grey film over it. A slice of toast at the left of his plate seemed to grin at her with the semi-circular wedge that he had bitten out of it.

Terry stared down at this congealing remnant. Then she laughed, a hard, high little laugh, pushed a plate away contemptuously with her hand, and walked into the sitting room. On the piano was the piece of music (Bennie Gottschalk's great song hit, "Hicky Bloo") which she had been playing the night before. She picked it up, tore it straight across, once, placed the pieces back to back and tore it across again. Then she dropped the pieces to the floor.

"You bet I'm going," she said, as though concluding a train of thought. "You just bet I'm going. Right now!"

And Terry went. She went for much the same reason as that given by the ladye of high degree in the old English song—she who had left her lord and bed and board to go with the raggle-taggle gipsies-O! The thing that was sending Terry Platt away was much more than a conjugal quarrel precipitated by a soft-boiled egg and a flap of the arm. It went so much deeper that if psychology had not become a cant word we might drag it into the explanation. It went so deep that it's necessary to delve back to the days when Theresa Platt was Terry Sheehan to get the real significance of it, and of the things she did after she went.

When Mrs. Orville Platt had been Terry Sheehan she had played the piano, afternoons and evenings, in the orchestra of the Bijou theatre, on Cass street, Wetona, Wisconsin. Any one with a name like Terry Sheehan would, perforce, do well anything she might set out to do. There was nothing of genius in Terry, but there was something of fire, and much that was Irish. The combination makes for what is known as imagination in playing. Which meant that the Watson Team, Eccentric Song and Dance Artists, never needed a rehearsal when they played the Bijou. Ruby Watson used merely to approach Terry before the Monday performance, sheet-music in hand, and say, "Listen, dearie. We've got some new business I want to wise you to. Right here it goes 'Tum dee-dee dum dee-dee tum dum dum. See? Like that. And then Jim vamps. Get me?"

Terry, at the piano, would pucker her pretty brow a moment. Then, "Like this, you mean?"

"That's it! You've got it."

"All right. I'll tell the drum."

She could play any tune by ear, once heard. She got the spirit of a thing, and transmitted it. When Terry played a march number you tapped the floor with your foot, and unconsciously straightened your shoulders. When she played a home-and-mother song that was heavy on the minor wail you hoped that the man next to you didn't know you were crying (which he probably didn't, because he was weeping, too).

At that time motion pictures had not attained their present virulence. Vaudeville, polite or otherwise, had not yet been crowded out by the ubiquitous film. The Bijou offered entertainment of the cigar-box tramp variety, interspersed with trick bicyclists, soubrettes in slightly soiled pink, trained seals, and Family Fours with lumpy legs who tossed each other about and struck Goldbergian attitudes.

Contact with these gave Terry Sheehan a semi-professional tone. The more conservative of her townspeople looked at her askance. There never had been an evil thing about Terry, but Wetona considered her rather fly. Terry's hair was very black, and she had a fondness for those little, close-fitting scarlet velvet turbans. A scarlet velvet turban would have made Martha Washington look fly. Terry's mother had died when the girl was eight, and Terry's father had been what is known as easy-going. A good-natured, lovable, shiftless chap in the contracting business. He drove around Wetona in a sagging, one-seated cart and never made any money because he did honest work and charged as little for it as men who did not. His mortar stuck, and his bricks did not crumble, and his lumber did not crack. Riches are not acquired in the contracting business in that way. Ed Sheehan and his daughter were great friends. When he died (she was nineteen) they say she screamed once, like a banshee, and dropped to the floor.

After they had straightened out the muddle of books in Ed Sheehan's gritty, dusty little office Terry turned her piano-playing talent to practical account. At twenty-one she was still playing at the Bijou, and into her face was creeping the first hint of that look of sophistication which comes from daily contact with the artificial world of the footlights. It is the look of those who must make believe as a business, and are a-weary. You see it developed into its highest degree in the face of a veteran comedian. It is the thing that gives the look of utter pathos and tragedy to the relaxed expression of a circus clown.

There are, in a small, Mid-West town like Wetona, just two kinds of girls. Those who go down town Saturday nights, and those who don't. Terry, if she had not been busy with her job at the Bijou, would have come in the first group. She craved excitement. There was little chance to satisfy such craving in Wetona, but she managed to find certain means. The travelling men from the Burke House just across the street used to drop in at the Bijou for an evening's entertainment. They usually sat well toward the front, and Terry's expert playing, and the gloss of her black hair, and her piquant profile as she sometimes looked up toward the stage for a signal from one of the performers, caught their fancy, and held it.

Terry did not accept their attentions promiscuously. She was too decent a girl for that. But she found herself, at the end of a year or two, with a rather large acquaintance among these peripatetic gentlemen. You occasionally saw one of them strolling home with her. Sometimes she went driving with one of them of a Sunday afternoon. And she rather enjoyed taking Sunday dinner at the Burke Hotel with a favoured friend. She thought those small-town hotel Sunday dinners the last word in elegance. The roast course was always accompanied by an aqueous, semi-frozen concoction which the bill of fare revealed as Roman punch. It added a royal touch to the repast, even when served with roast pork. I don't say that any of these Lotharios snatched a kiss during a Sunday afternoon drive. Or that Terry slapped him promptly. But either seems extremely likely.

Terry was twenty-two when Orville Platt, making his initial Wisconsin trip for the wholesale grocery house he represented, first beheld Terry's piquant Irish profile, and heard her deft manipulation of the keys. Orville had the fat man's sense of rhythm and love of music. He had a buttery tenor voice, too, of which he was rather proud.

82

He spent three days in Wetona that first trip, and every evening saw him at the Bijou, first row, centre. He stayed through two shows each time, and before he had been there fifteen minutes Terry was conscious of him through the back of her head. In fact I think that, in all innocence, she rather played up to him. Orville Platt paid no more heed to the stage, and what was occurring thereon, than if it had not been. He sat looking at Terry, and waggling his head in time to the music. Not that Terry was a beauty. But she was one of those immaculately clean types. That look of fragrant cleanliness was her chief charm. Her clear, smooth skin contributed to it, and the natural pencilling of her eyebrows. But the thing that accented it, and gave it a last touch, was the way in which her black hair came down in a little point just in the centre of her forehead, where hair meets brow. It grew to form what is known as a cow-lick. (A prettier name for it is widow's peak.) Your eye lighted on it, pleased, and from it travelled its gratified way down her white temples, past her little ears, to the smooth black coil at the nape of her neck. It was a trip that rested you.

At the end of the last performance on the second night of his visit to the Bijou, Orville waited until the audience had begun to file out. Then he leaned forward over the rail that separated orchestra from audience.

"Could you," he said, his tones dulcet, "could you oblige me with the name of that last piece you played?"

Terry was stacking her music. "George!" she called, to the drum. "Gentleman wants to know the name of that last piece." And prepared to leave.

"'My Georgia Crackerjack'," said the laconic drum.

Orville Platt took a hasty side-step in the direction of the door toward which Terry was headed. "It's a pretty thing," he said, fervently. "An awful pretty thing. Thanks. It's beautiful."

Terry flung a last insult at him over her shoulder: "Don't thank me for it. I didn't write it."

Orville Platt did not go across the street to the hotel. He wandered up Cass street, and into the ten-o'clock quiet of Main street, and down as far as the park and back. "Pretty as a pink! And play!... And good, too. Good."

A fat man in love.

At the end of six months they were married. Terry was surprised into it. Not that she was not fond of him. She was; and grateful to him, as well. For, pretty as she was, no man had ever before asked Terry to be his wife. They had made love to her. They had paid court to her. They had sent her large boxes of stale drug-

83

store chocolates, and called her endearing names as they made cautious declaration such as:

"I've known a lot of girls, but you've got something different. I don't know. You've got so much sense. A fellow can chum around with you. Little pal."

Orville's headquarters were Wetona. They rented a comfortable, seven-room house in a comfortable, middle-class neighbourhood, and Terry dropped the red velvet turbans and went in for picture hats and paradise aigrettes. Orville bought her a piano whose tone was so good that to her ear, accustomed to the metallic discords of the Bijou instrument, it sounded out of tune. She played a great deal at first, but unconsciously she missed the sharp spat of applause that used to follow her public performance. She would play a piece, brilliantly, and then her hands would drop to her lap. And the silence of her own sitting room would fall flat on her ears. It was better on the evenings when Orville was home. He sang, in his throaty, fat man's tenor, to Terry's expert accompaniment.

"This is better than playing for those bum actors, isn't it, hon?" And he would pinch her ear.

"Sure"—listlessly.

But after the first year she became accustomed to what she termed private life. She joined an afternoon sewing club, and was active in the ladies' branch of the U.C.T. She developed a knack at cooking, too, and Orville, after a week or ten days of hotel fare in small Wisconsin towns, would come home to sea-foam biscuits, and real soup, and honest pies and cake. Sometimes, in the midst of an appetising meal he would lay down his knife and fork and lean back in his chair, and regard the cool and unruffled Terry with a sort of reverence in his eyes. Then he would get up, and come around to the other side of the table, and tip her pretty face up to his.

"I'll bet I'll wake up, some day, and find out it's all a dream. You know this kind of thing doesn't really happen—not to a dub like me."

One year; two; three; four. Routine. A little boredom. Some impatience. She began to find fault with the very things she had liked in him: his super-neatness; his fondness for dashing suit patterns; his throaty tenor; his worship of her. And the flap. Oh, above all, that flap! That little, innocent, meaningless mannerism that made her tremble with nervousness. She hated it so that she could not trust herself to speak of it to him. That was the trouble. Had she spoken of it, laughingly or in earnest, before it became an obsession with her, that hideous breakfast quarrel, with its taunts, and revilings, and open hate, might never have come to pass. For that matter, any one of those foreign fellows with the guttural

84

names and the psychoanalytical minds could have located her trouble in one séance.

Terry Platt herself didn't know what was the matter with her. She would have denied that anything was wrong. She didn't even throw her hands above her head and shriek: "I want to live! I want to live! I want to live!" like a lady in a play. She only knew she was sick of sewing at the Wetona West-End Red Cross shop; sick of marketing, of home comforts, of Orville, of the flap.

Orville, you may remember, left at 8.19. The 11.23 bore Terry Chicagoward. She had left the house as it was—beds unmade, rooms unswept, breakfast table uncleared. She intended never to come back.

Now and then a picture of the chaos she had left behind would flash across her order-loving mind. The spoon on the table-cloth. Orville's pajamas dangling over the bathroom chair. The coffee-pot on the gas stove.

"Pooh! What do I care?"

In her pocketbook she had a tidy sum saved out of the housekeeping money. She was naturally thrifty, and Orville had never been niggardly. Her meals when Orville was on the road, had been those sketchy, haphazard affairs with which women content themselves when their household is manless. At noon she went into the dining car and ordered a flaunting little repast of chicken salad and asparagus, and Neapolitan ice cream. The men in the dining car eyed her speculatively and with appreciation. Then their glance dropped to the third finger of her left hand, and wandered away. She had meant to remove it. In fact, she had taken it off and dropped it into her bag. But her hand felt so queer, so unaccustomed, so naked, that she had found herself slipping the narrow band on again, and her thumb groped for it, gratefully.

It was almost five o'clock when she reached Chicago. She felt no uncertainty or bewilderment. She had been in Chicago three or four times since her marriage. She went to a down town hotel. It was too late, she told herself, to look for a more inexpensive room that night. When she had tidied herself she went out. The things she did were the childish, aimless things that one does who finds herself in possession of sudden liberty. She walked up State Street, and stared in the windows; came back, turned into Madison, passed a bright little shop in the window of which taffy—white and gold—was being wound endlessly and fascinatingly about a double-jointed machine. She went in and bought a sackful, and wandered on down the street, munching.

She had supper at one of those white-tiled sarcophagi that emblazon Chicago's down town side streets. It had been her original intention to dine in state in the rose-and-gold dining room of her hotel. She had even thought daringly of lobster. But at the last moment she recoiled from the idea of dining alone in that wilderness of tables so obviously meant for two.

After her supper she went to a picture show. She was amazed to find there, instead of the accustomed orchestra, a pipe-organ that panted and throbbed and rumbled over lugubrious classics. The picture was about a faithless wife. Terry left in the middle of it.

She awoke next morning at seven, as usual, started up wildly, looked around, and dropped back. Nothing to get up for. The knowledge did not fill her with a rush of relief. She would have her breakfast in bed! She telephoned for it, languidly. But when it came she got up and ate it from the table, after all. Terry was the kind of woman to whom a pink gingham all-over apron, and a pink dust-cap are ravishingly becoming at seven o'clock in the morning. That sort of woman congenitally cannot enjoy her breakfast in bed.

That morning she found a fairly comfortable room, more within her means, on the north side in the boarding house district. She unpacked and hung up her clothes and drifted down town again, idly. It was noon when she came to the corner of State and Madison streets. It was a maelstrom that caught her up, and buffeted her about, and tossed her helplessly this way and that. The corner of Broadway and Forty-second streets has been exploited in song and story as the world's most hazardous human whirlpool. I've negotiated that corner. I've braved the square in front of the American Express Company's office in Paris, June, before the War. I've crossed the Strand at 11 p.m. when the theatre crowds are just out. And to my mind the corner of State and Madison streets between twelve and one, mid-day, makes any one of these dizzy spots look bosky, sylvan, and deserted.

The thousands jostled Terry, and knocked her hat awry, and dug her with unheeding elbows, and stepped on her feet.

"Say, look here!" she said, once futilely. They did not stop to listen. State and Madison has no time for Terrys from Wetona. It goes its way, pellmell. If it saw Terry at all it saw her only as a prettyish person, in the wrong kind of suit and hat, with a bewildered, resentful look on her face.

Terry drifted on down the west side of State Street, with the hurrying crowd. State and Monroe. A sound came to Terry's ears. A sound familiar, beloved. To her ear, harassed with the roar and crash, with the shrill scream of the crossing policemen's whistle, with the hiss of feet shuffling on cement, it was a celestial strain. She looked up, toward the sound. A great second-story window opened wide to the street. In it a girl at a piano, and a man, red-

86

faced, singing through a megaphone. And on a flaring red and green sign:

BERNIE GOTTSCHALK'S MUSIC HOUSE!

COME IN! HEAR BERNIE GOTTSCHALK'S LATEST
HIT! THE HEART-THROB SONG THAT HAS GOT 'EM ALL!
THE SONG THAT MADE THE KAISER CRAWL!

"I COME FROM PARIS, ILLINOIS, BUT OH!
YOU PARIS, FRANCE!
I USED TO WEAR BLUE OVERALLS BUT
NOW ITS KHAKI PANTS."

COME IN! COME IN!

Terry accepted.

She followed the sound of the music. Around the corner. Up a little flight of stairs. She entered the realm of Euterpe; Euterpe with her back hair frizzed; Euterpe with her flowing white robe replaced by soiled white boots that failed to touch the hem of an empire-waisted blue serge; Euterpe abandoning her lyre for jazz. She sat at the piano, a red-haired young lady whose familiarity with the piano had bred contempt. Nothing else could have accounted for her treatment of it. Her fingers, tipped with sharp-pointed grey and glistening nails, clawed the keys with a dreadful mechanical motion. There were stacks of music-sheets on counters, and shelves, and dangling from overhead wires. The girl at the piano never ceased playing. She played mostly by request. A prospective purchaser would mumble something in the ear of one of the clerks. The fat man with the megaphone would bawl out, "'Hicky Bloo!' Miss Ryan." And Miss Ryan would oblige. She made a hideous rattle and crash and clatter of sound compared to which an Indian tom-tom would have seemed as dulcet as the strumming of a lute in a lady's boudoir.

Terry joined the crowds about the counter. The girl at the piano was not looking at the keys. Her head was screwed around over her left shoulder and as she played she was holding forth animatedly to a girl friend who had evidently dropped in from some store or office during the lunch hour. Now and again the fat man paused in his vocal efforts to reprimand her for her slackness. She paid no heed. There was something gruesome, uncanny, about the way her fingers went their own way over the defenceless keys. Her conversation with the frowzy little girl went on.

87

"Wha'd he say?" (Over her shoulder).

"Oh, he laffed."

"Well, didja go?"

"Me! Well, whutya think I yam, anyway?"

"I woulda took a chanst."

The fat man rebelled.

"Look here! Get busy! What are you paid for? Talkin' or playin'? Huh?"

The person at the piano, openly reproved thus before her friend, lifted her uninspired hands from the keys and spake. When she had finished she rose.

"But you can't leave now," the megaphone man argued. "Right in the rush hour."

"I'm gone," said the girl. The fat man looked about, helplessly. He gazed at the abandoned piano, as though it must go on of its own accord. Then at the crowd. "Where's Miss Schwimmer?" he demanded of a clerk.

"Out to lunch."

Terry pushed her way to the edge of the counter and leaned over. "I can play for you," she said.

The man looked at her. "Sight?"

"Yes."

"Come on."

Terry went around to the other side of the counter, took off her hat and coat, rubbed her hands together briskly, sat down and began to play. The crowd edged closer.

It is a curious study, this noonday crowd that gathers to sate its music-hunger on the scraps vouchsafed it by Bernie Gottschalk's Music House. Loose-lipped, slope-shouldered young men with bad complexions and slender hands. Girls whose clothes are an unconscious satire on present-day fashions. On their faces, as they listen to the music, is a look of peace and dreaming. They stand about, smiling a wistful half smile. It is much the same expression that steals over the face of a smoker who has lighted his after-dinner cigar, or of a drug victim who is being lulled by his opiate. The music seems to satisfy a something within them. Faces dull, eyes lustreless, they listen in a sort of trance.

Terry played on. She played as Terry Sheehan used to play. She played as no music hack at Bernie Gottschalk's had ever played before. The crowd swayed a little to the sound of it. Some kept time with little jerks of the shoulder—the little hitching movement of the rag-time dancer whose blood is filled with the fever of syncopation. Even the crowd flowing down State Street must have caught the rhythm of it, for the room soon filled.

At two o'clock the crowd began to thin. Business would be slack, now, until five, when it would again pick up until closing time at six.

The fat vocalist put down his megaphone, wiped his forehead, and regarded Terry with a warm blue eye. He had just finished singing "I've Wandered Far from Dear Old Mother's Knee." (Bernie Gottschalk Inc. Chicago. New York. You can't get bit with a Gottschalk hit. 15 cents each.)

"Girlie," he said, emphatically, "You sure—can—play!" He came over to her at the piano and put a stubby hand on her shoulder. "Yessir! Those little fingers—"

Terry just turned her head to look down her nose at the moist hand resting on her shoulder. "Those little fingers are going to meet your face—suddenly—if you don't move on."

"Who gave you your job?" demanded the fat man.

"Nobody. I picked it myself. You can have it if you want it."

"Can't you take a joke?"

"Label yours."

As the crowd dwindled she played less feverishly, but there was nothing slipshod about her performance. The chubby songster found time to proffer brief explanations in asides. "They want the patriotic stuff. It used to be all that Hawaiian dope, and Wild Irish Rose junk, and songs about wanting to go back to every place from Dixie to Duluth. But now seems it's all these here flag raisers. Honestly, I'm so sick of 'em I got a notion to enlist to get away from it."

Terry eyed him with, withering briefness. "A little training wouldn't ruin your figure."

She had never objected to Orville's embonpoint. But then, Orville was a different sort of fat man; pink-cheeked, springy, immaculate.

At four o'clock, as she was in the chorus of "Isn't There Another Joan of Arc?" a melting masculine voice from the other side of the counter said, "Pardon me. What's that you're playing?"

Terry told him. She did not look up.

"I wouldn't have known it. Played like that—a second Marseillaise. If the words—what are the words? Let me see a—"

"Show the gentleman a 'Joan'," Terry commanded briefly, over her shoulder. The fat man laughed a wheezy laugh. Terry glanced around, still playing, and encountered the gaze of two melting masculine eyes that matched the melting masculine voice. The songster waved a hand uniting Terry and the eyes in informal introduction.

"Mr. Leon Sammett, the gentleman who sings the Gottschalk

89

songs wherever songs are heard. And Mrs.—that is—and Mrs. Sammett—"

Terry turned. A sleek, swarthy world-old young man with the fashionable concave torso, and alarmingly convex bone-rimmed glasses. Through them his darkly luminous gaze glowed upon Terry. To escape their warmth she sent her own gaze past him to encounter the arctic stare of the large blonde person who had been included so lamely in the introduction. And at that the frigidity of that stare softened, melted, dissolved.

"Why Terry Sheehan! What in the world!"

Terry's eyes bored beneath the layers of flabby fat. "It's—why, it's Ruby Watson, isn't it? Eccentric Song and Dance—"

She glanced at the concave young man and faltered. He was not Jim, of the Bijou days. From him her eyes leaped back to the fur-bedecked splendour of the woman. The plump face went so painfully red that the makeup stood out on it, a distinct layer, like thin ice covering flowing water. As she surveyed that bulk Terry realised that while Ruby might still claim eccentricity, her song and dance days were over. "That's ancient history, m'dear. I haven't been working for three years. What're you doing in this joint? I'd heard you'd done well for yourself. That you were married."

"I am. That is I—well, I am. I—"

At that the dark young man leaned over and patted Terry's hand that lay on the counter. He smiled. His own hand was incredibly slender, long, and tapering.

"That's all right," he assured her, and smiled. "You two girls can have a reunion later. What I want to know is can you play by ear?"

"Yes, but—"

He leaned far over the counter. "I knew it the minute I heard you play. You've got the touch. Now listen. See if you can get this, and fake the bass."

He fixed his sombre and hypnotic eyes on Terry. His mouth screwed up into a whistle. The tune—a tawdry but haunting little melody—came through his lips. And Terry's quick ear sensed that every note was flat. She turned back to the piano. "Of course you know you flatted every note," she said.

This time it was the blonde woman who laughed, and the man who flushed. Terry cocked her head just a little to one side, like a knowing bird, looked up into space beyond the piano top, and played the lilting little melody with charm and fidelity. The dark young man followed her with a wagging of the head and little jerks of both outspread hands. His expression was beatific, enraptured. He hummed a little under his breath and any one who was music wise would have known that he was just a half-beat behind her all the way.

When she had finished he sighed deeply, ecstatically. He bent his lean frame over the counter and, despite his swart colouring, seemed to glitter upon her—his eyes, his teeth, his very finger-nails.

"Something led me here. I never come up on Tuesdays. But something—"

"You was going to complain," put in his lady, heavily, "about that Teddy Sykes at the Palace Gardens singing the same songs this week that you been boosting at the Inn."

He put up a vibrant, peremptory hand. "Bah! What does that matter now! What does anything matter now! Listen Miss—ah—Miss?—"

"Pl—Sheehan. Terry Sheehan."

He gazed off a moment into space. "H'm. 'Leon Sammett in Songs. Miss Terry Sheehan at the Piano.' That doesn't sound bad. Now listen, Miss Sheehan. I'm singing down at the University Inn. The Gottschalk song hits. I guess you know my work. But I want to talk to you, private. It's something to your interest. I go on down at the Inn at six. Will you come and have a little something with Ruby and me? Now?"

"Now?" faltered Terry, somewhat helplessly. Things seemed to be moving rather swiftly for her, accustomed as she was to the peaceful routine of the past four years.

"Get your hat. It's your life chance. Wait till you see your name in two-foot electrics over the front of every big-time house in the country. You've got music in you. Tie to me and you're made." He turned to the woman beside him. "Isn't that so, Rube?"

"Sure. Look at me!" One would not have thought there could be so much subtle vindictiveness in a fat blonde.

Sammett whipped out a watch. "Just three-quarters of an hour. Come on, girlie."

His conversation had been conducted in an urgent undertone, with side glances at the fat man with the megaphone. Terry approached him now.

"I'm leaving now," she said.

"Oh, no you're not. Six o'clock is your quitting time."

In which he touched the Irish in Terry. "Any time I quit is my quitting time." She went in quest of hat and coat much as the girl had done whose place she had taken early in the day. The fat man followed her, protesting. Terry, pinning on her hat tried to ignore him. But he laid one plump hand on her arm and kept it there, though she tried to shake him off.

"Now, listen to me. That boy wouldn't mind putting his heel on

91

your face if he thought it would bring him up a step. I know'm. Y'see that walking stick he's carrying? Well, compared to the yellow stripe that's in him, that cane is a lead pencil. He's a song tout, that's all he is." Then, more feverishly, as Terry tried to pull away: "Wait a minute. You're a decent girl. I want to—Why, he can't even sing a note without you give it to him first. He can put a song over, yes. But how? By flashin' that toothy grin, of his and talkin' every word of it. Don't you—"

But Terry freed herself with a final jerk and whipped around the counter. The two, who had been talking together in an undertone, turned to welcome her. "We've got a half hour. Come on. It's just over to Clark and up a block or so."

If you know Chicago at all, you know the University Inn, that gloriously intercollegiate institution which welcomes any graduate of any school of experience, and guarantees a post-graduate course in less time than any similar haven of knowledge. Down a flight of stairs and into the unwonted quiet that reigns during the hour of low potentiality, between five and six, the three went, and seated themselves at a table in an obscure corner. A waiter brought them things in little glasses, though no order had been given. The woman who had been Ruby Watson was so silent as to be almost wordless. But the man talked rapidly. He talked well, too. The same quality that enabled him, voiceless though he was, to boost a song to success, was making his plea sound plausible in Terry's ears now.

"I've got to go and make up in a few minutes. So get this. I'm not going to stick down in this basement eating house forever. I've got too much talent. If I only had a voice—I mean a singing voice. But I haven't. But then, neither has Georgie Cohan, and I can't see that it's wrecked his life any. Look at Elsie Janis! But she sings. And they like it! Now listen. I've got a song. It's my own. That bit you played for me up at Gottschalk's is part of the chorus. But it's the words that'll go big. They're great. It's an aviation song, see? Airship stuff. They're yelling that it's the airyoplanes that're going to win this war. Well, I'll help 'em. This song is going to put the aviator where he belongs. It's going to be the big song of the war. It's going to make 'Tipperary' sound like a Moody and Sankey hymn. It's the-"

Ruby lifted her heavy-lidded eyes and sent him a meaning look. "Get down to business, Leon. I'll tell her how good you are while you're making up."

He shot her a malignant glance, but took her advice. "Now what I've been looking for for years is somebody who has got the music knack to give me the accompaniment just a quarter of a jump ahead of my voice, see? I can follow like a lamb, but I've got to have that feeler first. It's more than a knack. It's a gift. And you've got it. I

92

know it when I see it. I want to get away from this cabaret thing. There's nothing in it for a man of my talent. I'm gunning for vaudeville. But they won't book me without a tryout. And when they hear my voice they—Well, if me and you work together we can fool 'em. The song's great. And my makeup's one of these av-iation costumes to go with the song, see? Pants tight in the knee and baggy on the hips. And a coat with one of those full skirt whaddyoucall'ems—"

"Peplums," put in Ruby, placidly.

"Sure. And the girls'll be wild about it. And the words!" he began to sing, gratingly off-key:

> "Put on your sky clothes,
> Put on your fly clothes
> And take a trip with me.
> We'll sail so high
> Up in the sky
> We'll drop a bomb from Mercury."

"Why, that's awfully cute!" exclaimed Terry. Until now her opinion of Mr. Sammett's talents had not been on a level with his.

"Yeh, but wait till you hear the second verse. That's only part of the chorus. You see, he's supposed to be talking to a French girl. He says:

> I'll parlez-vous in Français plain,
> You'll answer, 'Cher Américain,
> We'll both. . . . ."

The six o'clock lights blazed up, suddenly. A sad-looking group of men trailed in and made for a corner where certain bulky, shapeless bundles were soon revealed as those glittering and tortuous instruments which go to make a jazz band.

"You better go, Lee. The crowd comes in awful early now, with all those buyers in town."

Both hands on the table he half rose, reluctantly, still talking. "I've got three other songs. They make Gottschalk's stuff look sick. All I want's a chance. What I want you to do is accompaniment. On the stage, see? Grand piano. And a swell set. I haven't quite made up my mind to it. But a kind of an army camp room, see? And maybe you dressed as Liberty. Anyway, it'll be new, and a knock-out. If only we can get away with the voice thing. Say, if Eddie Foy, all those years never had a—"

The band opened with a terrifying clash of cymbal, and thump of drum. "Back at the end of my first turn," he said as he fled. Terry

93

followed his lithe, electric figure. She turned to meet the heavy-lidded gaze of the woman seated opposite. She relaxed, then, and sat back with a little sigh. "Well! If he talks that way to the managers I don't see—"

Ruby laughed a mirthless little laugh. "Talk doesn't get it over with the managers, honey. You've got to deliver."

"Well, but he's—that song is a good one. I don't say it's as good as he thinks it is, but it's good."

"Yes," admitted the woman, grudgingly, "it's good."

"Well, then?"

The woman beckoned a waiter; he nodded and vanished, and reappeared with a glass that was twin to the one she had just emptied. "Does he look like he knew French? Or could make a rhyme?"

"But didn't he? Doesn't he?"

"The words were written by a little French girl who used to skate down here last winter, when the craze was on. She was stuck on a Chicago kid who went over to fly for the French."

"But the music?"

"There was a Russian girl who used to dance in the cabaret and she—"

Terry's head came up with a characteristic little jerk. "I don't believe it!"

"Better." She gazed at Terry with the drowsy look that was so different from the quick, clear glance of the Ruby Watson who used to dance so nimbly in the Old Bijou days. "What'd you and your husband quarrel about, Terry?"

Terry was furious to feel herself flushing. "Oh, nothing. He just—I—it was—Say, how did you know we'd quarrelled?"

And suddenly all the fat woman's apathy dropped from her like a garment and some of the old sparkle and animation illumined her heavy face. She pushed her glass aside and leaned forward on her folded arms, so that her face was close to Terry's.

"Terry Sheehan, I know you've quarrelled, and I know just what it was about. Oh, I don't mean the very thing it was about; but the kind of thing. I'm going to do something for you, Terry, that I wouldn't take the trouble to do for most women. But I guess I ain't had all the softness knocked out of me yet, though it's a wonder. And I guess I remember too plain the decent kid you was in the old days. What was the name of that little small-time house me and Jim used to play? Bijou, that's it; Bijou."

The band struck up a new tune. Leon Sammett—slim, sleek, lithe in his evening clothes—appeared with a little fair girl in pink chiffon. The woman reached across the table and put one pudgy,

94

jewelled hand on Terry's arm. "He'll be through in ten minutes. Now listen to me. I left Jim four years ago, and there hasn't been a minute since then, day or night, when I wouldn't have crawled back to him on my hands and knees if I could. But I couldn't. He wouldn't have me now. How could he? How do I know you've quarrelled? I can see it in your eyes. They look just the way mine have felt for four years, that's how. I met up with this boy, and there wasn't anybody to do the turn for me that I'm trying to do for you. Now get this. I left Jim because when he ate corn on the cob he always closed his eyes and it drove me wild. Don't laugh."

"I'm not laughing," said Terry.

"Women are like that. One night—we was playing Fond du Lac; I remember just as plain—we was eating supper and Jim reached for one of those big yellow ears, and buttered and salted it, and me kind of hanging on to the edge of the table with my nails. Seemed to me if he shut his eyes when he put his teeth into that ear of corn I'd scream. And he did. And I screamed. And that's all."

Terry sat staring at her with a wide-eyed stare, like a sleep walker. Then she wet her lips, slowly. "But that's almost the very—"

"Kid, go on back home. I don't know whether it's too late or not, but go anyway. If you've lost him I suppose it ain't any more than you deserve, but I hope to God you don't get your desserts this time. He's almost through. If he sees you going he can't quit in the middle of his song to stop you. He'll know I put you wise, and he'll prob'ly half kill me for it. But it's worth it. You get."

And Terry—dazed, shaking, but grateful—fled. Down the noisy aisle, up the stairs, to the street. Back to her rooming house. Out again, with her suitcase, and into the right railroad station somehow, at last. Not another Wetona train until midnight. She shrank into a remote corner of the waiting room and there she huddled until midnight watching the entrances like a child who is fearful of ghosts in the night.

The hands of the station clock seemed fixed and immovable. The hour between eleven and twelve was endless. She was on the train. It was almost morning. It was morning. Dawn was breaking. She was home! She had the house key clutched tightly in her hand long before she turned Schroeder's corner. Suppose he had come home! Suppose he had jumped a town and come home ahead of his schedule. They had quarrelled once before, and he had done that.

Up the front steps. Into the house. Not a sound. She stood there a moment in the early morning half-light. She peered into the dining room. The table, with its breakfast débris, was as she had left it. In the kitchen the coffee pot stood on the gas stove. She was home. She was safe. She ran up the stairs, got out of her clothes and

95

into crisp gingham morning things. She flung open windows everywhere. Down-stairs once more she plunged into an orgy of cleaning. Dishes, table, stove, floor, rugs. She washed, scoured, flapped, swabbed, polished. By eight o'clock she had done the work that would ordinarily have taken until noon. The house was shining, orderly, and redolent of soapsuds.

During all this time she had been listening, listening, with her sub-conscious ear. Listening for something she had refused to name definitely in her mind, but listening, just the same; waiting.

And then, at eight o'clock, it came. The rattle of a key in the lock. The boom of the front door. Firm footsteps.

He did not go to meet her, and she did not go to meet him. They came together and were in each other's arms. She was weeping.

"Now, now, old girl. What's there to cry about? Don't, honey; don't. It's all right."

She raised her head then, to look at him. How fresh, and rosy, and big he seemed, after that little sallow, yellow restaurant rat.

"How did you get here? How did you happen—?"

"Jumped all the way from Ashland. Couldn't get a sleeper, so I sat up all night. I had to come back and square things with you, Terry. My mind just wasn't on my work. I kept thinking how I'd talked—how I'd talked—"

"Oh, Orville, don't! I can't bear—Have you had your breakfast?"

"Why, no. The train was an hour late. You know that Ashland train."

But she was out of his arms and making for the kitchen. "You go and clean up. I'll have hot biscuits and everything in fifteen minutes. You poor boy. No breakfast!"

She made good her promise. It could not have been more than twenty minutes later when he was buttering his third feathery, golden brown biscuit. But she had eaten nothing. She watched him, and listened, and again her eyes were sombre, but for a different reason. He broke open his egg. His elbow came up just a fraction of an inch. Then he remembered, and flushed like a schoolboy, and brought it down again, carefully. And at that she gave a little tremulous cry, and rushed around the table to him.

"Oh, Orville!" She took the offending elbow in her two arms, and bent and kissed the rough coat sleeve.

"Why, Terry! Don't, honey. Don't!"

"Oh, Orville, listen—"

"Yes."

"Listen, Orville—"

"I'm listening, Terry."

96

"I've got something to tell you. There's something you've got to know."

"Yes, I know it, Terry. I knew you'd out with it, pretty soon, if I just waited."

She lifted an amazed face from his shoulder then, and stared at him. "But how could you know? You couldn't! How could you?"

He patted her shoulder then, gently. "I can always tell. When you have something on your mind you always take up a spoon of coffee, and look at it, and kind of joggle it back and forth in the spoon, and then dribble it back into the cup again, without once tasting it. It used to get me nervous when we were first married watching you. But now I know it just means you're worried about something, and I wait, and pretty soon—"

"Oh, Orville!" she cried, then. "Oh, Orville!"

"Now, Terry. Just spill it, hon. Just spill it to daddy. And you'll feel better."

VI

THE WOMAN WHO TRIED TO BE GOOD

Before she tried to be a good woman she had been a very bad woman—so bad that she could trail her wonderful apparel up and down Main Street, from the Elm Tree Bakery to the railroad tracks, without once having a man doff his hat to her or a woman bow. You passed her on the street with a surreptitious glance, though she was well worth looking at—in her furs and laces and plumes. She had the only full-length sealskin coat in our town, and Ganz' shoe store sent to Chicago for her shoes. Hers were the miraculously small feet you frequently see in stout women.

Usually she walked alone; but on rare occasions, especially round Christmas time, she might have been seen accompanied by some silent, dull-eyed, stupid-looking girl, who would follow her dumbly in and out of stores, stopping now and then to admire a cheap comb or a chain set with flashy imitation stones—or, queerly enough, a doll with yellow hair and blue eyes and very pink cheeks. But, alone or in company, her appearance in the stores of our town was the signal for a sudden jump in the cost of living. The storekeepers mulcted her; and she knew it and paid in silence, for she was of the class that has no redress. She owned the House With the Closed Shutters, near the freight depot—did Blanche Devine. And beneath her silks and laces and furs there was a scarlet letter on her breast.

In a larger town than ours she would have passed unnoticed. She did not look like a bad woman. Of course she used too much perfumed white powder, and as she passed you caught the oversweet breath of a certain heavy scent. Then, too, her diamond eardrops would have made any woman's features look hard; but her plump face, in spite of its heaviness, wore an expression of good-humoured intelligence, and her eyeglasses gave her somehow a look of respectability. We do not associate vice with eyeglasses. So in a large city she would have passed for a well-dressed prosperous, comfortable wife and mother, who was in danger of losing her figure from an overabundance of good living; but with us she was a town character, like Old Man Givins, the drunkard, or the weak-minded Binns girl. When she passed the drug-store corner there would be a sniggering among the vacant-eyed loafers idling there, and they would leer at each other and jest in undertones.

So, knowing Blanche Devine as we did, there was something

resembling a riot in one of our most respectable neighbourhoods when it was learned that she had given up her interest in the house near the freight depot and was going to settle down in the white cottage on the corner and be good. All the husbands in the block, urged on by righteously indignant wives, dropped in on Alderman Mooney after supper to see if the thing could not be stopped. The fourth of the protesting husbands to arrive was the Very Young Husband, who lived next door to the corner cottage that Blanche Devine had bought. The Very Young Husband had a Very Young Wife, and they were the joint owners of Snooky. Snooky was three-going-on-four, and looked something like an angel—only healthier and with grimier hands. The whole neighbourhood borrowed her and tried to spoil her; but Snooky would not spoil.

Alderman Mooney was down in the cellar fooling with the furnace. He was in his furnace overalls—a short black pipe in his mouth. Three protesting husbands had just left. As the Very Young Husband, following Mrs. Mooney's directions, cautiously descended the cellar stairs, Alderman Mooney looked up from his tinkering. He peered through a haze of pipe-smoke.

"Hello!" he called, and waved the haze away with his open palm. "Come on down! Been tinkering with this blamed furnace since supper. She don't draw like she ought. 'Long toward spring a furnace always gets balky. How many tons you used this winter?"

"Oh—ten," said the Very Young Husband shortly. Alderman Mooney considered it thoughtfully. The Young Husband leaned up against the side of the cistern, his hands in his pockets. "Say, Mooney, is that right about Blanche Devine's having bought the house on the corner?"

"You're the fourth man that's been in to ask me that this evening. I'm expecting the rest of the block before bedtime. She's bought it all right."

The Young Husband flushed and kicked at a piece of coal with the toe of his boot.

"Well, it's a darned shame!" he began hotly. "Jen was ready to cry at supper. This'll be a fine neighbourhood for Snooky to grow up in! What's a woman like that want to come into a respectable street for anyway? I own my home and pay my taxes—"

Alderman Mooney looked up.

"So does she," he interrupted. "She's going to improve the place—paint it, and put in a cellar and a furnace, and build a porch, and lay a cement walk all round."

The Young Husband took his hands out of his pockets in order to emphasize his remarks with gestures.

"What's that got to do with it? I don't care if she puts in

99

diamonds for windows and sets out Italian gardens and a terrace with peacocks on it. You're the alderman of this ward, aren't you? Well, it was up to you to keep her out of this block! You could have fixed it with an injunction or something. I'm going to get up a petition—that's what I'm going—"

Alderman Mooney closed the furnace door with a bang that drowned the rest of the threat. He turned the draft in a pipe overhead and brushed his sooty palms briskly together like one who would put an end to a profitless conversation.

"She's bought the house," he said mildly, "and paid for it. And it's hers. She's got a right to live in this neighbourhood as long as she acts respectable."

The Very Young Husband laughed.

"She won't last! They never do."

Alderman Mooney had taken his pipe out of his mouth and was rubbing his thumb over the smooth bowl, looking down at it with unseeing eyes. On his face was a queer look—the look of one who is embarrassed because he is about to say something honest.

"Look here! I want to tell you something: I happened to be up in the mayor's office the day Blanche signed for the place. She had to go through a lot of red tape before she got it—had quite a time of it, she did! And say, kid, that woman ain't so—bad."

The Very Young Husband exclaimed impatiently:

"Oh, don't give me any of that, Mooney! Blanche Devine's a town character. Even the kids know what she is. If she's got religion or something, and wants to quit and be decent, why doesn't she go to another town—Chicago or some place—where nobody knows her?"

That motion of Alderman Mooney's thumb against the smooth pipebowl stopped. He looked up slowly.

"That's what I said—the mayor too. But Blanche Devine said she wanted to try it here. She said this was home to her. Funny— ain't it? Said she wouldn't be fooling anybody here. They know her. And if she moved away, she said, it'd leak out some way sooner or later. It does, she said. Always! Seems she wants to live like—well, like other women. She put it like this: She says she hasn't got religion, or any of that. She says she's no different than she was when she was twenty. She says that for the last ten years the ambition of her life has been to be able to go into a grocery store and ask the price of, say, celery; and, if the clerk charged her ten when it ought to be seven, to be able to sass him with a regular piece of her mind—and then sail out and trade somewhere else until he saw that she didn't have to stand anything from storekeepers, any more than any other woman that did her own marketing. She's a smart woman, Blanche is! She's saved her money. God knows I ain't taking her part—exactly; but she talked a little, and the mayor and me got a little of her history."

A sneer appeared on the face of the Very Young Husband. He had been known before he met Jen as a rather industrious sower of that seed known as wild oats. He knew a thing or two, did the Very Young Husband, in spite of his youth! He always fussed when Jen wore even a V-necked summer gown on the street.

"Oh, she wasn't playing for sympathy," west on Alderman Mooney in answer to the sneer. "She said she'd always paid her way and always expected to. Seems her husband left her without a cent when she was eighteen—with a baby. She worked for four dollars a week in a cheap eating house. The two of 'em couldn't live on that. Then the baby—"

"Good night!" said the Very Young Husband. "I suppose Mrs. Mooney's going to call?"

"Minnie! It was her scolding all through supper that drove me down to monkey with the furnace. She's wild—Minnie is." He peeled off his overalls and hung them on a nail. The Young Husband started to ascend the cellar stairs. Alderman Mooney laid a detaining finger on his sleeve. "Don't say anything in front of Minnie! She's boiling! Minnie and the kids are going to visit her folks out West this summer; so I wouldn't so much as dare to say 'Good morning!' to the Devine woman. Anyway a person wouldn't talk to her, I suppose. But I kind of thought I'd tell you about her."

"Thanks!" said the Very Young Husband dryly.

In the early spring, before Blanche Devine moved in, there came stonemasons, who began to build something. It was a great stone fireplace that rose in massive incongruity at the side of the little white cottage. Blanche Devine was trying to make a home for herself. We no longer build fireplaces for physical warmth—we build them for the warmth of the soul; we build them to dream by, to hope by, to home by.

Blanche Devine used to come and watch them now and then as the work progressed. She had a way of walking round and round the house, looking up at it pridefully and poking at plaster and paint with her umbrella or fingertip. One day she brought with her a man with a spade. He spaded up a neat square of ground at the side of the cottage and a long ridge near the fence that separated her yard from that of the very young couple next door. The ridge spelled sweet peas and nasturtiums to our small-town eyes.

On the day that Blanche Devine moved in there was wild agitation among the white-ruffled bedroom curtains of the neighbourhood. Later on certain odours, as of burning dinners,

101

pervaded the atmosphere. Blanche Devine, flushed and excited, her hair slightly askew, her diamond eardrops flashing, directed the moving, wrapped in her great fur coat; but on the third morning we gasped when she appeared out-of-doors, carrying a little household ladder, a pail of steaming water and sundry voluminous white cloths. She reared the little ladder against the side of the house mounted it cautiously, and began to wash windows: with housewifely thoroughness. Her stout figure was swathed in a grey sweater and on her head was a battered felt hat—the sort of window-washing costume that has been worn by women from time immemorial. We noticed that she used plenty of hot water and clean rags, and that she rubbed the glass until it sparkled, leaning perilously sideways on the ladder to detect elusive streaks. Our keenest housekeeping eye could find no fault with the way Blanche Devine washed windows.

By May, Blanche Devine had left off her diamond eardrops—perhaps it was their absence that gave her face a new expression. When she went down town we noticed that her hats were more like the hats the other women in our town wore; but she still affected extravagant footgear, as is right and proper for a stout woman who has cause to be vain of her feet. We noticed that her trips down town were rare that spring and summer. She used to come home laden with little bundles; and before supper she would change her street clothes for a neat, washable housedress, as is our thrifty custom. Through her bright windows we could see her moving briskly about from kitchen to sitting room; and from the smells that floated out from her kitchen door, she seemed to be preparing for her solitary supper the same homely viands that were frying or stewing or baking in our kitchens. Sometimes you could detect the delectable scent of browning hot tea biscuit. It takes a brave, courageous, determined woman to make tea biscuit for no one but herself.

Blanche Devine joined the church. On the first Sunday morning she came to the service there was a little flurry among the ushers at the vestibule door. They seated her well in the rear. The second Sunday morning a dreadful thing happened. The woman next to whom they seated her turned, regarded her stonily for a moment, then rose agitatedly and moved to a pew across the aisle. Blanche Devine's face went a dull red beneath her white powder. She never came again—though we saw the minister visit her once or twice. She always accompanied him to the door pleasantly, holding it well open until he was down the little flight of steps and on the sidewalk. The minister's wife did not call—but, then, there are limits to the duties of a minister's wife.

She rose early, like the rest of us; and as summer came on we

102

used to see her moving about in her little garden patch in the dewy, golden morning. She wore absurd pale-blue kimonos that made her stout figure loom immense against the greenery of garden and apple tree. The neighbourhood women viewed these negligées with Puritan disapproval as they smoothed down their own prim, starched gingham skirts. They said it was disgusting—and perhaps it was; but the habit of years is not easily overcome. Blanche Devine—snipping her sweet peas; peering anxiously at the Virginia creeper that clung with such fragile fingers to the trellis; watering the flower baskets that hung from her porch—was blissfully unconscious of the disapproving eyes. I wish one of us had just stopped to call good morning to her over the fence, and to say in our neighbourly, small town way: "My, ain't this a scorcher! So early too! It'll be fierce by noon!" But we did not.

I think perhaps the evenings must have been the loneliest for her. The summer evenings in our little town are filled with intimate, human, neighbourly sounds. After the heat of the day it is infinitely pleasant to relax in the cool comfort of the front porch, with the life of the town eddying about us. We sew and read out there until it grows dusk. We call across-lots to our next-door neighbour. The men water the lawns and the flower boxes and get together in little quiet groups to discuss the new street paving. I have even known Mrs. Hines to bring her cherries out there when she had canning to do, and pit them there on the front porch partially shielded by her porch vine, but not so effectually that she was deprived of the sights and sounds about her. The kettle in her lap and the dishpan full of great ripe cherries on the porch floor by her chair, she would pit and chat and peer out through the vines, the red juice staining her plump bare arms.

I have wondered since what Blanche Devine thought of us those lonesome evenings—those evenings filled with little friendly sights and sounds. It is lonely, uphill business at best—this being good. It must have been difficult for her, who had dwelt behind closed shutters so long, to seat herself on the new front porch for all the world to stare at; but she did sit there—resolutely—watching us in silence.

She seized hungrily upon the stray crumbs of conversation that fell to her. The milkman and the iceman and the butcher boy used to hold daily conversation with her. They—sociable gentlemen—would stand on her doorstep, one grimy hand resting against the white of her doorpost, exchanging the time of day with Blanche in the doorway—a tea towel in one hand, perhaps, and a plate in the other. Her little house was a miracle of cleanliness. It was no uncommon sight to see her down on her knees on the kitchen floor,

103

wielding her brush and rag like the rest of us. In canning and preserving time there floated out from her kitchen the pungent scent of pickled crab apples; the mouth-watering, nostril-pricking smell that meant sweet pickles; or the cloying, tantalising, divinely sticky odour that meant raspberry jam. Snooky, from her side of the fence, often used to peer through the pickets, gazing in the direction of the enticing smells next door. Early one September morning there floated out from Blanche Devine's kitchen that clean, fragrant, sweet scent of fresh-baked cookies—cookies with butter in them, and spice, and with nuts on top. Just by the smell of them your mind's eye pictured them coming from the oven—crisp brown circlets, crumbly, toothsome, delectable. Snooky, in her scarlet sweater and cap, sniffed them from afar and straightway deserted her sandpile to take her stand at the fence. She peered through the restraining bars, standing on tiptoe. Blanche Devine, glancing up from her board and rolling-pin, saw the eager golden head. And Snooky, with guile in her heart, raised one fat, dimpled hand above the fence and waved it friendlily. Blanche Devine waved back. Thus encouraged, Snooky's two hands wigwagged frantically above the pickets. Blanche Devine hesitated a moment, her floury hand on her hip. Then she went to the pantry shelf and took out a clean white saucer. She selected from the brown jar on the table three of the brownest, crumbliest, most perfect cookies, with a walnut meat perched atop of each, placed them temptingly on the saucer and, descending the steps, came swiftly across the grass to the triumphant Snooky. Blanche Devine held out the saucer, her lips smiling, her eyes tender. Snooky reached up with one plump white arm.

"Snooky!" shrilled a high voice. "Snooky!" A voice of horror and of wrath. "Come here to me this minute! And don't you dare to touch those!" Snooky hesitated rebelliously, one pink finger in her pouting mouth. "Snooky! Do you hear me?"

And the Very Young Wife began to descend the steps of her back porch. Snooky, regretful eyes on the toothsome dainties, turned away aggrieved. The Very Young Wife, her lips set, her eyes flashing, advanced and seized the shrieking Snooky by one writhing arm and dragged her away toward home and safety.

Blanche Devine stood there at the fence, holding the saucer in her hand. The saucer tipped slowly, and the three cookies slipped off and fell to the grass. Blanche Devine followed them with her eyes and stood staring at them a moment. Then she turned quickly, went into the house and shut the door.

It was about this time we noticed that Blanche Devine was away much of the time. The little white cottage would be empty for a week. We knew she was out of town because the expressman would come for her trunk. We used to lift our eyebrows significantly. The newspapers and handbills would accumulate in a dusty little heap on the porch; but when she returned there was always a grand cleaning, with the windows open, and Blanche—her head bound turbanwise in a towel—appearing at a window every few minutes to shake out a dustcloth. She seemed to put an enormous amount of energy into those cleanings—as if they were a sort of safety valve.

As winter came on she used to sit up before her grate fire long, long after we were asleep in our beds. When she neglected to pull down the shades we could see the flames of her cosy fire dancing gnomelike on the wall.

There came a night of sleet and snow, and wind and rattling hail—one of those blustering, wild nights that are followed by morning-paper reports of trains stalled in drifts, mail delayed, telephone and telegraph wires down. It must have been midnight or past when there came a hammering at Blanche Devine's door—a persistent, clamorous rapping. Blanche Devine, sitting before her dying fire half asleep, started and cringed when she heard it; then jumped to her feet, her hand at her breast—her eyes darting this way and that, as though seeking escape.

She had heard a rapping like that before. It had meant bluecoats swarming up the stairway, and frightened cries and pleadings, and wild confusion. So she started forward now, quivering. And then she remembered, being wholly awake now—she remembered, and threw up her head and smiled a little bitterly and walked toward the door. The hammering continued, louder than ever. Blanche Devine flicked on the porch light and opened the door. The half-clad figure of the Very Young Wife next door staggered into the room. She seized Blanche Devine's arm with both her frenzied hands and shook her, the wind and snow beating in upon both of them.

"The baby!" she screamed in a high, hysterical voice. "The baby! The baby—"

Blanche Devine shut the door and shook the Young Wife smartly by the shoulders.

"Stop screaming," she said quietly. "Is she sick?"

The Young Wife told her, her teeth chattering:

"Come quick! She's dying! Will's out of town. I tried to get the doctor. The telephone wouldn't—I saw your light! For God's sake—"

Blanche Devine grasped the Young Wife's arm, opened the door, and together they sped across the little space that separated the two houses. Blanche Devine was a big woman, but she took the stairs like a girl and found the right bedroom by some miraculous

105

woman instinct. A dreadful choking, rattling sound was coming from Snooky's bed.

"Croup," said Blanche Devine, and began her fight.

It was a good fight. She marshalled her little inadequate forces, made up of the half-fainting Young Wife and the terrified and awkward hired girl.

"Get the hot water on—lots of it!" Blanche Devine pinned up her sleeves. "Hot cloths! Tear up a sheet—or anything! Got an oilstove? I want a teakettle boiling in the room. She's got to have the steam. If that don't do it we'll raise an umbrella over her and throw a sheet over, and hold the kettle under till the steam gets to her that way. Got any ipecac?"

The Young Wife obeyed orders, whitefaced and shaking. Once Blanche Devine glanced up at her sharply.

"Don't you dare faint!" she commanded.

And the fight went on. Gradually the breathing that had been so frightful became softer, easier. Blanche Devine did not relax. It was not until the little figure breathed gently in sleep that Blanche Devine sat back satisfied. Then she tucked a cover ever so gently at the side of the bed, took a last satisfied look at the face on the pillow, and turned to look at the wan, dishevelled Young Wife.

"She's all right now. We can get the doctor when morning comes—though I don't know's you'll need him."

The Young Wife came round to Blanche Devine's side of the bed and stood looking up at her.

"My baby died," said Blanche Devine simply. The Young Wife gave a little inarticulate cry, put her two hands on Blanche Devine's broad shoulders and laid her tired head on her breast.

"I guess I'd better be going," said Blanche Devine.

The Young Wife raised her head. Her eyes were round with fright.

"Going! Oh, please stay! I'm so afraid. Suppose she should take sick again! That awful—awful breathing—"

"I'll stay if you want me to."

"Oh, please! I'll make up your bed and you can rest—"

"I'm not sleepy. I'm not much of a hand to sleep anyway. I'll sit up here in the hall, where there's a light. You get to bed. I'll watch and see that every-thing's all right. Have you got something I can read out here—something kind of lively—with a love story in it?"

So the night went by. Snooky slept in her little white bed. The Very Young Wife half dozed in her bed, so near the little one. In the hall, her stout figure looming grotesque in wall-shadows, sat Blanche Devine pretending to read. Now and then she rose and tiptoed into the bedroom with miraculous quiet, and stooped over the little bed and listened and looked—and tiptoed away again, satisfied.

The Young Husband came home from his business trip next day with tales of snowdrifts and stalled engines. Blanche Devine breathed a sigh of relief when she saw him from her kitchen window. She watched the house now with a sort of proprietary eye. She wondered about Snooky; but she knew better than to ask. So she waited. The Young Wife next door had told her husband all about that awful night—had told him with tears and sobs. The Very Young Husband had been very, very angry with her—angry and hurt, he said, and astonished! Snooky could not have been so sick! Look at her now! As well as ever. And to have called such a woman! Well, really he did not want to be harsh; but she must understand that she must never speak to the woman again. Never!

So the next day the Very Young Wife happened to go by with the Young Husband. Blanche Devine spied them from her sitting-room window, and she made the excuse of looking in her mailbox in order to go to the door. She stood in the doorway and the Very Young Wife went by on the arm of her husband. She went by—rather white-faced—without a look or a word or a sign!

And then this happened! There came into Blanche Devine's face a look that made slits of her eyes, and drew her mouth down into an ugly, narrow line, and that made the muscles of her jaw tense and hard. It was the ugliest look you can imagine. Then she smiled—if having one's lips curl away from one's teeth can be called smiling.

Two days later there was great news of the white cottage on the corner. The curtains were down; the furniture was packed; the rugs were rolled. The wagons came and backed up to the house and took those things that had made a home for Blanche Devine. And when we heard that she had bought back her interest in the House With the Closed Shutters, near the freight depot, we sniffed.

"I knew she wouldn't last!" we said.

"They never do!" said we.

VII

THE GIRL WHO WENT RIGHT

There is a story—Kipling, I think—that tells of a spirited horse galloping in the dark suddenly drawing up tense, hoofs bunched, slim flanks quivering, nostrils dilated, ears pricked. Urging being of no avail the rider dismounts, strikes a match, advances a cautious step or so, and finds himself at the precipitous brink of a newly formed crevasse.

So it is with your trained editor. A miraculous sixth sense guides him. A mysterious something warns him of danger lurking within the seemingly innocent oblong white envelope. Without slitting the flap, without pausing to adjust his tortoise-rimmed glasses, without clearing his throat, without lighting his cigarette— he knows.

The deadly newspaper story he scents in the dark. Cub reporter. Crusty city editor. Cub fired. Stumbles on to a big story. Staggers into newspaper office wild-eyed. Last edition. "Hold the presses!" Crusty C.E. stands over cub's typewriter grabbing story line by line. Even foreman of pressroom moved to tears by tale. "Boys, this ain't just a story this kid's writin'. This is history!" Story finished. Cub faints. C.E. makes him star reporter.

The athletic story: "I could never marry a mollycoddle like you, Harold Hammond!" Big game of the year. Team crippled. Second half. Halfback hurt. Harold Hammond, scrub, into the game. Touchdown! Broken leg. Five to nothing. "Harold, can you ever, ever forgive me?"

The pseudo-psychological story: She had been sitting before the fire for a long, long time. The flame had flickered and died down to a smouldering ash. The sound of his departing footsteps echoed and re-echoed through her brain. But the little room was very, very still.

The shop-girl story: Torn boots and temptation, tears and snears, pathos and bathos, all the way from Zola to the vice inquiry.

Having thus attempted to hide the deadly commonplaceness of this story with a thin layer of cynicism, perhaps even the wily editor may be tricked into taking the leap.

Four weeks before the completion of the new twelve-story addition the store advertised for two hundred experienced saleswomen. Rachel Wiletzky, entering the superintendent's office after a wait of three hours, was Applicant No. 179. The superintendent did not look up as Rachel came in. He scribbled busily on a pad of paper at his desk, thus observing rules one and two in the proper conduct of superintendents when interviewing applicants. Rachel Wiletzky, standing by his desk, did not cough or wriggle or rustle her skirts or sag on one hip. A sense of her quiet penetrated the superintendent's subconsciousness. He glanced up hurriedly over his left shoulder. Then he laid down his pencil and sat up slowly. His mind was working quickly enough though. In the twelve seconds that intervened between the laying down of the pencil and the sitting up in his chair he had hastily readjusted all his well-founded preconceived ideas on the appearance of shop-girl applicants.

Rachel Wiletzky had the colouring and physique of a dairymaid. It was the sort of colouring that you associate in your mind with lush green fields, and Jersey cows, and village maids, in Watteau frocks, balancing brimming pails aloft in the protecting curve of one rounded upraised arm, with perhaps a Maypole dance or so in the background. Altogether, had the superintendent been given to figures of speech, he might have said that Rachel was as much out of place among the preceding one hundred and seventy-eight bloodless, hollow-chested, stoop-shouldered applicants as a sunflower would be in a patch of dank white fungi.

He himself was one of those bleached men that you find on the office floor of department stores. Grey skin, grey eyes, greying hair, careful grey clothes—seemingly as void of pigment as one of those sunless things you disclose when you turn over a board that has long lain on the mouldy floor of a damp cellar. It was only when you looked closely that you noticed a fleck of golden brown in the cold grey of each eye, and a streak of warm brown forming an unquenchable forelock that the conquering grey had not been able to vanquish. It may have been a something within him corresponding to those outward bits of human colouring that tempted him to yield to a queer impulse. He whipped from his breast-pocket the grey-bordered handkerchief, reached up swiftly and passed one white corner of it down the length of Rachel Wiletzky's Killarney-rose left cheek. The rude path down which the handkerchief had travelled deepened to red for a moment before both rose-pink cheeks bloomed into scarlet. The superintendent gazed rather ruefully from unblemished handkerchief to cheek and back again.

"Why—it—it's real!" he stammered.

Rachel Wiletzky smiled a good-natured little smile that had in it a dash of superiority.

"If I was putting it on," she said, "I hope I'd have sense enough to leave something to the imagination. This colour out of a box would take a spiderweb veil to tone it down."

Not much more than a score of words. And yet before the half were spoken you were certain that Rachel Wiletzky's knowledge of lush green fields and bucolic scenes was that gleaned from the condensed-milk ads that glare down at one from billboards and street-car chromos. Hers was the ghetto voice—harsh, metallic, yet fraught with the resonant music of tragedy.

"H'm—name?" asked the grey superintendent. He knew that vocal quality.

A queer look stole into Rachel Wiletzky's face, a look of cunning and determination and shrewdness.

"Ray Willets," she replied composedly. "Double l."

"Clerked before, of course. Our advertisement stated—"

"Oh yes," interrupted Ray Willets hastily, eagerly. "I can sell goods. My customers like me. And I don't get tired. I don't know why, but I don't."

The superintendent glanced up again at the red that glowed higher with the girl's suppressed excitement. He took a printed slip from the little pile of paper that lay on his desk.

"Well, anyway, you're the first clerk I ever saw who had so much red blood that she could afford to use it for decorative purposes. Step into the next room, answer the questions on this card and turn it in. You'll be notified."

Ray Willets took the searching, telltale blank that put its questions so pertinently. "Where last employed?" it demanded. "Why did you leave? Do you live at home?"

Ray Willets moved slowly away toward the door opposite. The superintendent reached forward to press the button that would summon Applicant No. 180. But before his finger touched it Ray Willets turned and came back swiftly. She held the card out before his surprised eyes.

"I can't fill this out. If I do I won't get the job. I work over at the Halsted Street Bazaar. You know—the Cheap Store. I lied and sent word I was sick so I could come over here this morning. And they dock you for time off whether you're sick or not."

The superintendent drummed impatiently with his fingers. "I can't listen to all this. Haven't time. Fill out your blank, and if—"

All that latent dramatic force which is a heritage of her race came to the girl's aid now.

"The blank! How can I say on a blank that I'm leaving because I want to be where real people are? What chance has a girl got over there on the West Side? I'm different. I don't know why, but I am.

Look at my face! Where should I get red cheeks from? From not having enough to eat half the time and sleeping three in a bed?"

She snatched off her shabby glove and held one hand out before the man's face.

"From where do I get such hands? Not from selling hardware over at Twelfth and Halsted. Look at it! Say, couldn't that hand sell silk and lace?"

Some one has said that to make fingers and wrists like those which Ray Willets held out for inspection it is necessary to have had at least five generations of ancestors who have sat with their hands folded in their laps. Slender, tapering, sensitive hands they were, pink-tipped, temperamental. Wistful hands they were, speaking hands, an inheritance, perhaps, from some dreamer ancestor within the old-world ghetto, some long-haired, velvet-eyed student of the Talmud dwelling within the pale with its squalor and noise, and dreaming of unseen things beyond the confining gates—things rare and exquisite and fine.

"Ashamed of your folks?" snapped the superintendent.

"N-no—No! But I want to be different. I am different! Give me a chance, will you? I'm straight. And I'll work. And I can sell goods. Try me."

That all-pervading greyness seemed to have lifted from the man at the desk. The brown flecks in the eyes seemed to spread and engulf the surrounding colourlessness. His face, too, took on a glow that seemed to come from within. It was like the lifting of a thick grey mist on a foggy morning, so that the sun shines bright and clear for a brief moment before the damp curtain rolls down again and effaces it.

He leaned forward in his chair, a queer half-smile on his face.

"I'll give you your chance," he said, "for one month. At the end of that time I'll send for you. I'm not going to watch you. I'm not going to have you watched. Of course your sale slips will show the office whether you're selling goods or not. If you're not they'll discharge you. But that's routine. What do you want to sell?"

"What do I want to—Do you mean—Why, I want to sell the lacy things."

"The lacy—"

Ray, very red-cheeked, made the plunge. "The—the lawnjeree, you know. The things with ribbon and handwork and yards and yards of real lace. I've seen 'em in the glass case in the French Room. Seventy-nine dollars marked down from one hundred."

The superintendent scribbled on a card. "Show this Monday morning. Miss Jevne is the head of your department. You'll spend

111

two hours a day in the store school of instruction for clerks. Here, you're forgetting your glove."

The grey look had settled down on him again as he reached out to press the desk button. Ray Willets passed out at the door opposite the one through which Rachel Wiletzky had entered.

Some one in the department nick-named her Chubbs before she had spent half a day in the underwear and imported lingerie. At the store school she listened and learned. She learned how important were things of which Halsted Street took no cognisance. She learned to make out a sale slip as complicated as an engineering blueprint. She learned that a clerk must develop suavity and patience in the same degree as a customer waxes waspish and insulting, and that the spectrum's colours do not exist in the costume of the girl-behind-the-counter. For her there are only black and white. These things she learned and many more, and remembered them, for behind the rosy cheeks and the terrier-bright eyes burned the indomitable desire to get on. And the finished embodiment of all of Ray Willets' desires and ambitions was daily before her eyes in the presence of Miss Jevne, head of the lingerie and negligées.

Of Miss Jevne it might be said that she was real where Ray was artificial, and artificial where Ray was real. Everything that Miss Jevne wore was real. She was as modish as Ray was shabby, as slim as Ray was stocky, as artificially tinted and tinctured as Ray was naturally rosy-cheeked and buxom. It takes real money to buy clothes as real as those worn by Miss Jevne. The soft charmeuse in her graceful gown was real and miraculously draped. The cobweb-lace collar that so delicately traced its pattern against the black background of her gown was real. So was the ripple of lace that cascaded down the front of her blouse. The straight, correct, hideously modern lines of her figure bespoke a real eighteen-dollar corset. Realest of all, there reposed on Miss Jevne's bosom a bar pin of platinum and diamonds—very real diamonds set in a severely plain but very real bar of precious platinum. So if you except Miss Jevne's changeless colour, her artificial smile, her glittering hair and her undulating head-of-the-department walk, you can see that everything about Miss Jevne was as real as money can make one.

Miss Jevne, when she deigned to notice Ray Willets at all, called her "girl," thus: "Girl, get down one of those Number Seventeens for me—with the pink ribbons." Ray did not resent the tone. She thought about Miss Jevne as she worked. She thought about her at night when she was washing and ironing her other shirtwaist for next day's wear. In the Halsted Street Bazaar the girls had been on terms of dreadful intimacy with those affairs in each other's lives which popularly are supposed to be private knowledge.

They knew the sum which each earned per week; how much they turned in to help swell the family coffers and how much they were allowed to keep for their own use. They knew each time a girl spent a quarter for a cheap sailor collar or a pair of near-silk stockings. Ray Willets, who wanted passionately to be different, whose hands so loved the touch of the lacy, silky garments that made up the lingerie and negligee departments, recognised the perfection of Miss Jevne's faultless realness—recognised it, appreciated it, envied it. It worried her too. How did she do it? How did one go about attaining the same degree of realness?

Meanwhile she worked. She learned quickly. She took care always to be cheerful, interested, polite. After a short week's handling of lacy silken garments she ceased to feel a shock when she saw Miss Jevne displaying a robe-de-nuit made up of white cloud and sea-foam and languidly assuring the customer that of course it wasn't to be expected that you could get a fine handmade lace at that price—only twenty-seven-fifty. Now if she cared to look at something really fine—made entirely by hand—why—

The end of the first ten days found so much knowledge crammed into Ray Willets' clever, ambitious little head that the pink of her cheeks had deepened to carmine, as a child grows flushed and too bright-eyed when overstimulated and overtired.

Miss Myrtle, the store beauty, strolled up to Ray, who was straightening a pile of corset covers and brassieres. Miss Myrtle was the store's star cloak-and-suit model. Tall, svelte, graceful, lovely in line and contour, she was remarkably like one of those exquisite imbeciles that Rossetti used to love to paint. Hers were the great cowlike eyes, the wonderful oval face, the marvellous little nose, the perfect lips and chin. Miss Myrtle could don a forty-dollar gown, parade it before a possible purchaser, and make it look like an imported model at one hundred and twenty-five. When Miss Myrtle opened those exquisite lips and spoke you got a shock that hurt. She laid one cool slim finger on Ray's ruddy cheek.

"Sure enough!" she drawled nasally. "Whereja get it anyway, kid? You must of been brought up on peaches 'n' cream and slept in a pink cloud somewheres."

"Me!" laughed Ray, her deft fingers busy straightening a bow here, a ruffle of lace there. "Me! The L-train runs so near my bed that if it was ever to get a notion to take a short cut it would slice off my legs to the knees."

"Live at home?" Miss Myrtle's grasshopper mind never dwelt long on one subject.

"Well, sure," replied Ray. "Did you think I had a flat up on the Drive?"

113

"I live at home too," Miss Myrtle announced impressively. She was leaning indolently against the table. Her eyes followed the deft, quick movements of Ray's slender, capable hands. Miss Myrtle always leaned when there was anything to lean on. Involuntarily she fell into melting poses. One shoulder always drooped slightly, one toe always trailed a bit like the picture on the cover of the fashion magazines, one hand and arm always followed the line of her draperies while the other was raised to hip or breast or head.

Ray's busy hands paused a moment. She looked up at the picturesque Myrtle. "All the girls do, don't they?"

"Huh?" said Myrtle blankly.

"Live at home, I mean? The application blank says—"

"Say, you've got clever hands, ain't you?" put in Miss Myrtle irrelevantly. She looked ruefully at her own short, stubby, unintelligent hands, that so perfectly reflected her character in that marvellous way hands have. "Mine are stupid-looking. I'll bet you'll get on." She sagged to the other hip with a weary gracefulness. "I ain't got no brains," she complained.

"Where do they live then?" persisted Ray.

"Who? Oh, I live at home"—again virtuously—"but I've got some heart if I am dumb. My folks couldn't get along without what I bring home every week. A lot of the girls have flats. But that don't last. Now Jevne—"

"Yes?" said Ray eagerly. Her plump face with its intelligent eyes was all aglow.

Miss Myrtle lowered her voice discreetly. "Her own folks don't know where she lives. They says she sends 'em money every month, but with the understanding that they don't try to come to see her. They live way over on the West Side somewhere. She makes her buying trip to Europe every year. Speaks French and everything. They say when she started to earn real money she just cut loose from her folks. They was a drag on her and she wanted to get to the top."

"Say, that pin's real, ain't it?"

"Real? Well, I should say it is! Catch Jevne wearing anything that's phony. I saw her at the theatre one night. Dressed! Well, you'd have thought that birds of paradise were national pests, like English sparrows. Not that she looked loud. But that quiet, rich elegance, you know, that just smells of money. Say, but I'll bet she has her lonesome evenings!"

Ray Willets' eyes darted across the long room and rested upon the shining black-clad figure of Miss Jevne moving about against the luxurious ivory-and-rose background of the French Room.

"She—she left her folks, h'm?" she mused aloud.

114

Miss Myrtle, the brainless, regarded the tips of her shabby boots.

"What did it get her?" she asked as though to herself. "I know what it does to a girl, seeing and handling stuff that's made for millionaires, you get a taste for it yourself. Take it from me, it ain't the six-dollar girl that needs looking after. She's taking her little pay envelope home to her mother that's a widow and it goes to buy milk for the kids. Sometimes I think the more you get the more you want. Somebody ought to turn that vice inquiry on to the tracks of that thirty-dollar-a-week girl in the Irish crochet waist and the diamond bar pin. She'd make swell readin'."

There fell a little silence between the two—a silence of which neither was conscious. Both were thinking, Myrtle disjointedly, purposelessly, all unconscious that her slow, untrained mind had groped for a great and vital truth and found it; Ray quickly, eagerly, connectedly, a new and daring resolve growing with lightning rapidity.

"There's another new baby at our house," she said aloud suddenly. "It cries all night pretty near."

"Ain't they fierce?" laughed Myrtle. "And yet I dunno—"

She fell silent again. Then with the half-sign with which we waken from day dreams she moved away in response to the beckoning finger of a saleswoman in the evening-coat section. Ten minutes later her exquisite face rose above the soft folds of a black charmeuse coat that rippled away from her slender, supple body in lines that a sculptor dreams of and never achieves.

Ray Willets finished straightening her counter. Trade was slow. She moved idly in the direction of the black-garbed figure that flitted about in the costly atmosphere of the French section. It must be a very special customer to claim Miss Jevne's expert services. Ray glanced in through the half-opened glass and ivory-enamel doors.

"Here, girl," called Miss Jevne. Ray paused and entered. Miss Jevne was frowning. "Miss Myrtle's busy. Just slip this on. Careful now. Keep your arms close to your head."

She slipped a marvellously wrought garment over Ray's sleek head. Fluffy drifts of equally exquisite lingerie lay scattered about on chairs, over mirrors, across showtables. On one of the fragile little ivory-and-rose chairs, in the centre of the costly little room, sat a large, blonde, perfumed woman who clanked and rustled and swished as she moved. Her eyes were white-lidded and heavy, but strangely bright. One ungloved hand was very white too, but pudgy and covered so thickly with gems that your eye could get no clear picture of any single stone or setting.

Ray, clad in the diaphanous folds of the robe-de-nuit that was

115

so beautifully adorned with delicate embroideries wrought by the patient, needle-scarred fingers of some silent, white-faced nun in a far-away convent, paced slowly up and down the short length of the room that the critical eye of this coarse, unlettered creature might behold the wonders woven by this weary French nun, and, beholding, approve.

"It ain't bad," spake the blonde woman grudgingly. "How much did you say?"

"Ninety-five," Miss Jevne made answer smoothly. "I selected it myself when I was in France my last trip. A bargain."

She slid the robe carefully over Ray's head. The frown came once more to her brow. She bent close to Ray's ear. "Your waist's ripped under the left arm. Disgraceful!"

The blonde woman moved and jangled a bit in her chair. "Well, I'll take it," she sighed. "Look at the colour on that girl! And it's real too." She rose heavily and came over to Ray, reached up and pinched her cheek appraisingly with perfumed white thumb and forefinger.

"That'll do, girl," said Miss Jevne sweetly. "Take this along and change these ribbons from blue to pink."

Ray Willets bore the fairy garment away with her. She bore it tenderly, almost reverently. It was more than a garment. It represented in her mind a new standard of all that was beautiful and exquisite and desirable.

Ten days before the formal opening of the new twelve-story addition there was issued from the superintendent's office an order that made a little flurry among the clerks in the sections devoted to women's dress. The new store when thrown open would mark an epoch in the retail drygoods business of the city, the order began. Thousands were to be spent on perishable decorations alone. The highest type of patronage was to be catered to. Therefore the women in the lingerie, negligée, millinery, dress, suit and corset sections were requested to wear during opening week a modest but modish black one-piece gown that would blend with the air of elegance which those departments were to maintain.

Ray Willets of the lingerie and negligée sections read her order slip slowly. Then she reread it. Then she did a mental sum in simple arithmetic. A childish sum it was. And yet before she got her answer the solving of it had stamped on her face a certain hard, set, resolute look.

The store management had chosen Wednesday to be the opening day. By eight-thirty o'clock Wednesday morning the French lingerie, millinery and dress sections, with their women clerks garbed in modest but modish black one-piece gowns, looked like a levee at Buckingham when the court is in mourning. But the ladies-in-waiting, grouped about here and there, fell back in respectful silence when there paced down the aisle the queen royal in the person of Miss Jevne. There is a certain sort of black gown that is more startling and daring than scarlet. Miss Jevne's was that style. Fast black you might term it. Miss Jevne was aware of the flurry and flutter that followed her majestic progress down the aisle to her own section. She knew that each eye was caught in the tip of the little dog-eared train that slipped and slunk and wriggled along the ground, thence up to the soft drapery caught so cunningly just below the knee, up higher to the marvelously simple sash that swayed with each step, to the soft folds of black against which rested the very real diamond and platinum bar pin, up to the lace at her throat, and then stopping, blinking and staring again gazed fixedly at the string of pearls that lay about her throat, pearls rosily pink, mistily grey. An aura of self-satisfaction enveloping her, Miss Jevne disappeared behind the rose-garlanded portals of the new cream-and-mauve French section. And there the aura vanished, quivering. For standing before one of the plate-glass cases and patting into place with deft fingers the satin bow of a hand-wrought chemise was Ray Willets, in her shiny little black serge skirt and the braver of her two white shirtwaists.

Miss Jevne quickened her pace. Ray turned. Her bright brown eyes grew brighter at sight of Miss Jevne's wondrous black. Miss Jevne, her train wound round her feet like an actress' photograph, lifted her eyebrows to an unbelievable height.

"Explain that costume!" she said.

"Costume?" repeated Ray, fencing.

Miss Jevne's thin lips grew thinner. "You understood that women in this department were to wear black one-piece gowns this week!"

Ray smiled a little twisted smile. "Yes, I understood."

"Then what—"

Ray's little smile grew a trifle more uncertain. "—I had the money—last week—I was going to—The baby took sick—the heat I guess, coming so sudden. We had the doctor—and medicine—I— Say, your own folks come before black one-piece dresses!"

Miss Jevne's cold eyes saw the careful patch under Ray's left arm where a few days before the torn place had won her a reproof. It was the last straw.

"You can't stay in this department in that rig!"

"Who says so?" snapped Ray with a flash of Halsted Street bravado. "If my customers want a peek at Paquin I'll send 'em to you."

117

"I'll show you who says so!" retorted Miss Jevne, quite losing sight of the queen business. The stately form of the floor manager was visible among the glass showcases beyond. Miss Jevne sought him agitatedly. All the little sagging lines about her mouth showed up sharply, defying years of careful massage.

The floor manager bent his stately head and listened. Then, led by Miss Jevne, he approached Ray Willets, whose deft fingers, trembling a very little now, were still pretending to adjust the perfect pink-satin bow.

The manager touched her on the arm not unkindly. "Report for work in the kitchen utensils, fifth floor," he said. Then at sight of the girl's face: "We can't have one disobeying orders, you know. The rest of the clerks would raise a row in no time."

Down in the kitchen utensils and household goods there was no rule demanding modest but modish one-piece gowns. In the kitchenware one could don black sateen sleevelets to protect one's clean white waist without breaking the department's tenets of fashion. You could even pin a handkerchief across the front of your waist, if your job was that of dusting the granite ware.

At first Ray's delicate fingers, accustomed to the touch of soft, sheer white stuff and ribbon and lace and silk, shrank from contact with meat grinders, and aluminum stewpans, and egg beaters, and waffle irons, and pie tins. She handled them contemptuously. She sold them listlessly. After weeks of expatiating to customers on the beauties and excellencies of gossamer lingerie she found it difficult to work up enthusiasm over the virtues of dishpans and spice boxes. By noon she was less resentful. By two o'clock she was saying to a fellow clerk:

"Well, anyway, in this section you don't have to tell a woman how graceful and charming she's going to look while she's working the washing machine."

She was a born saleswoman. In spite of herself she became interested in the buying problems of the practical and plain-visaged housewives who patronised this section. By three o'clock she was looking thoughtful—thoughtful and contented.

Then came the summons. The lingerie section was swamped! Report to Miss Jevne at once! Almost regretfully Ray gave her customer over to an idle clerk and sought out Miss Jevne. Some of that lady's statuesqueness was gone. The bar pin on her bosom rose and fell rapidly. She espied Ray and met her halfway. In her hand she carried a soft black something which she thrust at Ray.

"Here, put that on in one of the fitting rooms. Be quick about it. It's your size. The department's swamped. Hurry now!"

Ray took from Miss Jevne the black silk gown, modest but

118

modish. There was no joy in Ray's face. Ten minutes later she emerged in the limp and clinging little frock that toned down her colour and made her plumpness seem but rounded charm.

The big store will talk for many a day of that afternoon and the three afternoons that followed, until Sunday brought pause to the thousands of feet beating a ceaseless tattoo up and down the thronged aisles. On the Monday following thousands swarmed down upon the store again, but not in such overwhelming numbers. There were breathing spaces. It was during one of these that Miss Myrtle, the beauty, found time for a brief moment's chat with Ray Willets.

Ray was straightening her counter again. She had a passion for order. Myrtle eyed her wearily. Her slender shoulders had carried an endless number and variety of garments during those four days and her feet had paced weary miles that those garments might the better be displayed.

"Black's grand on you," observed Myrtle. "Tones you down." She glanced sharply at the gown. "Looks just like one of our eighteen-dollar models. Copy it?"

"No," said Ray, still straightening petticoats and corset covers. Myrtle reached out a weary, graceful arm and touched one of the lacy piles adorned with cunning bows of pink and blue to catch the shopping eye.

"Ain't that sweet!" she exclaimed. "I'm crazy about that shadow lace. It's swell under voiles. I wonder if I could take one of them home to copy it."

Ray glanced up. "Oh, that!" she said contemptuously. "That's just a cheap skirt. Only twelve-fifty. Machine-made lace. Imitation embroidery—"

She stopped. She stared a moment at Myrtle with the fixed and wide-eyed gaze of one who does not see.

"What'd I just say to you?"

"Huh?" ejaculated Myrtle, mystified.

"What'd I just say?" repeated Ray.

Myrtle laughed, half understanding. "You said that was a cheap junk skirt at only twelve-fifty, with machine lace and imitation—"

But Ray Willets did not wait to hear the rest. She was off down the aisle toward the elevator marked "Employées." The superintendent's office was on the ninth floor. She stopped there. The grey superintendent was writing at his desk. He did not look up as Ray entered, thus observing rules one and two in the proper conduct of superintendents when interviewing employees. Ray Willets, standing by his desk, did not cough or wriggle or rustle her skirts or sag on one hip. A consciousness of her quiet penetrated the

119

superintendent's mind. He glanced up hurriedly over his left shoulder. Then he laid down his pencil and sat up slowly.

"Oh, it's you!" he said.

"Yes, it's me," replied Ray Willets simply. "I've been here a month to-day."

"Oh, yes." He ran his fingers through his hair so that the brown forelock stood away from the grey. "You've lost some of your roses," he said, and tapped his cheek. "What's the trouble?"

"I guess it's the dress," explained Ray, and glanced down at the folds of her gown. She hesitated a moment awkwardly. "You said you'd send for me at the end of the month. You didn't."

"That's all right," said the grey superintendent. "I was pretty sure I hadn't made a mistake. I can gauge applicants pretty fairly. Let's see—you're in the lingerie, aren't you?"

"Yes."

Then with a rush: "That's what I want to talk to you about. I've changed my mind. I don't want to stay in the lingeries. I'd like to be transferred to the kitchen utensils and household goods."

"Transferred! Well, I'll see what I can do. What was the name now? I forget."

A queer look stole into Ray Willets' face, a look of determination and shrewdness.

"Name?" she said. "My name is Rachel Wiletzky."

VIII

THE HOOKER-UP-THE-BACK

Miss Sadie Corn was not a charmer, but when you handed your room-key to her you found yourself stopping to chat a moment. If you were the right kind you showed her your wife's picture in the front of your watch. If you were the wrong kind, with your scant hair carefully combed to hide the bald spot, you showed her the newspaper clipping that you carried in your vest pocket. Following inspection of the first, Sadie Corn would say: "Now that's what I call a sweet face! How old is the youngest?" Upon perusal the second was returned with dignity and: "Is that supposed to be funny?" In each case Sadie Corn had you placed for life.

She possessed the invaluable gift of the floor clerk, did Sadie Corn—that of remembering names and faces. Though you had registered at the Hotel Magnifique but the night before, for the first time, Sadie Corn would look up at you over her glasses as she laid your key in its proper row, and say: "Good morning, Mr. Schultz! Sleep well?"

"Me!" you would stammer, surprised and gratified. "Me! Fine! H'm—Thanks!" Whereupon you would cross your right foot over your left nonchalantly and enjoy that brief moment's chat with Floor Clerk Number Two. You went back to Ishpeming, Michigan, with three new impressions: The first was that you were becoming a personage of considerable importance. The second was that the Magnifique realised this great truth and was grateful for your patronage. The third was that New York was a friendly little hole after all!

Miss Sadie Corn was dean of the Hotel Magnifique's floor clerks. The primary requisite in successful floor clerkship is homeliness. The second is discreet age. The third is tact. And for the benefit of those who think the duties of a floor clerk end when she takes your key when you leave your room, and hands it back as you return, it may be mentioned that the fourth, fifth, sixth and seventh requisites are diplomacy, ingenuity, unlimited patience and a comprehensive knowledge of human nature. Ambassadors have been known to keep their jobs on less than that.

She had come to the Magnifique at thirty-three, a plain, spare, sallow woman, with a quiet, capable manner, a pungent trick of the tongue on occasion, a sparse fluff of pale-coloured hair, and big, bony-knuckled hands, such as you see on women who have the gift

121

of humanness. She was forty-eight now—still plain, still spare, still sallow. Those bony, big-knuckled fingers had handed keys to potentates, and pork-packers, and millinery buyers from Seattle; and to princes incognito, and paupers much the same—the difference being that the princes dressed down to the part, while the paupers dressed up to it.

Time, experience, understanding and the daily dealing with ever-changing humanity had brought certain lines into Sadie Corn's face. So skilfully were they placed that the unobservant put them down as wrinkles on the countenance of a homely, middle-aged woman; but he who read as he ran saw that the lines about the eyes were quizzical, shrewd lines, which come from the practice of gauging character at a glance; that the mouth-markings meant tolerance and sympathy and humour; that the forehead furrows had been carved there by those master chisellers, suffering and sacrifice.

In the last three or four years Sadie Corn had taken to wearing a little lavender-and-white crocheted shawl about her shoulders on cool days, and when Two-fifty-seven, who was a regular, caught his annual heavy cold late in the fall, Sadie would ask him sharply whether he had on his winter flannels. On his replying in the negative she would rebuke him scathingly and demand a bill of sizable denomination; and when her watch was over she would sally forth to purchase four sets of men's winter underwear. As captain of the Magnifique's thirty-four floor clerks Sadie Corn's authority extended from the parlours to the roof, but her especial domain was floor two. Ensconced behind her little desk in a corner, blocked in by mailracks, pantry signals, pneumatic-tube chutes and telephone, with a clear view of the elevators and stairway, Sadie Corn was mistress of the moods, manners and morals of the Magnifique's second floor.

It was six thirty p.m. on Monday of Automobile Show Week when Sadie Corn came on watch. She came on with a lively, well-developed case of neuralgia over her right eye and extending down into her back teeth. With its usual spitefulness the attack had chosen to make its appearance during her long watch. It never selected her short-watch days, when she was on duty only from eleven a.m. until six-thirty p.m.

Now with a peppermint bottle held close to alternately sniffing nostrils Sadie Corn was running her eye over the complex report sheet of the floor clerk who had just gone off watch. The report was even more detailed and lengthy than usual. Automobile Show Week meant that the always prosperous Magnifique was filled to the eaves and turning them away. It meant twice the usual number of inside telephone calls anent rooms too hot, rooms too cold, radiators hammering, radiators hissing, windows that refused to open, windows that refused to shut, packages undelivered, hot water not forthcoming. As the human buffers between guests and hotel management, it was the duty of Sadie Corn and her diplomatic squad to pacify the peevish, to smooth the path of the paying.

Down the hall strolled Donahue, the house detective—Donahue the leisurely. Donahue the keen-eyed, Donahue the guileless—looking in his evening clothes for all the world like a prosperous diner-out. He smiled benignly upon Sadie Corn, and Sadie Corn had the bravery to smile back in spite of her neuralgia, knowing well that men have no sympathy with that anguishing ailment and no understanding of it.

"Everything serene, Miss Corn?" inquired Donahue.

"Everything's serene," said Sadie Corn. "Though Two-thirty-three telephoned a minute ago to say that if the valet didn't bring his pants from the presser in the next two seconds he'd come down the hall as he is and get 'em. Perhaps you'd better stay round."

Donahue chuckled and passed on. Half way down the hall he retraced his steps, and stopped again before Sadie Corn's busy desk. He balanced a moment thoughtfully from toe to heel, his chin lifted inquiringly: "Keep your eye on Two-eighteen and Two-twenty-three this morning?"

"Like a lynx!" answered Sadie.

"Anything?"

"Not a thing. I guess they just scraped acquaintance in the Alley after dinner, like they sometimes do. A man with eyelashes like his always speaks to any woman alone who isn't pockmarked and toothless. Two minutes after he's met a girl his voice takes on the 'cello note. I know his kind. Why, say, he even tried waving those eyelashes of his at me first time he turned in his key; and goodness knows I'm so homely that pretty soon I'll be ripe for bachelor floor thirteen. You know as well as I that to qualify for that job a floor clerk's got to look like a gargoyle."

"Maybe they're all right," said Donahue thoughtfully. "If it's just a flirtation, why—anyway, watch 'em this evening. The day watch listened in and says they've made some date for to-night."

He was off down the hall again with his light, quick step that still had the appearance of leisureliness.

The telephone at Sadie's right buzzed warningly. Sadie picked up the receiver and plunged into the busiest half hour of the evening. From that moment until seven o'clock her nimble fingers and eyes and brain and tongue directed the steps of her little world. She held the telephone receiver at one ear and listened to the demands of incoming and outgoing guests with the other. She jotted

123

down reports, dealt out mail and room-keys, kept her neuralgic eye on stairs and elevators and halls, her sound orb on tube and pantry signals, while through and between and above all she guided the stream of humanity that trickled past her desk—bellhops, Polish chambermaids, messenger boys, guests, waiters, parlour maids.

Just before seven there disembarked at floor two out of the cream-and-gold elevator one of those visions that have helped to make Fifth Avenue a street of the worst-dressed women in the world. The vision was Two-eighteen, and her clothes were of the kind that prepared you for the shock that you got when you looked at her face. Plume met fur, and fur met silk, and silk met lace, and lace met gold—and the whole met and ran into a riot of colour, and perfume—and little jangling, swishing sounds. Just by glancing at Two-eighteen's feet in their inadequate openwork silk and soft kid you knew that Two-eighteen's lips would be carmined.

She came down the corridor and stopped at Sadie Corn's desk. Sadie Corn had her key ready for her. Two-eighteen took it daintily between white-gloved fingers.

"I'll want a maid in fifteen minutes," she said. "Tell them to send me the one I had yesterday. The pretty one. She isn't so clumsy as some."

Sadie Corn jotted down a note without looking up.

"Oh, Julia? Sorry—Julia's busy," she lied.

Two-eighteen knew she lied, because at that moment there came round the bend in the broad, marble stairway that led up from the parlour floor the trim, slim figure of Julia herself.

Two-eighteen took a quick step forward. "Here, girl! I'll want you to hook me in fifteen minutes," she said.

"Very well, ma'am," replied Julia softly.

There passed between Sadie Corn and Two-eighteen a—well, you could hardly call it a look, it was so fleeting, so ephemeral; that electric, pregnant, meaning something that flashes between two women who dislike and understand each other. Then Two-eighteen was off down the hall to her room.

Julia stood at the head of the stairway just next to Sadie's desk and watched Two-eighteen until the bend in the corridor hid her. Julia, of the lady's-maid staff, could never have qualified for the position of floor clerk, even if she had chosen to bury herself in lavender-and-white crocheted shawls to the tip of her marvellous little Greek nose. In her frilly white cap, her trim black gown, her immaculate collar and cuffs and apron, Julia looked distractingly like the young person who, in the old days of the furniture-dusting drama, was wont to inform you that it was two years since young master went away—all but her feet. The feather-duster person was

124

addicted to French-heeled, beaded slippers. Not so Julia. Julia was on her feet for ten hours or so a day. When you subject your feet to ten-hour tortures you are apt to pass by French-heeled effects in favour of something flat-heeled, laced, with an easy, comfortable crack here and there at the sides, and stockings with white cotton soles.

Julia, at the head of the stairway, stood looking after Two-eighteen until the tail of her silken draperies had whisked round the corner. Then, still staring, Julia spoke resentfully:

"Life for her is just one darned pair of long white kid gloves after another! Look at her! Why is it that kind of a face is always wearing the sables and diamonds?"

"Sables and diamonds," replied Sadie Corn, sniffing essence of peppermint, "seem a small enough reward for having to carry round a mug like that!"

Julia came round to the front of Sadie Corn's desk. Her eyes were brooding, her lips sullen.

"Oh, I don't know!" she said bitterly. "Being pretty don't get you anything—just being pretty! When I first came I used to wonder at those women that paint their faces and colour their hair, and wear skirts that are too tight and waists that are too low. But—I don't know! This town's so big and so—so kind of uninterested. When you see everybody wearing clothes that are more gorgeous than yours, and diamonds bigger, and limousines longer and blacker and quieter, it gives you a kind of fever. You—you want to make people look at you too."

Sadie Corn leaned back in her chair. The peppermint bottle was held at her nose. It may have been that which caused her eyes to narrow to mere slits as she gazed at the drooping Julia. She said nothing. Suddenly Julia seemed to feel the silence. She looked down at Sadie Corn. As by a miracle all the harsh, sullen lines in the girl's face vanished, to be replaced by a lovely compassion.

"Your neuralgy again, dearie?" she asked in pretty concern.

Sadie sniffed long and audibly at the peppermint bottle.

"If you ask me I think there's some imp inside of my head trying to push my right eye out with his thumb. Anyway it feels like that."

"Poor old dear!" breathed Julia. "It's the weather. Have them send you up a pot of black tea."

"When you've got neuralgy over your right eye," observed Sadie Corn grimly, "there's just one thing helps—that is to crawl into bed in a flannel nightgown, with the side of your face resting on the red rubber bosom of a hot-water bottle. And I can't do it; so let's talk about something cheerful. Seen Jo to-day?"

125

There crept into Julia's face a wave of colour—not the pink of pleasure, but the dull red of pain. She looked away from Sadie's eyes and down at her shabby boots. The sullen look was in her face once more.

"No; I ain't seen him," she said.

"What's the trouble?" Sadie asked.

"I've been busy," replied Julia airily. Then, with a forced vivacity: "Though it's nothing to Auto Show Week last year. I remember that week I hooked up until my fingers were stiff. You know the way the dresses fastened last winter. Some of 'em ought to have had a map to go by, they were that complicated. And now, just when I've got so's I can hook any dress that was ever intended for the human form—"

"Wasn't it Jo who said they ought to give away an engineering blueprint with every dress, when you told him about the way they hooked?" put in Sadie. "What's the trouble between you and—"

Julia rattled on, unheeding:

"You wouldn't believe what a difference there's been since these new peasant styles have come in! And the Oriental craze! Hook down the side, most of 'em—and they can do 'em themselves if they ain't too fat."

"Remember Jo saying they ought to have a hydraulic press for some of those skintight dames, when your fingers were sore from trying to squeeze them into their casings? By the way, what's the trouble between you and—"

"Makes an awful difference in my tips!" cut in Julia deftly. "I don't believe I've hooked up six this evening, and two of them sprung the haven't-anything-but-a-five-dollar-bill-see-you-to-morrow! Women are devils! I wish—"

Sadie Corn leaned forward, placed her hand on Julia's arm, and turned the girl about so that she faced her. Julia tried miserably to escape her keen eyes and failed.

"What's the trouble between you and Jo?" she demanded for the fourth time. "Out with it or I'll telephone down to the engine room and ask him myself."

"Oh, well, if you want to know—" She paused, her eyelids drooping again; then, with a rush: "Me and Jo have quarrelled again—for good, this time. I'm through!"

"What about?"

"I s'pose you'll say I'm to blame. Jo's mother's sick again. She's got to go to the hospital and have another operation. You know what that means—putting off the wedding again until God knows when! I'm sick of it—putting off and putting off! I told him we might as well quit and be done with it. We'll never get married at this rate.

126

Soon's Jo gets enough put by to start us on, something happens. Last three times it's been his ma. Pretty soon I'll be as old and wrinkled and homely as—"

"As me!" put in Sadie calmly. "Well, I don't know's that's the worst thing that can happen to you. I'm happy. I had my plans, too, when I was a girl like you—not that I was ever pretty; but I had my trials. Funny how the thing that's easy and the thing that's right never seem to be the same!"

"Oh, I'm fond of Jo's ma," said Julia, a little shamefacedly. "We get along all right. She knows how it is, I guess; and feels—well, in the way. But when Jo told me, I was tired I guess. We had words. I told him there were plenty waiting for me if he was through. I told him I could have gone out with a real swell only last Saturday if I'd wanted to. What's a girl got her looks for if not to have a good time?"

"Who's this you were invited out by?" asked Sadie Corn.

"You must have noticed him," said Julia, dimpling. "He's as handsome as an actor. Name's Venner. He's in two-twenty-three."

There came the look of steel into Sadie Corn's eyes.

"Look here, Julia! You've been here long enough to know that you're not to listen to the talk of the men guests round here. Two-twenty-three isn't your kind—and you know it! If I catch you talking to him again I'll—"

The telephone at her elbow sounded sharply. She answered it absently, her eyes, with their expression of pain and remonstrance, still unshrinking before the onslaught of Julia's glare. Then her expression changed. A look of consternation came into her face.

"Right away, madam!" she said, at the telephone. "Right away! You won't have to wait another minute." She hung up the receiver and waved Julia away with a gesture. "It's Two-eighteen. You promised to be there in fifteen minutes. She's been waiting and her voice sounds like a saw. Better be careful how you handle her."

Julia's head, with its sleek, satiny coils of black hair that waved away so bewitchingly from the cream of her skin, came up with a jerk.

"I'm tired of being careful of other people's feelings. Let somebody be careful of mine for a change." She walked off down the hall, the little head still held high. A half dozen paces and she turned. "What was it you said you'd do to me if you caught me talking to him again?" she sneered.

A miserable twinge of pain shot through Sadie Corn's eye, to be followed by a wave of nausea that swept over her. They alone were responsible for her answer.

"I'll report you!" she snapped, and was sorry at once.

127

Julia turned again, walked down the corridor and round the corner in the direction of two-eighteen.

Long after Julia had disappeared Sadie Corn stared after her—miserable, regretful.

Julia knocked once at the door of two-eighteen and turned the knob before a high, shrill voice cried:

"Come!"

Two-eighteen was standing in the centre of the floor in scant satin knickerbockers and tight brassière. The blazing folds of a cerise satin gown held in her hands made a great, crude patch of colour in the neutral-tinted bedroom. The air was heavy with scent. Hair, teeth, eyes, fingernails—Two-eighteen glowed and glistened. Chairs and bed held odds and ends.

"Where've you been, girl?" shrilled Two-eighteen. "I've been waiting like a fool! I told you to be here in fifteen minutes."

"My stop-watch isn't working right," replied Julia impudently and took the cerise satin gown in her two hands.

She made a ring of the gown's opening, and through that cerise frame her eyes met those of Two-eighteen.

"Careful of my hair!" Two-eighteen warned her, and ducked her head to the practised movement of Julia's arms. The cerise gown dropped to her shoulders without grazing a hair. Two-eighteen breathed a sigh of relief. She turned to face the mirror.

"It starts at the left, three hooks; then to the centre; then back four—under the arm and down the middle again. That chiffon comes over like a drape."

She picked up a buffer from the litter of ivory and silver on the dresser and began to polish her already glittering nails, turning her head this way and that, preening her neck, biting her scarlet lips to deepen their crimson, opening her eyes wide and half closing them languorously. Julia, down on her knees in combat with the trickiest of the hooks, glanced up and saw. Two-eighteen caught the glance in the mirror. She stopped her idle polishing and preening to study the glowing and lovely little face that looked up at her. A certain queer expression grew in her eyes—a speculative, eager look.

"Tell me, little girl," she said, "What do you do round here?"

Julia turned from the mirror to the last of the hooks, her fingers working nimbly.

"Me? My regular job is working. Don't jerk, please. I've fastened this one three times."

"Working!" laughed Two-eighteen, fingering the diamonds at her throat. "What does a pretty girl like you want to do that for?"

"Hook off here," said Julia. "Shall I sew it?"

"Pin it!" snapped Two-eighteen.

128

Julia's tidy nature revolted.

"It'll take just a minute to catch it with thread—"

Two-eighteen whirled about in one of the sudden hot rages of her kind:

"Pin it, you fool! Pin it! I told you I was late!"

Julia paused a moment, the red surging into her face. Then in silence she knelt and wove a pin deftly in and out. When she rose from her knees her face was quite white.

"There, that's the girl!" said Two-eighteen blithely, her rage forgotten. "Just pat this over my shoulders."

She handed a powder-puff to Julia and turned her back to the broad mirror, holding a hand-glass high as she watched the powder-laden puff leaving a snowy coat on the neck and shoulders and back so generously displayed in the cherry-coloured gown. Julia's face was set and hard.

"Oh, now, don't sulk!" coaxed Two-eighteen good-naturedly, all of a sudden. "I hate sulky girls. I like people to be cheerful round me."

"I'm not used to being yelled at," Julia said resentfully.

Two-eighteen patted her cheek lightly. "You come out with me to-morrow and I'll buy you something pretty. Don't you like pretty clothes?"

"Yes; but—"

"Of course you do. Every girl does—especially pretty ones like you. How do you like this dress? Don't you think it smart?"

She turned squarely to face Julia, trying on her the tricks she had practised in the mirror. A little cruel look came into Julia's face.

"Last year's, isn't it?" she asked coolly.

"This!" cried Two-eighteen, stiffening. "Last year's! I got it yesterday on Fifth Avenue, and paid two hundred and fifty for it. What do you—"

"Oh, I believe you," drawled Julia. "They can tell a New Yorker from an out-of-towner every time. You know the really new thing is the Bulgarian effect!"

"Well, of all the nerve!" began Two-eighteen, turning to the mirror in a sort of fright. "Of all the—"

What she saw there seemed to reassure. She raised one hand to push the gown a little more off the left shoulder.

"Will there be anything else?" inquired Julia, standing aloof.

Two-eighteen turned reluctantly from the mirror and picked up a jewelled gold-mesh bag that lay on the bed. From it she extracted a coin and held it out to Julia. It was a generous coin. Julia looked at it. Her smouldering wrath burst into flame.

129

"Keep it!" she said savagely, and was out of the room and down the hall.

Sadie Corn, at her desk, looked up quickly as Julia turned the corner. Julia, her head held high, kept her eyes resolutely away from Sadie.

"Oh, Julia, I want to talk to you!" said Sadie Corn as Julia reached the stairway. Julia began to descend the stairs, unheeding. Sadie Corn rose and leaned over the railing, her face puckered with anxiety. "Now, Julia, girl, don't hold that up against me! I didn't mean it. You know that. You wouldn't be mad at a poor old woman that's half crazy with neuralgy!" Julia hesitated, one foot poised to take the next step. "Come on up," coaxed Sadie Corn, "and tell me what Two-eighteen's wearing this evening. I'm that lonesome, with nothing to do but sit here and watch the letter-ghosts go flippering down the mailchute! Come on!"

"What made you say you'd report me?" demanded Julia bitterly.

"I'd have said the same thing to my own daughter if I had one. You know yourself I'd bite my tongue out first!"

"Well!" said Julia slowly, and relented. She came up the stairs almost shyly. "Neuralgy any better?"

"Worse!" said Sadie Corn cheerfully.

Julia leaned against the desk sociably and glanced down the hall.

"Would you believe it," she snickered, "she's wearing red! With that hair! She asked me if I didn't think she looked too pale. I wanted to tell her that if she had any more colour, with that dress, they'd be likely to use the chemical sprinklers on her when she struck the Alley."

"Sh-sh-sh!" breathed Sadie in warning. Two-eighteen, in her shimmering, flame-coloured costume, was coming down the hall toward the elevators. She walked with the absurd and stumbling step that her scant skirt necessitated. With each pace the slashed silken skirt parted to reveal a shameless glimpse of cerise silk stocking. In her wake came Venner, of Two-twenty-three—a strange contrast in his black and white.

Sadie and Julia watched them from the corner nook. Opposite the desk Two-eighteen stopped and turned to Julia.

"Just run into my room and pick things up and hang them away, will you?" she said. "I didn't have time—and I hate things all about when I come in dead tired."

The little formula of service rose automatically to Julia's lips.

"Very well, madam," she said.

Her eyes and Sadie's followed the two figures until they had

130

stepped into the cream-and-gold elevator and had vanished. Sadie, peppermint bottle at nose, spoke first:

"She makes one of those sandwich men with a bell, on Sixth Avenue, look like a shrinking violet!"

Julia's lower lip was caught between her teeth. The scent that had enveloped Two-eighteen as she passed was still in the air. Julia's nostrils dilated as she sniffed it. Her breath came a little quickly. Sadie Corn sat very still, watching her.

"Look at her!" said Julia, her voice vibrant. "Look at her! Old and homely, and all made up! I powdered her neck. Her skin's like tripe.

"Now Julia—" remonstrated Sadie Corn soothingly.

"I don't care," went on Julia with a rush. "I'm young. And I'm pretty too. And I like pretty things. It ain't fair! That was one reason why I broke with Jo. It wasn't only his mother. I told him he couldn't ever give me the things I want anyway. You can't help wanting 'em—seeing them all round every day on women that aren't half as good-looking as you are! I want low-cut dresses too. My neck's like milk. I want silk underneath, and fur coming up on my coat collar to make my cheeks look pink. I'm sick of hooking other women up. I want to stand in front of a mirror, looking at myself, polishing my pink nails with a silver thing and having somebody else hook me up!"

In Sadie Corn's eyes there was a mist that could not be traced to neuralgia or peppermint.

"Julia, girl," said Sadie Corn, "ever since the world began there's been hookers and hooked. And there always will be. I was born a hooker. So were you. Time was when I used to cry out against it too. But shucks! I know better now. I wouldn't change places. Being a hooker gives you such an all-round experience like of mankind. The hooked only get a front view. They only see faces and arms and chests. But the hookers—they see the necks and shoulderblades of this world, as well as faces. It's mighty broadening—being a hooker. It's the hookers that keep this world together, Julia, and fastened up right. It wouldn't amount to much if it had to depend on such as that!" She nodded her head in the direction the cerise figure had taken. "The height of her ambition is to get the cuticle of her nails trained back so perfectly that it won't have to be cut; and she don't feel decently dressed to be seen in public unless she's wearing one of those breastplates of orchids. Envy her! Why, Julia, don't you know that as you were standing here in your black dress as she passed she was envying you!"

"Envying me!" said Julia, and laughed a short laugh that had little of mirth in it. "You don't understand, Sadie!"

131

Sadie Corn smiled a rather sad little smile.

"Oh, yes, I do understand. Don't think because a woman's homely, and always has been, that she doesn't have the same heartaches that a pretty woman has. She's built just the same inside."

Julia turned her head to stare at her wide-eyed. It was a long and trying stare, as though she now saw Sadie Corn for the first time.

Sadie, smiling up at the girl, stood it bravely. Then, with a sudden little gesture, Julia patted the wrinkled, sallow cheek and was off down the hall and round the corner to two-eighteen.

The lights still blazed in the bedroom. Julia closed the door and stood with her back to it, looking about the disordered chamber. In that marvellous way a room has of reflecting the very personality of its absent owner, room two-eighteen bore silent testimony to the manner of woman who had just left it. The air was close and overpoweringly sweet with perfume—sachet, powder—the scent of a bedroom after a vain and selfish woman has left it. The litter of toilet articles lay scattered about on the dresser. Chairs and bed held garments of lace and silk. A bewildering negligée hung limply over a couch; and next it stood a patent-leather slipper, its mate on the floor.

Julia saw these things in one accustomed glance. Then she advanced to the middle of the room and stooped to pick up a pink wadded bedroom slipper from where it lay under the bed. And her hand touched a coat of velvet and fur that had been flung across the counterpane—touched it and rested there.

The coat was of stamped velvet and fur. Great cuffs of fur there were, and a sumptuous collar that rolled from neck to waist. There was a lining of vivid orange. Julia straightened up and stood regarding the garment, her hands on her hips.

"I wonder if it's draped in the back," she said to herself, and picked it up. It was draped in the back—bewitchingly. She held it at arm's length, turning it this way and that. Then, as though obeying some powerful force she could not resist, Julia plunged her arms into the satin of the sleeves and brought the great soft revers up about her throat. The great, gorgeous, shimmering thing completely hid her grubby little black gown. She stepped to the mirror and stood surveying herself in a sort of ecstasy. Her cheeks glowed rose-pink against the dark fur, as she had known they would. Her lovely little head, with its coils of black hair, rose flowerlike from the clinging garment. She was still standing there, lips parted, eyes wide with delight, when the door opened and closed—and Venner, of two-twenty-three, strode into the room.

132

"You little beauty!" exclaimed Two-twenty-three.

Julia had wheeled about. She stood staring at him, eyes and lips wide with fright now. One hand clutched the fur at her breast.

"Why, what—" she gasped.

Two-twenty-three laughed.

"I knew I'd find you here. I made an excuse to come up. Old Nutcracker Face in the hall thinks I went to my own room." He took two quick steps forward. "You raving little Cinderella beauty, you!"—And he gathered Julia, coat and all, into his arms.

"Let me go!" panted Julia, fighting with all the strength of her young arms. "Let me go!"

"You'll have coats like this," Two-twenty-three was saying in her ear—"a dozen of them! And dresses too; and laces and furs! You'll be ten times the beauty you are now! And that's saying something. Listen! You meet me to-morrow—"

There came a ring—sudden and startling—from the telephone on the wall near the door. The man uttered something and turned. Julia pushed him away, loosened the coat with fingers that shook and dropped it to the floor. It lay in a shimmering circle about the tired feet in their worn, cracked boots. And one foot was raised suddenly and kicked the silken garment into a heap.

The telephone bell sounded again. Venner, of two-twenty-three, plunged his hand into his pocket, took out something and pressed it in Julia's palm, shutting her fingers over it. Julia did not need to open them and look to see—she knew by the feel of the crumpled paper, stiff and crackling. He was making for the door, with some last instructions that she did not hear, before she spoke. The telephone bell had stopped its insistent ringing.

Julia raised her arm and hurled at him with all her might the yellow-backed paper he had thrust in her hand.

"I'll—I'll get my man to whip you for this!" she panted. "Jo'll pull those eyelashes of yours out and use 'em for couplings. You miserable little—"

The outside door opened again, striking Two-twenty-three squarely in the back. He crumpled up against the wall with an oath.

Sadie Corn, in the doorway, gave no heed to him. Her eyes searched Julia's flushed face. What she saw there seemed to satisfy her. She turned to him then grimly.

"What are you doing here?" Sadie asked briskly.

Two-twenty-three muttered something about the wrong room by mistake. Julia laughed.

"He lies!" she said, and pointed to the floor. "That bill belongs to him."

Sadie Corn motioned to him.

133

"Pick it up!" she said.

"I don't—want it!" snarled Two-twenty-three.

"Pick—it—up!" articulated Sadie Corn very carefully. He came forward, stooped, put the bill in his pocket. "You check out to-night!" said Sadie Corn. Then, at a muttered remonstrance from him: "Oh, yes, you will! So will Two-eighteen. Huh? Oh, I guess she will! Say, what do you think a floor clerk's for? A human keyrack? I'll give you until twelve. I'm off watch at twelve-thirty." Then, to Julia, as he slunk off: "Why didn't you answer the phone? That was me ringing!"

A sob caught Julia in the throat, but she turned it into a laugh.

"I didn't hardly hear it. I was busy promising him a licking from Jo."

Sadie Corn opened the door.

"Come on down the hall. I've left no one at the desk. It was Jo I was telephoning you for."

Julia grasped her arm with gripping fingers.

"Jo! He ain't—"

Sadie Corn took the girl's hand in hers.

"Jo's all right! But Jo's mother won't bother you any more, Sadie. You'll never need to give up your housekeeping nest-egg for her again. Jo told me to tell you."

Julia stared at her for one dreadful moment, her fist, with the knuckles showing white, pressed against her mouth. A little moan came from her that, repeated over and over, took the form of words:

"Oh, Sadie, if I could only take back what I said to Jo! If I could only take back what I said to Jo! He'll never forgive me now! And I'll never forgive myself!"

"He'll forgive you," said Sadie Corn; "but you'll never forgive yourself. That's as it should be. That, you know, is our punishment for what we say in thoughtlessness and anger."

They turned the corridor corner. Standing before the desk near the stairway was the tall figure of Donahue, house detective. Donahue had always said that Julia was too pretty to be a hotel employé.

"Straighten up, Julia!" whispered Sadie Corn. "And smile if it kills you—unless you want to make me tell the whole of it to Donahue."

Donahue, the keen-eyed, balancing, as was his wont, from toe to heel and back again, his chin thrust out inquiringly, surveyed the pair.

"Off watch?" inquired Donahue pleasantly, staring at Julia's eyes. "What's wrong with Julia?"

"Neuralgy!" said Sadie Corn crisply. "I've just told her to quit rubbing her head with peppermint. She's got the stuff into her eyes."

She picked up the bottle on her desk and studied its label, frowning. "Run along downstairs, Julia. I'll see if they won't send you some hot tea."

Donahue, hands clasped behind him, was walking off in his leisurely, light-footed way.

"Everything serene?" he called back over his big shoulder.

The neuralgic eye closed and opened, perhaps with another twinge.

"Everything's serene!" said Sadie Corn.

IX

THE GUIDING MISS GOWD

It has long been the canny custom of writers on travel bent to defray the expense of their journeyings by dashing off tales filled with foreign flavour. Dickens did it, and Dante. It has been tried all the way from Tasso to Twain; from Raskin to Roosevelt. A pleasing custom it is and thrifty withal, and one that has saved many a one but poorly prepared for the European robber in uniform the moist and unpleasant task of swimming home.

Your writer spends seven days, say, in Paris. Result? The Latin Quarter story. Oh, mes enfants! That Parisian student-life story! There is the beautiful young American girl—beautiful, but as earnest and good as she is beautiful, and as talented as she is earnest and good. And wedded, be it understood, to her art—preferably painting or singing. From New York! Her name must be something prim, yet winsome. Lois will do—Lois, la belle Américaine. Then the hero—American too. Madly in love with Lois. Tall he is and always clean-limbed—not handsome, but with one of those strong, rugged faces. His name, too, must be strong and plain, yet snappy. David is always good. The villain is French, fascinating, and wears a tiny black moustache to hide his mouth, which is cruel.

The rest is simple. A little French restaurant—Henri's. Know you not Henri's? Tiens! But Henri's is not for the tourist. A dim little shop and shabby, modestly tucked away in the shadows of the Rue Brie. But the food! Ah, the—whadd'you-call'ems—in the savoury sauce, that is Henri's secret! The tender, broiled poularde, done to a turn! The bottle of red wine! Mais oui; there one can dine under the watchful glare of Rosa, the plump, black-eyed wife of the concierge. With a snowy apron about her buxom waist, and a pot of red geraniums somewhere, and a sleek, lazy cat contentedly purring in the sunny window!

Then Lois starving in a garret. Temptation! Sacré bleu! Zut! Also nom d'un nom! Enter David. Bon! Oh, David, take me away! Take me back to dear old Schenectady. Love is more than all else, especially when no one will buy your pictures.

The Italian story recipe is even simpler. A pearl necklace; a low, clear whistle. Was it the call of a bird or a signal? His-s-s-st! Again! A black cape; the flash of steel in the moonlight; the sound of a splash in the water; a sickening gurgle; a stifled cry! Silence! His-st! Vendetta!

136

There is the story made in Germany, filled with students and steins and scars; with beer and blonde, blue-eyed Mädchen garbed—the Mädchen, that is—in black velvet bodice, white chemisette, scarlet skirt with two rows of black ribbon at the bottom, and one yellow braid over the shoulder. Especially is this easily accomplished if actually written in the Vaterland, German typewriting machines being equipped with umlauts.

And yet not one of these formulas would seem to fit the story of Mary Gowd. Mary Gowd, with her frumpy English hat and her dreadful English fringe, and her brick-red English cheeks, which not even the enervating Italian sun, the years of bad Italian food or the damp and dim little Roman room had been able to sallow. Mary Gowd, with her shabby blue suit and her mangy bit of fur, and the glint of humour in her pale blue eyes. Many, many times that same glint of humour had saved English Mary Gowd from seeking peace in the muddy old Tiber.

Her card read imposingly thus: Mary M. Gowd, Cicerone. Certificated and Licensed Lecturer on Art and Archaeology. Via del Babbuino, Roma.

In plain language Mary Gowd was a guide. Now, Rome is swarming with guides; but they are men guides. They besiege you in front of Cook's. They perch at the top of the Capitoline Hill, ready to pounce on you when you arrive panting from your climb up the shallow steps. They lie in wait in the doorway of St. Peter's. Bland, suave, smiling, quiet, but insistent, they dog you from the Vatican to the Catacombs.

Hundreds there are of these little men—undersized, even in this land of small men—dapper, agile, low-voiced, crafty. In his inner coat pocket each carries his credentials, greasy, thumb-worn documents, but precious. He glances at your shoes—this insinuating one—or at your hat, or at any of those myriad signs by which he marks you for his own. Then up he steps and speaks to you in the language of your country, be you French, German, English, Spanish or American.

And each one of this clan—each slim, feline little man in blue serge, white-toothed, gimlet-eyed, smooth-tongued, brisk—hated Mary Gowd. They hated her with the hate of an Italian for an outlander—with the hate of an Italian for a woman who works with her brain—with the hate of an Italian who sees another taking the bread out of his mouth. All this, coupled with the fact that your Italian is a natural-born hater, may indicate that the life of Mary Gowd had not the lyric lilt that life is commonly reputed to have in sunny Italy.

Oh, there is no formula for Mary Gowd's story. In the first

place, the tale of how Mary Gowd came to be the one woman guide in Rome runs like melodrama. And Mary herself, from her white cotton gloves, darned at the fingers, to her figure, which mysteriously remained the same in spite of fifteen years of scant Italian fare, does not fit gracefully into the rôle of heroine.

Perhaps that story, scraped to bedrock, shorn of all floral features, may gain in force what it loses in artistry.

She was twenty-two when she came to Rome—twenty-two and art-mad. She had been pretty, with that pink-cheesecloth prettiness of the provincial English girl, who degenerates into blowsiness at thirty. Since seventeen she had saved and scrimped and contrived for this modest Roman holiday. She had given painting lessons— even painted on loathsome china—that the little hoard might grow. And when at last there was enough she had come to this Rome against the protests of the fussy English father and the spinster English sister.

The man she met quite casually one morning in the Sistine Chapel—perhaps he bumped her elbow as they stood staring up at the glorious ceiling. A thousand pardons! Ah, an artist too? In five minutes they were chattering like mad—she in bad French and exquisite English; he in bad English and exquisite French. He knew Rome—its pictures, its glories, its history—as only an Italian can. And he taught her art, and he taught her Italian, and he taught her love.

And so they were married, or ostensibly married, though Mary did not know the truth until three months later when he left her quite as casually as he had met her, taking with him the little hoard, and Mary's English trinkets, and Mary's English roses, and Mary's broken pride.

So! There was no going back to the fussy father or the spinster sister. She came very near resting her head on Father Tiber's breast in those days. She would sit in the great galleries for hours, staring at the wonder-works. Then, one day, again in the Sistine Chapel, a fussy little American woman had approached her, her eyes snapping. Mary was sketching, or trying to.

"Do you speak English?"

"I am English," said Mary.

The feathers in the hat of the fussy little woman quivered.

"Then tell me, is this ceiling by Raphael?"

"Ceiling!" gasped Mary Gowd. "Raphael!"

Then, very gently, she gave the master's name.

"Of course!" snapped the excited little American. "I'm one of a party of eight. We're all school-teachers And this guide"—she waved a hand in the direction of a rapt little group standing in the

138

agonising position the ceiling demands—"just informed us that the ceiling is by Raphael. And we're paying him ten lire!"

"Won't you sit here?" Mary Gowd made a place for her. "I'll tell you."

And she did tell her, finding a certain relief from her pain in unfolding to this commonplace little woman the glory of the masterpiece among masterpieces.

"Why—why," gasped her listener, who had long since beckoned the other seven with frantic finger, "how beautifully you explain it! How much you know! Oh, why can't they talk as you do?" she wailed, her eyes full of contempt for the despised guide.

"I am happy to have helped you," said Mary Gowd.

"Helped! Why, there are hundreds of Americans who would give anything to have some one like you to be with them in Rome."

Mary Gowd's whole body stiffened. She stared fixedly at the grateful little American school-teacher.

"Some one like me—"

The little teacher blushed very red.

"I beg your pardon. I wasn't thinking. Of course you don't need to do any such work, but I just couldn't help saying—"

"But I do need work," interrupted Mary Gowd. She stood up, her cheeks pink again for the moment, her eyes bright. "I thank you. Oh, I thank you!"

"You thank me!" faltered the American.

But Mary Gowd had folded her sketchbook and was off, through the vestibule, down the splendid corridor, past the giant Swiss guard, to the noisy, sunny Piazza di San Pietro.

That had been fifteen years ago. She had taken her guide's examinations and passed them. She knew her Rome from the crypt of St. Peter's to the top of the Janiculum Hill; from the Campagna to Tivoli. She read and studied and learned. She delved into the past and brought up strange and interesting truths. She could tell you weird stories of those white marble men who lay so peacefully beneath St. Peter's dome, their ringed hands crossed on their breasts. She learned to juggle dates with an ease that brought gasps from her American clients, with their history that went back little more than one hundred years.

She learned to designate as new anything that failed to have its origin stamped B.C.; and the Magnificent Augustus, he who boasted of finding Rome brick and leaving it marble, was a mere nouveau riche with his miserable A.D. 14.

She was as much at home in the Thermae of Caracalla as you in your white-and-blue-tiled bath. She could juggle the history of emperors with one hand and the scandals of half a dozen kings with the other. No ruin was too unimportant for her attention—no picture too faded for her research. She had the centuries at her tongue's end. Michelangelo and Canova were her brothers in art, and Rome was to her as your back-garden patch is to you.

Mary Gowd hated this Rome as only an English woman can who has spent fifteen years in that nest of intrigue. She fought the whole race of Roman guides day after day. She no longer turned sick and faint when they hissed after her vile Italian epithets that her American or English clients quite failed to understand. Quite unconcernedly she would jam down the lever of the taximeter the wily Italian cabby had pulled only halfway so that the meter might register double. And when that foul-mouthed one crowned his heap of abuse by screaming "Camorrista! Camor-r-rista!" at her, she would merely shrug her shoulders and say "Andate presto!" to show him she was above quarrelling with a cabman.

She ate eggs and bread, and drank the red wine, never having conquered her disgust for Italian meat since first she saw the filthy carcasses, fly-infested, dust-covered, loathsome, being carted through the swarming streets.

It was six o'clock of an evening early in March when Mary Gowd went home to the murky little room in the Via Babbuino. She was too tired to notice the sunset. She was too tired to smile at the red-eyed baby of the cobbler's wife, who lived in the rear. She was too tired to ask Tina for the letters that seldom came. It had been a particularly trying day, spent with a party of twenty Germans, who had said "Herrlich!" when she showed them the marvels of the Vatican and "Kolossal!" at the grandeur of the Colosseum and, for the rest, had kept their noses buried in their Baedekers.

She groped her way cautiously down the black hall. Tina had a habit of leaving sundry brushes, pans or babies lying about. After the warmth of the March sun outdoors the house was cold with that clammy, penetrating, tomblike chill of the Italian home.

"Tina!" she called.

From the rear of the house came a cackle of voices. Tina was gossiping. There was no smell of supper in the air. Mary Gowd shrugged patient shoulders. Then, before taking off the dowdy hat, before removing the white cotton gloves, she went to the window that overlooked the noisy Via Babbuino, closed the massive wooden shutters, fastened the heavy windows and drew the thick curtains. Then she stood a moment, eyes shut. In that little room the roar of Rome was tamed to a dull humming. Mary Gowd, born and bred amid the green of Northern England, had never become hardened to the maddening noises of the Via Babbuino: The rattle and clatter of cab wheels; the clack-clack of thousands of iron-shod hoofs; the shrill, high cry of the street venders; the blasts of motor horns that seemed to rend the narrow street; the roar and rumble of the electric trams; the wail of fretful babies; the chatter of gossiping women; and above and through and below it all the cracking of the cabman's whip—that sceptre of the Roman cabby, that wand which is one part whip and nine parts crack. Sometimes it seemed to Mary Gowd that her brain was seared and welted by the pistol-shot reports of those eternal whips.

She came forward now and lighted a candle that stood on the table and another on the dresser. Their dim light seemed to make dimmer the dark little room. She looked about with a little shiver. Then she sank into the chintz-covered chair that was the one bit of England in the sombre chamber. She took off the dusty black velvet hat, passed a hand over her hair with a gesture that was more tired than tidy, and sat back, her eyes shut, her body inert, her head sagging on her breast.

The voices in the back of the house had ceased. From the kitchen came the slipslop of Tina's slovenly feet. Mary Gowd opened her eyes and sat up very straight as Tina stood in the doorway. There was nothing picturesque about Tina. Tina was not one of those olive-tinted, melting-eyed daughters of Italy that one meets in fiction. Looking at her yellow skin and her wrinkles and her coarse hands, one wondered whether she was fifty, or sixty, or one hundred, as is the way with Italian women of Tina's class at thirty-five.

Ah, the signora was tired! She smiled pityingly. Tired! Not at all, Mary Gowd assured her briskly. She knew that Tina despised her because she worked like a man.

"Something fine for supper?" Mary Gowd asked mockingly. Her Italian was like that of the Romans themselves, so soft, so liquid, so perfect.

Tina nodded vigorously, her long earrings shaking.

"Vitello"—she began, her tongue clinging lovingly to the double l sound—"Vee-tail-loh—"

"Ugh!" shuddered Mary Gowd. That eternal veal and mutton, pinkish, flabby, sickening!

"What then?" demanded the outraged Tina.

Mary Gowd stood up, making gestures, hat in hand.

"Clotted cream, with strawberries," she said in English, an unknown language, which always roused Tina to fury. "And a steak—a real steak of real beef, three inches thick and covered with onions fried in butter. And creamed chicken, and English hothouse tomatoes, and fresh peaches and little hot rolls, and coffee that isn't licorice and ink, and—and—"

141

Tina's dangling earrings disappeared in her shoulders. Her outspread palms were eloquent.

"Crazy, these English!" said the shoulders and palms. "Mad!"

Mary Gowd threw her hat on the bed, pushed aside a screen and busied herself with a little alcohol stove.

"I shall prepare an omelet," she said over her shoulder in Italian. "Also, I have here bread and wine."

"Ugh!" granted Tina.

"Ugh, veal!" grunted Mary Gowd. Then, as Tina's flapping feet turned away: "Oh, Tina! Letters?"

Tina fumbled at the bosom of her gown, thought deeply and drew out a crumpled envelope. It had been opened and clumsily closed again. Fifteen years ago Mary Gowd would have raged. Now she shrugged philosophic shoulders. Tina stole hairpins, opened letters that she could not hope to decipher, rummaged bureau drawers, rifled cupboards and fingered books; but then, so did most of the other Tinas in Rome. What use to complain?

Mary Gowd opened the thumb-marked letter, bringing it close to the candlelight. As she read, a smile appeared.

"Huh! Gregg," she said, "Americans!" She glanced again at the hotel letterhead on the stationery—the best hotel in Naples. "Americans—and rich!"

The pleased little smile lingered as she beat the omelet briskly for her supper.

The Henry D. Greggs arrived in Rome on the two o'clock train from Naples. And all the Roman knights of the waving palm espied them from afar and hailed them with whoops of joy. The season was still young and the Henry D. Greggs looked like money—not Italian money, which is reckoned in lire, but American money, which mounts grandly to dollars. The postcard men in the Piazza delle Terme sped after their motor taxi. The swarthy brigand, with his wooden box of tawdry souvenirs, marked them as they rode past. The cripple who lurked behind a pillar in the colonnade threw aside his coat with a practised hitch of his shoulder to reveal the sickeningly maimed arm that was his stock in trade.

Mr. and Mrs. Henry D. Gregg had left their comfortable home in Batavia, Illinois, with its sleeping porch, veranda and lawn, and seven-passenger car; with its two glistening bathrooms, and its Oriental rugs, and its laundry in the basement, and its Sunday fried chicken and ice cream, because they felt that Miss Eleanora Gregg ought to have the benefit of foreign travel. Miss Eleanora Gregg thought so too: in fact, she had thought so first.

Her name was Eleanora, but her parents called her Tweetie, which really did not sound so bad as it might if Tweetie had been

142

one whit less pretty. Tweetie was so amazingly, Americanly pretty that she could have triumphed over a pet name twice as absurd.

The Greggs came to Rome, as has been stated, at two P.M. Wednesday. By two P.M. Thursday Tweetie had bought a pair of long, dangling earrings, a costume with a Roman striped collar and sash, and had learned to loll back in her cab in imitation of the dashing, black-eyed, sallow women she had seen driving on the Pincio. By Thursday evening she was teasing Papa Gregg for a spray of white aigrets, such as those same languorous ladies wore in feathery mists atop their hats.

"But, Tweet," argued Papa Gregg, "what's the use? You can't take them back with you. Custom-house regulations forbid it."

The rather faded but smartly dressed Mrs. Gregg asserted herself:

"They're barbarous! We had moving pictures at the club showing how they're torn from the mother birds. No daughter of mine—"

"I don't care!" retorted Tweetie. "They're perfectly stunning; and I'm going to have them."

And she had them—not that the aigret incident is important; but it may serve to place the Greggs in their respective niches.

At eleven o'clock Friday morning Mary Gowd called at the Gregg's hotel, according to appointment. In far-away Batavia, Illinois, Mrs. Gregg had heard of Mary Gowd. And Mary Gowd, with her knowledge of everything Roman—from the Forum to the best place at which to buy pearls—was to be the staff on which the Greggs were to lean.

"My husband," said Mrs. Gregg; "my daughter Twee—er— Eleanora. We've heard such wonderful things of you from my dear friend Mrs. Melville Peters, of Batavia."

"Ah, yes!" exclaimed Mary Gowd. "A most charming person, Mrs. Peters."

"After she came home from Europe she read the most wonderful paper on Rome before the Women's West End Culture Club, of Batavia. We're affiliated with the National Federation of Women's Clubs, as you probably know; and—"

"Now, Mother," interrupted Henry Gregg, "the lady can't be interested in your club."

"Oh, but I am!" exclaimed Mary Gowd very vivaciously. "Enormously!"

Henry Gregg eyed her through his cigar smoke with suddenly narrowed lids.

"M-m-m! Well, let's get to the point anyway. I know Tweetie here is dying to see St. Peter's, and all that."

143

Tweetie had settled back inscrutably after one comprehensive, disdainful look at Mary Gowd's suit, hat, gloves and shoes. Now she sat up, her bewitching face glowing with interest.

"Tell me," she said, "what do they call those officers with the long pale-blue capes and the silver helmets and the swords? And the ones in dark-blue uniform with the maroon stripe at the side of the trousers? And do they ever mingle with the—that is, there was one of the blue capes here at tea yesterday—"

Papa Gregg laughed a great, comfortable laugh.

"Oh, so that's where you were staring yesterday, young lady! I thought you acted kind of absent-minded." He got up to walk over and pinch Tweetie's blushing cheek.

So it was that Mary Gowd began the process of pouring the bloody, religious, wanton, pious, thrilling, dreadful history of Rome into the pretty and unheeding ear of Tweetie Gregg.

On the fourth morning after that introductory meeting Mary Gowd arrived at the hotel at ten, as usual, to take charge of her party for the day. She encountered them in the hotel foyer, an animated little group centred about a very tall, very dashing, very black-mustachioed figure who wore a long pale blue cape thrown gracefully over one shoulder as only an Italian officer can wear such a garment. He was looking down into the brilliantly glowing face of the pretty Eleanora, and the pretty Eleanora was looking up at him; and Pa and Ma Gregg were standing by, placidly pleased.

A grim little line appeared about Miss Gowd's mouth. Blue Cape's black eyes saw it, even as he bent low over Mary Gowd's hand at the words of introduction.

"Oh, Miss Gowd," pouted Tweetie, "it's too bad you haven't a telephone. You see, we shan't need you to-day."

"No?" said Miss Gowd, and glanced at Blue Cape.

"No; Signor Caldini says it's much too perfect a day to go poking about among old ruins and things."

Henry D. Gregg cleared his throat and took up the explanation. "Seems the—er—Signor thinks it would be just the thing to take a touring car and drive to Tivoli, and have a bite of lunch there."

"And come back in time to see the Colosseum by moonlight!" put in Tweetie ecstatically.

"Oh, yes!" said Mary Gowd.

Pa Gregg looked at his watch.

"Well, I'll be running along," he said. Then, in answer to something in Mary Gowd's eyes: "I'm not going to Tivoli, you see. I met a man from Chicago here at the hotel. He and I are going to chin awhile this morning. And Mrs. Gregg and his wife are going on

144

a shopping spree. Say, ma, if you need any more money speak up now, because I'm—"

Mary Gowd caught his coat sleeve.

"One moment!"

Her voice was very low. "You mean—you mean Miss Eleanora will go to Tivoli and to the Colosseum alone—with—with Signor Caldini?"

Henry Gregg smiled indulgently.

"The young folks always run round alone at home. We've got our own car at home in Batavia, but Tweetie's beaus are always driving up for her in—"

Mary Gowd turned her head so that only Henry Gregg could hear what she said.

"Step aside for just one moment. I must talk to you."

"Well, what?"

"Do as I say," whispered Mary Gowd.

Something of her earnestness seemed to convey a meaning to Henry Gregg.

"Just wait a minute, folks," he said to the group of three, and joined Mary Gowd, who had chosen a seat a dozen paces away. "What's the trouble?" he asked jocularly. "Hope you're not offended because Tweet said we didn't need you to-day. You know young folks—"

"They must not go alone," said Mary Gowd.

"But—"

"This is not America. This is Italy—this Caldini is an Italian."

"Why, look here; Signor Caldini was introduced to us last night. His folks really belong to the nobility."

"I know; I know," interrupted Mary Gowd. "I tell you they cannot go alone. Please believe me! I have been fifteen years in Rome. Noble or not, Caldini is an Italian. I ask you"—she had clasped her hands and was looking pleadingly up into his face—"I beg of you, let me go with them. You need not pay me to-day. You—"

Henry Gregg looked at her very thoughtfully and a little puzzled. Then he glanced over at the group again, with Blue Cape looking down so eagerly into Tweetie's exquisite face and Tweetie looking up so raptly into Blue Cape's melting eyes and Ma Gregg standing so placidly by. He turned again to Mary Gowd's earnest face.

"Well, maybe you're right. They do seem to use chaperons in Europe—duennas, or whatever you call 'em. Seems a nice kind of chap, though."

He strolled back to the waiting group. From her seat Mary Gowd heard Mrs. Gregg's surprised exclamation, saw Tweetie's pout, understood Caldini's shrug and sneer. There followed a little burst of conversation. Then, with a little frown which melted into a smile for Blue Cape, Tweetie went to her room for motor coat and trifles that the long day's outing demanded. Mrs. Gregg, still voluble, followed.

Blue Cape, with a long look at Mary Gowd, went out to confer with the porter about the motor. Papa Gregg, hand in pockets, cigar tilted, eyes narrowed, stood irresolutely in the centre of the great, gaudy foyer. Then, with a decisive little hunch of his shoulders, he came back to where Mary Gowd sat.

"Did you say you've been fifteen years in Rome?"

"Fifteen years," answered Mary Gowd.

Henry D. Gregg took his cigar from his mouth and regarded it thoughtfully.

"Well, that's quite a spell. Must like it here." Mary Gowd said nothing. "Can't say I'm crazy about it—that is, as a place to live. I said to Mother last night: 'Little old Batavia's good enough for Henry D.' Of course it's a grand education, travelling, especially for Tweetie. Funny, I always thought the fruit in Italy was regular hothouse stuff—thought the streets would just be lined with trees all hung with big, luscious oranges. But, Lord! Here we are at the best hotel in Rome, and the fruit is worse than the stuff the pushcart men at home feed to their families—little wizened bananas and oranges. Still, it's grand here in Rome for Tweetie. I can't stay long— just ran away from business to bring 'em over; but I'd like Tweetie to stay in Italy until she learns the lingo. Sings, too—Tweetie does; and she and Ma think they'll have her voice cultivated over here. They'll stay here quite a while, I guess."

"Then you will not be here with them?" asked Mary Gowd.

"Me? No."

They sat silent for a moment.

"I suppose you're crazy about Rome," said Henry Gregg again. "There's a lot of culture here, and history, and all that; and—"

"I hate Rome!" said Mary Gowd.

Henry Gregg stared at her in bewilderment.

"Then why in Sam Hill don't you go back to England?"

"I'm thirty-seven years old. That's one reason why. And I look older. Oh, yes, I do. Thanks just the same. There are too many women in England already—too many half-starving shabby genteel. I earn enough to live on here—that is, I call it living. You couldn't. In the bad season, when there are no tourists, I live on a lire a day, including my rent."

Henry Gregg stood up.

146

"My land! Why don't you come to America?" He waved his arms. "America!"

Mary Gowd's brick-red cheeks grew redder.

"America!" she echoed. "When I see American tourists here throwing pennies in the Fountain of Trevi, so that they'll come back to Rome, I want to scream. By the time I save enough money to go to America I'll be an old woman and it will be too late. And if I did contrive to scrape together enough for my passage over I couldn't go to the United States in these clothes. I've seen thousands of American women here. If they look like that when they're just travelling about, what do they wear at home!"

"Clothes?" inquired Henry Gregg, mystified. "What's wrong with your clothes?"

"Everything! I've seen them look at my suit, which hunches in the back and strains across the front, and is shiny at the seams. And my gloves! And my hat! Well, even though I am English I know how frightful my hat is."

"You're a smart woman," said Henry D. Gregg.

"Not smart enough," retorted Mary Gowd, "or I shouldn't be here."

The two stood up as Tweetie came toward them from the lift. Tweetie pouted again at sight of Mary Gowd, but the pout cleared as Blue Cape, his arrangements completed, stood in the doorway, splendid hat in hand.

It was ten o'clock when the three returned from Tivoli and the Colosseum—Mary Gowd silent and shabbier than ever from the dust of the road; Blue Cape smiling; Tweetie frankly pettish. Pa and Ma Gregg were listening to the after-dinner concert in the foyer.

"Was it romantic—the Colosseum, I mean—by moonlight?" asked Ma Gregg, patting Tweetie's cheek and trying not to look uncomfortable as Blue Cape kissed her hand.

"Romantic!" snapped Tweetie. "It was as romantic as Main Street on Circus Day. Hordes of people tramping about like buffaloes. Simply swarming with tourists—German ones. One couldn't find a single ruin to sit on. Romantic!" She glared at the silent Mary Gowd.

There was a strange little glint in Mary Gowd's eyes, and the grim line was there about the mouth again, grimmer than it had been in the morning.

"You will excuse me?" she said. "I am very tired. I will say good night."

"And I," announced Caldini.

Mary Gowd turned swiftly to look at him.

"You!" said Tweetie Gregg.

147

"I trust that I may have the very great happiness to see you in the morning," went on Caldini in his careful English. "I cannot permit Signora Gowd to return home alone through the streets of Rome." He bowed low and elaborately over the hands of the two women.

"Oh, well; for that matter—" began Henry Gregg gallantly.

Caldini raised a protesting, white-gloved hand.

"I cannot permit it."

He bowed again and looked hard at Mary Gowd. Mary Gowd returned the look. The brick-red had quite faded from her cheeks. Then, with a nod, she turned and walked toward the door. Blue Cape, sword clanking, followed her.

In silence he handed her into the fiacre. In silence he seated himself beside her. Then he leaned very close.

"I will talk in this damned English," he began, "that the pig of a fiaccheraio may not understand. This—this Gregg, he is very rich, like all Americans. And the little Eleanora! Bellissima! You must not stand in my way. It is not good." Mary Dowd sat silent. "You will help me. To-day you were not kind. There will be much money— money for me; also for you."

Fifteen years before—ten years before—she would have died sooner than listen to a plan such as he proposed; but fifteen years of Rome blunts one's English sensibilities. Fifteen years of privation dulls one's moral sense. And money meant America. And little Tweetie Gregg had not lowered her voice or her laugh when she spoke that afternoon of Mary Gowd's absurd English fringe and her red wrists above her too-short gloves.

"How much?" asked Mary Gowd. He named a figure. She laughed.

"More—much more!"

He named another figure; then another.

"You will put it down on paper," said Mary Gowd, "and sign your name—to-morrow."

They drove the remainder of the way in silence. At her door in the Via Babbuino:

"You mean to marry her?" asked Mary Gowd.

Blue Cape shrugged eloquent shoulders:

"I think not," he said quite simply.

It was to be the Appian Way the next morning, with a stop at the Catacombs. Mary Gowd reached the hotel very early, but not so early as Caldini.

"Think the five of us can pile into one carriage?" boomed Henry Gregg cheerily.

"A little crowded, I think," said Mary Gowd, "for such a long

148

drive. May I suggest that we three"—she smiled on Henry Gregg and his wife—"take this larger carriage, while Miss Eleanora and Signor Caldini follow in the single cab?"

A lightning message from Blue Cape's eyes.

"Yes; that would be nice!" cooed Tweetie.

So it was arranged. Mary Gowd rather outdid herself as a guide that morning. She had a hundred little intimate tales at her tongue's end. She seemed fairly to people those old ruins again with the men and women of a thousand years ago. Even Tweetie—little frivolous, indifferent Tweetie—was impressed and interested.

As they were returning to the carriages after inspecting the Baths of Caracalla, Tweetie even skipped ahead and slipped her hand for a moment into Mary Gowd's.

"You're simply wonderful!" she said almost shyly. "You make things sound so real. And—and I'm sorry I was so nasty to you yesterday at Tivoli."

Mary Dowd looked down at the glowing little face. A foolish little face it was, but very, very pretty, and exquisitely young and fresh and sweet. Tweetie dropped her voice to a whisper:

"You should hear him pronounce my name. It is like music when he says it—El-e-a-no-ra; like that. And aren't his kid gloves always beautifully white? Why, the boys back home—"

Mary Gowd was still staring down at her. She lifted the slim, ringed little hand which lay within her white-cotton paw and stared at that too.

Then with a jerk she dropped the girl's hand and squared her shoulders like a soldier, so that the dowdy blue suit strained more than ever at its seams; and the line that had settled about her mouth the night before faded slowly, as though a muscle too tightly drawn had relaxed.

In the carriages they were seated as before. The horses started up, with the smaller cab but a dozen paces behind. Mary Gowd leaned forward. She began to speak—her voice very low, her accent clearly English, her brevity wonderfully American.

"Listen to me!" she said. "You must leave Rome to-night!"

"Leave Rome to-night!" echoed the Greggs as though rehearsing a duet.

"Be quiet! You must not shout like that. I say you must go away."

Mamma Gregg opened her lips and shut them, wordless for once. Henry Gregg laid one big hand on his wife's shaking knees and eyed Mary Gowd very quietly.

"I don't get you," he said.

149

Mary Gowd looked straight at him as she said what she had to say:

"There are things in Rome you cannot understand. You could not understand unless you lived here many years. I lived here many months before I learned to step meekly off into the gutter to allow a man to pass on the narrow sidewalk. You must take your pretty daughter and go away. To-night! No—let me finish. I will tell you what happened to me fifteen years ago, and I will tell you what this Caldini has in his mind. You will believe me and forgive me; and promise me that you will go quietly away."

When she finished Mrs. Gregg was white-faced and luckily too frightened to weep. Henry Gregg started up in the carriage, his fists white-knuckled, his lean face turned toward the carriage crawling behind.

"Sit down!" commanded Mary Gowd. She jerked his sleeve. "Sit down!"

Henry Gregg sat down slowly. Then he wet his lips slightly and smiled.

"Oh, bosh!" he said. "This—this is the twentieth century and we're Americans, and it's broad daylight. Why, I'll lick the—"

"This is Rome," interrupted Mary Gowd quietly, "and you will do nothing of the kind, because he would make you pay for that too, and it would be in all the papers; and your pretty daughter would hang her head in shame forever." She put one hand on Henry Gregg's sleeve. "You do not know! You do not! Promise me you will go." The tears sprang suddenly to her English blue eyes. "Promise me! Promise me!"

"Henry!" cried Mamma Gregg, very grey-faced. "Promise, Henry!"

"I promise," said Henry Gregg, and he turned away.

Mary Gowd sank back in her seat and shut her eyes for a moment.

"Presto!" she said to the half-sleeping driver. Then she waved a gay hand at the carriage in the rear. "Presto!" she called, smiling. "Presto!"

At six o'clock Mary Gowd entered the little room in the Via Babbuino. She went first to the window, drew the heavy curtains. The roar of Rome was hushed to a humming. She lighted a candle that stood on the table. Its dim light emphasized the gloom. She took off the battered black velvet hat and sank into the chintz-covered English chair. Tina stood in the doorway. Mary Gowd sat up with a jerk.

"Letters, Tina?"

150

Tina thought deeply, fumbled at the bosom of her gown and drew out a sealed envelope grudgingly.

Mary Gowd broke the seal, glanced at the letter. Then, under Tina's startled gaze, she held it to the flaming candle and watched it burn.

"What is it that you do?" demanded Tina.

Mary Gowd smiled.

"You have heard of America?"

"America! A thousand—a million time! My brother Luigi—"

"Naturally! This, then"—Mary Gowd deliberately gathered up the ashes into a neat pile and held them in her hand, a crumpled heap—"this then, Tina, is my trip to America."

X

SOPHY-AS-SHE-MIGHT-HAVE-BEEN

The key to the heart of Paris is love. He whose key-ring lacks that open sesame never really sees the city, even though he dwell in the shadow of the Sorbonne and comprehend the fiacre French of the Paris cabman. Some there are who craftily open the door with a skeleton key; some who ruthlessly batter the panels; some who achieve only a wax impression, which proves to be useless. There are many who travel no farther than the outer gates. You will find them staring blankly at the stone walls; and their plaint is:

"What do they find to rave about in this town?"

Sophy Gold had been eight days in Paris and she had not so much as peeked through the key-hole. In a vague way she realised that she was seeing Paris as a blind man sees the sun—feeling its warmth, conscious of its white light beating on the eyeballs, but never actually beholding its golden glory.

This was Sophy Gold's first trip to Paris, and her heart and soul and business brain were intent on buying the shrewdest possible bill of lingerie and infants' wear for her department at Schiff Brothers', Chicago; but Sophy under-estimated the powers of those three guiding parts. While heart, soul, and brain were bent dutifully and indefatigably on the lingerie and infants'-wear job they also were registering a series of kaleidoscopic outside impressions.

As she drove from her hotel to the wholesale district, and from the wholesale district to her hotel, there had flashed across her consciousness the picture of the chic little modistes' models and ouvrières slipping out at noon to meet their lovers on the corner, to sit over their sirop or wine at some little near-by café, hands clasped, eyes glowing.

Stepping out of the lift to ask for her room key, she had come on the black-gowned floor clerk, deep in murmured conversation with the valet, and she had seemed not to see Sophy at all as she groped subconsciously for the key along the rows of keyboxes. She had seen the workmen in their absurdly baggy corduroy trousers and grimy shirts strolling along arm in arm with the women of their class—those untidy women with the tidy hair. Bareheaded and happy, they strolled along, a strange contrast to the glitter of the fashionable boulevard, stopping now and then to gaze wide-eyed at a million-franc necklace in a jeweller's window; then on again with a laugh and a shrug and a caress. She had seen the silent couples in the Tuileries Gardens at twilight.

Once, in the Bois de Boulogne, a slim, sallow élégant had bent for what seemed an interminable time over a white hand that was stretched from the window of a motor car. He was standing at the curb; in either greeting or parting, and his eyes were fastened on other eyes within the car even while his lips pressed the white hand.

Then one evening—Sophy reddened now at memory of it—she had turned a quiet corner and come on a boy and a girl. The girl was shabby and sixteen; the boy pale, voluble, smiling.

Evidently they were just parting. Suddenly, as she passed, the boy had caught the girl in his arms there on the street corner in the daylight, and had kissed her—not the quick, resounding smack of casual leave-taking, but a long, silent kiss that left the girl limp.

Sophy stood rooted to the spot, between horror and fascination. The boy's arm brought the girl upright and set her on her feet.

She took a long breath, straightened her hat, and ran on to rejoin her girl friend awaiting her calmly up the street. She was not even flushed; but Sophy was. Sophy was blushing hotly and burning uncomfortably, so that her eyes smarted.

Just after her late dinner on the eighth day of her Paris stay, Sophy Gold was seated in the hotel lobby. Paris thronged with American business buyers—those clever, capable, shrewd-eyed women who swarm on the city in June and strip it of its choicest flowers, from ball gowns to back combs. Sophy tried to pick them from the multitude that swept past her. It was not difficult. The women visitors to Paris in June drop easily into their proper slots.

There were the pretty American girls and their marvellously young-looking mammas, both out-Frenching the French in their efforts to look Parisian; there were rows of fat, placid, jewel-laden Argentine mothers, each with a watchful eye on her black-eyed, volcanically calm, be-powdered daughter; and there were the buyers, miraculously dressy in next week's styles in suits and hats— of the old-girl type most of them, alert, self-confident, capable.

They usually returned to their hotels at six, limping a little, dog-tired; but at sight of the brightly lighted, gay hotel foyer they would straighten up like war-horses scenting battle and achieve an effective entrance from the doorway to the lift.

In all that big, busy foyer Sophy Gold herself was the one person distinctly out of the picture. One did not know where to place her. To begin with, a woman as irrevocably, irredeemably ugly as Sophy was an anachronism in Paris. She belonged to the gargoyle period. You found yourself speculating on whether it was her mouth or her nose that made her so devastatingly plain, only to bring up at

153

her eyes and find that they alone were enough to wreck any ambitions toward beauty. You knew before you saw it that her hair would be limp and straggling.

You sensed without a glance at them that her hands would be bony, with unlovely knuckles.

The Fates, grinning, had done all that. Her Chicago tailor and milliner had completed the work. Sophy had not been in Paris ten minutes before she noticed that they were wearing 'em long and full. Her coat was short and her skirt scant. Her hat was small. The Paris windows were full of large and graceful black velvets of the Lillian Russell school.

"May I sit here?"

Sophy looked up into the plump, pink, smiling face of one of those very women of the buyer type on whom she had speculated ten minutes before—a good-natured face with shrewd, twinkling eyes. At sight of it you forgave her her skittish white-kid-topped shoes.

"Certainly," smiled Sophy, and moved over a bit on the little French settee.

The plump woman sat down heavily. In five minutes Sophy was conscious she was being stared at surreptitiously. In ten minutes she was uncomfortably conscious of it. In eleven minutes she turned her head suddenly and caught the stout woman's eyes fixed on her, with just the baffled, speculative expression she had expected to find in them. Sophy Gold had caught that look in many women's eyes. She smiled grimly now.

"Don't try it," she said, "It's no use."

The pink, plump face flushed pinker.

"Don't try—"

"Don't try to convince yourself that if I wore my hair differently, or my collar tighter, or my hat larger, it would make a difference in my looks. It wouldn't. It's hard to believe that I'm as homely as I look, but I am. I've watched women try to dress me in as many as eleven mental changes of costume before they gave me up."

"But I didn't mean—I beg your pardon—you mustn't think—"

"Oh, that's all right! I used to struggle, but I'm used to it now. It took me a long time to realise that this was my real face and the only kind I could ever expect to have."

The plump woman's kindly face grew kinder.

"But you're really not so—"

"Oh, yes, I am. Upholstering can't change me. There are various kinds of homely women—some who are hideous in blue maybe, but who soften up in pink. Then there's the one you read about, whose features are lighted up now and then by one of those rare, sweet

154

smiles that make her plain face almost beautiful. But once in a while you find a woman who is ugly in any colour of the rainbow; who is ugly smiling or serious, talking or in repose, hair down low or hair done high—just plain dyed-in-the-wool, sewed-in-the-seam homely. I'm that kind. Here for a visit?"

"I'm a buyer," said the plump woman.

"Yes; I thought so. I'm the lingerie and infants'-wear buyer for Schiff, Chicago."

"A buyer!" The plump woman's eyes jumped uncontrollably again to Sophy Gold's scrambled features. "Well! My name's Miss Morrissey—Ella Morrissey. Millinery for Abelman's, Pittsburgh. And it's no snap this year, with the shops showing postage-stamp hats one day and cart-wheels the next. I said this morning that I envied the head of the tinware department. Been over often?"

Sophy made the shamefaced confession of the novice: "My first trip."

The inevitable answer came:

"Your first! Really! This is my twentieth crossing. Been coming over twice a year for ten years. If there's anything I can tell you, just ask. The first buying trip to Paris is hard until you know the ropes. Of course you love this town?"

Sophy Gold sat silent a moment, hesitating. Then she turned a puzzled face toward Miss Morrissey.

"What do people mean when they say they love Paris?"

Ella Morrissey stared. Then a queer look came into her face—a pitying sort of look. The shrewd eyes softened. She groped for words.

"When I first came over here, ten years ago, I—well, it would have been easier to tell you then. I don't know—there's something about Paris—something in the atmosphere—something in the air. It—it makes you do foolish things. It makes you feel queer and light and happy. It's nothing you can put your finger on and say 'That's it!' But it's there."

"Huh!" grunted Sophy Gold. "I suppose I could save myself a lot of trouble by saying that I feel it; but I don't. I simply don't react to this town. The only things I really like in Paris are the Tomb of Napoleon, the Seine at night, and the strawberry tart you get at Vian's. Of course the parks and boulevards are a marvel, but you can't expect me to love a town for that. I'm no landscape gardener."

That pitying look deepened in Miss Morrissey's eyes.

"Have you been out in the evening? The restaurants! The French women! The life!"

Sophy Gold caught the pitying look and interpreted it without

155

resentment; but there was perhaps an added acid in her tone when she spoke.

"I'm here to buy—not to play. I'm thirty years old, and it's taken me ten years to work my way up to foreign buyer. I've worked. And I wasn't handicapped any by my beauty. I've made up my mind that I'm going to buy the smoothest-moving line of French lingerie and infants' wear that Schiff Brothers ever had."

Miss Morrissey checked her.

"But, my dear girl, haven't you been round at all?"

"Oh, a little; as much as a woman can go round alone in Paris—even a homely woman. But I've been disappointed every time. The noise drives me wild, to begin with. Not that I'm not used to noise. I am. I can stand for a town that roars, like Chicago. But this city yelps. I've been going round to the restaurants a little. At noon I always picked the restaurant I wanted, so long as I had to pay for the lunch of the commissionnaire who was with me anyway. Can you imagine any man at home letting a woman pay for his meals the way those shrimpy Frenchmen do?

"Well, the restaurants were always jammed full of Americans. The men of the party would look over the French menu in a helpless sort of way, and then they'd say: 'What do you say to a nice big steak with French-fried potatoes?' The waiter would give them a disgusted look and put in the order. They might just as well have been eating at a quick lunch place. As for the French women, every time I picked what I took to be a real Parisienne coming toward me I'd hear her say as she passed: 'Henry, I'm going over to the Galerie Lafayette. I'll meet you at the American Express at twelve. And, Henry, I think I'll need some more money.'"

Miss Ella Morrissey's twinkling eyes almost disappeared in wrinkles of laughter; but Sophy Gold was not laughing. As she talked she gazed grimly ahead at the throng that shifted and glittered and laughed and chattered all about her.

"I stopped work early one afternoon and went over across the river. Well! They may be artistic, but they all looked as though they needed a shave and a hair-cut and a square meal. And the girls!"

Ella Morrissey raised a plump, protesting palm.

"Now look here, child, Paris isn't so much a city as a state of mind. To enjoy it you've got to forget you're an American. Don't look at it from a Chicago, Illinois, viewpoint. Just try to imagine you're a mixture of Montmartre girl, Latin Quarter model and duchess from the Champs Élysées. Then you'll get it."

"Get it!" retorted Sophy Gold. "If I could do that I wouldn't be buying lingerie and infants' wear for Schiffs'. I'd be crowding Duse and Bernhardt and Mrs. Fiske off the boards."

156

Miss Morrissey sat silent and thoughtful, rubbing one fat forefinger slowly up and down her knee. Suddenly she turned.

"Don't be angry—but have you ever been in love?"

"Look at me!" replied Sophy Gold simply. Miss Morrissey reddened a little. "As head of the lingerie section I've selected trousseaus for I don't know how many Chicago brides; but I'll never have to decide whether I'll have pink or blue ribbons for my own."

With a little impulsive gesture Ella Morrissey laid one hand on the shoulder of her new acquaintance.

"Come on up and visit me, will you? I made them give me an inside room, away from the noise. Too many people down here. Besides, I'd like to take off this armour-plate of mine and get comfortable. When a girl gets as old and fat as I am—"

"There are some letters I ought to get out," Sophy Gold protested feebly.

"Yes; I know. We all have; but there's such a thing as overdoing this duty to the firm. You get up at six to-morrow morning and slap off those letters. They'll come easier and sound less tired."

They made for the lift; but at its very gates:

"Hello, little girl!" cried a masculine voice; and a detaining hand was laid on Ella Morrissey's plump shoulder.

That lady recognised the voice and the greeting before she turned to face their source. Max Tack, junior partner in the firm of Tack Brothers, Lingerie and Infants' Wear, New York, held out an eager hand.

"Hello, Max!" said Miss Morrissey not too cordially. "My, aren't you dressy!"

He was undeniably dressy—not that only, but radiant with the self-confidence born of good looks, of well-fitting evening clothes, of a fresh shave, of glistening nails. Max Tack, of the hard eye and the soft smile, of the slim figure and the semi-bald head, of the flattering tongue and the business brain, bent his attention full on the very plain Miss Sophy Gold.

"Aren't you going to introduce me?" he demanded.

Miss Morrissey introduced them, buyer fashion—names, business connection, and firms.

"I knew you were Miss Gold," began Max Tack, the honey-tongued. "Some one pointed you out to me yesterday. I've been trying to meet you ever since."

"I hope you haven't neglected your business," said Miss Gold without enthusiasm.

Max Tack leaned closer, his tone lowered.

"I'd neglect it any day for you. Listen, little one: aren't you going to take dinner with me some evening?"

157

Max Tack always called a woman "Little one." It was part of his business formula. He was only one of the wholesalers who go to Paris yearly ostensibly to buy models, but really to pay heavy diplomatic court to those hundreds of women buyers who flock to that city in the interests of their firms. To entertain those buyers who were interested in goods such as he manufactured in America; to win their friendship; to make them feel under obligation at least to inspect his line when they came to New York—that was Max Tack's mission in Paris. He performed it admirably.

"What evening?" he said now. "How about to-morrow?" Sophy Gold shook her head. "Wednesday then? You stick to me and you'll see Paris. Thursday?"

"I'm buying my own dinners," said Sophy Gold.

Max Tack wagged a chiding forefinger at her.

"You little rascal!" No one had ever called Sophy Gold a little rascal before. "You stingy little rascal! Won't give a poor lonesome fellow an evening's pleasure, eh! The theatre? Want to go slumming?"

He was feeling his way now, a trifle puzzled. Usually he landed a buyer at the first shot. Of course you had to use tact and discrimination. Some you took to supper and to the naughty revues. Occasionally you found a highbrow one who preferred the opera. Had he not sat through Parsifal the week before? And nearly died! Some wanted to begin at Tod Sloan's bar and work their way up through Montmartre, ending with breakfast at the Pré Catalan. Those were the greedy ones. But this one!

"What's she stalling for—with that face?" he asked himself.

Sophy Gold was moving toward the lift, the twinkling-eyed Miss Morrissey with her.

"I'm working too hard to play. Thanks, just the same. Good-night."

Max Tack, his face blank, stood staring up at them as the lift began to ascend.

"Trazyem," said Miss Morrissey grandly to the lift man.

"Third," replied that linguistic person, unimpressed.

It turned out to be soothingly quiet and cool in Ella Morrissey's room. She flicked on the light and turned an admiring glance on Sophy Gold.

"Is that your usual method?"

"I haven't any method," Miss Gold seated herself by the window. "But I've worked too hard for this job of mine to risk it by putting myself under obligations to any New York firm. It simply means that you've got to buy their goods. It isn't fair to your firm."

Miss Morrissey was busy with hooks and eyes and strings. Her utterance was jerky but concise. At one stage of her disrobing she breathed a great sigh of relief as she flung a heavy garment from her.

"There! That's comfort! Nights like this I wish I had that back porch of our flat to sit on for just an hour. Ma has flower boxes all round it, and I bought one of those hammock couches last year. When I come home from the store summer evenings I peel and get into my old blue-and-white kimono and lie there, listening to the girl stirring the iced tea for supper, and knowing that Ma has a platter of her swell cold fish with egg sauce!" She relaxed into an armchair. "Tell me, do you always talk to men that way?"

Sophy Gold was still staring out the open window.

"They don't bother me much, as a rule."

"Max Tack isn't a bad boy. He never wastes much time on me. I don't buy his line. Max is all business. Of course he's something of a smarty, and he does think he's the first verse and chorus of Paris-by-night; but you can't help liking him."

"Well, I can," said Sophy Gold, and her voice was a little bitter, "and without half trying."

"Oh, I don't say you weren't right. I've always made it a rule to steer clear of the ax-grinders myself. There are plenty of girls who take everything they can get. I know that Max Tack is just padded with letters from old girls, beginning 'Dear Kid,' and ending, 'Yours with a world of love!' I don't believe in that kind of thing, or in accepting things. Julia Harris, who buys for three departments in our store, drives up every morning in the French car that Parmentier's gave her when she was here last year. That's bad principle and poor taste. But—Well, you're young; and there ought to be something besides business in your life."

Sophy Gold turned her face from the window toward Miss Morrissey. It served to put a stamp of finality on what she said:

"There never will be. I don't know anything but business. It's the only thing I care about. I'll be earning my ten thousand a year pretty soon."

"Ten thousand a year is a lot; but it isn't everything. Oh, no, it isn't. Look here, dear; nobody knows better than I how this working and being independent and earning your own good money puts the stopper on any sentiment a girl might have in her; but don't let it sour you. You lose your illusions soon enough, goodness knows! There's no use in smashing 'em out of pure meanness."

"I don't see what illusions have got to do with Max Tack," interrupted Sophy Gold.

Miss Morrissey laughed her fat, comfortable chuckle.

"I suppose you're right, and I guess I've been getting a lee-tle bit nosey; but I'm pretty nearly old enough to be your mother. The girls kind of come to me and I talk to 'em. I guess they've spoiled me. They—"

There came a smart rapping at the door, followed by certain giggling and swishing. Miss Morrissey smiled.

"That'll be some of 'em now. Just run and open the door, will you, like a nice little thing? I'm too beat out to move."

The swishing swelled to a mighty rustle as the door opened. Taffeta was good this year, and the three who entered were the last in the world to leave you in ignorance of that fact. Ella Morrissey presented her new friend to the three, giving the department each represented as one would mention a title or order.

"The little plump one in black?—Ladies' and Misses' Ready-to-wear, Gates Company, Portland.... That's a pretty hat, Carrie. Get it to-day? Give me a big black velvet every time. You can wear 'em with anything, and yet they're dressy too. Just now small hats are distinctly passy.

"The handsome one who's dressed the way you always imagined the Parisiennes would dress, but don't?—Fancy Goods, Stein & Stack, San Francisco. Listen, Fan: don't go back to San Francisco with that stuff on your lips. It's all right in Paris, where all the women do it; but you know as well as I do that Morry Stein would take one look at you and then tell you to go upstairs and wash your face. Well, I'm just telling you as a friend.

"That little trick is the biggest lace buyer in the country.... No, you wouldn't, would you? Such a mite! Even if she does wear a twenty-eight blouse she's got a forty-two brain—haven't you, Belle? You didn't make a mistake with that blue crêpe de chine, child. It's chic and yet it's girlish. And you can wear it on the floor, too, when you get home. It's quiet if it is stunning."

These five, as they sat there that June evening, knew what your wife and your sister and your mother would wear on Fifth Avenue or Michigan Avenue next October. On their shrewd, unerring judgment rested the success or failure of many hundreds of feminine garments. The lace for Miss Minnesota's lingerie; the jewelled comb in Miss Colorado's hair; the hat that would grace Miss New Hampshire; the dress for Madam Delaware—all were the results of their farsighted selection. They were foragers of feminine fal-lals, and their booty would be distributed from oyster cove to orange grove.

They were marcelled and manicured within an inch of their lives. They rustled and a pleasant perfume clung about them. Their hats were so smart that they gave you a shock. Their shoes were correct. Their skirts bunched where skirts should bunch that year or lay smooth where smoothness was decreed. They looked like the essence of frivolity—until you saw their eyes; and then you noticed that that which is liquid in sheltered women's eyes was crystallised in theirs.

Sophy Gold, listening to them, felt strangely out of it and plainer than ever.

"I'm taking tango lessons, Ella," chirped Miss Laces. "Every time I went to New York last year I sat and twiddled my thumbs while every one else was dancing. I've made up my mind I'll be in it this year."

"You girls are wonders!" Miss Morrissey marvelled. "I can't do it any more. If I was to work as hard as I have to during the day and then run round the way you do in the evening they'd have to hold services for me at sea. I'm getting old."

"You—old!" This from Miss Ready-to-Wear. "You're younger now than I'll ever be. Oh, Ella, I got six stunning models at Estelle Mornet's. There's a business woman for you! Her place is smart from the ground floor up—not like the shabby old junk shops the others have. And she greets you herself. The personal touch! Let me tell you, it counts in business!"

"I'd go slow on those cape blouses if I were you; I don't think they're going to take at home. They look like regular Third Avenue style to me."

"Don't worry. I've hardly touched them."

They talked very directly, like men, when they discussed clothes; for to them a clothes talk meant a business talk.

The telephone buzzed. The three sprang up, rustling.

"That'll be for us, Ella," said Miss Fancy Goods. "We told the office to call us here. The boys are probably downstairs." She answered the call, turned, nodded, smoothed her gloves and preened her laces.

Ella Morrissey, in kimonoed comfort, waved a good-bye from her armchair. "Have a good time! You all look lovely. Oh, we met Max Tack downstairs, looking like a grand duke!"

Pert Miss Laces turned at the door, giggling.

"He says the French aristocracy has nothing on him, because his grandfather was one of the original Ten Ikes of New York."

A final crescendo of laughter, a last swishing of silks, a breath of perfume from the doorway and they were gone.

Within the room the two women sat looking at the closed door for a moment. Then Ella Morrissey turned to look at Sophy Gold just as Sophy Gold turned to look at Ella Morrissey.

"Well?" smiled Ella.

Sophy Gold smiled too—a mirthless, one-sided smile.

161

"I felt just like this once when I was a little girl. I went to a party, and all the other little girls had yellow curls. Maybe some of them had brown ones; but I only remember a maze of golden hair, and pink and blue sashes, and rosy cheeks, and ardent little boys, and the sureness of those little girls—their absolute faith in their power to enthrall, and in the perfection of their curls and sashes. I went home before the ice cream. And I love ice cream!"

Ella Morrissey's eyes narrowed thoughtfully.

"Then the next time you're invited to a party you wait for the ice cream, girlie."

"Maybe I will," said Sophy Gold.

The party came two nights later. It was such a very modest affair that one would hardly call it that—least of all Max Tack, who had spent seventy-five dollars the night before in entertaining an important prospective buyer.

On her way to her room that sultry June night Sophy had encountered the persistent Tack. Ella Morrissey, up in her room, was fathoms deep in work. It was barely eight o'clock and there was a wonderful opal sky—a June twilight sky, of which Paris makes a specialty—all grey and rose and mauve and faint orange.

"Somebody's looking mighty sweet to-night in her new Paris duds!"

Max Tack's method of approach never varied in its simplicity.

"They're not Paris—they're Chicago."

His soul was in his eyes.

"They certainly don't look it!" Then, with a little hurt look in those same expressive features: "I suppose, after the way you threw me down hard the other night, you wouldn't come out and play somewhere, would you—if I sat up and begged and jumped through this?"

"It's too warm for most things," Sophy faltered.

"Anywhere your little heart dictates," interrupted Max Tack ardently. "Just name it."

Sophy looked up.

"Well, then, I'd like to take one of those boats and go down the river to St.-Cloud. The station's just back of the Louvre. We've just time to catch the eight-fifteen boat."

"Boat!" echoed Max Tack stupidly. Then, in revolt: "Why, say, girlie, you don't want to do that! What is there in taking an old tub and flopping down that dinky stream? Tell you what we'll do: we'll-"

"No, thanks," said Sophy. "And it really doesn't matter. You simply asked me what I'd like to do and I told you. Thanks. Good-night."

"Now, now!" pleaded Max Tack in a panic. "Of course we'll go. I

162

just thought you'd rather do something fussier—that's all. I've never gone down the river; but I think that's a classy little idea—yes, I do. Now you run and get your hat and we'll jump into a taxi and—"

"You don't need to jump into a taxi; it's only two blocks. We'll walk."

There was a little crowd down at the landing station. Max Tack noticed, with immense relief, that they were not half-bad-looking people either. He had been rather afraid of workmen in red sashes and with lime on their clothes, especially after Sophy had told him that a trip cost twenty centimes each.

"Twenty centimes! That's about four cents! Well, my gad!"

They got seats in the prow. Sophy took off her hat and turned her face gratefully to the cool breeze as they swung out into the river. The Paris of the rumbling, roaring auto buses, and the honking horns, and the shrill cries, and the mad confusion faded away. There was the palely glowing sky ahead, and on each side the black reflection of the tree-laden banks, mistily mysterious now and very lovely. There was not a ripple on the water and the Pont Alexandre III and the golden glory of the dome of the Hôtel des Invalides were ahead.

"Say, this is Venice!" exclaimed Max Tack.

A soft and magic light covered the shore, the river, the sky, and a soft and magic something seemed to steal over the little boat and work its wonders. The shabby student-looking chap and his equally shabby and merry little companion, both Americans, closed the bag of fruit from which they had been munching and sat looking into each other's eyes.

The long-haired artist, who looked miraculously like pictures of Robert Louis Stevenson, smiled down at his queer, slender-legged little daughter in the curious Cubist frock; and she smiled back and snuggled up and rested her cheek on his arm. There seemed to be a deep and silent understanding between them. You knew, somehow, that the little Cubist daughter had no mother, and that the father's artist friends made much of her and that she poured tea for them prettily on special days.

The bepowdered French girl who got on at the second station sat frankly and contentedly in the embrace of her sweetheart. The stolid married couple across the way smiled and the man's arm rested on his wife's plump shoulder.

So the love boat glided down the river into the night. And the shore faded and became grey, and then black. And the lights came out and cast slender pillars of gold and green and scarlet on the water.

Max Tack's hand moved restlessly, sought Sophy's, found it,

clasped it. Sophy's hand had never been clasped like that before. She did not know what to do with it, so she did nothing—which was just what she should have done.

"Warm enough?" asked Max Tack tenderly.

"Just right," murmured Sophy.

The dream trip ended at St.-Cloud. They learned to their dismay that the boat did not return to Paris. But how to get back? They asked questions, sought direction—always a frantic struggle in Paris. Sophy, in the glare of the street light, looked uglier than ever.

"Just a minute," said Max Tack. "I'll find a taxi."

"Nonsense! That man said the street car passed right here, and that we should get off at the Bois. Here it is now! Come on!"

Max Tack looked about helplessly, shrugged his shoulders and gave it up.

"You certainly make a fellow hump," he said, not without a note of admiration. "And why are you so afraid that I'll spend some money?" as he handed the conductor the tiny fare.

"I don't know—unless it's because I've had to work so hard all my life for mine."

At Porte Maillot they took one of the flock of waiting fiacres.

"But you don't want to go home yet!" protested Max Tack.

"I—I think I should like to drive in the Bois Park—if you don't mind—that is—"

"Mind!" cried the gallant and game Max Tack.

Now Max Tack was no villain; but it never occurred to him that one might drive in the Bois with a girl and not make love to her. If he had driven with Aurora in her chariot he would have held her hand and called her tender names. So, because he was he, and because this was Paris, and because it was so dark that one could not see Sophy's extreme plainness, he took her unaccustomed hand again in his.

"This little hand was never meant for work," he murmured.

Sophy, the acid, the tart, said nothing. The Bois Park at night is a mystery maze and lovely beyond adjectives. And the horse of that particular fiacre wore a little tinkling bell that somehow added to the charm of the night. A waterfall, unseen, tumbled and frothed near by. A turn in the winding road brought them to an open stretch, and they saw the world bathed in the light of a yellow, mellow, roguish Paris moon. And Max Tack leaned over quietly and kissed Sophy Gold on the lips.

Now Sophy Gold had never been kissed in just that way before. You would have thought she would not know what to do; but the plainest woman, as well as the loveliest, has the centuries back of

164

her. Sophy's mother, and her mother's mother, and her mother's mother's mother had been kissed before her. So they told her to say:

"You shouldn't have done that."

And the answer, too, was backed by the centuries:

"I know it; but I couldn't help it. Don't be angry!"

"You know," said Sophy with a little tremulous laugh, "I'm very, very ugly—when it isn't moonlight."

"Paris," spake Max Tack, diplomat, "is so full of medium-lookers who think they're pretty, and of pretty ones who think they're beauties, that it sort of rests my jaw and mind to be with some one who hasn't any fake notions to feed. They're all right; but give me a woman with brains every time." Which was a lie!

They drove home down the Bois—the cool, spacious, tree-bordered Bois—and through the Champs Élysées. Because he was an artist in his way, and because every passing fiacre revealed the same picture, Max Tack sat very near her and looked very tender and held her hand in his. It would have raised a laugh at Broadway and Forty-second. It was quite, quite sane and very comforting in Paris.

At the door of the hotel:

"I'm sailing Wednesday," said Max Tack. "You—you won't forget me?"

"Oh, no—no!"

"You'll call me up or run into the office when you get to New York?"

"Oh, yes!"

He walked with her to the lift, said good-bye and returned to the fiacre with the tinkling bell. There was a stunned sort of look in his face. The fiacre meter registered two francs seventy. Max Tack did a lightning mental calculation. The expression on his face deepened. He looked up at the cabby—the red-faced, bottle-nosed cabby, with his absurd scarlet vest, his mustard-coloured trousers and his glazed top hat.

"Well, can you beat that? Three francs thirty for the evening's entertainment! Why—why, all she wanted was just a little love!"

To the bottle-nosed one all conversation in a foreign language meant dissatisfaction with the meter. He tapped that glass-covered contrivance impatiently with his whip. A flood of French bubbled at his lips.

"It's all right, boy! It's all right! You don't get me!" And Max Tacked pressed a five-franc piece into the outstretched palm. Then to the hotel porter: "Just grab a taxi for me, will you? These tubs make me nervous."

Sophy, on her way to her room, hesitated, turned, then ran up the stairs to the next floor and knocked gently at Miss Morrissey's door. A moment later that lady's kimonoed figure loomed large in the doorway.

"Who is—oh, it's you! Well, I was just going to have them drag the Seine for you. Come in!"

She went back to the table. Sheets of paper, rough sketches of hat models done from memory, notes and letters lay scattered all about. Sophy leaned against the door dreamily.

"I've been working this whole mortal evening," went on Ella Morrissey, holding up a pencil sketch and squinting at it disapprovingly over her working spectacles, "and I'm so tired that one eye's shut and the other's running on first. Where've you been, child?"

"Oh, driving!" Sophy's limp hair was a shade limper than usual, and a strand of it had become loosened and straggled untidily down over her ear. Her eyes looked large and strangely luminous. "Do you know, I love Paris!"

Ella Morrissey laid down her pencil sketch and turned slowly. She surveyed Sophy Gold, her shrewd eyes twinkling.

"That so? What made you change your mind?"

The dreamy look in Sophy's eyes deepened.

"Why—I don't know. There's something in the atmosphere— something in the air. It makes you do and say foolish things. It makes you feel queer and light and happy."

Ella Morrissey's bright twinkle softened to a glow. She stared for another brief moment. Then she trundled over to where Sophy stood and patted her leathery cheek. "Welcome to our city!" said Miss Ella Morrissey.

166

XI

THE THREE OF THEM

For eleven years Martha Foote, head housekeeper at the Senate Hotel, Chicago, had catered, unseen, and ministered, unknown, to that great, careless, shifting, conglomerate mass known as the Travelling Public. Wholesale hostessing was Martha Foote's job. Senators and suffragists, ambassadors and first families had found ease and comfort under Martha Foote's régime. Her carpets had bent their nap to the tread of kings, and show girls, and buyers from Montana. Her sheets had soothed the tired limbs of presidents, and princesses, and prima donnas. For the Senate Hotel is more than a hostelry; it is a Chicago institution. The whole world is churned in at its revolving front door.

For eleven years Martha Foote, then, had beheld humanity throwing its grimy suitcases on her immaculate white bedspreads; wiping its muddy boots on her bath towels; scratching its matches on her wall paper; scrawling its pencil marks on her cream woodwork; spilling its greasy crumbs on her carpet; carrying away her dresser scarfs and pincushions. There is no supremer test of character. Eleven years of hotel housekeepership guarantees a knowledge of human nature that includes some things no living being ought to know about her fellow men. And inevitably one of two results must follow. You degenerate into a bitter, waspish, and fault-finding shrew; or you develop into a patient, tolerant, and infinitely understanding woman. Martha Foote dealt daily with Polack scrub girls, and Irish porters, and Swedish chambermaids, and Swiss waiters, and Halsted Street bell-boys. Italian tenors fried onions in her Louis-Quinze suite. College boys burned cigarette holes in her best linen sheets. Yet any one connected with the Senate Hotel, from Pete the pastry cook to H.G. Featherstone, lessee-director, could vouch for Martha Foote's serene unacidulation.

Don't gather from this that Martha Foote was a beaming, motherly person who called you dearie. Neither was she one of those managerial and magnificent blonde beings occasionally encountered in hotel corridors, engaged in addressing strident remarks to a damp and crawling huddle of calico that is doing something sloppy to the woodwork. Perhaps the shortest cut to Martha Foote's character is through Martha Foote's bedroom. (Twelfth floor. Turn to your left. That's it; 1246. Come in!)

In the long years of its growth and success the Senate Hotel had known the usual growing pains. Starting with walnut and red plush it had, in its adolescence, broken out all over into brass beds and birds'-eye maple. This, in turn, had vanished before mahogany veneer and brocade. Hardly had the white scratches on these ruddy surfaces been doctored by the house painter when—whisk! Away with that sombre stuff! And in minced a whole troupe of near-French furnishings; cream enamel beds, cane-backed; spindle-legged dressing tables before which it was impossible to dress; perilous chairs with raspberry complexions. Through all these changes Martha Foote, in her big, bright twelfth floor room, had clung to her old black walnut set.

The bed, to begin with, was a massive, towering edifice with a headboard that scraped the lofty ceiling. Head and foot-board were fretted and carved with great blobs representing grapes, and cornucopias, and tendrils, and knobs and other bedevilments of the cabinet-maker's craft. It had been polished and rubbed until now it shone like soft brown satin. There was a monumental dresser too, with a liver-coloured marble top. Along the wall, near the windows, was a couch; a heavy, wheezing, fat-armed couch decked out in white ruffled cushions. I suppose the mere statement that, in Chicago, Illinois, Martha Foote kept these cushions always crisply white, would make any further characterization superfluous. The couch made you think of a plump grandmother of bygone days, a beruffled white fichu across her ample, comfortable bosom. Then there was the writing desk; a substantial structure that bore no relation to the pindling rose-and-cream affairs that graced the guest rooms. It was the solid sort of desk at which an English novelist of the three-volume school might have written a whole row of books without losing his dignity or cramping his style. Martha Foote used it for making out reports and instruction sheets, for keeping accounts, and for her small private correspondence.

Such was Martha Foote's room. In a modern and successful hotel, whose foyer was rose-shaded, brass-grilled, peacock-alleyed and tessellated, that bed-sitting-room of hers was as wholesome, and satisfying, and real as a piece of home-made rye bread on a tray of French pastry; and as incongruous.

It was to the orderly comfort of these accustomed surroundings that the housekeeper of the Senate Hotel opened her eyes this Tuesday morning. Opened them, and lay a moment, bridging the morphean chasm that lay between last night and this morning. It was 6:30 A.M. It is bad enough to open one's eyes at 6:30 on Monday morning. But to open them at 6:30 on Tuesday morning, after an indigo Monday.... The taste of yesterday lingered, brackish, in Martha's mouth.

"Oh, well, it won't be as bad as yesterday, anyway. It can't." So she assured herself, as she lay there. "There never were two days like that, hand running. Not even in the hotel business."

For yesterday had been what is known as a muddy Monday. Thick, murky, and oozy with trouble. Two conventions, three banquets, the lobby so full of khaki that it looked like a sand-storm, a threatened strike in the laundry, a travelling man in two-twelve who had the grippe and thought he was dying, a shortage of towels (that bugaboo of the hotel housekeeper) due to the laundry trouble that had kept the linen-room telephone jangling to the tune of a hundred damp and irate guests. And weaving in and out, and above, and about and through it all, like a neuralgic toothache that can't be located, persisted the constant, nagging, maddening complaints of the Chronic Kicker in six-eighteen.

Six-eighteen was a woman. She had arrived Monday morning, early. By Monday night every girl on the switchboard had the nervous jumps when they plugged in at her signal. She had changed her rooms, and back again. She had quarrelled with the room clerk. She had complained to the office about the service, the food, the linen, the lights, the noise, the chambermaid, all the bell-boys, and the colour of the furnishings in her suite. She said she couldn't live with that colour. It made her sick. Between 8:30 and 10:30 that night, there had come a lull. Six-eighteen was doing her turn at the Majestic.

Martha Foote knew that. She knew, too, that her name was Geisha McCoy, and she knew what that name meant, just as you do. She had even laughed and quickened and responded to Geisha McCoy's manipulation of her audience, just as you have. Martha Foote knew the value of the personal note, and it had been her idea that had resulted in the rule which obliged elevator boys, chambermaids, floor clerks, doormen and waiters if possible, to learn the names of Senate Hotel guests, no matter how brief their stay.

"They like it," she had said, to Manager Brant. "You know that better than I do. They'll be flattered, and surprised, and tickled to death, and they'll go back to Burlington, Iowa, and tell how well known they are at the Senate."

When the suggestion was met with the argument that no human being could be expected to perform such daily feats of memory Martha Foote battered it down with:

"That's just where you're mistaken. The first few days are bad. After that it's easier every day, until it becomes mechanical. I

169

remember when I first started waiting on table in my mother's quick lunch eating house in Sorghum, Minnesota. I'd bring 'em wheat cakes when they'd ordered pork and beans, but it wasn't two weeks before I could take six orders, from soup to pie, without so much as forgetting the catsup. Habit, that's all."

So she, as well as the minor hotel employés, knew six-eighteen as Geisha McCoy. Geisha McCoy, who got a thousand a week for singing a few songs and chatting informally with the delighted hundreds on the other side of the footlights. Geisha McCoy made nothing of those same footlights. She reached out, so to speak, and shook hands with you across their amber glare. Neither lovely nor alluring, this woman. And as for her voice!—And yet for ten years or more this rather plain person, somewhat dumpy, no longer young, had been singing her every-day, human songs about every-day, human people. And invariably (and figuratively) her audience clambered up over the footlights, and sat in her lap. She had never resorted to cheap music-hall tricks. She had never invited the gallery to join in the chorus. She descended to no finger-snapping. But when she sang a song about a waitress she was a waitress. She never hesitated to twist up her hair, and pull down her mouth, to get an effect. She didn't seem to be thinking about herself, at all, or about her clothes, or her method, or her effort, or anything but the audience that was plastic to her deft and magic manipulation.

Until very recently. Six months had wrought a subtle change in Geisha McCoy. She still sang her every-day, human songs about every-day, human people. But you failed, somehow, to recognise them as such. They sounded sawdust-stuffed. And you were likely to hear the man behind you say, "Yeh, but you ought to have heard her five years ago. She's about through."

Such was six-eighteen. Martha Foote, luxuriating in that one delicious moment between her 6:30 awakening, and her 6:31 arising, mused on these things. She thought of how, at eleven o'clock the night before, her telephone had rung with the sharp zing! of trouble. The voice of Irish Nellie, on night duty on the sixth floor, had sounded thick-brogued, sure sign of distress with her.

"I'm sorry to be a-botherin' ye, Mis' Phut. It's Nellie speakin'—Irish Nellie on the sixt'."

"What's the trouble, Nellie?"

"It's that six-eighteen again. She's goin' on like mad. She's carryin' on something fierce."

"What about?"

"Th'—th' blankets, Mis' Phut."

"Blankets?—"

170

"She says—it's her wurruds, not mine—she says they're vile. Vile, she says."

Martha Foote's spine had stiffened. "In this house! Vile!"

If there was one thing more than another upon which Martha Foote prided herself it was the Senate Hotel bed coverings. Creamy, spotless, downy, they were her especial fad. "Brocade chairs, and pink lamps, and gold snake-work are all well and good," she was wont to say, "and so are American Beauties in the lobby and white gloves on the elevator boys. But it's the blankets on the beds that stamp a hotel first or second class." And now this, from Nellie.

"I know how ye feel, an' all. I sez to 'er, I sez: 'There never was a blanket in this house,' I sez, 'that didn't look as if it cud be sarved up wit' whipped cr-ream,' I sez, 'an' et,' I sez to her; 'an' fu'thermore,' I sez—"

"Never mind, Nellie. I know. But we never argue with guests. You know that rule as well as I. The guest is right—always. I'll send up the linen-room keys. You get fresh blankets; new ones. And no arguments. But I want to see those—those vile—"

"Listen, Mis' Phut." Irish Nellie's voice, until now shrill with righteous anger, dropped a discreet octave. "I seen 'em. An' they are vile. Wait a minnit! But why? Becus that there maid of hers—that yella' hussy—give her a body massage, wit' cold cream an' all, usin' th' blankets f'r coverin', an' smearin' 'em right an' lift. This was afther they come back from th' theayter. Th' crust of thim people, using the iligent blankets off'n the beds t'—"

"Good night, Nellie. And thank you."

"Sure, ye know I'm that upset f'r distarbin' yuh, an' all, but—"

Martha Foote cast an eye toward the great walnut bed. "That's all right. Only, Nellie—"

"Yesm'm."

"If I'm disturbed again on that woman's account for anything less than murder—"

"Yesm'm?"

"Well, there'll be one, that's all. Good night."

Such had been Monday's cheerful close.

Martha Foote sat up in bed, now, preparatory to the heroic flinging aside of the covers. "No," she assured herself, "it can't be as bad as yesterday." She reached round and about her pillow, groping for the recalcitrant hairpin that always slipped out during the night; found it, and twisted her hair into a hard bathtub bun.

With a jangle that tore through her half-wakened senses the telephone at her bedside shrilled into life. Martha Foote, hairpin in mouth, turned and eyed it, speculatively, fearfully. It shrilled on in her very face, and there seemed something taunting and vindictive

171

about it. One long ring, followed by a short one; a long ring, a short. "Ca-a-an't it? Ca-a-an't it?"

"Something tells me I'm wrong," Martha Foote told herself, ruefully, and reached for the blatant, snarling thing.

"Yes?"

"Mrs. Foote? This is Healy, the night clerk. Say, Mrs. Foote, I think you'd better step down to six-eighteen and see what's—"

"I am wrong," said Martha Foote.

"What's that?"

"Nothing. Go on. Will I step down to six-eighteen and—?"

"She's sick, or something. Hysterics, I'd say. As far as I could make out it was something about a noise, or a sound or—Anyway, she can't locate it, and her maid says if we don't stop it right away—"

"I'll go down. Maybe it's the plumbing. Or the radiator. Did you ask?"

"No, nothing like that. She kept talking about a wail."

"A what!"

"A wail. A kind of groaning, you know. And then dull raps on the wall, behind the bed."

"Now look here, Ed Healy; I get up at 6:30, but I can't see a joke before ten. If you're trying to be funny!—"

"Funny! Why, say, listen, Mrs. Foote. I may be a night clerk, but I'm not so low as to get you out at half past six to spring a thing like that in fun. I mean it. So did she."

"But a kind of moaning! And then dull raps!"

"Those are her words. A kind of m—"

"Let's not make a chant of it. I think I get you. I'll be down there in ten minutes. Telephone her, will you?"

"Can't you make it five?"

"Not without skipping something vital."

Still, it couldn't have been a second over ten, including shoes, hair, and hooks-and-eyes. And a fresh white blouse. It was Martha Foote's theory that a hotel housekeeper, dressed for work, ought to be as inconspicuous as a steel engraving. She would have been, too, if it hadn't been for her eyes.

She paused a moment before the door of six-eighteen and took a deep breath. At the first brisk rat-tat of her knuckles on the door there had sounded a shrill "Come in!" But before she could turn the knob the door was flung open by a kimonoed mulatto girl, her eyes all whites. The girl began to jabber, incoherently but Martha Foote passed on through the little hall to the door of the bedroom.

Six-eighteen was in bed. At sight of her Martha Foote knew that she had to deal with an over-wrought woman. Her hair was pushed back wildly from her forehead. Her arms were clasped about her

172

knees. At the left her nightgown had slipped down so that one plump white shoulder gleamed against the background of her streaming hair. The room was in almost comic disorder. It was a room in which a struggle has taken place between its occupant and that burning-eyed hag, Sleeplessness. The hag, it was plain, had won. A half-emptied glass of milk was on the table by the bed. Warmed, and sipped slowly, it had evidently failed to soothe. A tray of dishes littered another table. Yesterday's dishes, their contents congealed. Books and magazines, their covers spread wide as if they had been flung, sprawled where they lay. A little heap of grey-black cigarette stubs. The window curtain awry where she had stood there during a feverish moment of the sleepless night, looking down upon the lights of Grant Park and the sombre black void beyond that was Lake Michigan. A tiny satin bedroom slipper on a chair, its mate, sole up, peeping out from under the bed. A pair of satin slippers alone, distributed thus, would make a nun's cell look disreputable. Over all this disorder the ceiling lights, the wall lights, and the light from two rosy lamps, beat mercilessly down; and upon the white-faced woman in the bed.

She stared, hollow-eyed, at Martha Foote. Martha Foote, in the doorway, gazed serenely back upon her. And Geisha McCoy's quick intelligence and drama-sense responded to the picture of this calm and capable figure in the midst of the feverish, over-lighted, over-heated room. In that moment the nervous pucker between her eyes ironed out ever so little, and something resembling a wan smile crept into her face. And what she said was:

"I wouldn't have believed it."

"Believed what?" inquired Martha Foote, pleasantly.

"That there was anybody left in the world who could look like that in a white shirtwaist at 6:30 A.M. Is that all your own hair?"

"Strictly."

"Some people have all the luck," sighed Geisha McCoy, and dropped listlessly back on her pillows. Martha Foote came forward into the room. At that instant the woman in the bed sat up again, tense, every nerve strained in an attitude of listening. The mulatto girl had come swiftly to the foot of the bed and was clutching the footboard, her knuckles showing white.

"Listen!" A hissing whisper from the haggard woman in the bed. "What's that?"

"Wha' dat!" breathed the coloured girl, all her elegance gone, her every look and motion a hundred-year throwback to her voodoo-haunted ancestors.

The three women remained rigid, listening. From the wall somewhere behind the bed came a low, weird monotonous sound, half wail, half croaking moan, like a banshee with a cold. A clanking, then, as of chains. A s-s-swish. Then three dull raps, seemingly from within the very wall itself.

The coloured girl was trembling. Her lips were moving, soundlessly. But Geisha McCoy's emotion was made of different stuff.

"Now look here," she said, desperately, "I don't mind a sleepless night. I'm used to 'em. But usually I can drop off at five, for a little while. And that's been going on—well, I don't know how long. It's driving me crazy. Blanche, you fool, stop that hand wringing! I tell you there's no such thing as ghosts. Now you"—she turned to Martha Foote again—"you tell me, for God's sake, what is that!"

And into Martha Foote's face there came such a look of mingled compassion and mirth as to bring a quick flame of fury into Geisha McCoy's eyes.

"Look here, you may think it's funny but—"

"I don't. I don't. Wait a minute." Martha Foote turned and was gone. An instant later the weird sounds ceased. The two women in the room looked toward the door, expectantly. And through it came Martha Foote, smiling. She turned and beckoned to some one without. "Come on," she said. "Come on." She put out a hand, encouragingly, and brought forward the shrinking, cowering, timorous figure of Anna Czarnik, scrub-woman on the sixth floor. Her hand still on her shoulder Martha Foote led her to the centre of the room, where she stood, gazing dumbly about. She was the scrub-woman you've seen in every hotel from San Francisco to Scituate. A shapeless, moist, blue calico mass. Her shoes turned up ludicrously at the toes, as do the shoes of one who crawls her way backward, crab-like, on hands and knees. Her hands were the shrivelled, unlovely members that bespeak long and daily immersion in dirty water. But even had these invariable marks of her trade been lacking, you could not have failed to recognise her type by the large and glittering mock-diamond comb which failed to catch up her dank and stringy hair in the back.

One kindly hand on the woman's arm, Martha Foote performed the introduction.

"This is Mrs. Anna Czarnik, late of Poland. Widowed. Likewise childless. Also brotherless. Also many other uncomfortable things. But the life of the crowd in the scrub-girls' quarters on the top floor. Aren't you, Anna? Mrs. Anna Czarnik, I'm sorry to say, is the source of the blood-curdling moan, and the swishing, and the clanking, and the ghost-raps. There is a service stairway just on the other side of this wall. Anna Czarnik was performing her morning job of scrubbing it. The swishing was her wet rag. The clanking was her

174

pail. The dull raps her scrubbing brush striking the stair corner just behind your wall."

"You're forgetting the wail," Geisha McCoy suggested, icily.

"No, I'm not. The wail, I'm afraid, was Anna Czarnik, singing."

"Singing?"

Martha Foote turned and spoke a gibberish of Polish and English to the bewildered woman at her side. Anna Czarnik's dull face lighted up ever so little.

"She says the thing she was singing is a Polish folk-song about death and sorrow, and it's called a—what was that, Anna?"

"Dumka."

"It's called a dumka. It's a song of mourning, you see? Of grief. And of bitterness against the invaders who have laid her country bare."

"Well, what's the idea!" demanded Geisha McCoy. "What kind of a hotel is this, anyway? Scrub-girls waking people up in the middle of the night with a Polish cabaret. If she wants to sing her hymn of hate why does she have to pick on me!"

"I'm sorry. You can go, Anna. No sing, remember! Sh-sh-sh!"

Anna Czarnik nodded and made her unwieldy escape.

Geisha McCoy waved a hand at the mulatto maid. "Go to your room, Blanche. I'll ring when I need you." The girl vanished, gratefully, without a backward glance at the disorderly room. Martha Foote felt herself dismissed, too. And yet she made no move to go. She stood there, in the middle of the room, and every housekeeper inch of her yearned to tidy the chaos all about her, and every sympathetic impulse urged her to comfort the nerve-tortured woman before her. Something of this must have shone in her face, for Geisha McCoy's tone was half-pettish, half-apologetic as she spoke.

"You've no business allowing things like that, you know. My nerves are all shot to pieces anyway. But even if they weren't, who could stand that kind of torture? A woman like that ought to lose her job for that. One word from me at the office and she—"

"Don't say it, then," interrupted Martha Foote, and came over to the bed. Mechanically her fingers straightened the tumbled covers, removed a jumble of magazines, flicked away the crumbs. "I'm sorry you were disturbed. The scrubbing can't be helped, of course, but there is a rule against unnecessary noise, and she shouldn't have been singing. But—well, I suppose she's got to find relief, somehow. Would you believe that woman is the cut-up of the top floor? She's a natural comedian, and she does more for me in the way of keeping the other girls happy and satisfied than—"

"What about me? Where do I come in? Instead of sleeping until

175

eleven I'm kept awake by this Polish dirge. I go on at the Majestic at four, and again at 9.45 and I'm sick, I tell you! Sick!"

She looked it, too. Suddenly she twisted about and flung herself, face downward, on the pillow. "Oh, God!" she cried, without any particular expression. "Oh, God! Oh, God!"

That decided Martha Foote.

She crossed over to the other side of the bed, first flicking off the glaring top lights, sat down beside the shaken woman on the pillows, and laid a cool, light hand on her shoulder.

"It isn't as bad as that. Or it won't be, anyway, after you've told me about it."

She waited. Geisha McCoy remained as she was, face down. But she did not openly resent the hand on her shoulder. So Martha Foote waited. And as suddenly as Six-eighteen had flung herself prone she twisted about and sat up, breathing quickly. She passed a hand over her eyes and pushed back her streaming hair with an oddly desperate little gesture. Her lips were parted, her eyes wide.

"They've got away from me," she cried, and Martha Foote knew what she meant. "I can't hold 'em any more. I work as hard as ever— harder. That's it. It seems the harder I work the colder they get. Last week, in Indianapolis, they couldn't have been more indifferent if I'd been the educational film that closes the show. And, oh my God! They sit and knit."

"Knit!" echoed Martha Foote. "But everybody's knitting nowadays."

"Not when I'm on. They can't. But they do. There were three of them in the third row yesterday afternoon. One of 'em was doing a grey sock with four shiny needles. Four! I couldn't keep my eyes off of them. And the second was doing a sweater, and the third a helmet. I could tell by the shape. And you can't be funny, can you, when you're hypnotised by three stony-faced females all doubled up over a bunch of olive-drab? Olive-drab! I'm scared of it. It sticks out all over the house. Last night there were two young kids in uniform right down in the first row, centre, right. I'll bet the oldest wasn't twenty-three. There they sat, looking up at me with their baby faces. That's all they are. Kids. The house seems to be peppered with 'em. You wouldn't think olive-drab could stick out the way it does. I can see it farther than red. I can see it day and night. I can't seem to see anything else. I can't—"

Her head came down on her arms, that rested on her tight-hugged knees.

"Somebody of yours in it?" Martha Foote asked, quietly. She waited. Then she made a wild guess—an intuitive guess. "Son?"

"How did you know?" Geisha McCoy's head came up.

"I didn't."

"Well, you're right. There aren't fifty people in the world, outside my own friends, who know I've got a grown-up son. It's bad business to have them think you're middle-aged. And besides, there's nothing of the stage about Fred. He's one of those square-jawed kids that are just cut out to be engineers. Third year at Boston Tech."

"Is he still there, then?"

"There! He's in France, that's where he is. Somewhere—in France. And I've worked for twenty-two years with everything in me just set, like an alarm-clock, for the time when that kid would step off on his own. He always hated to take money from me, and I loved him for it. I never went on that I didn't think of him. I never came off with a half dozen encores that I didn't wish he could hear it. Why, when I played a college town it used to be a riot, because I loved every fresh-faced boy in the house, and they knew it. And now—and now—what's there in it? What's there in it? I can't even hold 'em any more. I'm through, I tell you. I'm through!"

And waited to be disputed. Martha Foote did not disappoint her.

"There's just this in it. It's up to you to make those three women in the third row forget what they're knitting for, even if they don't forget their knitting. Let 'em go on knitting with their hands, but keep their heads off it. That's your job. You're lucky to have it."

"Lucky?"

"Yes ma'am! You can do all the dumka stuff in private, the way Anna Czarnik does, but it's up to you to make them laugh twice a day for twenty minutes."

"It's all very well for you to talk that cheer-o stuff. It hasn't come home to you, I can see that."

Martha Foote smiled. "If you don't mind my saying it, Miss McCoy, you're too worn out from lack of sleep to see anything clearly. You don't know me, but I do know you, you see. I know that a year ago Anna Czarnik would have been the most interesting thing in this town, for you. You'd have copied her clothes, and got a translation of her sob song, and made her as real to a thousand audiences as she was to us this morning; tragic history, patient animal face, comic shoes and all. And that's the trouble with you, my dear. When we begin to brood about our own troubles we lose what they call the human touch. And that's your business asset."

Geisha McCoy was looking up at her with a whimsical half-smile. "Look here. You know too much. You're not really the hotel housekeeper, are you?"

"I am."

177

"Well, then, you weren't always—"

"Yes I was. So far as I know I'm the only hotel housekeeper in history who can't look back to the time when she had three servants of her own, and her private carriage. I'm no decayed black-silk gentlewoman. Not me. My father drove a hack in Sorgham, Minnesota, and my mother took in boarders and I helped wait on table. I married when I was twenty, my man died two years later, and I've been earning my living ever since."

"Happy?"

"I must be, because I don't stop to think about it. It's part of my job to know everything that concerns the comfort of the guests in this hotel."

"Including hysterics in six-eighteen?"

"Including. And that reminds me. Up on the twelfth floor of this hotel there's a big, old-fashioned bedroom. In half an hour I can have that room made up with the softest linen sheets, and the curtains pulled down, and not a sound. That room's so restful it would put old Insomnia himself to sleep. Will you let me tuck you away in it?"

Geisha McCoy slid down among her rumpled covers, and nestled her head in the lumpy, tortured pillows. "Me! I'm going to stay right here."

"But this room's—why, it's as stale as a Pullman sleeper. Let me have the chambermaid in to freshen it up while you're gone."

"I'm used to it. I've got to have a room mussed up, to feel at home in it. Thanks just the same."

Martha Foote rose, "I'm sorry. I just thought if I could help—"

Geisha McCoy leaned forward with one of her quick movements and caught Martha Foote's hand in both her own, "You have! And I don't mean to be rude when I tell you I haven't felt so much like sleeping in weeks. Just turn out those lights, will you? And sort of tiptoe out, to give the effect." Then, as Martha Foote reached the door, "And oh, say! D'you think she'd sell me those shoes?"

Martha Foote didn't get her dinner that night until almost eight, what with one thing and another. Still as days go, it wasn't so bad as Monday; she and Irish Nellie, who had come in to turn down her bed, agreed on that. The Senate Hotel housekeeper was having her dinner in her room. Tony, the waiter, had just brought it on and had set it out for her, a gleaming island of white linen, and dome-shaped metal tops. Irish Nellie, a privileged person always, waxed conversational as she folded back the bed covers in a neat triangular wedge.

"Six-eighteen kinda ca'med down, didn't she? High toime, the divil. She had us jumpin' yist'iddy. I loike t' went off me head wid her, and th' day girl th' same. Some folks ain't got no feelin', I dunno."

Martha Foote unfolded her napkin with a little tired gesture. "You can't always judge, Nellie. That woman's got a son who has gone to war, and she couldn't see her way clear to living without him. She's better now. I talked to her this evening at six. She said she had a fine afternoon."

"Shure, she ain't the only wan. An' what do you be hearin' from your boy, Mis' Phut, that's in France?"

"He's well, and happy. His arm's all healed, and he says he'll be in it again by the time I get his letter."

"Humph," said Irish Nellie. And prepared to leave. She cast an inquisitive eye over the little table as she made for the door—inquisitive, but kindly. Her wide Irish nostrils sniffed a familiar smell. "Well, fur th' land, Mis' Phut! If I was housekeeper here, an' cud have hothouse strawberries, an' swatebreads undher glass, an' sparrowgrass, an' chicken, an' ice crame, the way you can, whiniver yuh loike, I wouldn't be a-eatin' cornbeef an' cabbage. Not me."

"Oh, yes you would, Nellie," replied Martha Foote, quietly, and spooned up the thin amber gravy. "Oh, yes you would."

XII

SHORE LEAVE

Tyler Kamps was a tired boy. He was tired from his left great toe to that topmost spot at the crown of his head where six unruly hairs always persisted in sticking straight out in defiance of patient brushing, wetting, and greasing. Tyler Kamps was as tired as only a boy can be at 9.30 P.M. who has risen at 5.30 A.M. Yet he lay wide awake in his hammock eight feet above the ground, like a giant silk-worm in an incredible cocoon and listened to the sleep-sounds that came from the depths of two hundred similar cocoons suspended at regular intervals down the long dark room. A chorus of deep regular breathing, with an occasional grunt or sigh, denoting complete relaxation. Tyler Kamps should have been part of this chorus, himself. Instead he lay staring into the darkness, thinking mad thoughts of which this is a sample:

"Gosh! Wouldn't I like to sit up in my hammock and give one yell! The kind of a yell a movie cowboy gives on a Saturday night. Wake 'em up and stop that—darned old breathing."

Nerves. He breathed deeply himself, once or twice, because it seemed, somehow to relieve his feeling of irritation. And in that unguarded moment of unconscious relaxation Sleep, that had been lying in wait for him just around the corner, pounced on him and claimed him for its own. From his hammock came the deep, regular inhalation, exhalation, with an occasional grunt or sigh. The normal sleep-sounds of a very tired boy.

The trouble with Tyler Kamps was that he missed two things he hadn't expected to miss at all. And he missed not at all the things he had been prepared to miss most hideously.

First of all, he had expected to miss his mother. If you had known Stella Kamps you could readily have understood that. Stella Kamps was the kind of mother they sing about in the sentimental ballads; mother, pal, and sweetheart. Which was where she had made her big mistake. When one mother tries to be all those things to one son that son has a very fair chance of turning out a mollycoddle. The war was probably all that saved Tyler Kamps from such a fate.

In the way she handled this son of hers Stella Kamps had been as crafty and skilful and velvet-gloved as a girl with her beau. The proof of it is that Tyler had never known he was being handled. Some folks in Marvin, Texas, said she actually flirted with him, and they were almost justified. Certainly the way she glanced up at him from beneath her lashes was excused only by the way she scolded him if he tracked up the kitchen floor. But then, Stella Kamps and her boy were different, anyway. Marvin folks all agreed about that. Flowers on the table at meals. Sitting over the supper things talking and laughing for an hour after they'd finished eating, as if they hadn't seen each other in years. Reading out loud to each other, out of books and then going on like mad about what they'd just read, and getting all het up about it. And sometimes chasing each other around the yard, spring evenings, like a couple of fool kids. Honestly, if a body didn't know Stella Kamps so well, and what a fight she had put up to earn a living for herself and the boy after that good-for-nothing Kamps up and left her, and what a housekeeper she was, and all, a person'd think—well—

So, then, Tyler had expected to miss her first of all. The way she talked. The way she fussed around him without in the least seeming to fuss. Her special way of cooking things. Her laugh which drew laughter in its wake. The funny way she had of saying things, vitalising commonplaces with the spark of her own electricity.

And now he missed her only as the average boy of twenty-one misses the mother he has been used to all his life. No more and no less. Which would indicate that Stella Kamps, in her protean endeavours, had overplayed the parts just a trifle.

He had expected to miss the boys at the bank. He had expected to miss the Mandolin Club. The Mandolin Club met, officially, every Thursday and spangled the Texas night with their tinkling. Five rather dreamy-eyed adolescents slumped in stoop-shouldered comfort over the instruments cradled in their arms, each right leg crossed limply over the left, each great foot that dangled from the bony ankle, keeping rhythmic time to the plunketty-plink-tinketty-plunk.

He had expected to miss the familiar faces on Main Street. He had even expected to miss the neighbours with whom he and his mother had so rarely mingled. All the hundred little, intimate, trivial, everyday things that had gone to make up his life back home in Marvin, Texas—these he had expected to miss.

And he didn't.

After ten weeks at the Great Central Naval Training Station so near Chicago, Illinois, and so far from Marvin, Texas, there were two things he missed.

He wanted the decent privacy of his small quiet bedroom back home.

He wanted to talk to a girl.

He knew he wanted the first, definitely. He didn't know he

181

wanted the second. The fact that he didn't know it was Stella Kamps' fault. She had kept his boyhood girlless, year and year, by sheer force of her own love for him, and need of him, and by the charm and magnetism that were hers. She had been deprived of a more legitimate outlet for these emotions. Concentrated on the boy, they had sufficed for him. The Marvin girls had long ago given him up as hopeless. They fell back, baffled, their keenest weapons dulled by the impenetrable armour of his impersonal gaze.

The room? It hadn't been much of a room, as rooms go. Bare, clean, asceptic, with a narrow, hard white bed and a maple dresser whose second drawer always stuck and came out zig-zag when you pulled it; and a swimmy mirror that made one side of your face look sort of lumpy, and higher than the other side. In one corner a bookshelf. He had made it himself at manual training. When he had finished it—the planing, the staining, the polishing—Chippendale himself, after he had designed and executed his first gracious, wide-seated, back-fitting chair, could have felt no finer creative glow. As for the books it held, just to run your eye over them was like watching Tyler Kamps grow up. Stella Kamps had been a Kansas school teacher in the days before she met and married Clint Kamps. And she had never quite got over it. So the book case contained certain things that a fond mother (with a teaching past) would think her small son ought to enjoy. Things like "Tom Brown At Rugby" and "Hans Brinker, Or the Silver Skates." He had read them, dutifully, but they were as good as new. No thumbed pages, no ragged edges, no creases and tatters where eager boy hands had turned a page over—hastily. No, the thumb-marked, dog's-eared, grimy ones were, as always, "Tom Sawyer" and "Huckleberry Finn" and "Marching Against the Iroquois."

A hot enough little room in the Texas summers. A cold enough little room in the Texas winters. But his own. And quiet. He used to lie there at night, relaxed, just before sleep claimed him, and he could almost feel the soft Texas night enfold him like a great, velvety, invisible blanket, soothing him, lulling him. In the morning it had been pleasant to wake up to its bare, clean whiteness, and to the tantalising breakfast smells coming up from the kitchen below. His mother calling from the foot of the narrow wooden stairway:

"Ty-ler!," rising inflection. "Ty-ler," falling inflection. "Get up, son! Breakfast'll be ready."

It was always a terrific struggle between a last delicious stolen five minutes between the covers, and the scent of the coffee and bacon.

"Ty-ler! You'll be late!"

A mighty stretch. A gathering of his will forces. A swing of his

182

long legs over the side of the bed so that they described an arc in the air.

"Been up years."

Breakfast had won.

Until he came to the Great Central Naval Training Station Tyler's nearest approach to the nautical life had been when, at the age of six, he had sailed chips in the wash tub in the back yard. Marvin, Texas, is five hundred miles inland. And yet he had enlisted in the navy as inevitably as though he had sprung from a long line of Vikings. In his boyhood his choice of games had always been pirate. You saw him, a red handkerchief binding his brow, one foot advanced, knee bent, scanning the horizon for the treasure island from the vantage point of the woodshed roof, while the crew, gone mad with thirst, snarled and shrieked all about him, and the dirt yard below became a hungry, roaring sea. His twelve-year-old vocabulary boasted such compound difficulties as mizzentopsail-yard and main-topgallantmast. He knew the intricate parts of a full-rigged ship from the mainsail to the deck, from the jib-boom to the chart-house. All this from pictures and books. It was the roving, restless spirit of his father in him, I suppose. Clint Kamps had never been meant for marriage. When the baby Tyler was one year old Clint had walked over to where his wife sat, the child in her lap, and had tilted her head back, kissed her on the lips, and had gently pinched the boy's roseleaf cheek with a quizzical forefinger and thumb. Then, indolently, negligently, gracefully, he had strolled out of the house, down the steps, into the hot and dusty street and so on and on and out of their lives. Stella Kamps had never seen him again. Her letters back home to her folks in Kansas were triumphs of bravery and bare-faced lying. The kind of bravery, and the kind of lying that only a woman could understand. She managed to make out, somehow, at first. And later, very well indeed. As the years went on she and the boy lived together in a sort of closed corporation paradise of their own. At twenty-one Tyler, who had gone through grammar school, high school and business college had never kissed a girl or felt a love-pang. Stella Kamps kept her age as a woman does whose brain and body are alert and busy. When Tyler first went to work in the Texas State Savings Bank of Marvin the girls would come in on various pretexts just for a glimpse of his charming blondeur behind the little cage at the rear. It is difficult for a small-town girl to think of reasons for going into a bank. You have to be moneyed to do it. They say that the Davies girl saved up nickels until she had a dollar's worth and then came into the bank and asked to have a bill in exchange for it. They gave her one—a crisp, new, crackly dollar bill. She reached for it, gropingly, her eyes fixed on a point at the rear of the bank. Two days later she came in and brazenly asked to have it changed into nickels again. She might have gone on indefinitely thus if Tyler's country hadn't given him something more important to do than to change dollars into nickels and back again.

On the day he left for the faraway naval training station Stella Kamps for the second time in her life had a chance to show the stuff she was made of, and showed it. Not a whimper. Down at the train, standing at the car window, looking up at him and smiling, and saying futile, foolish, final things, and seeing only his blond head among the many thrust out of the open window.

"... and Tyler, remember what I said about your feet. You know. Dry.... And I'll send a box every week, only don't eat too many of the nut cookies. They're so rich. Give some to the other—yes, I know you will. I was just ... Won't it be grand to be right there on the water all the time! My!... I'll write every night and then send it twice a week.... I don't suppose you ... Well once a week, won't you, dear?... You're—you're moving. The train's going! Good-b—" she ran along with it for a few feet, awkwardly, as a woman runs. Stumblingly.

And suddenly, as she ran, his head always just ahead of her, she thought, with a great pang:

"O my God, how young he is! How young he is, and he doesn't know anything. I should have told him.... Things.... He doesn't know anything about ... and all those other men—"

She ran on, one arm outstretched as though to hold him a moment longer while the train gathered speed. "Tyler!" she called, through the din and shouting. "Tyler, be good! Be good!" He only saw her lips moving, and could not hear, so he nodded his head, and smiled, and waved, and was gone.

So Tyler Kamps had travelled up to Chicago. Whenever they passed a sizable town they had thrown open the windows and yelled, "Youp! Who-ee! Yow!"

People had rushed to the streets and had stood there gazing after the train. Tyler hadn't done much youping at first, but in the later stages of the journey he joined in to keep his spirits up. He, who had never been more than a two-hours' ride from home was flashing past villages, towns, cities—hundreds of them.

The first few days had been unbelievably bad, what with typhoid inoculations, smallpox vaccinations, and loneliness. The very first day, when he had entered his barracks one of the other boys, older in experience, misled by Tyler's pink and white and gold colouring, had leaned forward from amongst a group and had called in glad surprise, at the top of a leathery pair of lungs:

"Why, hello, sweetheart!" The others had taken it up with cruelty of their age. "Hello, sweetheart!" It had stuck. Sweetheart. In the hard years that followed—years in which the blood-thirsty and piratical games of his boyhood paled to the mildest of imaginings—the nickname still clung, long after he had ceased to resent it; long after he had stripes and braid to refute it.

But in that Tyler Kamps we are not interested. It is the boy Tyler Kamps with whom we have to do. Bewildered, lonely, and a little resentful. Wondering where the sea part of it came in. Learning to say "on the station" instead of "at the station," the idea being that the great stretch of land on which the station was located was not really land, but water; and the long wooden barracks not really barracks at all, but ships. Learning to sleep in a hammock (it took him a full week). Learning to pin back his sailor collar to save soiling the white braid on it (that meant scrubbing). Learning—but why go into detail? One sentence covers it.

Tyler met Gunner Moran. Moran, tattooed, hairy-armed, hairy-chested as a gorilla and with something of the sadness and humour of the gorilla in his long upper lip and short forehead. But his eyes did not bear out the resemblance. An Irish blue; bright, unravaged; clear beacon lights in a rough and storm-battered countenance. Gunner Moran wasn't a gunner at all, or even a gunner's mate, but just a seaman who knew the sea from Shanghai to New Orleans; from Liverpool to Barcelona. His knowledge of knots and sails and rifles and bayonets and fists was a thing to strike you dumb. He wasn't the stuff of which officers are made. But you should have seen him with a Springfield! Or a bayonet! A bare twenty-five, Moran, but with ten years' sea experience. Into those ten years he had jammed a lifetime of adventure. And he could do expertly all the things that Tyler Kamps did amateurishly. In a barrack, or in a company street, the man who talks the loudest is the man who has the most influence. In Tyler's barrack Gunner Moran was that man.

Because of what he knew they gave him two hundred men at a time and made him company commander, without insignia or official position. In rank, he was only a "gob" like the rest of them. In influence a captain. Moran knew how to put the weight lunge behind the bayonet. It was a matter of balance, of poise, more than of muscle.

Up in the front of his men, "G'wan," he would yell. "Whatddye think you're doin'! Tickling 'em with a straw! That's a bayonet you got there, not a tennis rackit. You couldn't scratch your initials on a Fritz that way. Put a little guts into it. Now then!"

He had been used to the old Krag, with a cam that jerked out, and threw back, and fed one shell at a time. The new Springfield, that was a gloriously functioning thing in its simplicity, he regarded with a sort of reverence and ecstasy mingled. As his fingers slid lightly, caressingly along the shining barrel they were like a man's fingers lingering on the soft curves of a woman's throat. The sight of a rookie handling this metal sweetheart clumsily filled him with fury.

"Whatcha think you got there, you lubber, you! A section o' lead pipe! You ought t' be back carryin' a shovel, where you belong. Here. Just a touch. Like that. See? Easy now."

He could box like a professional. They put him up against Slovatsky, the giant Russian, one day. Slovatsky put up his two huge hands, like hams, and his great arms, like iron beams and looked down on this lithe, agile bantam that was hopping about at his feet. Suddenly the bantam crouched, sprang, and recoiled like a steel trap. Something had crashed up against Slovatsky's chin. Red rage shook him. He raised his sledge-hammer right for a slashing blow. Moran was directly in the path of it. It seemed that he could no more dodge it than he could hope to escape an onrushing locomotive, but it landed on empty air, with Moran around in back of the Russian, and peering impishly up under his arm. It was like an elephant worried by a mosquito. Then Moran's lightning right shot out again, smartly, and seemed just to tap the great hulk on the side of the chin. A ludicrous look of surprise on Slovatsky's face before he crumpled and crashed.

This man it was who had Tyler Kamps' admiration. It was more than admiration. It was nearer adoration. But there was nothing unnatural or unwholesome about the boy's worship of this man. It was a legitimate thing, born of all his fatherless years; years in which there had been no big man around the house who could throw farther than Tyler, and eat more, and wear larger shoes and offer more expert opinion. Moran accepted the boy's homage with a sort of surly graciousness.

In Tyler's third week at the Naval Station mumps developed in his barracks and they were quarantined. Tyler escaped the epidemic but he had to endure the boredom of weeks of quarantine. At first they took it as a lark, like schoolboys. Moran's hammock was just next Tyler's. On his other side was a young Kentuckian named Dabney Courtney. The barracks had dubbed him Monicker the very first day. Monicker had a rather surprising tenor voice. Moran a salty bass. And Tyler his mandolin. The trio did much to make life bearable, or unbearable, depending on one's musical knowledge and views. The boys all sang a great deal. They bawled everything they knew, from "Oh, You Beautiful Doll" and "Over There" to "The End of a Perfect Day." The latter, ad nauseum. They even revived "Just

186

Break the News to Mother" and seemed to take a sort of awful joy in singing its dreary words and mournful measures. They played everything from a saxophone to a harmonica. They read. They talked. And they grew so sick of the sight of one another that they began to snap and snarl.

Sometimes they gathered round Moran and he told them tales they only half believed. He had been in places whose very names were exotic and oriental, breathing of sandalwood, and myrrh, and spices and aloes. They were places over which a boy dreams in books of travel. Moran bared the vivid tattooing on hairy arms and chest—tattooing representing anchors, and serpents, and girls' heads, and hearts with arrows stuck through them. Each mark had its story. A broad-swathed gentleman indeed, Gunner Moran. He had an easy way with him that made you feel provincial and ashamed. It made you ashamed of not knowing the sort of thing you used to be ashamed of knowing.

Visiting day was the worst. They grew savage, somehow, watching the mothers and sisters and cousins and sweethearts go streaming by to the various barracks. One of the boys to whom Tyler had never even spoken suddenly took a picture out of his blouse pocket and showed it to Tyler. It was a cheap little picture—one of the kind they sell two for a quarter if one sitter; two for thirty-five if two. This was a twosome. The boy, and a girl. A healthy, wide-awake wholesome looking small-town girl, who has gone through high school and cuts out her own shirtwaists.

"She's vice-president of the Silver Star Pleasure Club back home," the boy confided to Tyler. "I'm president. We meet every other Saturday."

Tyler looked at the picture seriously and approvingly. Suddenly he wished that he had, tucked away in his blouse, a picture of a clear-eyed, round-cheeked vice-president of a pleasure club. He took out his mother's picture and showed it.

"Oh, yeh," said the boy, disinterestedly.

The dragging weeks came to an end. The night of Tyler's restlessness was the last night of quarantine. To-morrow morning they would be free. At the end of the week they were to be given shore leave. Tyler had made up his mind to go to Chicago. He had never been there.

Five thirty. Reveille.

Tyler awoke with the feeling that something was going to happen. Something pleasant. Then he remembered, and smiled. Dabney Courtney, in the next hammock, was leaning far over the side of his perilous perch and delivering himself of his morning speech. Tyler did not quite understand this young southern elegant.

187

Monicker had two moods, both of which puzzled Tyler. When he awoke feeling gay he would lean over the extreme edge of his hammock and drawl, with an affected English accent:

"If this is Venice, where are the canals?"

In his less cheerful moments he would groan, heavily, "There ain't no Gawd!"

This last had been his morning observation during their many weeks of durance vile. But this morning he was, for the first time in many days, enquiring about Venetian waterways.

Tyler had no pal. His years of companionship with his mother had bred in him a sort of shyness, a diffidence. He heard the other boys making plans for shore leave. They all scorned Waukegan, which was the first sizable town beyond the Station. Chicago was their goal. They were like a horde of play-hungry devils after their confinement. Six weeks of restricted freedom, six weeks of stored-up energy made them restive as colts.

"Goin' to Chicago, kid?" Moran asked him, carelessly. It was Saturday morning.

"Yes. Are you?" eagerly.

"Kin a duck swim?"

At the Y.M.C.A. they had given him tickets to various free amusements and entertainments. They told him about free canteens, and about other places where you could get a good meal, cheap. One of the tickets was for a dance. Tyler knew nothing of dancing. This dance was to be given at some kind of woman's club on Michigan Boulevard. Tyler read the card, glumly. A dance meant girls. He knew that. Why hadn't he learned to dance?

Tyler walked down to the station and waited for the train that would bring him to Chicago at about one o'clock. The other boys, in little groups, or in pairs, were smoking and talking. Tyler wanted to join them, but he did not. They seemed so sufficient unto themselves, with their plans, and their glib knowledge of places, and amusements, and girls. On the train they all bought sweets from the train butcher—chocolate maraschinos, and nut bars, and molasses kisses—and ate them as greedily as children, until their hunger for sweets was surfeited.

Tyler found himself in the same car with Moran. He edged over to a seat near him, watching him narrowly. Moran was not mingling with the other boys. He kept aloof, his sea-blue eyes gazing out at the flat Illinois prairie. All about him swept and eddied the currents and counter-currents of talk.

"They say there's a swell supper in the Tower Building for fifty cents."

"Fifty nothing. Get all you want in the Library canteen for nix."

188

"Where's this dance, huh?"

"Search me."

"Heh, Murph! I'll shoot you a game of pool at the club."

"Naw, I gotta date."

Tyler's glance encountered Moran's, and rested there. Scorn curled the Irishman's broad upper lip. "Navy! This ain't no navy no more. It's a Sunday school, that's what! Phonographs, an' church suppers, an' pool an' dances! It's enough t' turn a fella's stomick. Lot of Sunday school kids don't know a sail from a tablecloth when they see it."

He relapsed into contemptuous silence.

Tyler, who but a moment before had been envying them their familiarity with these very things now nodded and smiled understanding at Moran. "That's right," he said. Moran regarded him a moment, curiously. Then he resumed his staring out of the window. You would never have guessed that in that bullet head there was bewilderment and resentment almost equalling Tyler's, but for a much different reason. Gunner Moran was of the old navy—the navy that had been despised and spat upon. In those days his uniform alone had barred him from decent theatres, decent halls, decent dances, contact with decent people. They had forced him to a knowledge of the burlesque houses, the cheap theatres, the shooting galleries, the saloons, the dives. And now, bewilderingly, the public had right-about faced. It opened its doors to him. It closed its saloons to him. It sought him out. It offered him amusement. It invited him to its home, and sat him down at its table, and introduced him to its daughter.

"Nix!" said Gunner Moran, and spat between his teeth. "Not f'r me. I pick me own lady friends."

Gunner Moran was used to picking his own lady friends. He had picked them in wicked Port Said, and in Fiume; in Yokohama and Naples. He had picked them unerringly, and to his taste, in Cardiff, and Hamburg, and Vladivostok.

When the train drew in at the great Northwestern station shed he was down the steps and up the long platform before the wheels had ceased revolving.

Tyler came down the steps slowly. Blue uniforms were streaming past him—a flood of them. White leggings twinkled with the haste of their wearers. Caps, white or blue, flowed like a succession of rippling waves and broke against the great doorway, and were gone.

In Tyler's town, back home in Marvin, Texas, you knew the train numbers and their schedules, and you spoke of them by name,

189

familiarly and affectionately, as Number Eleven and Number Fifty-five. "I reckon Fifty-five'll be late to-day, on account of the storm."

Now he saw half a dozen trains lined up at once, and a dozen more tracks waiting, empty. The great train shed awed him. The vast columned waiting room, the hurrying people, the uniformed guards gave him a feeling of personal unimportance. He felt very negligible, and useless, and alone. He stood, a rather dazed blue figure, in the vastness of that shining place. A voice—the soft, cadenced voice of the negro—addressed him.

"Lookin' fo' de sailors' club rooms?"

Tyler turned. A toothy, middle-aged, kindly negro in a uniform and red cap. Tyler smiled friendlily. Here was a human he could feel at ease with. Texas was full of just such faithful, friendly types of negro.

"Reckon I am, uncle. Show me the way?"

Red Cap chuckled and led the way. "Knew you was f'om de south minute Ah see yo'. Cain't fool me. Le'ssee now. You-all f'om-?"

"I'm from the finest state in the Union. The most glorious state in the—"

"H'm—Texas," grinned Red Cap.

"How did you know!"

"Ah done heah 'em talk befoh, son. Ah done heah 'em talk befoh."

It was a long journey through the great building to the section that had been set aside for Tyler and boys like him. Tyler wondered how any one could ever find it alone. When the Red Cap left him, after showing him the wash rooms, the tubs for scrubbing clothes, the steam dryers, the bath-tubs, the lunch room, Tyler looked after him regretfully. Then he sped after him and touched him on the arm.

"Listen. Could I—would they—do you mean I could clean up in there—as much as I wanted? And wash my things? And take a bath in a bathtub, with all the hot water I want?"

"Yo' sho' kin. On'y things look mighty grabby now. Always is Sat'days. Jes' wait aroun' an' grab yo' tu'n."

Tyler waited. And while he waited he watched to see how the other boys did things. He saw how they scrubbed their uniforms with scrubbing brushes, and plenty of hot water and soap. He saw how they hung them carefully, so that they might not wrinkle, in the dryers. He saw them emerge, glowing, from the tub rooms. And he waited, the fever of cleanliness burning in his eye.

His turn came. He had waited more than an hour, reading, listening to the phonograph and the electric piano, and watching.

Now he saw his chance and seized it. And then he went through

190

a ceremony that was almost a ritual. Stella Kamps, could she have seen it, would have felt repaid for all her years of soap-and-water insistence.

First he washed out the stationary tub with soap, and brush, and scalding water. Then he scalded the brush. Then the tub again. Then, deliberately, and with the utter unconcern of the male biped he divested himself, piece by piece, of every stitch of covering wherewith his body was clothed. And he scrubbed them all. He took off his white leggings and his white cap and scrubbed those, first. He had seen the other boys follow that order of procedure. Then his flapping blue flannel trousers, and his blouse. Then his underclothes, and his socks. And finally he stood there, naked and unabashed, slim, and pink and silver as a mountain trout. His face, as he bent over the steamy tub, was very red, and moist and earnest. His yellow hair curled in little damp ringlets about his brow. Then he hung his trousers and blouse in the dryers without wringing them (wringing, he had been told, wrinkled them). He rinsed and wrung, and flapped the underclothes, though, and shaped his cap carefully, and spread his leggings, and hung those in the dryer, too. And finally, with a deep sigh of accomplishment, he filled one of the bathtubs in the adjoining room—filled it to the slopping-over point with the luxurious hot water, and he splashed about in this, and reclined in it, gloriously, until the waiting ones threatened to pull him out. Then he dried himself and issued forth all flushed and rosy. He wrapped himself in a clean coarse sheet, for his clothes would not be dry for another half hour. Swathed in the sheet like a Roman senator he lay down on one of the green velvet couches, relics of past Pullman glories, and there, with the rumble and roar of steel trains overhead, with the smart click of the billiard balls sounding in his ears, with the phonograph and the electric piano going full blast, with the boys dancing and larking all about the big room, he fell sound asleep as only a boy cub can sleep.

When he awoke an hour later his clothes were folded in a neat pile by the deft hand of some jackie impatient to use the drying space for his own garments. Tyler put them on. He stood before a mirror and brushed his hair until it glittered. He drew himself up with the instinctive pride and self respect that comes of fresh clean clothes against the skin. Then he placed his absurd round hat on his head at what he considered a fetching angle, though precarious, and sallied forth on the streets of Chicago in search of amusement and adventure.

He found them.

Madison and Canal streets, west, had little to offer him. He sensed that the centre of things lay to the east, so he struck out

191

along Madison, trying not to show the terror with which the grim, roaring, clamorous city filled him. He jingled the small coins in his pocket and strode along, on the surface a blithe and carefree jackie on shore leave; a forlorn and lonely Texas boy, beneath.

It was late afternoon. His laundering, his ablutions and his nap had taken more time than he had realised. It was a mild spring day, with just a Lake Michigan evening snap in the air. Tyler, glancing about alertly, nevertheless felt dreamy, and restless, and sort of melting, like a snow-heap in the sun. He wished he had some one to talk to. He thought of the man on the train who had said, with such easy confidence, "I got a date." Tyler wished that he too had a date— he who had never had a rendezvous in his life. He loitered a moment on the bridge. Then he went on, looking about him interestedly, and comparing Chicago, Illinois, with Marvin, Texas, and finding the former sadly lacking. He passed LaSalle, Clark. The streets were packed. The noise and rush tired him, and bewildered him. He came to a moving picture theatre—one of the many that dot the district. A girl occupied the little ticket kiosk. She was rather a frowsy girl, not too young, and with a certain look about the jaw. Tyler walked up to the window and shoved his money through the little aperture. The girl fed him a pink ticket without looking up. He stood there looking at her. Then he asked her a question. "How long does the show take?" He wanted to see the colour of her eyes. He wanted her to talk to him.

"'Bout a hour," said the girl, and raised wise eyes to his.

"Thanks," said Tyler, fervently, and smiled. No answering smile curved the lady's lips. Tyler turned and went in. There was an alleged comic film. Tyler was not amused. It was followed by a war picture. He left before the show was over. He was very hungry by now. In his blouse pocket were the various information and entertainment tickets with which the Y.M.C.A. man had provided him. He had taken them out, carefully, before he had done his washing. Now he looked them over. But a dairy lunch room invited him, with its white tiling, and its pans of baked apples, and browned beans and its coffee tank. He went in and ate a solitary supper that was heavy on pie and cake.

When he came out to the street again it was evening. He walked over to State Street (the wrong side). He took the dance card out of his pocket and looked at it again. If only he had learned to dance. There'd be girls. There'd have to be girls at a dance. He stood staring into the red and tin-foil window display of a cigar store, turning the ticket over in his fingers, and the problem over in his mind.

Suddenly, in his ear, a woman's voice, very soft and low. "Hello,

Sweetheart!" the voice said. His nickname! He whirled around, eagerly.

The girl was a stranger to him. But she was smiling, friendlily, and she was pretty, too, sort of. "Hello, Sweetheart!" she said, again.

"Why, how-do, ma'am," said Tyler, Texas fashion.

"Where you going, kid?" she asked.

Tyler blushed a little. "Well, nowhere in particular, ma'am. Just kind of milling around."

"Come on along with me," she said, and linked her arm in his.

"Why—why—thanks, but—"

And yet Texas people were always saying easterners weren't friendly. He felt a little uneasy, though, as he looked down into her smiling face. Something—

"Hello, Sweetheart!" said a voice, again. A man's voice, this time. Out of the cigar store came Gunner Moran, the yellow string of a tobacco bag sticking out of his blouse pocket, a freshly rolled cigarette between his lips.

A queer feeling of relief and gladness swept over Tyler. And then Moran looked sharply at the girl and said, "Why, hello, Blanche!"

"Hello yourself," answered the girl, sullenly.

"Thought you was in 'Frisco."

"Well, I ain't."

Moran shifted his attention from the girl to Tyler. "Friend o' yours?"

Before Tyler could open his lips to answer the girl put in, "Sure he is. Sure I am. We been around together all afternoon."

Tyler jerked. "Why, ma'am, I guess you've made a mistake. I never saw you before in my life. I kind of thought when you up and spoke to me you must be taking me for somebody else. Well, now, isn't that funny—"

The smile faded from the girl's face, and it became twisted with fury. She glared at Moran, her lips drawn back in a snarl. "Who're you to go buttin' into my business! This guy's a friend of mine, I tell yuh!"

"Yeh? Well, he's a friend of mine, too. Me an' him had a date to meet here right now and we're goin' over to a swell little dance on Michigan Avenoo. So it's you who's buttin' in, Blanche, me girl."

The girl stood twisting her handkerchief savagely. She was panting a little. "I'll get you for this."

"Beat it!" said Moran. He tucked his arm through Tyler's, with a little impelling movement, and Tyler found himself walking up the street at a smart gait, leaving the girl staring after them.

Tyler Kamps was an innocent, but he was not a fool. At what he

193

had vaguely guessed a moment before, he now knew. They walked along in silence, the most ill-sorted pair that you might hope to find in all that higgledy-piggledy city. And yet with a new, strong bond between them. It was more than fraternal. It had something of the character of the feeling that exists between a father and son who understand each other.

Man-like, they did not talk of that which they were thinking.

Tyler broke the silence.

"Do you dance?"

"Me! Dance! Well, I've mixed with everything from hula dancers to geisha girls, not forgettin' the Barbary Coast in the old days, but—well, I ain't what you'd rightly call a dancer. Why you askin'?"

"Because I can't dance, either. But we'll just go up and see what it's like, anyway."

"See wot wot's like?"

Tyler took out his card again, patiently. "This dance we're going to."

They had reached the Michigan Avenue address given on the card, and Tyler stopped to look up at the great, brightly lighted building. Moran stopped too, but for a different reason. He was staring, open-mouthed, at Tyler Kamps.

"You mean t' say you thought I was goin'—"

He choked. "Oh, my Gawd!"

Tyler smiled at him, sweetly. "I'm kind of scared, too. But Monicker goes to these dances and he says they're right nice. And lots of—of pretty girls. Nice girls. I wouldn't go alone. But you—you're used to dancing, and parties and—girls."

He linked his arm through the other man's. Moran allowed himself to be propelled along, dazedly. Still protesting, he found himself in the elevator with a dozen red-cheeked, scrubbed-looking jackies. At which point Moran, game in the face of horror, accepted the inevitable. He gave a characteristic jerk from the belt.

"Me, I'll try anything oncet. Lead me to it."

The elevator stopped at the ninth floor. "Out here for the jackies' dance," said the elevator boy.

The two stepped out with the others. Stepped out gingerly, caps in hand. A corridor full of women. A corridor a-flutter with girls. Talk. Laughter. Animation. In another moment the two would have turned and fled, terrified. But in that half-moment of hesitation and bewilderment they were lost.

A woman approached them hand outstretched. A tall, slim, friendly looking woman, low-voiced, silk-gowned, inquiring.

"Good-evening!" she said, as if she had been haunting the halls

194

in the hope of their coming. "I'm glad to see you. You can check your caps right there. Do you dance?"

Two scarlet faces. Four great hands twisting at white caps in an agony of embarrassment. "Why, no ma'am."

"That's fine. We'll teach you. Then you'll go into the ball room and have a wonderful time."

"But—" in choked accents from Moran.

"Just a minute. Miss Hall!" She beckoned a diminutive blonde in blue. "Miss Hall, this is Mr.—ah—Mr. Moran. Thanks. And Mr.?— yes—Mr. Kamps. Tyler Kamps. They want to learn to dance. I'll turn them right over to you. When does your class begin?"

Miss Hall glanced at a toy watch on the tiny wrist. Instinctively and helplessly Moran and Tyler focused their gaze on the dials that bound their red wrists. "Starting right now," said Miss Hall, crisply. She eyed the two men with calm appraising gaze. "I'm sure you'll both make wonderful dancers. Follow me."

She turned. There was something confident, dauntless, irresistible about the straight little back. The two men stared at it. Then at each other. Panic was writ large on the face of each. Panic, and mutiny. Flight was in the mind of both. Miss Hall turned, smiled, held out a small white hand. "Come on," she said. "Follow me."

And the two, as though hypnotised, followed.

A fair-sized room, with a piano in one corner and groups of fidgeting jackies in every other corner. Moran and Tyler sighed with relief at sight of them. At least they were not to be alone in their agony.

Miss Hall wasted no time. Slim ankles close together, head held high, she stood in the centre of the room. "Now then, form a circle please!"

Twenty six-foot, well-built specimens of manhood suddenly became shambling hulks. They clumped forward, breathing hard, and smiling mirthlessly, with an assumption of ease that deceived no one, least of all, themselves. "A little lively, please. Don't look so scared. I'm not a bit vicious. Now then, Miss Weeks! A fox trot."

Miss Weeks, at the piano, broke into spirited strains. The first faltering steps in the social career of Gunner Moran and Tyler Kamps had begun.

To an onlooker, it might have been mirth-provoking if it hadn't been, somehow, tear-compelling. The thing that little Miss Hall was doing might have seemed trivial to one who did not know that it was magnificent. It wasn't dancing merely that she was teaching these awkward, serious, frightened boys. She was handing them a key that would unlock the social graces. She was presenting them with a

195

magic something that would later act as an open sesame to a hundred legitimate delights.

She was strictly business, was Miss Hall. No nonsense about her. "One-two-three-four! And a one-two three-four. One-two-three-four! And a turn-two, turn-four. Now then, all together. Just four straight steps as if you were walking down the street. That's it! One-two-three-four! Don't look at me. Look at my feet. And a one-two three-four."

Red-faced, they were. Very earnest. Pathetically eager and docile. Weeks of drilling had taught them to obey commands. To them the little dancing teacher whose white spats twinkled so expertly in the tangle of their own clumsy clumping boots was more than a pretty girl. She was knowledge. She was power. She was the commanding officer. And like children they obeyed.

Moran's Barbary Coast experience stood him in good stead now, though the stern and watchful Miss Hall put a quick stop to a certain tendency toward shoulder work. Tyler possessed what is known as a rhythm sense. An expert whistler is generally a natural dancer. Stella Kamps had always waited for the sound of his cheerful whistle as he turned the corner of Vernon Street. High, clear, sweet, true, he would approach his top note like a Tettrazini until, just when you thought he could not possibly reach that dizzy eminence he did reach it, and held it, and trilled it, bird-like, in defiance of the laws of vocal equilibrium.

His dancing was much like that. Never a half-beat behind the indefatigable Miss Weeks. It was a bit laboured, at first, but it was true. Little Miss Hall, with the skilled eye of the specialist, picked him at a glance.

"You've danced before?"

"No ma'am."

"Take the head of the line, please. Watch Mr. Kamps. Now then, all together, please."

And they were off again.

At 9.45 Tyler Kamps and Gunner Moran were standing in the crowded doorway of the ballroom upstairs, in a panic lest some girl should ask them to dance; fearful lest they be passed by. Little Miss Hall had brought them to the very door, had left them there with a stern injunction not to move, and had sped away in search of partners for them.

Gunner Moran's great scarlet hands were knotted into fists. His Adam's apple worked convulsively.

"Le's duck," he whispered hoarsely. The jackie band in the corner crashed into the opening bars of a fox trot.

"Oh, it don't seem—" But it was plain that Tyler was weakening.

196

Another moment and they would have turned and fled. But coming toward them was little Miss Hall, her blonde head bobbing in and out among the swaying couples. At her right and left was a girl. Her bright eyes held her two victims in the doorway. They watched her approach, and were helpless to flee. They seemed to be gripped by a horrible fascination. Their limbs were fluid.

A sort of groan rent Moran. Miss Hall and the two girls stood before them, cool, smiling, unruffled.

"Miss Cunningham, this is Mr. Tyler Kamps. Mr. Moran, Miss Cunningham. Miss Drew—Mr. Moran, Mr. Kamps."

The boy and the man gulped, bowed, mumbled something.

"Would you like to dance?" said Miss Cunningham, and raised limpid eyes to Tyler's.

"Why—I—you see I don't know how. I just started to—"

"Oh, that's all right," Miss Cunningham interrupted, cheerfully. "We'll try it." She stood in position and there seemed to radiate from her a certain friendliness, a certain assurance and understanding that was as calming as it was stimulating. In a sort of daze Tyler found himself moving over the floor in time to the music. He didn't know that he was being led, but he was. She didn't try to talk. He breathed a prayer of thanks for that. She seemed to know, somehow, about those four straight steps and two to the right and two to the left, and four again, and turn-two, turn-four. He didn't know that he was counting aloud, desperately. He didn't even know, just then, that this was a girl he was dancing with. He seemed to move automatically, like a marionette. He never was quite clear about those first ten minutes of his ballroom experience.

The music ceased. A spat of applause. Tyler mopped his head, and his hands, and applauded too, like one in a dream. They were off again for the encore.

Five minutes later he found himself seated next Miss Cunningham in a chair against the wall. And for the first time since their meeting the mists of agony cleared before his gaze and he saw Miss Cunningham as a tall, slim, dark-haired girl, with a glint of mischief in her eye, and a mouth that looked as if she were trying to keep from smiling.

"Why don't you?" Tyler asked, and was aghast.

"Why don't I what?"

"Smile if you want to."

At which the glint in her eye and the hidden smile on her lips sort of met and sparked and she laughed. Tyler laughed, too, and then they laughed together and were friends.

Miss Cunningham's conversation was the kind of conversation that a nice girl invariably uses in putting at ease a jackie whom she has just met at a war recreation dance. Nothing could have been more commonplace or unoriginal, but to Tyler Kamps the brilliance of a Madame de Stael would have sounded trivial and uninteresting in comparison.

"Where are you from?"

"Why, I'm from Texas, ma'am. Marvin, Texas."

"Is that so? So many of the boys are from Texas. Are you out at the station or on one of the boats?"

"I'm on the Station. Yes ma'am."

"Do you like the navy?"

"Yes ma'am, I do. I sure do. You know there isn't a drafted man in the navy. No ma'am! We're all enlisted men."

"When do you think the war will end, Mr. Kamps?"

He told her, gravely. He told her many other things. He told her about Texas, at length and in detail, being a true son of that Brobdingnagian state. Your Texan born is a walking mass of statistics. Miss Cunningham made a sympathetic and interested listener. Her brown eyes were round and bright with interest. He told her that the distance from Texas to Chicago was only half as far as from here to there in the state of Texas itself. Yes ma'am! He had figures about tons of grain, and heads of horses and herds of cattle. Why, say, you could take little ol' meachin' Germany and tuck it away in a corner of Texas and you wouldn't any more know it was there than if it was somebody's poor no-'count ranch. Why, Big Y ranch alone would make the whole country of Germany look like a cattle grazin' patch. It was bigger than all those countries in Europe strung together, and every man in Texas would rather fight than eat. Yes ma'am. Why, you couldn't hold 'em.

"My!" breathed Miss Cunningham.

They danced again. Miss Cunningham introduced him to some other girls, and he danced with them, and they in turn asked him about the station, and Texas, and when he thought the war would end. And altogether he had a beautiful time of it, and forgot completely and entirely about Gunner Moran. It was not until he gallantly escorted Miss Cunningham downstairs for refreshments that he remembered his friend. He had procured hot chocolate for himself and Miss Cunningham; and sandwiches, and delectable chunks of caramel cake. And they were talking, and eating, and laughing and enjoying themselves hugely, and Tyler had gone back for more cake at the urgent invitation of the white-haired, pink-cheeked woman presiding at the white-clothed table in the centre of the charming room. And then he had remembered. A look of horror settled down over his face. He gasped.

"W-what's the matter?" demanded Miss Cunningham.

"My—my friend. I forgot all about him." He regarded her with stricken eyes.

"Oh, that's all right," Miss Cunningham assured him for the second time that evening. "We'll just go and find him. He's probably forgotten all about you, too."

And for the second time she was right. They started on their quest. It was a short one. Off the refreshment room was a great, gracious comfortable room all deep chairs, and soft rugs, and hangings, and pictures and shaded lights. All about sat pairs and groups of sailors and girls, talking, and laughing and consuming vast quantities of cake. And in the centre of just such a group sat Gunner Moran, lolling at his ease in a rosy velvet-upholstered chair. His little finger was crookt elegantly over his cup. A large and imposing square of chocolate cake in the other hand did not seem to cramp his gestures as he talked. Neither did the huge bites with which he was rapidly demolishing it seem in the least to stifle his conversation. Four particularly pretty girls, and two matrons surrounded him. And as Tyler and Miss Cunningham approached him he was saying, "Well, it's got so I can't sleep in anything but a hammick. Yessir! Why, when I was fifteen years old I was—" He caught Tyler's eye. "Hello!" he called, genially. "Meet me friend." This to the bevy surrounding him. "I was just tellin' these ladies here—"

And he was off again. All the tales that he told were not necessarily true. But that did not detract from their thrill. Moran's audience grew as he talked. And he talked until he and Tyler had to run all the way to the Northwestern station for the last train that would get them on the Station before shore leave expired. Moran, on leaving, shook hands like a presidential candidate.

"I never met up with a finer bunch of ladies," he assured them, again and again. "Sure I'm comin' back again. Ask me. I've had a elegant time. Elegant. I never met a finer bunch of ladies."

They did not talk much in the train, he and Tyler. It was a sleepy lot of boys that that train carried back to the Great Central Naval Station. Tyler was undressed and in his hammock even before Moran, the expert. He would not have to woo sleep to-night. Finally Moran, too, had swung himself up to his precarious nest and relaxed with a tired, happy grunt.

Quiet again brooded over the great dim barracks. Tyler felt himself slipping off to sleep, deliciously. She would be there next Saturday. Her first name, she had said, was Myrtle. An awful pretty name for a girl. Just about the prettiest he had ever heard. Her folks invited jackies to dinner at the house nearly every Sunday. Maybe, if they gave him thirty-six hours' leave next time—

"Hey, Sweetheart!" sounded in a hissing whisper from Moran's hammock.

"What?"

"Say, was that four steps and then turn-turn, or four and two steps t' the side? I kinda forgot."

"O, shut up!" growled Monicker, from the other side. "Let a fellow sleep, can't you! What do you think this is? A boarding school!"

"Shut up yourself!" retorted Tyler, happily. "It's four steps, and two to the right and two to the left, and four again, and turn two, turn two."

"I was pretty sure," said Moran, humbly. And relaxed again.

Quiet settled down upon the great room. There were only the sounds of deep regular breathing, with an occasional grunt or sigh. The normal sleep sounds of very tired boys.

THE END